MERCHANT'S BOOK

BOOK ONE OF THE MERCHANT SERIES

MAP OF GERENNT

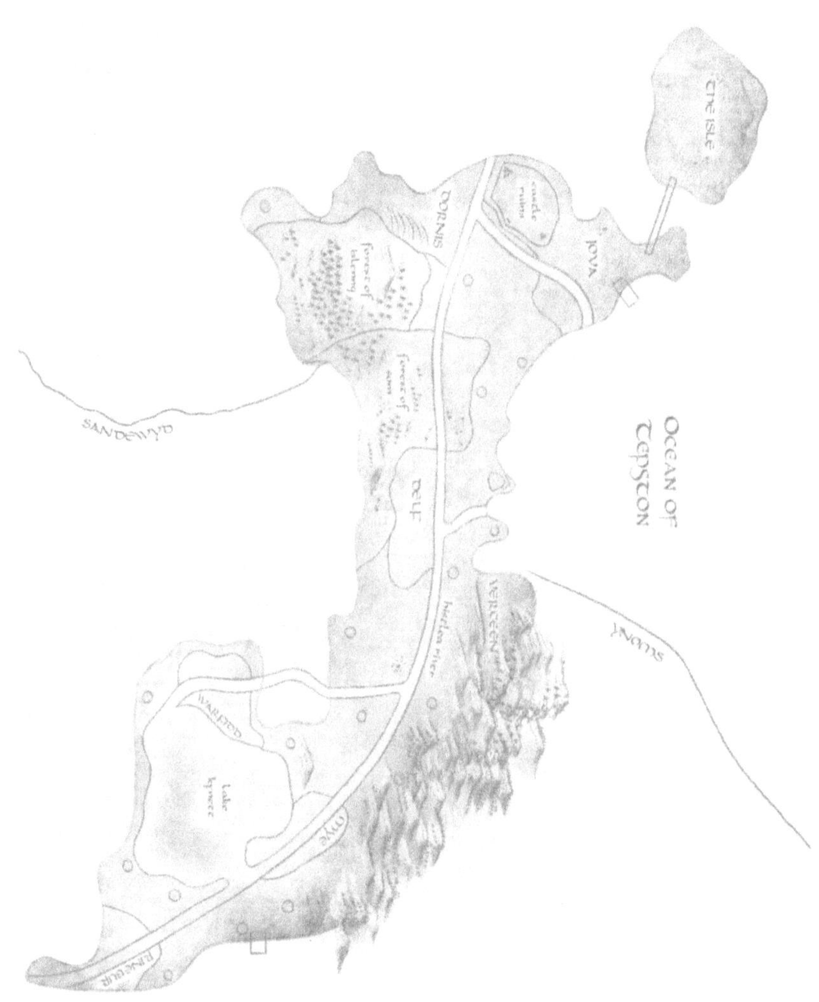

THE MERCHANT SERIES

In reading order:

Merchant's Book

A Border's Call

(Coming: October 2026)

MERCHANT'S BOOK

BOOK ONE OF THE MERCHANT SERIES

EMILY GREY

WICKED INK

PUBLISHING

Published by Wicked Ink Publishing Ltd.
www.wickedinkpublishing.com

Cover and book design © 2025 by Wicked Ink Publishing Ltd.
Editors: Raymond Griffiths & Adam Bamford

First Edition: October 2025
Printed in Canada

Library and Archives Canada Cataloguing in Publication

Title: Merchant's book / Emily Grey.
Names: Grey, Emily (Author of Merchant's book), author.
Description: Series statement: The merchant's series ; book one
Identifiers: Canadiana (print) 20250265109
Canadiana (ebook) 20250265087
ISBN 9781998278251 (softcover)
ISBN 9781998278268 (EPUB)
Subjects: LCGFT: Fantasy fiction. | LCGFT: Romance fiction. | LCGFT: Novels.
Classification: LCC PS8613.R483 M47 2025 | DDC C813/.6—dc23

To my mum, for the encouragement of books & the magic of other worlds

To H & K, listening and responding at nauseum
To L, for being my backbone when I started to weaken

To my readers…This story started with a costume and imagination.

I hope it inspires your imagination too.

MERCHANT'S BOOK

BOOK ONE OF THE MERCHANT SERIES

In a Land where Magick Thrives, Freedom is the Ultimate Prize.

Chapter 1

My eyelashes were stuck together and my mind wanted to stay asleep. But something poked at me to get up. As I did, my spine ached and I couldn't stop from groaning. The worst pain was throbbing along my ribs, like I was hit by a tree branch. Rubbing my eyes to loosen the crud, a grey-coloured, wooden floor appeared in my field of vision. Why was I on the ground?

"Owyn?"

Lyris Pennev, my friend of almost a decade, sat next to me. Her forehead was scrunched, slightly hidden by slick raven hair, with her body balled up in an awkward position. The dishevelled state of her clothes came into my field of vision when she winced and clutched her side, hand disappearing under her top. Ignoring the silent bells of danger, I weakly peeled her limp hand away.

An enormous bruise was barely noticeable against her dark skin. Thin veins protrude out, highlighting the raisin-coloured stain. Bending to my curiosity, I rested my fingertip against the most obvious vein. She hissed at the sensation and I mumbled an apology, removing my hand.

"You have one too," Lyris half-heartedly commented, her hand resting where mine just was.

A noticeable discomfort became more pronounced under my skin and, reaching back, I felt my top was destroyed like hers. Twisting my head, a stained version of Lyris' bruise against my lighter coloured skin. Black and purple with blotches of yellow and red, discoloured my ribcage. Blue veins looked like lightning through the sand. Heat radiated off the spot. Voices grew louder around us.

I peered around the room, wincing as my skin pinched the bruise. The room wasn't normal; I noticed as I looked for the source. No definitive walls, only infinitely thick fog and empty, nothing distinct for me to understand where we were. Surrounding us, other people were splayed out on the floor and were waking up with the same looks of confusion and torn white shirts. Confusion and mental fog made it harder to understand what I was seeing. Rolling my head against my arm, my mouth opened to ask Lyris about the others.

But she was gone.

Without warning, a soundless light violently engulfed the room. My eyelids squeezed shut, waiting for it to disappear. The ground no longer felt solid beneath me. I could be floating.

The space changed. Rather than the floor, an uncomfortable tabletop pressed against my back. Unfamiliar faces circled above me. They muttered between themselves with no reaction when my eyes opened, their words undistinguishable. Fueled by fear, I jerked upwards, but hands forced me back, pressing too hard.

"Let's begin," a calm woman's voice announced. The people remained expressionless, and I wondered if I'd only heard her inside my head. The muscles in my arms ached, making me wonder if my blood was trying to pump faster.

A grey-haired woman's voice echoed through my head, and the words dissolved over my head like mist. All hands disappeared until a single one remained against my bruise. My muscles were entirely relaxed and I no longer felt the need to get up. More words began to form, but I couldn't recognize any of them. Her voice melting away any uneasiness.

Silence. An excruciating icy pinch grabbed at every point of exposed skin, a scream forcing out from my chest. I fought to throw *my body away from the pain and the expressionless people who caused it, but it was useless. It didn't matter that I couldn't comprehend where it came from. I couldn't get away.*

The feeling slithered inside my skin and into my mind, unable to find the edges. The inside of my head was hurting. My eardrums felt on the edge of bursting as the internal pressure fought to exit. No reactions happened around me. I was alone in pain.

Another blinding light and my eyes snapped closed.

As I opened them again, I had control over my senses, like nothing happened. But I was back on the hard floor, in the same position as before. How long ago was that? I lifted myself up into a sitting position. The tightness pulsing along my left side.

"Owyn?"

My lungs burned for air as my eyelids snapped open. I wasn't in a wall-less room of terrifying strangers. It was another nightmare; I thought comfortingly as my fingers ran through the hairs that fell loose from my thick braid. Sunlight peaked between mahogany curtains covering the window that overlooked the town of Rinebur.

Staring at the crack of visible sky, the nightmare replayed over in my head. It was the same dream I experienced for a month straight. A twisted version of the same day repeated; my unasked-for and unexpected trip to the Isle. The very real bruise on my rib cage twinged as I relived the painful experience again.

A boisterous laughter from the hallway broke through the wooden door, making me jump before scolding myself. The old tavern was never entirely quiet, always some noise happening. Some people were already enjoying the day, probably still awake from the night before and as drunk as when the moon rose. I planted my feet on the creaking wood floor, knowing the lodging would only get louder and it was better to give up on sleep now.

My rented room wasn't too big; it only fit the double bed, a side table, dresser, and a single chair. None of it was built in the last fifty years and it matched so well, it could have grown from the same cherry tree. The addition of a small closet-sized washroom incorporated the rest of the tree in its sink and furnishings.

In front of a hanging full-length mirror, I scrunched up my nightshirt. The unchanging ugly bruise, a gift from the Council's magickal practitioner, stared back mockingly. Dropping the shirt, my hands slipped to my waist, and I met my gaze in the mirror. The little voice inside my head pointed out my ivory skin was already appearing grey. The gold floating in my blue eyes was nearly gone.

Not having my pyx, the essence born inside me and every other being to keep our bodies functioning, was already changing me. Inhaling sharply, I grabbed a washcloth and soaked it in hot water. Starting my day by thinking about a dismal ending to my life wasn't a good way to boost my mood.

My arrival in Rinebur a day early wasn't intentional, but I was anxious and my horses sensed it. I caught my foot shaking several times during yesterday's ride. Rinebur was a town that functioned on its own. It was separated from the next towns, Warfidd and Mye, by thick woods. The entire town used the Histlea River to keep itself functioning.

Once I'd found myself a room to stay in for the night, I wasted time buying supplies and artefacts that could turn into future transactions. A few of my customers in Jova, Gerennt's capital town, were novice collectors and Rinebur, the town at the farthest end of the country, was the perfect spot to get pieces they would never find. The cart pulled behind my horses would carry back any haul.

I avoided the Guards as best as I could, not needing to catch their attention and delay my return. Walking along the singular large road of Rinebur, older shopkeepers recognized me from prior visits and were eager to discuss transactions. The conversations stayed quiet, unable to be heard by strangers over the consistent thundering of rushing water.

Each shop was unique inside buildings that were all designed with the same eye. Live animals, plants, jars of dismembered bodies and spells. It was a comforting routine that would keep me going through the day and not hiding away in a pub to wallow in my situation.

When the sun disappeared behind the buildings, I hid my purchases in my rented and magickally protected room before leaving to track down the Dusty Pirate. The Dusty Pirate was the only bar where the patrons wouldn't stare with wide eyes and ask for horror stories of being a Merchant. Turning off the cobblestone road onto a path that was close to nearly grown over, the Delegate's house appeared.

Removing the leather band holding my hair back and I ruffled some long strands in front of my face as a poor disguise. Through the uncovered windows, laughter and energetic conversation seeped out. The Delegate, a person elected by the Council to run each town, seemed to be entertaining tonight. Ignoring my curiosity, I kept my head down.

The lights from the lamp posts melted away, causing me to squint as I checked each tree, trying to remember how many past the Delegate's house was the entrance. Thankfully, I didn't have to try hard when there became an obvious difference in the grass. The path didn't disappear, but came back to life.

At the base of the maple tree, hidden in the shadow of weeds, was a familiar, swirly symbol that caught my attention. Lining my foot up against the carving, I kicked once. Bugs flew up in my face and there was a discernible pause of silence around me. With a stiff groan, the ground shook with a rumble that caused my hands to shoot out for balance and a long rectangular strip of ground sunk into the earth, revealing a dull light. Lifting a handful of my skirt so as not to trip, I descended into the hole.

"Evening ma'am."

I raised my head once my feet hit the stable rock floor. A teenage boy, not much younger than me, stood next to a rusted pulley system. He looked sickly with ghostly white skin and dirty formal clothes, with stains haunting the fabric. No matter how many times he scrubbed them, the waistcoat and buttoned trousers would always look the way they did. I couldn't remember if he was the same teenager who manned the entrance during my last visit months prior. There couldn't be that many Igor children bound to this town, serving its needs until their death.

"Evening," I responded, releasing my skirt.

The constant dirt covering the unnaturally carved floors didn't bother me. My clothes always got dirty. The boy wrapped his hands around the chain and heaved. The rusted pulley system rotated and the ground rose back into place, bits of dirt falling as it settled.

With the outside world cut off, the familiar scent of alcohol now emanated from the walls. It was a large room where I didn't risk hitting my head. There was nowhere for the boy to sit, only standing next to the system.

"Are you meeting anybody, ma'am?" he asked, rubbing his palms against his scratchy pants.

He sounded and appeared younger than the life festering behind his ochre eyes.

I smiled at him. "No, thank you. Who's the bartender tonight?"

"Arin, I believe."

I reached into the small change pouch on my hip, nodding. Tossing a drak to him, his eyes widened at the coin.

"Don't spend that while you're working," I warned with a smile before walking towards the carved out entrance.

The short, twisted hallway connecting between the hidden entrance and the underground pub didn't have smooth walls. Chunks of stone brushing against my hair as I avoided hitting my head in the poorly lit space.

The volume rose drastically as I exited the hallway. For over a century, the pub stayed unchanged since its carving. The original designers knew what they were doing to keep it a secret. Bright lanterns and laughter of the Drao patrons welcomed me. I spent many of my early days as a solo-travelling Merchant here. Though not full, the two-levelled open 'room' was boisterous, every hand holding a drink.

The smell of spilled alcohol intensified in the space where at least two cups were spilled each night. Hundred-year-old gin probably soaked the wooden railings to the core. Through the moving bodies, I spotted a three-piece band playing in the corner. The voices were loud, but the strings could still be heard.

"Well, look what the mountain lion dragged in," a female voice called above the crowd.

I peered at the bartender, grinning. Her mess of red hair sat wrapped in a bun resembling a nest on the top of her head, shining in the dull light. Watching me walk over, she wiped down a stein with a smirk on her face.

"What's brought you here, little girl?" Arin asked as I sat on the empty stool in front of her, rolling my eyes at the greeting.

"You're five years older than me. Watch yourself," I said.

"A baseless threat from a Vek Merchant. How original," she sassed back, handing a shot to a short, horned Drao behind me.

"I'm surprised you remembered where we're hidden. What's it been? At least two springs." She raised her eyebrows accusingly, taking an empty mug from another patron with a nod. With her head turned, the pointed tips of her ears were noticeably sticking through her hair.

"I've been busy. Travelling across the country, doing my job. I don't have time to watch hooligans drink themselves silly all day."

"I seem to remember you spending a fair amount of time drinking yourself silly with those hooligans."

I couldn't stop the scoff coming out. "Could I get a drink to heal your verbal wounds?"

"The usual, coming up," she promised with a wink.

Glancing around the room, a few faces sparked recognition in my brain and we exchanged nods of greeting as if we made eye contact. A group of plainly dressed men sitting around a table in the back corner caught my attention.

Their clothing was loose-fitting natural fibre shirts with their hair unstyled and in their faces with no jewellery. They were doing their best not to be noticed. However, in a room of Drao and their electric auras and bejewelled fabrics, they stuck out. Leaning back in their chairs, nursing steins of alcohol, the men watched everyone. None of them spoke to each other.

"The unhappy men," I commented to Arin when she reappeared. "Guards?"

She nodded, taking a drink before passing the stein to me. The stout rolled down my throat, and my nose twitched at the familiar sensation. This alcohol could only be found in Rinebur. Once upon a time, smugglers brought it through the Fence. It was delicious, whether the first mug or the tenth.

"They've been here the past few days since opening. Other than a couple of glares, no one's giving them any attention."

I peeked at them again, and one man was looking back. He didn't react to being caught, taking a drink from the wooden stout. Even with the large scar running down his face, he was handsome. His eyebrows covered his eyes with shadows, making them hard to see, but his jaw was tight. Something in his expression made me uncomfortable. Arin leaned against the counter, her hands atop the bar top as she watched them too.

"I'm surprised you've let them stay."

She shrugged, focusing on her rag swiping across the countertop.

"They aren't causing trouble. Probably heard about us and they're checking it out. It's happened in the past. The number of Guards in town have doubled in the past few months. It was bound to happen. Gorg has an eye on them," she said, gesturing across the room with her chin.

Gorg, a Drao who filled every door frame as he walked through, stood against the back wall. His head was shadowed by the dark hair he kept cropped. The occasional twitch of his head was the only thing separating him from a statue. He was so still that I hadn't noticed him in my initial scan of the room. His crossed arms were tense in the dim candlelight and though I wasn't sure if he worked on his muscles, the limbs looked larger than the last time I saw him. Truthfully, I assumed he was born with defined muscles and they only got larger with age.

From the day we met, I knew he could crush my skull with a pinch of his fingers. It took three seconds for Gorg to sense my gaze. I sent him a closed smile and after raising his thick eyebrows for a split second; he returned to intensely watching the patrons. It was the most enthusiastic greeting I'd get.

"Gorg is the best deterrent available," I agreed, taking a drink.

She smirked, her sharp canine teeth poking out. "A moon cycle ago, a practitioner came through and tried to hustle some younger Drao. Gorg tossed him out with one hand. It was the hardest he's worked in a decade."

"He's gained a reputation over the last century. Anytime

Rinebur or the Dirty Pirate is mentioned, his name comes up. If he ever leaves, you'd be swarmed with trouble."

"Speaking of trouble," Arin mumbled, leaving to speak with someone else.

"Owyn Kellobyn!" a joyful shout rose above the sounds of patrons.

Whipping around, a smile grew on my face upon recognizing the familiar voice. Walking with his arms spread wide and spilling some of his drink on people's heads was Niko.

The same species as Gorg, but much friendlier. I didn't know what species they were, but they called each other cousins. Drao was the umbrella term, like Vek was for magickless people.

"Hello, my heart," I greeted, standing from my seat.

Niko flung his arms around my torso, locking me in a hug and squeezed the laughter out of me, my back getting wet. I didn't mind his jovial affection as my feet spun in the air, stuck in Niko's embrace. His long blonde hair brushed under my nose, but it was easy to ignore.

"My heart, look at you." Placing my feet back on the ground, the world continued to spin past my eyes. "It's been too long."

As I sat back on my stool, Niko glared at the man next to me. The stranger sighed in defeat, not wanting a confrontation with the giant, vacating his seat. Niko's toothy grin broke out again, planting himself down. The impact's thud resonated beneath me. He tilted his mug back, pausing when nothing came out.

"Arin, another!" He demanded loudly, slamming the mug against the counter.

"It's coming, you mountain," she called from the other end of the bar. He grinned at her, not meaning anything by his tone.

"What're you doing in dull, little Rinebur?" Niko asked, gripping my knee to turn my body closer to him.

Letting my tongue wet my bottom lip, I gazed into the hulking man's eyes. As my friend for the better part of ten years, he was genuinely interested, and I considered telling him. I didn't want to be the only one with the burden of what I was going through. If I asked for his help in saving my life and sanity, he would drop everything at a moment's notice without considering the personal risks.

Instead, I gave my best fake smile, hoping he was too drunk to notice the difference. "Finishing a transaction with the High Drao. I'm visiting her in the morning."

"The High Drao of Rinebur! I've met her a few times in passing. Wonderful woman. You know it's said she's lived forever?"

"You can't believe all the stories," I said before taking a drink. "No one has lived forever."

"That's what you'd like to think, my darling Owyn. No sense of adventure," Niko commented with raised eyebrows. I rolled my eyes in response.

Receiving a new pair of full steins from Arin, Niko and I made our way around the pub. He kept me hooked on his arm, introducing me to everyone. Truthfully, I wasn't sure who he knew and who he didn't. Niko was extremely friendly, and on the other hand, I wouldn't remember a single name.

The pub's occupants were all Drao. No Veks, regular magickless folks, were privy to the underground venue. They had their own establishments above the ground that Drao rarely entered. Some Drao bodies looked the same as Veks. It was undistinguishable. But there were others who you could tell were different. Unnaturally coloured eyes, tails, horns, scaled skin of different colours. It was obvious they weren't magickless. They enticed everyone to look in awe.

I entirely forgot about the Guards until Niko led us past them with a formal greeting. My gaze stuck to the handsomely scarred man's. The bubble of emotion appeared in my stomach again. and I wanted to hide from his gaze, but I was stuck with my arm through Niko's. With scrunched eyebrows, the guard looked between Niko and me. Was he trying to read the relationship?

We maintained eye contact until Niko spun me toward the dance floor. The natural magick radiating off the Drao patrons made its way into my veins. Along with the ale warming my body, laughter flowed out of me easily.

As Niko wrapped me in his arms and swayed to the music, I forgot about the Guard and my worries.

Chapter 2

It was nearly dawn when I escaped the blinding magick and left the underground pub. My body begged for sleep. Niko was snoring in a lounge chair, grumbling when I left a kiss on his forehead before Arin and I exchanged cheek kisses as I made for the exit.

Knowing it was likely her magick, I still felt a tinge of jealousy at how put together and not sweaty she was, as if she didn't work all night. The same boy stood at the entrance, swaying on his feet with his eyelids slipping shut. Silently, I tossed him another drak on my way up the grassy ramp.

The sky above Rinebur was turning a light pink as the sun grew over the skyline. I took the leather band from my pocket as the sun warmed my face. Tying my hair back into a ponytail, I cringed at the knots that my fingers hit. Stepping out of the woods, no one was travelling along the road. It was still too early for most to be awake.

Crossing the thick stone bridge over Histlea River, a few men stood at the river's edge, fishing rods extended over the water. Their voices could barely be heard over the river. All the houses had their windows closed and covered as the occupants still slept. The shops wouldn't be opening yet. The mist blowing off the river was refreshing on my sweat-covered skin. I couldn't stand here and enjoy it, though. I had a meeting in a few hours and I needed some sleep if I hoped for any success.

HOURS LATER, AND LESS EXHAUSTED, I DRESSED IN A FORMAL navy-blue corseted shirt and wide legged pants that would be easily mistaken for a skirt. I could ride in it, but appropriate to visit the High Drao.

As I walked down the stairs, I made sure my coin purse was in a second bag on my belt, securing it from snatchers. Rolling back my shoulders, I stepped onto the main floor and began my way through the tavern's pub. The sun may still be out and the day early, but the day drunks were already a bottle deep. Drunkards and thieves huddled in the bar, hiding from the Guards.

"'xcuse me, pretty lady. Got any pesa you could lend me?" An old man curled over on himself asked. In any other town, I would feel some compassion for how unkempt he was.

"No," I responded and kept walking. The people here were like parrots, hand out one shiny thing and they all flock.

"Girl, give me some coin," another man barked.

This one was drunk, leaning so far back on his stool that he almost fell off. Unlike the first, I ignored him. It wasn't a large pub, but people kept asking. I was used to it, the drunkards were part of travelling.

Reaching the door, a bony hand grabbed my wrist. The man was large and smelled horrible. Alcohol dried on his sweat-soaked clothes overnight, along with some sort of meat.

"Coin, now," he barked at me, reaching for the pack on my hip.

Before his fingers touched the fabric, I had the tip of my

dagger pressed under his chin. His hand released me immediately, but I didn't take away my weapon. I simply stared until he was far enough away that I couldn't smell him anymore. Without a look back, I exited the building.

As bold as they could be, drunkards always missed the weapons when they thought they spotted an easy mark.

While I napped, Rinebur opened up. The tavern sat next to a bakery and my stomach groaned for me to go inside. Traffic was forming outside of the essential shops and I couldn't get swept up in its natural flow.

Around me, mumbles of "excuse me" and grumpy huffs could be heard mixed in with the other conversations. A few tails smacked my legs. Leaving bruises, I'm sure.

Manoeuvring to the stables, I kept my head up and focused on keeping my nerves at bay when I noticed how right Arin was. Guards seemed to stand at every corner and walking through the crowd in pairs. They looked close to matching the citizens in numbers.

Even in the capital township of Jova, I had never seen so many navy coloured uniforms without an obvious threat nearby. Most citizens looked away from the Guards' eyes, not wanting the attention. In the doorways, people glared at the Guards that passed by.

Standing silently on the other side of the aged roofs, the Fence shimmered in the early sunlight and thinning fog. Through it, a forest was seen running along Gerennt's borders. The rumour was the forest was just an illusion, but I'd never heard of anyone challenging it. It was easy to ignore most days.

Whether or not it was real, Ynoms and Sandewyd, the countries bordering Gerennt, were hidden from view. When the Council overthrew the royal family two hundred years ago, Ynoms and Sandewyd were deemed threats to Gerennt's safety and wanted to demolish our way of life.

From the mouths of Drao, eventually reaching the ears of

Merchants, whispers circulated about what the true purpose of the Fence could be. To most, the Council didn't want Gerennt citizens knowing what our neighbours could teach us.

The ruling body wanted us sheltered and on our own, relying on them to lead us through our decisions and lives. I may have not liked the Council and how hungry they were for power, but it would land on deaf ears if I said it out loud.

As a Merchant, I was taught to keep my head down and supply any rebellions that were building without question. That's what my mentor taught me, at least.

Stepping into the crowd that was shuffling across the bridge, I had time to look at the housing across the river. The decay of Rinebur was noticeable. The Delegate wouldn't put any the country's currency, or pesa, into renovations. Like most of the people in his position, he decided it would go to Guards and their endeavours and making a bigger production of exporting wood up the river to Jova.

From the bridge, it wasn't far from the community stables. Building so close to the river was a risky decision, but the design of Rinebur looked as if no one planned how it would be finished; it just happened. So, the stable was stuck with as many safety measures as possible and the paddocks backing on to a rushing river.

Entering the brown and red barn, I nodded to the barn keepers when they greeted me. It was weird to be addressed as "ma'am" by anyone, especially those who looked my age. The first time it happened, and I showed obvious discomfort, my mentor Janna told me, as a Merchant, I deserved the recognition and respect. To show discomfort would be ungrateful.

The barn was large. It contained twenty stalls or so. Only a few large equestrian heads stuck out into the single, well-lit hallway. Riders stood in the spacious stalls, either preparing to leave town or just arriving. The community stable was well stocked. I was impressed. Saddle blankets filled shelving units in the corner, and a multitude of different sized ropes hung along the walls. Two particular creatures sticking their heads over the door, waiting, had me smiling as I got closer.

"Good morning, lovelies," I said, unlocking the wooden door.

My gorgeous cedar-coloured horse, Dill, bumped her nose against my forehead, which, after a decade of being together, was her normal greeting. I ran my hand along her unique bleached mane.

Seeing how my second horse, Marr, looked at me with sleepy eyes, had me shooting back a playful glare. He must've woken up just as I arrived, but the accusatory look was there. I knew days of pulling a half-empty cart with only a few hours' rest exhausted my aging workhorse.

"Don't worry, bud, I'm not here for you. It's your sister and me this morning," I assured him.

The spruce-grey horse huffed in appreciation. He accepted one last pat on the snout before moving to the bucket of oats hanging from the wall. With a quick inspection of his nose, he determined the buckets were empty and, with a brief sigh of disappointment, he prepared to go back to sleep. I rolled my eyes. Drama queen.

"Come on, girl, let's leave your brother to sleep." I said.

Chapter 3

THE EARLY MORNING CROWD OF BAKERS AND COOKS HAD disappeared back into their own buildings, no longer trying to panhandle to the crowds. With fewer people, Dill had an easier time walking on Rinebur's cobbled streets.

Like most of the other towns in Gerennt, the shopkeepers set up stalls outside their businesses to give a sample of what was inside. None of the stall roofs were too bright, the fabric having faded over years of use. Some shopkeepers were smart, half hidden under awnings of their buildings. The grey and crumbling buildings were taken care of by people cleaning windows and dusting their front steps.

As the sun rose higher, the buyers turned from mothers buying ingredients for breakfast or other shopkeepers needing to stock up to people idly picking at things, negotiating for lower prices. The day was warm, but the breeze coming off the river kept most people in cloaks, bags hanging across their bodies.

Keeping a tight grip on Dill's reins, my eyes flickered around. Not being a horse that's easily spooked, she also didn't care about children running dangerously close to her hooves. School hadn't started for the day yet and the kids were getting antsy while waiting for their parents. It was my job to make sure she didn't trample anybody and if she noticed, they would receive a disapproving huff.

Most of the shopping district was built between the river and the gates leading to the Crewynr Mountains. In the opposite direction, deep in the woods that made up the southern tip of the town, was where the High Drao of Rinebur lived.

Following the main road, the shops turned to houses that thinned out quickly. In my youth, I saw plans to expand Rinebur into the woods next to the Fence. It never happened. Outside of the well-loved houses, people hung laundry or picked at the vegetables in their small gardens. It was hard not to notice the grey tone that settled over the town. If you lived here, you wouldn't notice it eventually.

Histlea River flooded almost every year, but a few years ago was the worst they'd experienced and weren't ready for it. The stone houses nestled near the banks showed the damaging results. The population did what it could to save their homes, but it didn't result in beautiful or even safe remodels. Fixing the roads wasn't a priority, and the cobblestone became packed dirt.

Birds singing and the dirt kicking under Dill's feet replaced the manufactured sounds of people. The road ended and became a pathway wide enough for a single cart. Inhaling, the air seemed fresher the further into the trees I went and heavier, almost like it was going to rain, but the sky was clear and blue. The familiar smell of magick.

Some of the magick came from the Fence nearby. It was silent, meant to be invisible but from age or damage, the occasional iridescent glimmer could be spotted hanging alone in the air. An awkward pressure began against the side of my head, not growing into anything painful, but a quiet signal indicated I was close to somewhere I shouldn't be. Dill tilted her head away, not enjoying the sensation either.

The trees came to a hard stop, revealing a cottage that could be considered a large hut. The brownish red masonry was a welcoming sight. Deep green ivy grew up at the sides, gripping the stones tightly. The chimney on the roof puffed out a stream of smoke and around the front door was a wildflower garden. A few white goats mulled around, eating the lush tall grass for their breakfast. Peeking out from the back of the cottage were little paddocks holding cows and pigs. The cottage was a dream I would be happy to hide in.

One of the most powerful Drao in Gerennt, the High Drao of Rinebur, lived here. She didn't travel from her home to work, none of the seven High Drao did. Collectively, they had hundreds of years of experience, wisdom, and time to gain their reputations. People came to them without question.

Stopping Dill, I stared at the cottage and considered what I was here for. I thought I would have more anxiety being here, but I suspected it was held off by magick. The High Drao weren't champions of violence, so they kept it as far away from their homes as they could. If she could suppress my emotions, could she persuade me to feel something else that helped her?

Dismounting Dill, I led her over to the hitch post. Tying her reins, a giant butterfly landed on the end of Dill's nose. A sneeze of surprise puffed from her nostrils, suspiciously glaring at the shining green insect when it flew away. A giggle slipped from my lips to which I received a glare for.

The cottage door creaked open, making my head snap around and my smile to fall. An old woman stood in the doorway, her arms crossed with authority. I met every High Drao in Gerennt before, including Rinebur. Every time, I still felt intimidated. My fingers ran along Dill's coat for temporary comfort, but I couldn't cling to my horse. I had to be an adult.

"High Drao, good morning," I greeted, approaching

carefully. My discomfort made me feel like a mud-covered child after running through someone's garden.

"Orinthia, good morning."

My birth name caused an uncomfortable pinch along my spine. Her ice-blue eyes stared at me in a way I swore the ancient woman knew every thought crossing my mind.

It was a possibility she already knew why I was here as she watched me without a word. Purple and blue clothes adorned the short woman, with gold jewelry sparkling in the sunlight. If this was under different circumstances, I would find her grandmotherly.

There was a long moment of silence as she examined me and I tried to keep eye contact, but couldn't help look away. My fingers wove together to stop from pulling at the leather adorning my sword's handle. For my sake or not, her wrinkled face visibly softened as she stepped inside. Sighing through my nose, I followed her. No going back.

As I stepped into the cottage, a large blob flew past my face. Stunned, I spotted a grey Dragonette doing a lap around the roof. A common pet in Gerennt that resembled tiny versions of their severely more dangerous cousins. More of a nuisance than any actual danger themselves.

"Sit and we shall discuss the purpose of your visit?"

The High Drao was already at her aged dining table, with a steaming mug in front of her. Placing myself across from her, the Dragonette landed with a thump on the wood. On its two back legs and little claws attached to its wings, it waddled to its mother's mug and curled itself around the heat source.

Gazing down at the creature fondly, a smile curled at the corner of her lip. When her eyes met mine, I expected the smile to disappear, but it stayed. She had no reason to be concerned, being inside her house with a stranger. The High Drao was a practitioner, but what was she skilled in? I didn't know. I heard rumours during my travels, but all I knew was she generated enough power that no one attempted to fight her unless their goal was death.

"How can I help you, Orinthia?"

The room was lit with natural light flooding in through the multiple windows in unconventional spots along the walls. Every bit of furniture was embroidered with different floral patterns, including the lamp shades. From her attire, the High Drao's home being minimally decorated was a surprise.

Staring at one large chartreuse flower stitched into a pillowcase, I still hadn't figured out how to approach the situation. I didn't figure out a delicate way to say it, or without feeling as though I was breaking some imaginary rules. Shifting my eyes past her, I concentrated on the shut door encased in light from a window behind it.

"I need faerie eggs," I explained in a weaker voice than I expected. "The Council has…" pausing, considering my words. "Forcibly obtained my services. They request faerie eggs to deem my service complete."

The High Drao's smile tightened into pursed lips, as her intense gaze stayed on me, but her finger rubbed back and forth across the table's grain.

"How, may I ask, did they forcibly buy your services?"

My gaze dropped to my lap, where I continued to wring my hands. That's the embarrassing question, wasn't it?

"They removed my pyx," I meekly answered, knowing it sounded ridiculous. From the people's eyes, the Council ran Gerennt smoothly. They wouldn't steal the thing which kept their citizens whole and alive. Children's stories explained it to be another part of our hearts, our centre of emotions. It was the part of us where decisions were made, whether good or bad.

The High Drao leaned back in her chair, expression unreadable, but intense and I could barely look at her.

"I've heard of the Council manipulating Merchants and Drao not under their employment, but this is a new extreme."

She tapped her finger on her mouth. "Were you chosen at random or are you in the Council's debt?"

The polite tone I heard before was gone but I expected it. My head started shaking halfway through her question. "I owe them nothing. There were seven other Merchants in the Council Chambers with me that day. I'm sure not all of them catered to Drao. The couple I recognized, do."

The older woman rose from her chair, pacing in front of the house's warped front window. The Dragonette raised its head, following her with its large yellow eyes. When it understood she wasn't far, the creature returned to its nap.

I knew what I was implying. The Council were targeting Merchants who worked specifically with Drao. Some products could only be used by people with magick. Drao needed more than the bare essentials to live. And Merchants like myself were the only way that some could get what they needed.

Eighty years ago, the port in Jova became restricted, and the Council was allegedly trying to control the Drao and restrict their purchasing avenues. Force as many pockets to the Council and their bank as possible.

Veks and the most naïve Drao didn't believe the rumours, saying distrustful monarchy supporters created the lies and doubt. During my time as a Merchant, both apprentice and on my own, I'd heard the whispers and saw the treatment spoken about.

But it didn't make what I said any less conspiratorial.

"Those of us who've been around for a long time know the Council isn't innocent, caring less and less about the freedom of Drao in recent decades," the High Drao muttered. "This, however, is proof that a lot of people have searched for. We're risking more to live in their society than if we had stayed under the king's rule."

Her back was to me, but I could see her reflection in the glass pane. The deep wrinkles and down turned mouth reappeared as she stared at the goats crossing the lawn, but I wasn't sure if she was actually watching them.

Sliding down in the chair, I waited. For her to say something or give me a plan on how to get my pyx back. Because other than finding and handing over the faerie eggs, I didn't have any ideas.

"How does it feel?" It took a moment, even after she turned, to realise she was asking me. "Your waist, my dear. I'm familiar with the spell to remove a pyx. It's a painful process. Some would say tortuous."

My hand instinctively shifted across my torso to rest on my side.

"Sore. It's an internal throbbing now, as opposed to the burning when it first happened."

The mood in the room darkened as she nodded. "At least they hired a practitioner who knew what they were doing. When an amateur performs it, the subject dies within days."

Unable to hear her as she mumbled to herself, toddling into her kitchen. Her finger ran along the shelves of jars as she grabbed containers to read the labels and putting it back to its spot. Peeking back at me a few times, she tilting her head back and forth in consideration. I felt exposed, like she was reading something much deeper than my appearance.

The High Drao held an item out to me.

"Go to the food market. The one closest to the front gates. Ask for Julon and give him this. He will comply with whatever you ask."

It was a thick piece of parchment, folded and sealed with red wax. Embossed was the national seal of the High Drao. 'Rinebur' beautifully scripted in gold at the bottom.

"This will get me the faerie eggs?" I asked with hesitancy.

It didn't happen often, but no matter how sweet she appeared, I would need to prove myself before she would help. It made sense. No matter her position, the High Drao was risking her own safety with my request.

"Julon will give them without question. I warn you to go at night though and be careful. People frown upon selling faerie eggs, but I'm sure you know that. Illegal, if you ask some Drao. If anyone finds out you have them, you'll become a target for robbery. You'll need to keep them in something secure," she muttered, her eyes wandering as her thoughts took her away.

She riffled through the drawers of a dresser covered in books and jewelry boxes. Whatever was inside clanged as she pushed it aside without care. A quiet squawk came from below me and tiny claws pinched into my shoulder. The Dragonette perched, wide snake-like eyes staring at me.

I smiled at the creature, its scaly grey wing grazing my cheek. Unexpectedly, the small dragon sneezed, and a puff of smoke rushed from its nose. After shaking its head, the creature looked surprised by the sound. The hints of smoke rose into my nostrils, and I did my best to hold back a sneeze too. Footsteps pattered against the wooden floors towards me.

"Put the eggs in this. It's enchanted, so nothing inside will break. Wear it around your neck and do not take it off unless you're putting it somewhere only you have access." She explained, extending her hand. "Once they find out you're a Merchant for Drao, Guards will use any excuse to arrest you for having faerie eggs."

A thick gold chain anchored to the top of a small bird cage dropped into my hand. The gold was in pristine condition, but it felt old. Like with most physical magick, it was hard to explain the sensation correctly. A red velvet pillow was stuffed into the cage's base, and most importantly, at any time, the eggs would be visible inside. I dropped the chain around my neck, the cage rested at the edge of my corset. It would fit between my breasts if I needed to.

"Thank you," I said, peering at the High Drao of Rinebur. "You didn't have to do this. It's more than what I came for."

"But I did, Orinthia. Your reputation is whispered amongst my people. Janna may have raised you, but you have left your own mark amongst the Drao."

I nodded, tightly smiling. It was uncomfortable accepting a compliment that I didn't entirely understand and I wasn't going to ask her to explain. The mention of my mentor's name threw me off. It always did. She was a Drao Merchant, but sometimes it sounded like Drao resented that fact. The High Drao made a clicking sound, and patted her shoulder.

With a single flap of its wings, the Dragonette pushed off from me and landed on the High Drao's shoulder. Giving her pet a warm smile, the elderly woman looked back at me. Whatever stress she felt during our conversation, had disappeared.

"You should get some rest. I expect you'll be leaving in the morning for your journey back to Jova."

"Yes, I plan to." I stood from my seat and moved to the door. "Thank you again. I appreciate it."

She didn't say another word. I left the cottage with my chest feeling lighter, clutching the scroll of parchment as I got closer to Dill. She had spotted more butterflies and watched them closely, ignoring the goat that took up residence between her front legs to continue its breakfast. I slipped the parchment into a small saddle pouch.

Hiking my pants, I mounted Dill. I didn't look back. The weight on my shoulders felt a little lighter, knowing I was getting the faerie eggs and didn't have to make shady deals with people I didn't know.

If I could get the eggs and get onto the country-wide highway, my chances of getting my pyx back were smooth and painless.

Chapter 4

I rode Dill down the main road with Marr and my cart in tow. Dill avoided the children, but old Marr almost stepped on a few. He lacked the build for speed or swift decisions, but also, he didn't care.

After leaving the High Drao's, I went back to my rented room for another nap. It was brief, as none of the other guests were considerate of anyone sleeping during the day. I contemplated getting the faerie eggs when I left the cottage, but I was nervous. What if the High Drao betrayed me? What if someone saw me and alerted the Guards? Waiting until dark was my safest option.

Instead, I decided the rest of my day would be updating the protection potions and spells on my horses and cart. The current ones I bought before I left Jova and the magick should still be potent, but it couldn't hurt.

I tied both horses to the hitching posts between an apothecary and potions shop. Giving Dill a kiss on the nose, I jogged across the street. With my hand around the door handle, I glanced back at an uproar of young voices. Little kids had converged and were running their hands along the horses' coats.

They were lucky Marr and Dill were nice; I knew a few horses that bit fingers of those who got too curious. Dill glanced down at them, not sure how to feel about getting attention. On the other hand, Marr was loving it and I couldn't hear his noises, but the little giggles meant he was definitely grunting pleasantly. A grumpy horse until people wanted to love on him. Hopefully, the children knew better than to try stealing anything. The spells on my property could take a person's hand off.

A calming scent of vanilla and herbal tea enveloped me as I pushed open the shop's door. The apothecary reflected the busy street. Hands reached for and pointed at jars with dried bits of plants and dead animals that covered shelves.

From the ceiling, long strands of drying herbs hung in bunches, and a faint smell of each as I walked underneath. Each step came with a pause as people walked in front of me. Amphibians and reptiles were in a small section along the wall, with a group of boys standing close to a frog tank as I squeezed past them.

"They're so weird looking," one boy said, his nose wrinkled.

"I should buy one. My mum would scream but she would let me keep it," the tallest of the group said confidently.

I wondered if they knew the animals were being sold for other not cute and magickal reasons.

Joining the short line of assorted people, I waited for the shopkeepers.

"Following me, Orinthia?"

Arin appeared, joining me in line not in her Vek attire of a barkeeper. Red hair tied at her neck, her curled horns were on full display unlike when she worked and they stayed hidden after hearing hundreds of sexual innuendos from patrons.

"I'm leaving in the morning. I figured for the trip home, I should refresh a few spells," I said after we exchanged cheek kisses.

"We've got similar thoughts it seems. I've run low on my veiling potion. Would hate for some drunk Vek to stumble upon me in the middle of the night when the potion fails and my horns appear," she said with a twisted grin.

"I'm sure the Delegate would be pleased," I answered, the sarcasm seeping out.

Arin raised her eyebrows in agreement. A loud wailing screeched through the shop, making us flinch. The customers searched for the source, some covering their ears. The shop keeper, a portly woman with shining violet eyes, approached a young boy frozen in the doorway with his hand under his jacket. He stared at her, terrified, as she stretched out her hand, to which his head dropped in shame, producing a large toad from under his jacket.

A quiet snort slipped through my nose at the attempted theft and the amphibian leapt into the keeper's arms. The boy dashed out, his friends following without a word. As the door shut, their voices mocking him flooded back inside. Arin and I shook our heads in unison, moving up in the line. The keeper muttered to herself, holding the uninjured toad close to her body.

"Damn children," she grumbled as the creature thumped back in its enclosure. Arin glanced at me, trying to hide her smile.

A second attendant stood behind the counter and like her partner, her eyes shone violet. After looking at them long enough, swirls visibly moved. I heard it produced an enchantment, but if I wanted to keep my pesa coins, I wouldn't dare.

Both women were piskies, a species of Drao with the ability to manipulate anyone they made extended eye contact with. Their desires were mainly financial.

"What can I do for you today, Merchant?" she asked, shifting her posture.

It was slight enough that I wouldn't have noticed if I

didn't know she was attempting to make eye contact. I kept my eyes on the back wall.

"Protection spells, deterrent charms, horses' wound salves. The usual travelling Merchant's bundle," I requested.

The pisky didn't give me a reaction, moving to the large cabinet behind her. When her eyes no longer were a risk, my gaze roamed across her back, exposed by her clothing. Her spine was noticeable, but not concerning. The dress draped at the base of her spine, falling around her full hips. It wasn't just a pisky's eyes that were enticing, each pisky used its physicality to entice victims.

A sharp thud hit my chest, and my focus removed from the building fog of temptation. My whole body felt warm, like I was wearing too many layers on the hottest day of the year. Arin chuckled as she lowered her hand. Having caught the mental trap I was unknowingly slipping into. I raised my eyebrows shortly in thanks as the pisky returned with a wooden box.

"This should support you until Delf, if used correctly. Would you like a lesson?"

I smirked. "No thank you, I'm fairly educated. What do I owe you?"

The pisky rolled her hand out. "Six hundred and fifty pesa."

I dropped tokk and meso coins into her waiting palm. She shut her hand when the metal barely made contact before tossing the coins into a bucket on the counter. If someone wanted to steal the pisky's payment, they risked their skin turning red and violently itchy. I accidentally did it in my younger days, having dropped a button inside. Whatever was inside was not worth the punishment.

"And you, Arin? How can I fulfil your needs today?"

Arin responded in a smooth tone, "the usual, Galley."

The pisky nodded, bending down. She rose from behind the counter with another dark wood box, larger than the one she gave me. Arin already had the pesa she owed sitting on the counter. It was a swift exchange, and we nodded thanks to the pisky as her attention moved past us to the next customer.

The next person, a man with wide eyes, basically forced us aside to talk with her. He was under the pisky's natural spell already.

"As always, the trip to see the piskies is enjoyable," Arin said, as the shop's door fell shut behind us.

I snorted, nodding. Piskies would go to desperate lengths to get coins. Owning a shop was probably the most civilized. Yet some people were still unlucky. I'm sure being with Arin, a regular customer, saved me some hassle.

Crossing the road, I shooed the children away from the horses. They ran away without a 'thanks' or 'have a good day'. An overwhelmed Dill appeared relieved not to have little hands poking at her. Smiling at the tall horse, I placed a kiss on her nose, which she then bumped against my shoulder.

"Can you hold this?" I asked Arin, holding out the box.

Putting it on top of her own, she watched as I opened the lid and removed two largest identical vials, one in my pocket and opening the second. I positioned myself at Dill's head and stuck my finger inside. When it was soaked in the potion, I drew a protection symbol that looked like a poorly drawn tree on her forehead. Dill's chestnut eyes shut, the sensation of magick overwhelming over her.

The magick wasn't reactive to the air and it wouldn't roll off, so no one else would feel it. Even though I felt more peaceful after putting my finger in, I wasn't sure if the potion worked the same on me as it did on horses. It was calming. I poured the rest of the liquid between her ears. Taking the second one out, I repeated the actions on Marr.

Swapping the empty bottles with on labelled 'Travel Protection - Unliving'. Potions rarely had creative names unless very specific and rare. I traced the same symbol more carefully on the cart's lid. It was an unnoticeable potion, so much the liquid didn't effect the colour of the wood.

"Where you headed next?" Arin asked, watching as I worked.

"Jova, but I have a few transactions to finish on my way," I said, pouring the liquid over the cart.

"Picked up anything for Eira?"

Hand halfway into the wooden box, I paused and gave my friend a half-hearted glare. She grinned at her purposefully mentioning my friend, who lived in the capital. I snatched a smaller, squared bottle meant to help muscular reaction and began walking behind Dill.

"She asked me to pick up a new dagger," I mumbled back.

"Did she? Or do you think she needs a dagger? You know, for when you're not home in Jova?" Her emphasis on certain words made my jaw clench.

"I don't live in Jova," I answered between my teeth. This was a repetitive conversation and a reminder why I didn't spend much time in Rinebur.

Arin snorted. "You may not live in Jova, but you live with Eira."

Turning my head to snap back, she had already placed the box on top of my cart and was walking away, laughter ringing in the air. Shaking my head to myself, I went back to the potions.

Bringing a refreshed Marr and the cart back to the communal stables, it was dark enough to pay a visit to the food market. Making the choice to ride Dill felt like an overreaction, knowing I wasn't likely to be robbed in town, but being physically above everyone gave the opportunity to know what was happening. The familiar squawk of wild dragonettes flew close to my head. The pubs a few streets over had the drunk laughs flowing in the air.

Rinebur's front gates were barely visible through the dull

lamplight. Tying Dill to a post, the Guards' sharp voices by the gates broke over the river. My nerves put me on edge, the constant feeling I was doing something wrong sat in my stomach.

Running my hand along Dill's neck, I stared at the shop's door. The lights were on, but there wasn't any movement through the windows.

"I'll be back," I muttered to the horse.

Stepping inside, I felt the urge to leave. The shelves looked close to collapsing under the weight of the produce. A quick glance to the back revealed vegetables lying on the floor and somewhere in the building's wall, something scuttered away. I didn't expect it to really be a food market. Even if it was unwelcoming and felt unsafe, I thought it would be creepier. But I was still itching to leave.

"We're closing soon."

A man I hadn't noticed stood behind the counter, leaning on his bony elbows. His bulging eyes watched from inside a sunken face, intensifying my discomfort.

My hand stayed on the old door handle, contemplating if I should leave without another word as he stared at my chest longer than necessary. But on his face when he looked up, there was enjoyment in my discomfort.

It made me let go of the handle and stepped confidently into the shop. The door closed with a thud, determined to make him cower by the end of our conversation.

"Julon?" I asked from my spot, adjusting my shoulders.

His suspicious eyes snapped up to mine, squinting instinctually. The lanky man shifted his weight, standing straighter.

"Who's asking?"

The shrinking of his shoulders and leaning away showed his true colours behind his casual behaviour.

Stopping across the counter, I gave him an invasive once over and allowed my judgement spill out, making his gaze drop to the unpolished counter. He wore layers of unclean and semi-destroyed clothing, body odour and uncleanliness clinging to every thread.

Pressing my tongue against the roof of my mouth, I removed the parchment from my jacket. He flinched back at the sudden movement. His mouth dropped open slightly, his gaze flickering between my expressionless face and the parchment.

"The High Drao sent you."

Wordlessly, I held the parchment closer to him. Julon's hand shot out but froze, waiting for my reaction. I stared, giving nothing away. Changing his tactic, he took it delicately. The suspicion never disappeared, but it was met with a sparkle of interest. The seal popped off and he unravelled it.

There was a shift in his posture from seedy rat to unpleasant shop worker. "How can I help you this evening, ma'am?"

I produced a smirk at the attitude change. The door opened before I could speak and, glancing over my shoulder, I tensed. A Guard stood half in the store, reading the situation he'd walked into. In a moment, he analyzed the clothes I was wearing and with the shift of his jaw, I knew I'd been made as a Merchant.

"Give me a moment," Julon muttered, walking around the counter. His pants were in the worst condition, but the new boots were a surprise.

Turning to lean my elbow on the counter, I watched over my shoulder. The Guard towered over Julon, his arms crossed. The pair whispered; the words were unclear. Julon twisted his hands together, listening to the Guard's gruff voice.

Acting like my attention naturally shifted to the shelves behind the counter, the clinking of pesa echoed in the store. I wouldn't witness anything that put me at future risk.

"I'll have your order prepared in the morning, sir," Julon said politely.

The door banged shut, the scuffing footsteps got louder as the clerk returned.

"I'm sorry about that. He's a regular." Julon stood behind the counter, less uncomfortable than before. "How may I help a friend of the High Drao?"

"Faerie eggs. Three of them."

His eyebrows shot up. "Those are illegal."

I pushed my lips together. This wouldn't be a middle of the night purchase if I didn't know that. "Do you have them or not?"

"I may, but I must ask what you're going to use them for?" Julon paused. "Ethical purposes."

I stared at him, running my tongue along my bottom lip. I had a look of authority mastered during my apprenticeship that Janna claimed helped difficult situations without violence. The silence made him shift uncomfortably, his eyes flickering away as he tried not to shy away.

"I'll take the faerie eggs now. Thank you."

I was ready to bribe him with a few pesa, but he entirely lost his composure. Vigorously nodding, he rushed through an open door frame behind him. My hand rested on my dagger at all the crashing and moving items.

The back room went quiet and my hand tightened. Julon reappeared with a small wooden crate. When he put it down, the metal top reflected the candlelight above us.

The box was well taken care of, no dents or scratches on the metal or wood details. He glanced around the shop as if expecting someone to appear before removing the lid.

"What kind are you looking for, ma'am?"

I kept the cringe off my face at the formal term and removed the chain from my neck. The movement caught his attention, eyes snapping to it. His pupils grew the longer he stared, and he swallowed heavily, fingers tapped against the counter. Would the High Drao appreciate if I had to fight her trusted shop keeper?

Keeping the thick chain wrapped tightly around my palm, I looked at the eggs. The delicate vessels matched the description in every textbook; small as robin eggs, but with texture like a dragon's. The shell was rippled and puckered. Each one was a distinct colour, some had veins going through some while others had splotches. The image of tiny babies curled up inside made my stomach turn and I looked at Julon.

"I'm not picky."

He nodded, but his curiosity sparkled, why I was so impassive with my choice. Once the locks were unclipped, I picked up three eggs at random and carefully placed them on the inner cushion.

"How much do I owe you?" I asked, locking the cage again.

Closing the box, he shook his head. Once around my neck, I placed the cage under my shirt.

"No, ma'am, you don't owe me anything. A friend of the High Drao is a friend of mine."

Ignoring him, I dropped three drak on the counter. His eyes flicked down to them; his mouth tightened.

"Have a good evening," I said, exiting the shop.

Stepping out into the suddenly windy night, stress filled my chest. Crossing my arms to block against the wind, the weight in the cage tugged against my neck and my eyes checked every person who walked by.

Was I being set up? Were there Guards waiting to grab the faerie eggs from me and make my life even more difficult?

It felt like more people were out and looking my way, but I was paranoid. Lifting myself up on Dill's saddle provided a bit of comfort. No one we passed looked back or if they did, there was no care in their eyes.

After returning Dill to the community barn, I walked the covered pathway towards the tavern. It was close enough the patrons' voices drifted between the trees. Exhaustion crept up my spine, and I rolled my neck for some relief. My joints cracked when a second crack echoed that wasn't from my body.

The heel of my boot hovered in the air as I paused, hand going to my sword. I scanned the treeline, straining to hear other noises. A knowing tingle rushed through my body that it was more than a deer. Someone was watching me.

Continuing at the same pace, as if the person would think I didn't notice their noisy error, I went directly into the tavern.

The pub was full of drunks. Stepping around and over unconscious patrons didn't concern me. It was common. I stopped at the front desk, where the male attendant laughed at what a dainty woman next to him said. Both went silent, looking up with a tinge of annoyance that I'd interrupted their flirting.

"Owyn Kellobyn. Anything for me?"

The attendant nodded, reaching under the desk. "A letter arrived earlier."

I dropped a drak on the countertop in thanks before taking the letter. I was tempted to instruct the attendant that if anyone asked; I wasn't here. But if I was being followed, the point was moot.

The door barely closed when I flicked the lock into place. Tossing my outer jacket onto the bed, my hand rested on the chain to take it off, but the High Drao's words echoed in my mind. I turned my attention to the envelope instead.

Curling up on the vanity chair, I tore it open, even though I had an inkling of the sender.

> *Owyn Kellobyn,*
> *It's been a full moon cycle since I've last heard from you. I assume you're in Rinebur by now. If not,*

*you've become ridiculously distracted by some Drao
girl in Mye. I've sent this to your regular Rinebur
establishment of choice. If you've picked another, I'll
be highly disappointed. However, I'm never wrong,
and I plan never to be.*

*If you're in Rinebur, I hope you're making good
time on finishing this 'transaction'. I ask you to
hurry back. I'm eager for you every passing day. I
would like this to be over, as I'm sure you are too.
Your regular schedule and life are waiting. Stay
healthy.*

I expect your response promptly.
Eira Khrom, Jova

Chuckling, I folded the letter back inside the envelope. Only Eira could politely tell me off and to get moving with my responsibilities. I had to respond soon, or I could expect a letter at every stop on the way back to the capital.

A small part of me expected Eira to show up if she didn't hear from me. As enjoyable as that would be, she'd rush me back to Jova. Yes, I wanted to get back and deal with this, but I didn't want to hand over the eggs. It made me uncomfortable to think about and I wanted time to figure out another plan.

Staring down at the folded page, my thoughts drifted to the mystery person following me tonight. My instinctual assumption was whoever they were, knew what I just obtained. Faerie eggs were rare. They had a high survival rate, but faeries didn't reproduce often and only a few times in their long lives. Drao frowned at random people owning infernal faerie eggs, but the small objects were collectables. I agreed. Shifting my gaze from the eggs to the small lock meant to keep the wooden door shut.

I dragged a large decorative vase to the door. Crashing pottery would wake me if someone bypassed the lock. I turned to the last entry point, the windows. It was a two-story drop to the ground.

Like the other buildings in town, the bricks were smooth. No one could climb up unless they had sticky fingers. I didn't know any Drao with that ability, but it didn't mean magick wasn't available. There wasn't a successful flying spell, but I wasn't taking chances.

Hating to cut off the air flow, I locked the windows shut and placed breakable objects on the sill. I pulled the curtains shut for good measure. That would have to do.

Chapter 5

A ROOSTER'S SONG FORCED MY EYES TO OPEN AGAINST THEIR will. Once my brain stopped trying to fall back asleep, I remembered the faerie eggs and my hand instinctively shot up. Expecting it to have been a dream, it was a relief when I felt the thick chain lying on the mattress next to me.

My muscles ached as I pushed out of bed. My feet had barely hit the ground. As my vision spun it had me rushing into the next room, my knees hit the ground in time to empty my stomach's contents into the toilet bowl.

Slumping minutes later, the wooden floor cooled my cheek and lungs, forcing slow breaths. Entirely numb, my hand rested on the residual bruise marking my side. The rumoured side effects from a living body without a pyx prepared me for how my health would slowly worsen. I was determined not to focus on it, but the next weeks would become increasingly more miserable.

Once I was certain my stomach was calmed, I stood in front of the metal sink and looked in the mirror. The changes were noticeable, my skin paler than normal and the dark bags under my eyes became puffier and defined.

Cupping water in my hands, I soaked my face, then ran

my fingers through my hair repeatedly. Despite the aching and how badly I wanted to lie down, I needed to get out of Rinebur and back on the road.

Shuffling through my sack, I decided on pants. The weather wouldn't turn cold for a few months, but the Histlea River produced a breeze that wasn't comfortable in a skirt.

Tightening the leather belt with my sword and dagger sheaths attached, I started feeling more like myself. Tucking the thick white shirt into my pants, I double checked that everything was in place.

In Jova, most of my clothes were custom made by high-quality tailors, leaving everything comfortable, lasting a long time and hard to tear from physical labour. Strapping into my travelling corset, my spine physically straightened. The comfort from the well-constructed piece wouldn't last long, but I relished it for the time being. I felt powerful.

Before putting my handcrafted sword and daggers into their places, I examined them. The sword, made by a Drao blacksmith that trained with goblins and my first purchase that made me feel wealthy, was extremely well balanced. The handle's red leather wrapping complemented the gold accents on the pommel and rainguard.

For my birthday, Eira gifted me a matching dagger from the same blacksmith. The blade was smaller but just as beautifully crafted.

After removing any evidence I was here, I tied my sack closed and made sure I had the response letter for Eira I wrote last night in my pocket. With one last look, I shut the door. Another familiar yet temporary room.

The bar keeper wiped down the counter, gave me a wave as if unconscious slobbering drunks weren't surrounding him. I left the note with the front desk attendant, a different man than the night before, to be sent out in the next bag of mail. Stepping out the front door, I noticed I wasn't the only one up with the sun and roosters.

The consistency of Rinebur was comforting. Some towns and villages, the folks would begin their days whenever they felt like it. But here it was the same time every day.

Stepping out to slip through the horses already leaving town, I decided the long way to the community stables was best. The sad feeling in my chest of leaving different towns and people had diminished over the last couple of years. The friends and acquaintances knew as well as I did that I didn't know when I would be back. Finding a steady income near the capital of Jova, coming this far across Gerennt, was becoming more rare.

Paying the stable fee didn't take much time. The staff took care of them, feeding and cleaning them, ensuring they were well-rested. I wasn't concerned about blood being taken to be sold for spells. Before leaving their stall, I put Marr's harness on, tugging the buckles snug. It was the easiest part of their gear.

I led the horses out of the barn, reins attached to their bridles to the carts parked behind the barn. Dill stood patiently as I began backing Marr towards the cart. He knew the sequence without a stumble.

The break inside Rinebur's stables was needed, it seemed, since he usually grumbled as I snapped the cart clips into place. My more cooperative horse stepped into place next to her brother to allow their shared rein to be secured. With one last circle check, I lifted myself onto the saddle. With barely enough time to get settled, Dill began leading to the main road and I couldn't help but smile a little. *Impatient.*

The sun continued to rise over the treeline and shoppers flowed from their houses as we got closer to the gates.

Two dozen Guards pulled my attention from my grumbling stomach as I was forced to stop with a handful of citizens as they marched in two long lines. They weren't wearing chest plates or warm sweaters to be going for mountain patrol, just regular navy sweaters with the golden emblem and their swords bumping against their thighs.

With a glitch nearby, my assumption was they were heading to the Fence. A shiver sent an unrecognizable discomfort through me. Guards at the Fence tear weren't abnormal, but this felt different.

Passing under the towering archway, I nodded to the Guards. I could see them assessing if they needed to check my cart, but they made no move.

As the shadow covered me, I peered up at the enormous stone archway. A matching arch stood at every town entrance. Huge, grey boulders with intricate wild vines climbed around it with a stretch of wall in the same stone. Some bits of rock crumbled on the ground. Though Rinebur didn't keep their gateway maintained, it remained beautiful.

The cobble road eventually became the dirt highway and grew wide enough for three horses to walk side by side, with the trees growing in the ditch. Green leaves still grew on the trees carelessly, with barely any hints of changing soon. Between the trunks, animals hid in silence. The tapping of hooves and the crunching of dirt from wheels rolling over it were the only sounds.

Once upon a time, the silence that came with riding alone was spooky, but I prefer it now. The only issue I found was the lack of distraction from being tired. My mind wandered as I dug my nails into the palms of my hands, noticing again my stomach grumbling and how I could go back and buy more food. But with the plan being to arrive in Mye by nightfall, my meagre bag of snacks would have to do.

A familiar sight of deer grazed into the roadway. Noses to the ground, they searched for bits of food. Marr gruffed at their actions, even if it was still another minute before we reached them. He was already annoyed, knowing he would have to wait until they moved. A few of the deer watched us cautiously. Deer were hard creatures to read, their eyes not as expressive as others. It made me hesitate to assume their next moves.

Slowing Dill a dozen yards away, I waited to see if they'd choose to move off the road or I would have to help them. But their heads turned in sync, eerily staring into the woods. Then they scattered. A few seconds later, I heard what the deer had. Hooves thundering through the uneven undergrowth towards the road.

Three men on horseback rode up the road's edge ahead. With their horses slowed to a trot, the men watched me intently. Despite her slow steps, I stopped Dill. As they circled, I saw how dirty they were. Scratches and loose threads marred even the saddles and their facial hair was scruffy, hairs flying wild. My grip shifted on the reins, having travelled the roads of Gerennt long enough to recognize the people.

Thieves. And I was outnumbered.

The road was wide enough that I could turn around, but it wasn't an easy manoeuvre and the men were only controlling one horse. Dill moved to the far side of the road with my instruction, putting Marr closer to the road's edge than I was comfortable with. Trying to think of a route past, but with how close they were stopping, I was distracted.

The highway thieves spread out in a line, as if I would try to break through them. My heart began pounding harder, knowing I'd have to do my best to get through this conversation with as many of my possessions as possible.

Letting go of the reins, I gripped my sword in one hand. Glaring down at the men, I didn't let the sensation of nausea bubble up at their snarky grins.

"How can I help you, gentlemen?" I asked unworried.

My head twitched, but I kept from looking over my shoulder as another set of hooves pounded against the dirt behind me. How the sound echoed against the trees let me know it was a single rider. Assuming it was another thief, made my situation even worse. My thumb rubbed against the red leather handle comfortingly.

The centre man with shaggy long hair and extremely bad posture attempted to smile pleasantly. "We'd like to purchase your horses."

"They're not for sale," I responded, tracking the pounding steps.

"We could use fresh horses. Our journey is long, and your horses appear much younger than ours," the youngest of the three men, the greyest looking one from dried mud, said. "We're happy to exchange."

An obvious lie, as their horses were visibly younger than Dill and Marr, but that wasn't what they cared about. Rinebur was the town at the southern corner of the country. They wanted my cart and whatever they could sell inside.

The eldest man got off his horse and walked forwards. With hunched shoulders like his companion, he still managed a cocky facial expression. He thought he could get away with anything. The grip he had on his sword was anything but subtle. Dill backed up several steps instinctively. Her muscles tensed under my legs. If this man tried to pet her, he would get bit and I wouldn't be mad.

"You can meet mine if you'd like," he offered. "I've tamed her in all the best ways I know. She will do whatever you want."

The other two dismounted their horses. Dill huffed more aggressively as the men approached and Marr picked up on her fear, his feet shuffling uncomfortably. Staring at the men, I focused on keeping the horses under control with a neutral expression.

The thieves' eyes went past me as the lone horse slowed. My gaze followed to the side when the horse and its rider entered my vision. The stranger thudded around me, putting himself between the men and me. All their hands hovered over their weapons as he stared down at them and didn't look back at me.

"How're we this morning, gentlemen? Is this young woman bothering you?"

I snapped my eyes towards his head, but a glint of metal caught my attention. The pommel of his sword was at an angle that only I could see. A piece of bronze displayed a headless bird with its wings spread wide. Engraved in the bird's chest was a 'G'. The Guard's horse shifted and his profile was easier for me to see.

He looked familiar, and it took a moment to recognize him as one of the Guards in the pub. Still ignoring me, he watched the men on the road, unsure of what to do next.

The Guard lowered himself from his horse and I followed suit, feeling at a disadvantage being the only one on a horse. Passing the front of the Guard's grey horse, the creature bumped its nose gently against my shoulder. I patted her snout, smirking at her untroubled eyes.

The thieves ran their eyes along the Guard. He was larger than all of them in every way. As they faced each other, the youngest thief smacked his shaggy older cohort's side and nodded his chin towards the Guard. There was a look of shock on their faces, finally noticing the Council's emblem likely sewn onto his sweater.

The shaggy man tapped the older man and did the same thing. They shuffled together and whispered like children, deciding if the trouble was worth the fun. Killing a Merchant was one thing, but a Guard? Imprisonment awaited them. The Guard's grip adjusted on his sword, almost as antsy as I felt.

The youngest thief made the first decision, creeping closer to Marr. When he was too close, the tip of my long dagger slid from its sheath and rested against his throat. I raised my eyebrows at him and he froze, gaze sliding back to his companions for help, but there was little loyalty amongst thieves. Their attention remained on who they considered the bigger threat. I was a little offended.

"We're negotiating for the horses. No need to stop, Guard."

"I'm not sure about that." The Guard puffed out his chest casually with a deep breath. "I left Rinebur at a similar time as you, gentlemen, and noticed you rode in the forest instead of taking the road."

The eldest man shrugged, his only response.

"As I told you before, my horses aren't for sale," I answered in a monotone voice, glaring at the man I held at knifepoint.

The two oldest looked at each other, still unsure if they were going to instigate a fight. It would be closer now that I wasn't alone.

"I believe that's your cue to be on your way," the Guard said. "I'm sure the lady and I can help you with that, but I know none of us want that so early in the morning."

The eldest thief decided that three versus two were odds he liked as his sword came out from its sheath. Before I could respond by pulling the sword from my belt, the Guard flicked his wrist, throwing a short blade of his own and impaling it in the man's thigh.

Poorly assuming my attention was on the action, the young man launched forward but ignored my dagger. Through the awkward position, a gash sliced into his biceps. A screech escaped his lips as he jumped back, unprepared for the swift injury. Not getting far enough back, I kicked out and the bottom of my foot connected with his knee. It knocked him off balance, stumbling wildly and tripping over his own feet.

Knowing I needed to cause a wound so he couldn't fight back, I moved towards the downed man, but the unexpected sound of flesh against flesh caught my attention. With his first older opponent in a ball on the ground, the Guard turned on the third man, trembling with a sword he didn't know how to hold. The dark-haired Guard easily avoided uncontrolled swings, stepping close enough to snap a punch. From the crunch, the man's nose broke.

On the ground, the old man made the poor decision to yank the blade out. The blood soaking through his pants wasn't a concern as he tossed the blade to the ground and tried to stand. He didn't even make it to stand fully when his leg gave out again.

As he dropped, the one beside me shifted as he tried to get up. Not bothered about permanent damage, I stomped down on his hand.

Letting out another cry of pain, he cradled his newly wounded appendage to his chest. The broken-nosed thief took in the fact he was the only fighter standing, and dropped his sword before kneeling. All three thieves, so threatening minutes ago, no longer considered fighting back.

Putting my dirty dagger away, I approached their horses and smacked each one on the rear. I was eerily calm after the bloodshed and weapons. The first time I felt this calm after a fight scared me. But now, it was more uncomfortable if confrontation didn't happen.

"You'll have to buy some horses. Yours are going to better owners," I commented, the dust settling on the road.

The man whose thigh clearly needed medical attention rolled towards me and reached out, anger and pain contorting his features. Purposefully, I squished his hand too, as I walked past. Curses spewed from his mouth as the bones popped under my heel, the limbs digging into the dirt.

Wiping sweat off my upper lip, I felt a creeping disappointment. Was this how untrained thieves were nowadays? I knew retired thieves who would kill these men for how easily they lost.

I lifted myself onto Dill's back and peered down at the Guard, grabbing his dagger from the dirt. His brown hair flickered out of his eyes, glancing up at me, unphased. A cramping inside of my stomach twisted at our eye contact. Clearing my throat, I pushed away the feeling and tossed my ponytail off my shoulder.

"Thank you," I said before looking at the men covered in dirt. "You better move out of the way. I won't feel bad if my horses crush you."

Handicapped by their wounds, the men scrambled, blood soaking the road. Without instruction, Dill started walking with Marr, taking his cue. Neither were concerned by the violence. Having passed them, I permitted myself a backward glance. Rightfully, I didn't trust thieves.

Normally, they would do what they could for "free" coins, even with injuries. The men were still cowering as the Guard mounted his own horse. It wasn't uncommon to bump into thieves, but I hoped that was the last excitement.

Hooves thundered behind me, my shoulders tensing. Dill turned back upon hearing the sound, but wasn't concerned as the Guard slowed his horse. She gave the unfamiliar horse a thorough once over. Nothing bothered her about the stranger, weirdly comforting to me.

"Is there something I can help you with?" I asked, watching the road ahead.

His mouth opened a smidge, then shut it and I peered at him, raising my eyebrows for an answer.

He awkwardly coughed. "I'm sorry, I don't understand," he said finally.

I tugged Dill and Marr to a stop. The Guard continued forward on his horse until he realized I wasn't moving.

The horse turned until we faced each other. I stared at him, not budging without an explanation. Sighing quietly through his nose, his hand rested on the pommel of his sword.

"I don't require a riding partner," I told him.

His tongue flickered out to wet his bottom lip, but still

didn't move. Keeping eye contact, I reached into a saddle pocket and revealed an ugly, twisted bottle. The potion inside was a disgusting brown, like opaque muddy water. But it was potent, and I pointed the lid at him.

"If you don't explain why you're still here, I'll happily toss this paralyzing potion on you. I'm sure those rats will make their way down here and rob you dry." I paused, my gaze flickering down to his weapon.

"Including that Verceenian sword. Not standard issue for a Guard." I tilted my head. "I'm correct to guess it is from Verceen? I can guess the cost, and I'm sure you would hate to lose it."

His green eyes sparkled, staring at my face with barely a glance at the potion bottle. Fingers tapping against the expensive sword at his side, contemplating, and I began feeling restless under his amused stare. Prepared to get Dill moving again, I adjusted my grip on the reins, but the smirk appearing made me stop.

"I heard you knew your weaponry, but I didn't know you were ruthless too. But no worries, I'm not following you. I'm going the same way."

My eyebrows scrunched, but it was less suspicious for him to recognize me in some way. Everyone in Gerennt knew my mentor and, as her formal pupil, I too, was often recognized.

"Not good enough. You ride ahead," I said. "Try again."

His head dropped forwards, a smirk softening before peering up through his eyelashes. My stomach rolled again, like it did when we first made eye contact. The tingling sensation was unfamiliar.

"Could you accept a friendly travelling partner?"

My grip tightened on the bottle. "I don't need a travelling partner, friendly or not."

"Aren't you concerned about more highway thieves? With what you're carrying?"

My heart skipped a beat before clenching in my chest. "If

you don't move now, Guard, I will make you. I don't care what the consequences may be."

As if understanding my threat, his horse shifted back and forth uncomfortably. Shifting his grip, he dropped his eyes to get control of his horse and keep her in place. He sighed, almost a little defeated.

"Fine. I'm assigned to accompany you back to the Isle and deliver the faerie eggs without incident."

The moment he mentioned faerie eggs, I uncapped the bottle. The only way he could know was being the person who followed me through trees last night. I was shaking and my hands were clamming. If I threw the potion, I wasn't entirely sure I'd hit him. Hearing another person say they knew I possessed faerie eggs was terrifying.

Checking the forest line, I expected more Guards to reveal themselves. Instead of letting the highway thieves rob me, the Guard interfered and now stopped me from running away. The ghostly coloured horse stepped closer on her own and the movement caused me to drop the reins and reach for the hilt of my sword. The potion was a risk. To escape, I would need to kill him. Seeing the panic in my eyes, the Guard extended his hand towards me.

"Owyn, I'm not here to kill you. If I was, I would have let the thieves back there do it and keep my hands clean."

My grip tightened as I tried to plan my way out of this, but my focus wavered as my name passed his lips. This was more than being Janna's apprentice years ago. Two horses and a cart weren't fast enough for me to outrun him or even leave. Killing a Guard was a crime that I wouldn't be able to hide from. But I was tempted by the idea.

Could I throw the potion at him and wait for it to take effect? What if I mostly hit the horse? It was quick, but quick enough to leave me scratchless?

While I panicked inside my head, a metallic gleam around his neck caught my eye. It blended in with the dark colours of his clothing. My head leaned forwards instinctively, squinting to make sure I was seeing it correctly. Locking the potion bottle, I dismounted Dill and the Guard's hand moved to his sword, wearily watching me.

"Get down," I ordered, staring at his necklace.

Dropping the bottle back into my saddle seemed to calm him a little, but still slow to do as I instructed. Maintaining eye contact, I took my smallest dagger out, pointing towards the necklace. After a long moment, he glanced down.

"Where did you get that?" I demanded, studying every twitch of his face for a lie.

"Which are you talking about?" He picked up the items hanging off the leather strap.

There were grey feathers, dried flowers tied together, and a crystal wrapped in wire, but in between it all, was a long triangle with an uneven lump of metal attached. Although I couldn't see it clearly, I knew a High Drao imprinted their symbol on it.

"The metal talisman. Where did you get it?"

"The High Drao of Verceen," he carefully answered with his eyebrows pressed together.

"When?" I snapped. The lack of explanation didn't relieve the tightness in my chest.

"Coming from the Isle to find you in Rinebur."

When he let the bundle fall against his sweater gave me a better look at it. Exactly like I thought as the symbol stuck out, the sun hitting it purposefully. The metal remained lumpy in the middle, its embossing untouched, but was specific and defined. Not everyone knew what it was. Some would think it was just a gaudy piece of jewellery.

"Did you ask for it?"

"No, he showed up at the pub I was in. Approached me by name and handed it to me. I didn't even recognize him at first," the Guard answered. "Why?"

My mind was spiralling, trying to understand why the

High Drao gave it to him. A thick swallow went down my throat.

"What's the colour of the gemstone?" I asked, having a hard time finding strength in my voice.

His eyebrows twitched, noticing how tentative I'd become. "Sapphire with a gold line around it. Again, why?"

A shaky exhale fell from my lips, my eyelids fell shut. Somehow, the High Drao of Verceen knew this specific Guard was coming to escort me to the Isle and I wouldn't believe the words from his mouth when we met. The gemstone was a magickally grown sapphire, representing trust within the Drao community. Only the intended recipient could carry it.

The magick of the High Drao's symbol was old. My eyes followed the unbleached twine until I met his green eyes. The herbal colour was calm, but he was still confused. With his forehead wrinkled, the small scar on the right side of his face was noticeable. But the tingles that ran through me when I made eye contact with this Guard happened again. The tingling sensation buzzed inside of me as my worries about being arrested vanished the longer our eyes met. The High Drao's message suddenly made sense, and the dagger dropped to my side.

"What's your name?" I asked.

"Pax."

His eyes flickered down to the dagger hanging in my hand, concerned it was still a threat. A part of me screamed to pay him off and let me ride alone, but I trust the High Drao of Verceen and he would never stray me wrong. I wished that was enough for me to trust a stranger, even with the weird and nameless feelings he created inside of me.

I sheathed my dagger and held my hand out. "Do you have a written statement from the Council?"

He nodded, popping a pocket button open without breaking eye contact and revealed a folded parchment between his fingers. My stomach twisted in disgust at the wax seal as I took it from him.

Unfolding the sheet, I peeked at Pax before reading the words. The Council sent him to accompany me, whether I knew he was there or not. Staring at the ground over the edge of the parchment, I knew it made sense. They wanted me to know they were watching one of their prisoners. It was the trust from the High Drao that didn't, but I wasn't getting answers soon.

Pax watched me with a neutral expression, hand on his sword, patiently waiting. There wasn't any smugness on his face, only the observation that I would not kill him.

"Fine. You can ride back with me, but it's not because of this note," I said with the parchment between my fingers as I handed it back. "It's because of what's around your neck."

His eyebrow cocked, looking down at the bundle again. I mounted Dill as he stood on the road, parchment in his extended hand, watching me.

"Shall we?"

Chapter 6

The first half hour of riding was in silence as I continued to think about the talisman around Pax's neck. A piece of metal inside my cart displayed the same embossed symbol.

Upon my release from my apprenticeship five years ago, the High Drao of Verceen gave it to me for luck. The seven High Draos of Gerennt were what remained from the era of royalty. The Council couldn't get rid of them without risking retribution.

In my first years as a Merchant, I learned to have faith in the High Draos and their beliefs. They knew magick and how it worked better than anyone else, but I was still tense. The symbol wasn't handed out for no reason. It meant something. I just wasn't sure what.

From the beginning of this journey across Gerennt, I suspected the Council was watching me but through the Delegates, sending updates every time I passed through a town. I did my best not to overthink that fact and only stressed over getting the faerie eggs. To my surprise, it was a Guard.

For all they knew, I killed him the moment we met. Less dramatically, if I said no, Pax would've followed me back in the shadows and I would be hyper focused. Having an escort was better than knowing someone was behind me for weeks at a time.

As the horses walked along a natural curve, a blockage appeared a hundred yards down the road. Guards and their horses covered the space entirely, and my heart dropped. It was a trap! I was foolish to have thought anything else.

Yanking Dill to a halt, I began directing the horses and cart to turn around. Pax stopped his horse too, a few feet ahead. Glancing back, he noticed what I was doing.

"Wait, hold…"

His words became a gag as a foul stench burned my nostrils. I leaned as far from Dill as I could as my stomach flipped. Under me, Dill stomped her feet, letting out an uncomfortable whine. Pax's horse and Marr reacted the same way. Pax spat on the ground before letting out an expletive, covering his mouth.

"Morning." Our heads snapped up at the gruff voice.

The atrocious smell distracted us to see two Guards approaching us. Dirt covered their bronze chest plates and their khaki pants, but most noticeably, a thick piece of fabric covered the lower halves of their faces.

"Where are you two headed?" He asked, resting his thumbs around his belt.

The second man, dirtier than the one speaking, paced across the road, assessing our horses. His eyes were full of disinterest when I met his gaze.

"Hoping to stop in Mye," I answered, glancing between the Guards and Pax. Upon hearing the town, both men shook their heads.

"You'll have to travel around Lake Kynett. A dragon died and crashed across the road. Made a big ol' mess. Some sabretooth tigers and wolves have feasted on it."

Well, that gave an answer to the smell. One hand rested across my nose as the other gripped the reins. The smell would be imprinted on my brain, and I was almost certain I would have to burn these clothes.

"You've not been able to remove the predators?" Pax asked, his hands in fists trying to keep from throwing up.

They chuckled as one said, "If you'd like to try, go ahead. Every predator from the mountains came down once they smelt death. And as you can tell, it's a strong smell."

A polite way of saying the creatures were feral and hungry. It was why the Guards were in sight, but the dragon was not. They were waiting for the bones to be the only things left.

"We won't risk anyone getting near the corpse right now. We don't need any more of those things coming down," the other Guard said.

Sighing, my head dropped forwards. Riding around Lake Kynett added at least three days to my route. The thought of riding through the forest entered my mind, but the cart would never fit.

"Thank you, gentlemen," Pax said with a nod.

The Guards nodded back and walked away, waiting for the next travellers. I glanced between Pax and the Guards. It was ridiculous to assume all Guards in Gerennt knew each other, but it was naïve to assume they didn't. Especially in my situation.

"The road around Kynett starts there," Pax commented, pointing back to a fork in the road.

Staring at the turnoff, I contemplated my other option; wait in Rinebur another week and hope the dragon's carcass was decomposed to the point of inedibility and the carnivores went back up the mountain.

The large bruise on my side pulsed against my clothing, reminding me I didn't have time, and I squeezed my thighs into Dill. Around Kynett it was.

Once we made the turn and the smell disappeared, the tension was still in my chest. The expectation of being accosted and taken to the Isle's jailhouse wasn't going away. The guards treated every inmate with the same disdain, regardless of their crime.

Pax said nothing. His attention remained on the road. His horse made a loud noise of annoyance when a few rabbits ran in front of her feet and he chuckled, patting the side of her neck.

"What's her name?" I asked, nodding to the light grey horse.

"Neem." The horse tilted her head at her name. Again, Pax rubbed her neck.

"Dill," I ran my hand down her light blonde mane.

"The grumpy man pulling the cart is Marr." I chuckled to myself. "Actually, they're both pretty grumpy."

I glanced at him when I didn't get a reaction, and when he noticed, Pax made a sound of acknowledgement and nodded his head.

"You knew that already, didn't you?"

Pax cleared his throat, barely looking at me. "The Council gave me basic information. Did you know you've got a reputation for being a handful?"

"Sounds like an insult coming from them," I muttered, and he tittered in response. Good. The least he could do was pretend he hadn't read a file on me.

It didn't surprise me that the Council had compiled information on me. Was it generic information, or did they do their research? How much did they know?

The questions sat on the edge of my tongue, but I kept myself from asking them. It wouldn't do me any good to know. A particular dip in the road caused me to shift awkwardly on Dill's back. The cage bumped against my skin and gave me something to ask.

"You knew I had the faerie eggs," I stated.

"Yes," he said in the same matter-of-fact tone I used.

"Was that something else they told you?"

Pax glanced at me, but I kept my attention on the road. He cleared his throat.

"They told me it was what you were picking up in Rinebur. I confirmed it with that creepy shop attendant after you left."

The corner of my mouth twitched, but I ignored the comment about Julon. "What else did they tell you?"

"That your trip is important and nobody should interfere with it. I am to make sure of it."

I nodded, staying silent. He didn't know more than necessary. Which meant he didn't know why I had to get the faerie eggs and the situation I was in. It's how it would stay. I would never talk to this Guard again once we returned to Jova.

It took a few hours before the first signs of civilization came into view. The sixteen villages sporadically surrounded Gerennt's towns and had very few people living in them.

The villages didn't have actual names, identified by their surroundings. For example, this village was Rinebur's Kynett village. Crumbling bricks marred the bottom of the terribly conditioned houses. No pesa coins were contributed by the Council to the upkeep of villages.

Extremely simplistic, with only a few shops, the bare necessities of food, wood workers and tailors. Everything else required a trip into a town. The coins were spent on things they considered more important, people they found more important.

The dirt road turned into cobblestone and narrowed, forcing Pax closer to me. The entire village came out of their houses, hearing the unfamiliar hooves, and didn't look away as we passed. Clouds rolled over the lake as we rode by and the shadows already over the village appeared to grow, the buildings' cracks getting more defined. Trees loomed over the roadway and the people stood, taking in every detail of the strangers. The treeline between the road and lake did not silence the noise of crashing waves.

My shoulders rolled, scrunching more of my cape around my neck. A wet, rotting scent blew past my nose and I couldn't place it until large wooden beams pressed against the wall of a building came into view. Houses rotted and mould grew from years of unhindered water damage. There was no stopping in Rinebur's Kynett village. Hands would reach for our pockets before our feet hit the ground.

The houses ended without warning, and the wind got worse without the minimal coverage. Small animals scurried away, making their own noises against the natural sounds of the forest. Pax didn't require conversation, thankfully. His head was on a swivel, scanning the trees. He wasn't enjoying nature, but looking for threats.

Marr huffed in discomfort at the same moment my spine tingled. A disturbing energy was sneaking around us. As I looked for a threat, Dill began walking diagonally away from the forest next to her, pushing Marr towards the ditch. I tugged her straight, but still couldn't see what bothered us all.

"It's the Fence," Pax commented. "There's a Fence break coming up. The magick from it sets off an unsettling pulse. Animals can hear it and don't like it. We just feel it."

"How do you know that?" I asked.

"I know a Shifting Drao who's been through the break in Verceen."

His tone caught my attention. It looked neutral for him as he scanned the trees, but his hand was tight around his sword's pommel. His gaze flickered to mine momentarily, feeling my eyes on him. Everyone knew about the Fence breaks. No one was allowed through. It was illegal to travel between countries.

I don't know how the Fence breaks happened and why the Council didn't have their magick staff repair them. The

Council was the reason that the Fences were implemented, to keep Gerennt's citizens contained.

Three known Fence breaks existed.

One in the Forest of Som, where the risk of anyone passing through the Forest was extraordinarily low, seeing as they could expect their own death. The Forest generated consistent dark magick. No regular citizens went inside the very real and tall fence built around it and its neighbouring, more peaceful forest, the Forest of Islenng.

The second break was deep in the Crewnyr Mountains along the border of Verceen and Ynoms. A rumour circulated that people used this break to sneak out of the country. Merchants and powerful citizens knew it was an entry for black market products. I knew a few Merchants who used it to travel. Guards patrolled the border, but people still made their way through.

This was the third, leading into Sandewyd, the country to the south. It was another black market hub, but better secured and less used. No one wanted to travel to such a grim region.

A low hum rose from the quiet, accompanied by the jolting sound of sparks shooting into the air. It was only on my left side, which felt warmer than normal. Squinting my eyes, I tried to notice any changes in the scenery. Anything that showed a tear in the Fence. But it all seemed to be the same.

"You there!" Ahead of us, two Guards on horseback appeared out of the forest. "What's your purpose for travelling this road?"

Their horses stopped abruptly, shooting dust into the air. Absently, I waved my hand in front of my face to clear it from my eyes. Their swords were already out, hanging at their waists.

"We're trying to get to Mye, but there's a fresh dragon carcass across the road. We were sent this way," I responded.

On both sides of their horses' necks, daggers hung in sheaths. We were a threat to them.

Did they think we would be dumb enough to get through the Fence in the daylight?

"I'm going to have to look in your cart."

The younger Guard and Pax were having a stare down. Did the Guard realize Pax was one of them?

He wasn't wearing his armour but had on a sweater embroidered with the Guards' emblem. I glanced at the wrinkled older Guard who spoke and opened my mouth to answer, but Neem stepped forward to cover me and Dill.

"That won't be necessary. I'm escorting this Merchant on her travels and there's no need to look in her cart. I know all its contents," he stated, a very different persona coming out, revealing the sheath with the Council's emblem.

The Guard's expression changed. We were still a threat, but they weren't ready to kill us right away.

"Do you have your commands?" The Guard asked.

Having Neem get closer, Pax handed the same parchment over as before. It didn't take long for the man to read it and hand it back stiffly. With a nod of their heads, the Guards returned to the woods. As Neem moved to the side, all the horses began walking again. I glanced over my shoulder and made eye contact with the Guards watching us from inside the treeline. More Guards riding between the trees were revealed.

"You didn't need to intervene," I commented. "I know how to handle myself."

The road widened. My leg no longer brushed against Pax's with every step Dill took.

"That's the point of me being here. No one will question a Merchant being escorted by a Guard. I'm supposed to take on the attention. You're meant to be barely noticed."

"That's what everyone wants to hear," I muttered.

Pax smirked. "I figured you'd complain, but accept it. I'm

aware the Merchant's way of handling things is a lot messier."

I pursed my lips, not responding because he wasn't wrong. Janna taught me that if flirting or friendly conversation couldn't fix it, the weapons I carried would. The cart behind me was transporting potions and expensive or ancient Drao weapons. If I had to use them to defend myself, my clients would understand. They would be less understanding if I was arrested or killed and they never got their products.

THE SUN DISAPPEARED AS WE PASSED THROUGH THE GATES OF Warfidd. It was the only town on this side of Lake Kynett, isolated for a good reason. Like the village before, people stood and watched us with wide eyes.

Slumped against the building walls, they were curled in on themselves. A few shaky hands reached out to touch Dill, but she sent them into an angry huff and the hands shrunk back into the darkness.

"Do you know where the inn is?" Pax wearily asked, looking at every person we passed.

"Just up here," I answered, nodding with my chin and mostly ignoring the people, but Pax was tense, his hands flexing around Neem's reins. "Have you been to Warfidd before?"

He shook his head, suspiciously watching those closest to Neem. He wasn't giving any of them the benefit of the doubt, and his reaction was understandable.

Warfidd, at any time of day, presented a daunting sight, with its abandoned buildings, smashed windows, and boarded-up structures. Neglect left the gardens overgrown, spilling onto the road, while all the town's outer buildings crumbled, despite continued occupancy. Not just the poorest town in Gerennt with no pesa coming or leaving the town, but referred to as haunted, thanks to those who lived here.

Dismounting our horses near the faded paint-covered door, Pax followed me into Warfidd's community stable. Heavily armed Guards stood at the entrance to the building, scrutinizing each person as they entered. Pax only had to nod at them and we were let through without a second look. Different to my surprise of increased Guards in Rinebur, the number of them here was normal. We transferred the horses to the barn workers, shared their needs, and paid the fee.

Exiting the barn, a shrill laugh filled the air. It sent chills down my spine. The Guards twitched their hands to their pommels, on high alert.

Pax froze beside me, his shoulder brushing against mine, as his hand instinctively moved to the hilt of his sword. None of the stumbling people stuck out as the sound's source. Barely any of their heads moved in acknowledgement.

"It's fine. It's normal," I calmly said, ignoring my pounding heart. "I'm going to check in."

As I stepped across the threshold of the inn, its charming and cozy atmosphere was an immediate change. A young man shot to his feet out of a large armchair in the corner, sword hanging in his hand. We weren't who he was protecting the inn against. His wide eyes darted between Pax and me, taking in our attire before sitting down again.

With growing unease, Pax's eyes remained fixed on the man, the silence stretching uncomfortably between them. He was truthful when he said he had never come to Warfidd before. Evidently unfamiliar with the dynamics here, a place rife with the constant suspicion that people harboured for each other.

Turning my attention away from the hired security, I smiled at the man behind the desk and reached into my satchel for coins. The gleam of an enormous sword leaning against the desk beside the attendant caught my eye briefly.

"I'd like a room, please. One bed," I said, sliding the pesa on the counter.

"Can you make sure the room has a couch?" Pax added.

I glanced at him over my shoulder. "I think you should get your own room."

"I don't trust you enough not to leave without me. You don't think I'm that naïve, do you?" Pax whispered into my ear.

A wave of heat surged down my spine as his voice resonated close to my ear, a sensation I concealed.

The desk attendant stared boredly at us, rolling the pesa I handed him between his fingers. Pushing aside my frustration, I took a steadying breath and offered the attendant a polite smile, attempting to convey appreciation.

"One bed and a couch, please."

The attendant nodded. "Name?"

"Owyn Kellobyn," I answered, holding my hand up as Pax tried to answer. "We've got three horses in the barn. Stall six."

The attendant picked up a key from the counter and held it out. "How long are you planning on staying, Merchant?"

Pax, positioned behind me, became rigid, his muscles tensing. The attendant's gaze was drawn to Pax as he noticed the subtle shift and his eyes squinted, analysing the Guard travelling with a Merchant. Taking the key before he jumped to any insidious conclusions, I brought the attention back to myself.

"Just for the night. We'll be leaving early."

"How did he know you're a Merchant?" Pax asked, shutting the room door behind us.

I dropped my rucksack on the bed before reaching to loosen my corset, shrugging.

"Few people willingly come through Warfidd. Plus, I'm not exactly dressed like a Guard or a normal citizen. But let's be honest, I don't have what it takes to be a Guard."

Pax put his bag next to mine. "Ignoring what sounds like a jab, I have to ask. What's with this town that makes me want to run and never look back?"

I chuckled, throwing my sweaty corset onto the bed.

"Warfidd is a plagued town. The Council sends the Cursed to spend the rest of their lives after they're done messing with them," I explained, removing my weapons.

Digging out an apple, I glanced at the silent Guard. He stared into space as I pushed by and sat on the couch. Its limited furnishings emphasized the room's diminutive size, with a single bed, a solitary couch, and a simple dresser made up the entirety of its contents. The scratchy fabric hadn't seen an update in decades, frozen in time.

"The Cursed?" Turning around, he looked surprised. I didn't understand why it was a question.

"Yes," I said around a mouthful of apple. "The Cursed? The Drao that the Council experimented on? If the experiment ends and they're still alive, the Council sends the Drao here, regardless of their mental state."

His expression fell, and his eyes flickered around my face, making me the confused one now. As a Guard, this piece of information shouldn't be a surprise. When I became a Merchant, Gerennt's secrets were revealed. Every misconception and blindfold I lived with was erased. My entire young life, I believed the Cursed were Drao living in perpetual alcoholism and destroying their own lives.

"I wasn't aware of that," Pax muttered, crossing his arms.

If he was faking or digging for more, I couldn't tell. Overwhelmed by tiredness at the moment, I lacked the mental and emotional capacity to give a damn. Resting my head against the couch's back, I watched him closely. The unsettling, queasy sensation in my stomach, a feeling that was so confusing earlier, came back with a vengeance.

Why was I trusting a stranger, especially a Guard sent by the Council? What was this gnawing feeling to trust him? A clinking caught my attention. Pax's fingers anxiously tapped on his sword's pommel, trying not to look at me. I sighed. He needed to sleep if we didn't want to arrive in Mye tomorrow night.

As I moved closer, Pax tensed up noticeably as I bit down on the apple, freeing my hands to loosen his belt buckle. Once undone, I tossed the sword onto the bed. I raised my eyebrow at him and took the apple out of my mouth before putting my hands on my hips.

"Do I have to completely undress you to relax?"

A smirk tugged at the corners of Pax's mouth, betraying a hint of amusement. The alternate meaning of my words hung in the air and the gleam in his eyes made me roll my own.

"That isn't what I meant." I took my dagger thigh holster off, tossing it on the bed next to his sword. "I don't know you."

Pax snorted, walking past me. "I'm sure that hasn't stopped you before."

I spun as Pax stretched out along the length of the couch.

"And by that, you mean?" I snapped.

His eyes widened, not expecting my sudden anger. My eyebrows raised as he stuttered, trying to form words.

"I just...I've only met Merchants that tend to..." he paused, finding the words least likely to get him injured. "Live their lives to the fullest. They're very free individuals. Enjoying everything in their lives. I figured all Merchants were like that."

I pursed my lips, glaring at the Guard. He was right, a lot of Merchants loved to drink and go to bed with a new person every night. Mostly, those were Vek Merchants who transported regular and magickless products. Drao

Merchants, like myself, spent our nights trying not to get robbed of the high valued products we carried, or killed. All Merchants may appear to work together, being the same guild, but it was a jealous and silent hierarchy.

"You pulled the short straw on fun Merchants to travel with. I'm more of the 'inform you about the tortured beings outside your room' type of Merchant. From the group of Merchants the Council kidnapped, you could've gotten lucky with a couple. Hate to break it to you."

Pax stood from the couch, beginning to apologize. I turned away as the look in his eyes made goosebumps appear on my skin,walking into the bathroom. Shutting the door, I leaned against the wood and took a few breaths to slow my heart rate.

My nightmares forced their way to the front of my mind, replaying without consent. Suddenly, I felt as if my shirt was bound and restricting my breathing. I yanked it over my head and threw it against the opposite wall. Leaning over the washbasin, my chest heaved with a deep, ragged breath.

I had to get back to the Isle with these damn eggs. Doing it made me feel like the worst kind of traitor, filled with self-loathing. My eyes rested on the cage pointing out of my undergarments. A naïve part of me hoped my sleep would be peaceful again when I got them, to know there was an end in sight.

Taking my time scrubbing off the dirt over the basin. Something was missing, a feeling clawing its way to the surface in my chest. The world was muffled around me, but not enough to feel like a handicap. I didn't understand. With wet hair, I went back into the bedroom. Unmoving on the couch, a book lay open in Pax's lap. His head jerked up the instant I entered.

"Owyn, I'm sorry I..."

I raised my hand, silencing him. We only met earlier today. No matter how easy of a riding companion he was or how nice he was to look at, Pax the Guard was a stranger and he may have read some files on me, but I was a stranger too.

Rummaged through my sack, I searched for the book Eira gave me when I left Jova. If it was left unread, she would be disappointed. Dropping my sack on the floor, I sat on the bed with my back against the wall. Inside the cover was the small note she wrote. Just like the letter she sent in Rinebur, Eira instructed me to hurry back.

Since the incident occurred, she was more vocal than me about my lack of pyx. If I showed her how concerned I was, she wouldn't let me make this trip alone.

The lines of text blurred as my eyes closed, but the rest of me was wide awake. Tossing the book aside, the moon was visible high in the sky through the window.

Sunrise was still hours away. I shut my eyes, trying to convince my brain that sleep was the best idea. The town's pubs were closed, and the Warfidd's Delegate shut the stores and public areas early, as the Cursed tended to have more issues at night.

"You could sleep," Pax said from the couch. "Instead of brooding."

He moved during our reading session to lie down with the book over his head. Feeling the weight of my gaze upon him, he slowly turned his head.

"Will you be sleeping anytime soon?" I asked, crossing my arms.

Pax looked back at his book. "Don't plan on it. Like I said, need to make sure you don't leave without me."

"On top of the fact that staying up all night is a genuinely bad idea, I don't know how I feel about sleeping with a stranger staring at me."

Pax rested his shut book on his chest and looking over, he was trying to find more meaning in my words. When he said nothing, I shut my eyes again.

"I'm from Delf."

"Okay?" I asked with my eyes shut.

His clothes scratched against the couch fabric as he sat up.

"You said you didn't want a stranger staring at you and I don't want to ride with a stranger. I'll tell you a bit about me and I won't be a complete stranger." Pax paused. "I promise I won't stare. Your beauty will surely wear off once you start to drool and snore."

A single snort of laughter passed between my lips and my eyes opened to a smiling Pax. Glad to get a positive reaction, he patted the cushion next to him. Sighing, I moved to rest my back against the arm of the couch, facing Pax.

"What age did you become a Guard?" I asked.

His smile faded, but he recovered with pursed lips. Unintentionally, my question landed a blow.

"Sixteen," he answered stiffly, before adjusting his tone. "What about you? How old were you when you decided to become a Merchant?"

My gaze dropped, and I scolded myself for the reaction. 'Decide' wasn't exactly the right word, but I wasn't giving Pax the story. That was something I kept close to the chest. Clearing my throat, I tried to cover it up.

"My apprenticeship started at fourteen. Nothing different since."

A silent agreement passed between us. We weren't comfortable talking about our years leading to today. The past was off limits. Most Gerennt citizens had pretty simple lives. Mostly Veks like Pax and me. Recognizing the misery in Pax's voice matched mine. We weren't a part of that demographic.

"You have gold in your eyes. Did you know that?"

I couldn't help but look at the ratty ochre fabric under us, running my finger across it.

"Yeah, I know. No idea where it comes from. My parents have brown eyes. Don't think gold is a very common result of that combination."

"Maybe you're a Drao and you don't know it," he joked.

"Ever made anything levitate with your anger? Tried to cast a spell or change into an animal?"

A weak laugh slipped through my nostrils as I smirked. "Not that I've noticed. Getting new transactions would be easier. Drao don't trust Veks, no matter if they know them or not."

As he chuckled about his own joke, I studied him. Regular features. No horns protruding under his hair or skin, regular eye colour. Not even sharp canine teeth.

Before I could look away, he caught me and smirked. "I'm not a Drao. From what I know, I come from a strictly Vek heritage."

I should've guessed I didn't know any Drao-born Guards. The Council did their best to keep it out of their ranks. In the past two hundred years, less than ten Councilmen were Drao.

Hoping to move away from the topic of Drao and Veks, I searched for another topic.

"How long have you ridden, Neem?"

"Since she was three years old, so a few years. No idea who came up with the name, probably someone's daughter. She was donated to the Guards."

"She's beautiful. I haven't seen many light grey horses."

"Your horses are distinct, too. A dark brown horse with a blonde mane? Who did you steal her from?"

Smirking, I shrugged and picked at the couch.

"I've had Dill since she was a foal. The farmer who owned her mother planned on putting her down because she was too distinct. He feared someone would damage his farm trying to steal her. My parents knew I wanted to ride, and she was cheap. The farmer thinks a wild horse got into his paddock and impregnated one of his horses. It was the only answer he gave about her parentage."

"What about your other one? Marr, right?"

"He was a bit of a stray, too. My mother and sisters went into Mye and came home with him. Found him on the side of the road. The veterinarian guessed he was two or three years old at that point. Dill was six and basically raised him. When he was young, Marr was a lot smaller. My mother thought he'd be great for my sisters to ride. After a year passed, it was obvious he wasn't born for riding."

Pax chuckled. "I can see that. Have you ever tried to ride him?"

The memories surfacing made me smile.

"He's trained to be ridden if necessary. He doesn't love it. Doesn't understand what he's supposed to do. He walks like he expects you to go flying with every step. Training took a long time, and I ended up on the ground a lot. As much as I wouldn't want to make him, I don't plan on walking across the country if something happens to Dill."

"How old are they now?"

"Dill is fifteen, which makes Marr twelve or thirteen."

"I didn't realize Dill was so old," Pax commented with raised eyebrows.

My smile faltered, not enjoying the thought of my horse getting old, with Marr not far behind.

"She knows there's a job to do. It keeps her young," I answered, trying to be funny, but it came across dry.

Pax sensed the shift in my tone. Tossing his book onto the table, he adjusted his position to bring his feet up.

"Tell me your goriest Merchant story." I raised my eyebrows questioningly. "If we plan on staying up all night, we might as well get dramatic. Should we hunt down some coffee too? Or is alcohol more appropriate?"

He was right, so I mentally flipped through nine years of memories. The smirk naturally grew on my face as a particular story came to mind. Adjusting my position, I started the story.

CHAPTER 7

A ROOSTER'S CROW PULLED A GROAN FROM MY CHEST, AND I rolled over, wishing to stay in bed. I didn't get far, my forehead bumping into something not soft enough to be a pillow.

Confused, I opened my eyes and saw my head was on Pax's lap, with his flopped against the couch's back and softly snoring. Trying not to wake him up, I lifted my head.

Pax's hand sat on my hip and I reached to move it, but a snore caught in his throat. He groggily sat up, his curly hair falling into his eyes. Strands of my hair hung in my face as we made eye contact and his attention slowly focused as he remembered how we ended up in this position.

"Mornin'," he grunted, running the heel of his hand up his face.

"I didn't run away," I commented, stretching.

Subtly, I placed my hand on my diaphragm. The cage still was hiding safely under my shirt.

"Thanks for that. It would be a bummer trying to track you down."

I hid a smirk against my shoulder as I stretched. The

gravelly tone of his voice made it sound unconvincing that he was fully awake.

"Wouldn't be too hard. I'd be in Mye for a few days," I said, grabbing my bag from the floor.

"Good to know," he grumbled. "Why are you determined to go to Mye? Shouldn't we head right for the Isle?"

"I've got a transaction to finish," I told him, pulling out a new pair of undergarments and clothing. "I'm changing and then grabbing breakfast. You're welcome to come."

Pax made a sound in his throat, tugging his shirt off before rifling through his own bag. Looking back over my shoulder, my eyes ran down his back. Small, white scars marked his skin, but my cheeks flushed with warmth in reaction to his muscles. His arms reached into the air, loosening from an uncomfortable sleep on the couch, and his back muscles flexed as the skin tightened under the stretch.

Noticing that I was staring, I shook my head clear and put my focus on my stop in Mye. I didn't move until the warmth subsided, but the nausea hit. Startled by the unexpected sensation, my body curled towards the bed. Attempting to breathe through the flipping of my stomach, I shut my eyes.

"Are you okay?"

Straightening, I opened my eyes even though my stomach wasn't entirely settled.

"Yeah, I was thinking about something."

Not wanting an answer, I shut the bathroom door behind me before quietly leaning over the toilet. It would pass eventually, and Pax didn't need to know.

I slid on a wide legged pair of riding pants on top of stockings and socks. A fair amount of the day would be near Lake Kynett, and being cold was never a goal. I stared at myself in the mirror as I braided my hair back. The bags under my eyes were heavy even though I got sleep last night. It didn't make a difference.

Washing my face last, I scrubbed a layer of skin off.

Something to rejuvenate me, even if it was through pain or delusion. Unravelling the clothes I brought with me, a small familiar jar tumbled out into my hand. Fish tonic. It was disgusting, and I wanted to spit it out every time, but ironically, it helped with nausea and illness. As I stared down at the gross coloured liquid inside the thick glass, I hoped the day would just be easy.

It didn't take long to find a diner, even if it was unappealing. The dirt spattered the walls, and the windows were hard to see through. Pax held the diner door open for me. A fuzzy warmth, the kind that makes your heart feel light and happy, flooded back into my chest when he winked as I passed by.

Mentally, I smacked myself as I stepped inside. Was I really impressed with a wink and basic manners?

The diner, like the rest of Warfidd, was gloomy. It had ten people inside and no one looked to be enjoying their meals. With the door banging closed, all the heads turned.

"Can I help you?" the bald man behind the counter called.

His hand rested on his hip, the talons in place of his fingers shining in the low light.

"Oatmeal please. Two," I responded, sitting away from everyone else.

The anxiety reappeared on Pax's face as he sat down, gripping the strap of his bag even though it was tucked under the table. Glancing around the room, I made eye contact with most of the patrons and their multitude of eye colours and shapes. Horns stuck out from hoods. Some patrons had the noses of animals, but not a single smile. I don't think anyone in Warfidd felt genuine happiness.

I smiled in thanks to the waiter as he placed the oatmeal down. Not giving a response, his eyes fixed on Pax in a furious glare before turning his back and walked away.

The oatmeal's scent hit my nose, and I tried to keep it from scrunching against the unappealing smell. Poking at the mush with the spoon, I considered asking for some sugar or fruit. However, the vibe I got upon walking in, I suspected the food would be taken away entirely. Shutting my eyes, I ate the dirt flavoured mush.

The diner's door opened, and weak, shuffling footsteps replaced the silence behind me.

"No, you're not welcome here. Get out!" The attendant shouted.

The entire diner looked as the man stomped towards the doorway with a broom raised above his head. Under a ratty blanket, a figure cowered before the man got anywhere near them. The person spun for the door again but faced towards me for a moment.

From the blanket's shadows, a face emerged, and my heart sank. I didn't know if there were eyeballs or only sockets, as the eyes were so black. Poorly healed scars burned the being's face, making their disfigurement worse. The individual's face was visible for only a second before the broom harshly whacked the being's head.

My heart clenched as the Cursed Drao stumbled out of the diner.

Once the disturbance settled and the silence returned, I glanced at Pax. His face had paled significantly, his hand frozen holding a spoon. Unsure of what to think, his eyes darted between me and the door. His mouth opened, but I shook my head. This wasn't the spot for questions, too many ears.

Begrudgingly, I finished the meal and Pax picked at his oatmeal, only taking mouthfuls after I reminded him we would have nowhere to stop. The moment the bowls were empty, we left the pesa on the table and grabbed our bags. The gloom outside dissipated, a bit of sunlight coming through, but didn't get rid of the eerie feeling.

DILL AND NEEM HAD THEIR HEADS OVER THE GREY STALL DOOR as we walked into the barn. I handed the barn keepers extra pesa to help us prepare the horses. Getting them outside wasn't easy, since both were half asleep. I think it was this town. It affected every living thing.

Tossing the leather straps over Marr's back, I felt a small nip on my shoulder. Glancing back, my nose almost bumped into Neem's snout and my eyebrows raised in amusement at the horse.

"Can I help you?"

Neem bumped her nose against my shoulder, my heart aching at the sweet gesture. I ran my hand along her neck, and my breath slowed to match her deep ones. Peering over, Pax watched us with a soft smile. The expression made my stomach tense. I smiled back and turned to prepping Dill.

Unbuckling the leather saddlebags, I noted my supplies and decided that I may as well buy ingredients for basic potions and fish tonic while still in a town. I was going to need more and this detour wouldn't be an entire waste. Everything was cheaper here. I told Pax, and he nodded, still distracted by what happened in the diner as we walked the horses along the main road.

The Cursed were stumbling out of their hiding spots and, with us next to the horses, it kept their wandering hands at bay. The apothecary near the diner we ate in was one of the few buildings opened.

Pax followed me inside and I didn't complain. I wasn't sure he would do well alone for long. The shop door was stuck open, and I leaned inside. It smelt like cinnamon and vanilla, probably the only spot in Warfidd to not have an undertone of mould.

"What you lookin' for?"

A woman appeared from the darkness, glaring at us. Everyone was naturally suspicious here. When she decided I wasn't Cursed or a thief, her hand appeared from behind her back and put the dagger back in its sheath on her hip.

"Mostly, fish tonic. Maybe a few newt's eyes?" I asked, ignoring the weapon.

I understood. From behind me, Pax made a gagging sound at my requests. I glared at him before rolling my eyes.

"If you're going to be like that, go do something else then," I whispered.

He nodded his head, looking thankful. His eyes roamed over the shop again and stayed on the shopkeeper as he walked out.

The shopkeeper nodded. "Come in."

I exited the apothecary with a small fabric bag in hand. The sun had risen and more people were walking through the streets. There was a larger distinction between the Cursed and their family members, who were dragged to Warfidd to support their loved one.

I found Pax at the bakery a few doors down, handing pesa to the keeper for a bun. Turning away, he spotted me approaching.

"Find anything good?" he asked, taking a bite from the pastry.

He made a much better choice than staying with me and smelling all the potion ingredients. I started to answer him when shouting came from across the common space.

"Were you stealing from me?" a voice roared.

Under a ragged greying blanket, a Cursed stood at a stall, shrinking back from its large male owner. A few other Cursed rushed down the road, clutching their blankets. I watched the blanket shake as the person underneath shook their head before turning to scurry away.

As the tall man whose horns curled back towards his head shone in the sunlight, the Cursed Drao tripped over the blanket's hem, tripping awkwardly to the ground. With the fabric ripped away, the fragile and vulnerable body was exposed. It was the same Cursed from inside the diner.

His hands shot out to stop his head from smacking against the dirt road, but he had no strength. He couldn't hold up his own weight and dirt was thrown up in the air. Market customers laughed, openly enjoying the suffering.

Other Cursed circled the man and snatched the odds and ends that flew out across the dirt road. I shifted my weight, prepared to step forward and help the Cursed stand. Pax's hand wrapped around my upper arm, holding me back.

"Look," he whispered against my head.

I peeked to where Pax indicated. Through the crowd, the mustard-coloured robe stuck out. His hair slicked back and clean shaven, the Delegate of Warfidd had arrived on scene and he was staring at us. He was expecting me to step in and interrupt the natural flow of the day. He could instruct the Guards to stop and embarrass me.

From the grip Pax had and the look in the Delegate's eyes, it was a bad idea. My gaze returned to the splayed body. His blanket disappeared, taken by another Cursed. His limbs, contorted and misshapen as if repeatedly fractured and improperly healed, bore testament to a history of trauma.

I couldn't help when my heart dropped at the unnatural way the spine stuck out. The man hadn't eaten properly in a very long time. The exposed skin was a perfect match for the horrifically mutilated facial features. Pax squeezed my arm, his grip tightening.

The Delegate wasn't being coy about watching us as Guards spread throughout the townsfolk to break up the Cursed's unwanted attention. The people of Warfidd returned to their shopping as if nothing happened when the Guards got closer to them.

My attention returned to the exposed body when a gurgling sound erupted. The Drao's mouth hung open and as the body thrashed, green liquid spurted out. As their body rose, the person's head tilted backward, digging deeper into the dirt while their spine bent unnaturally.

Thicker than blood, the green liquid oozed from his eyes and nose. The Delegate continued to watch me as he smirked, challenging me to help. Warfidd was unsympathetic to the Council's failed experiments to 'live' out the rest of their lives. It wasn't a peaceful existence for anyone here and whispers of insanity lived. Interrupting the death would prove I disagreed with the Council.

The muscles in my side subconsciously nudged me, reminding me I disagreed or disappointed them somehow, and I was facing my punishment. I couldn't risk more of their wrath. The memory had me step back, Pax's chest stopping me.

To distract myself from the sadness threatening to overwhelm me, I closed my eyes tightly, focusing on his grip.

The gurgling slowed until a final crack made my eyes open. The Cursed Drao stopped moving. His back thumped into the dirt, body surrounded by the unknown dark green liquid. He broke his own spine.

"There's nothing you could do," Pax whispered. "Let's go before the Delegate comes to say hello. I'm sure that won't end peacefully."

I pulled my gaze from the corpse to the town official. He already turned his back to us, instructing the Guards surrounding him. I gently tugged my arm out of Pax's grip and walked back to the horses.

Reaching for my saddle, Pax's hand came to rest over mine. He looked down at me sympathetically. A silent communication passed between us.

"It would've been the right thing to do. I know."

I nodded sharply and he let go. After settling on Dill's back, I took a final glance at the Delegate. He seemed pleased we were leaving, and, mirroring his expression, I was equally prepared to leave.

The construction of the Warfidd gates matched those of Rinebur, except the ones in front of me, were crumbling. The grey boulders were grimy, chunks of it pushed off to the side. It fit the town it guarded. There was an overwhelming relief leaving the town. I knew I'd have to bathe when we got to Mye, to rid myself of the grim that built up overnight.

"Plan on visiting Warfidd again?" I asked, peering at Pax.

He huffed. "No, I'm okay. I don't know how people live there. It's miserable."

I shrugged. "Some have family members that are Cursed. A lot of fishermen live there because of the river access. It's a cheap town."

"I never realised that's what happened to Drao the Council tested on."

I made a sound in my throat, looking ahead on the road for any danger. Pax released a quiet scoff beside me. I glanced at him.

"What?"

"You don't believe me."

"I just find it surprising that a Guard doesn't know what happens on the Isle," I said.

"Not all of us are knowledgeable," he commented.

"Okay." I tried to sound convincing. Probably not working.

Chapter 8

The sun sat high in the sky as we reached the next village. Grey smoke rose over the treeline. Warfidd's village was another small hub of houses, close together. I couldn't remember ever visiting the village.

As we passed the fork in the road leading to the village, I spotted a group of children huddled at the edge of Lake Kynett. They weren't too old, young enough that they should've been in school. They squealed with laughter; one child jumping up and down in amusement. In the shallow water, something twitched as the children poked at it with a stick.

"Are you kidding me?" Pax muttered, making Neem speed up.

He yelled for their attention and the young kids stood, looking at him with wide eyes.

"Didn't your parents ever..." His scolding broke off with an exclamation. Neem reared back on two legs as she saw it, too.

The children stood with rocks in their hands, frozen that they were in trouble. Pax leapt off Neem, unexpectedly tossing her reins towards me. I could barely catch them. He pulled out his dagger, stomping towards the children.

One of the smallest boys began crying and I couldn't understand his reaction until the water moved again. I swore loudly and yanked back on Dill's reins, trying to keep control of all three horses. It was a secylla, a water-living humanoid carnivore that ate medium sized creatures, including children.

Secylla were ruthless creatures that hunted and killed out of a desired bloodlust. The children had no clue what they were taunting.

"Come over here," I told them. "Quickly!"

As they glanced back at the creature, it released a bloodcurdling scream. The children screamed, scrambling backwards and the horses became disturbed, but the smallest boy wasn't fast enough.

A single shot of its arm, the tall, grey-blue humanoid had his ankle in its grasp. Screaming and kicking aimlessly, the boy was left alone as his crying friends backed away. Its other limbs dug into the mud for better grip as the secylla dragged him towards the lake.

As the boy lost his footing, Pax leapt forward and grabbed his arm. He tried to get a better grip on the boy by reaching for his other arm, but was having a hard time from the jerking manoeuvres of the secylla. The horses' front hooves were rising off the ground in panic and the children's behaviour wasn't helping.

My focus needed to stay on the horses, keeping them from unintentionally hurting themselves or someone else. The screaming children ran back to their homes, leaving their friend to a brutal fate.

My heart dropped when Pax slipped in the mud, slamming into the ground. I could only watch with full hands as he raised his dagger in the air and awkwardly stabbed the secylla around the child.

The secylla screeched in pain, releasing the child to protect itself and slithered back into the lake's depths. Pax scrambled them back a few feet away before releasing him. Rushing to his feet, the sobbing boy ran home. He didn't look back.

I watched the surface of the water calm again, waiting for the secylla to make another appearance. The horses soothed themselves as the chaos disappeared. Carefully I dismounted Dill, weary that they were easier to spook after what just occurred. I jogged over to Pax's side, grabbed his shirt, and helped him stand up.

"Stupid kids don't even say thank you," Pax grumbled, trying to catch his breath.

He shoved his dagger into its sheath in frustration. A thick coating of mud soaked him, clinging to his clothes and skin.

The water across Lake Kynett was foggy, but didn't move. Today, Mye wasn't visible on the other shore. As Pax twisted his torso to look at his backside, seeing that the mud soaked his clothing completely. He scoffed, glaring out at the lake.

"Damn secylla," Pax muttered, chucking a rock into the water. "Kids didn't even know what they were messing with."

"Do you want to go into the village and get new clothes?"

Pax walked back to Neem. "Nah, I'll change into something I have and put these in a separate bag. I'll wash these in Mye."

I stood at Dill's head, petting her nose. She let out a huff, annoyed by being spooked. Tugging Neem to the roadside, Pax pulled out a handful of clothes from his rucksack.

With a toss of the clean clothes onto Neem's saddle, he shed his outer layers to reveal his upper body. My jaw dropped in surprise. His head turned, and I snapped my eyes down. Inspecting Dill's nose, a rush of embarrassment surged through me.

In my peripheral vision, Pax pulled his pants off in the middle of the road. I inhaled sharply, turning to Marr and fully giving him my back. My mind didn't need to wander to crude thoughts when the ride got quiet.

"Owyn?"

Clearing my throat far too aggressive, I turned with tiny hopes he was entirely dressed. He was wearing pants, but still only in an undershirt. I pressed my tongue to my bottom lip as my gaze absently flickered down to the tight fabric across his toned stomach.

Realizing I stared for far too long, I lifted my eyes but couldn't help running them over his torso and started roaming down to the loose pants when I heard my name again. Snapping my mouth shut, my eyes shot to Pax's face. The gleam in his eyes matched with the smirk on his face caused my blood to bubble. His hand moved, and I noticed a small hemp bag.

"Do you want a strawberry?"

My eyebrows scrunched as Pax rolled down the bag's edge, revealing the red fruit.

"When did you buy those?"

"You were in the apothecary," he said with a shrug.

I held my hand out, and Pax stepped closer, removing a fruit from the bag. He stopped close enough that his breath washed across on my face. My cohesive thoughts stuttered and I couldn't push him back. His green eyes looked around my face with a twinkle.

He raised a strawberry, unblinking. Opening my mouth, I accepted the fruit carefully. If he said anything, I didn't hear. My heartbeat was pounding in my ears as I chewed the fruit.

Pax watched me with a straight face. He swiped his thumb across my lower lip. I refrained from reacting when he put his thumb inside his mouth to clean off the juice. The blood rushed to my cheeks at the intimate action. His hand barely fell away from his face before aiming it towards my jaw.

"Where's the creature?"

My entire body flinched away from Pax, the shout breaking our trance. I glanced backwards at the village road, then to him. The colour in his eyes lost its intensity, and he looked confused now.

"Can we leave and not be accosted by angry village people?" I asked, my voice just above a whisper.

Hoping he wouldn't notice, I clenched my shaking hands. I didn't understand the overwhelming emotion. It was like I had just experienced a drunk crying episode.

"Right," he said, grabbing the clean sweater off the saddle and putting it on.

He was unphased as the pounding of boots got closer. Pax only grabbed his dirty sweater from the ground as I lifted myself onto Dill's back. He shoved it in a saddlebag and mounted Neem. Glancing across at me, he shrugged.

"Didn't like those pants much, anyway."

We set off as the adults appeared on the roadway, the children cowering behind them. They were carrying swords and other weapons, focused on the lake. The small voices told their parents where the incident had happened. We didn't even catch their attention.

***

PAX AND I STAYED SILENT AS WE CONTINUED TO RIDE AROUND Lake Kynett. Embarrassed by my behaviour, I couldn't bring myself to look over. It was out of character for me.

Yes, Pax is attractive, and I kept to myself since leaving Jova three weeks ago. I liked affection as much as the next person, but I met the man only a few days ago. I wasn't crippling in dire need. He was escorting me back to the Isle. I was his assignment. I was better contained than this.

Peeking at Pax, I saw him staring ahead, but I couldn't read his expression. The transformation of his eyes before flickered in my mind. He appeared as though he was possessed when I ate the strawberry.

What had I looked like when I felt so weird, being close to him?

THE FAMILIAR ARCHWAY OF MYE PEERED OUT FROM THE TREES with the faded red gates sitting open, dirt piling up at the base. They never were closed.

Mye was one of the few towns that had actual gates. The familiar sensation of my lungs seizing up began. It always did when I returned. My fingers ran along the leather of the reins, reminding me I wasn't staying here permanently. It was only for a night.

"Home sweet home, eh?" Pax said, smirking at me.

I returned it with a polite smile. "Yeah, sure."

He watched me, even after I returned to staring at the peeling red paint. Taking a deep breath that forced my lungs full of air, we passed under the stone arch. Ivy grew from both ends, meeting in the middle with small white flowers poking out.

The armoured Guards barely glanced our way. They nodded once before returning to their casual spots against the surrounding wall. They weren't worried about much going wrong. Mye was a casual town, the crime rates were low.

My tongue felt too big in my mouth when I prepared to speak.

"Follow me. I've got the way memorized."

I shut the door of the rented stalls and watched the horses quietly. They were comfortable as they pushed around the hay in a familiar space. I wish I could be that at ease.

This wasn't a town I enjoyed being in too long. Slinging my bag over my shoulder, I handed the workers a few extra pesa.

"Give them a scrub down after they eat?" They smiled in agreement, taking the coins.

Exiting the stables, I glanced up at the pink sky above the trees. I had two people in mind to visit while I was here, but there would be no time tonight. Pax stood beside me, holding his bag over his shoulder with his elbow stuck in the air. I couldn't stop myself from rolling my eyes. Even under the raggedy sweater, his muscles were obvious.

A pair of women passed, staring at him. They flirtatiously smiled, even though his skin was decorated with mud. He smiled back politely, but stepped behind my shoulder. The two women understood what he was trying to convey, even if it wasn't true. I rolled my eyes when he looked down at me.

"If you're done, I'll be renting a room for the night and eating dinner."

Pax's polite smile became smug. His eyes twinkled.

"Jealous?"

I scoffed, walking away from him. He jogged to catch up, chuckling. Barely moving my head, I checked to see if there was anything different from what I knew growing up. But Mye hadn't changed.

The buildings had renovations, like updating the raised patios that were damaged by the yearly flooding of the Histlea River. Some more gardens popped up, but it all looked the same. And it didn't give me a warm feeling of nostalgia.

"See anyone you know?" Pax asked, lightly jabbing me with his elbow. I smiled tightly at him but didn't answer.

My gaze rested on the first of two town bridges that crossed the Histlea River. The matching bridges were what I missed about Mye the most. Having been built hundreds of years ago during the reign of a royal family, the structures were beautifully constructed.

The thick pine wood with steel around it, the bridges were defining features. Before the Council put up the Fences, Mye was busier as a hub for travelling into the country before heading to Jova. Two hundred years ago, the Council took over and everything changed from there. The bridges didn't.

The warm night was being enjoyed by many people as children dashed by with sprinklers in hand. My boots tapped loudly against the cobblestones, the only sound ringing through my ears as I did my best to ignore the stares.

I didn't know if some recognized me or that Pax was an off-duty Guard. I understood their suspicion. Other than Jova, Guards were always in uniform outside of their homes.

"I didn't really know many people when I lived here," I answered, my gaze snapping from person to person.

I don't know what I was searching for, but I kept my voice fairly quiet.

"Why's that?"

I shrugged, not looking at him. "I didn't have a lot of friends."

"I guessed you were popular in school," Pax said, finally carrying his bag to his side.

"Thank you for the confidence, but no. I stayed only long enough to do my schoolwork."

"I'm happy to have met the fully developed Owyn then. I'm sure you would've broken my heart in school."

I didn't know how to answer the surprising comment other than the unintentional heat in my cheeks. Pax's gaze flicked to me before returning to the roadway.

Another amused smirk grew on his face. I huffed in frustration, knowing he said it to get a rise from me. My attention returned to where I was going when I felt the ground changed to wood. The cooling spray coming off the river calmed my spiralling nerves.

The impulsive feelings pushed aside, I could enjoy the town I grew up in. Most of the terrible memories were from home. The aged, dull school I spent my childhood at sat back from the road. My eyes barely paused on it. I never finished my proper education and the rest of my life pushed the memories away.

A thin line of trees separated the three-story cabin from the shops. The rushing sound of the river was in competition, with waves crashing against the shore. The inn sat almost directly between the Histlea River and Kynett Lake. It was a calming noise when I was falling asleep.

Pushing the door open, the warming smell flooded over me. I felt a sense of safety at its familiarity. There were other places to rent rooms, ones that Janna preferred to use, but I only chose here to stay.

"My, is that darling Orinthia?" The owner's wife, an older woman named Norma, walked around the front counter.

Her long grey hair hung over her limbs, loose like it always was. She wrapped her arms around my centre, squeezing tightly. I chuckled, using my free arm to hug her back. Norma was shorter than me enough that I could feel her stretching to rest her chin on my shoulder.

"Good evening. Do you have two beds available?"

Ignoring my question, she held me at arm's length and ran a hand down my hair soothingly.

"My dear, you need to wash your hair. You've got sticks and twigs in it." Her eyes flickered over my shoulder and widened, her smile freezing. "And who's this gentleman? Orinthia, I never considered you would snag a Guard."

I quietly laughed as she stepped past me, wrapping Pax in his own hug. His eyes widened with alarm, but returned the gesture politely. Norma gripped his face between both of her hands, staring at him. His eyes peeked at me briefly, begging for an explanation. My lips pulled back in between my teeth, enjoying the interaction.

Norma tapped his cheek, making him jump. He rested his fingertips on his cheek as she returned behind the counter.

"Two beds, you say? Are you sure you don't want just

one?" Norma asked, gazing up through her eyelashes with her brows raised.

I sighed at her suggestion, ignoring Pax's childish giggle.

"No, one room with two beds."

"Alright fine," Norma teasingly scolded. She finished scribbling in the inn's logbook before holding out an iron key. "How long will you be staying?"

"Just the night. I have some business in town," I answered. "I'll come see you after breakfast."

Norma winked as I took the key from her. She watched us leave the foyer, knowing she'd assume we wouldn't be using both beds.

"She's friendly," Pax commented as we climbed to the second floor.

I shrugged. "They're all friendly once you get to know them."

Chapter 9

Once in the room, I dropped my bag on the hardwood floor. Like the rest of the building, the room was familiar. I was already relaxed, knowing I would fall in the bed and be asleep in seconds.

However, since Norma mentioned my hair's condition, it was all I could think about.

"Unless you need it, I'm going to wash."

"Of course," Pax said. "You are starting to smell. I'm glad Norma mentioned it. I was afraid you'd kill me in my sleep if I did."

I glared at him, pulling at the laces of my corset. He winked, unconsciously thrusting his hips forward as he unbuckled his weaponry belt. My heart fluttered at the suggestive nature of the actions. I was proud of myself for not letting my eyes move down. What was with me today?

Turning away, I moved onto my own belt. I wore more weapons than the Guard, and not all of them were on top of my clothes.

I lit the boiler after topping off the pot of water. The tap was filling the tub quickly, but the water didn't heat fast enough to my liking. Mye was filled with inns and taverns, and the first time I ever stayed here, I appreciated just how clean it was.

The bathtub didn't look like someone used it every night. Not every inn owner was considerate of their guest's experience. They only cared about the pesa. Having kind owners was a bonus.

When the tub got close to full, I stripped out of my last layer of clothes and tossed the sweaty laundry on the floor. Carefully, I poured the boiling water in the standing bathtub. The tub was pushed under the window and the steam already fogged up the glass. My spine released its tension as my body slipped under the water.

Grabbing the bar of soap, I ran it along my arms. Watching the bubbles form, I stared at the white scars that rested underneath.

Memories flashed of a young teenage version of myself scrubbing my skin, trying to get rid of the forming scars. It only made them bleed and heal unevenly.

When my body was clean, I tilted my head back and soaked my head and hair. Scratching my nails against my scalp, I didn't realize I had a headache until it disappeared from the stimulation.

Before putting shampoo in my hair, I shut my eyes and placed my hands on the tub's edge. The muscles in my entire body released. The past two days contained more excitement than most of my year, not just the ride to Rinebur.

The bathroom door flew open and Pax's voice flooded in. "What's taking you-"

I sat up in surprise, eyes flying open. He stood with his hand around the handle, mouth hanging open with frozen words. I hid my chest behind the side of the bathtub, clearing my throat in annoyance. The sound snapped him out of his daze and he spun around.

"I'm sorry," he stated. "I thought you were only washing your hair. I didn't know what was taking you so long."

"Uh-huh," I said, my grip tightening on the edge of the tub. "Since you're here, bring my bag in? I forgot to grab something."

Pax came back with my large bag, hand slapped over his eyes. His dramatics made me smirk. Knowing he couldn't see me, I shamelessly glanced over his body. He was in another set of clean clothes.

The fabric of his lounging pants sculpted his thighs nicely. My already warm cheeks were set on fire when I noticed he was physically affected by my unexpected nudity.

"You can leave it there."

"Thank you," Pax sputtered, his voice weak. "I mean, okay."

Eyes still covered, Pax shut the door quickly as he backed out. I bit down on the tip of my tongue, holding in the laughter. He was more embarrassed than I was. Still smiling, I cleaned my hair and washed my body.

After sliding a huge shirt over my body and a pair of ripped up brown pants, I spun my hair in a bun on my head and stuck a metal pick through it. Putting the soiled clothes into a secondary bag, I opened the bathroom door.

Pax was lying on his bed, arm thrown across his face. His arm slightly raised, peeking at me before dropping back down. His chest rose, paused and slowly lowered as he loudly exhaled. The corner of my lips lifted as I tossed my bag to the corner.

"You're not the first person to see me naked. Don't feel like you took any virtue from me."

Pax muttered to himself, a grumble that didn't pass his chest. I stood at the end of his bed, watching the Guard. His reaction put me in a teasing mood. He didn't move as I moved around the bed. His arm flung from his face when I straddled his waist, resting my hands on his abdomen.

"Am I the first person you've seen naked? Is that why you're so embarrassed?" I asked, smirking at him.

Pax's other hand resting on his chest twitched. Staring him in his eye, I took the hand and placed it on my thigh, skin on skin, through a tear. His jaw clenched, a fire lighting in his eyes. My grin slipped until only the corners of my mouth lifted. I was challenging him to do more. The free hand dropped above his head on the pillow and the movement of his torso pulled my lower half forward, grinding me against him.

He inhaled sharply, fingers gripping my thigh. I felt what triggered the reaction. My teasing went too far, even if the voice inside of me screamed not to stop. Pax had yet to say a word. I pulled myself away from him, getting a weird sense of nausea as I did so.

Turning away from him, I took all the weapons off my bed. Pax sighed loudly and moved around on the bed. Staring at the bedsheets, I unravelled my hair and let it fall down my back. The hairs on the back of my neck tingled, and I knew he was staring at me, but I couldn't look at him. I kept my breathing quiet and slow, focusing on stopping my heart from pounding in my chest.

Facing away from him, I slid under the blankets of my bed. In the low light, he sighed again before shifting around himself.

Chapter 10

Opening my eyes to see the sleeping Guard across the room, I knew I had to get up. There was a transaction to finish, and I wanted to leave Mye as soon as possible.

Too much of my past could bubble out of the cracks and make this trip more stressful. Groaning as my feet connected with the ground, I rolled out of bed.

A voice in my head considered going back to bed, but it was easy to ignore. Tossing my bag onto the unmade bed, I rummaged through to find an appropriate outfit, knowing I'd required very specific clothing for this transaction. I had to appear mature, put together and like I knew what I was doing, but also I needed to run if things went wrong.

A wave of nausea twisted my stomach, forcing me to pause. I straightened, breathing through my nostrils. It would ruin my day if I puked all over my belongings.

"Leavin' me here?" Pax rubbed his eyes, head still on the pillow.

I smirked with my eyes closed, hand wrapped around the small cage hanging off my neck.

"No, I've got a transaction to finish. I need to get ready."

The feeling in my stomach passed, and I pushed clothes out of the way in my bag.

"Right. Where're we going?"

I paused with a dress in hand, looking at Pax. With droopy eyes full of sleep, he was interested. Nothing about him seemed to be waking up too quickly, and I sputtered out a laugh, able to reign it back enough to be a chuckle. The twist of his mouth made me feel a little bad.

"I can't take you with me," I said. "You have to stay here."

Pax sat up, offended. "Why not?"

"You're a Guard. Even wearing civilian clothing, it's obvious. Guards don't just hang around for no reason. You're too suspicious."

"So are you," he snapped.

I pushed my tongue against the back of my teeth, not laughing at the childish tone of his voice.

"I'm a Merchant, I usually have something illegal to sell or do. You've got very real authority and are meant to stop people who break rules. It's not something you can just turn off."

Pax turned, resting his feet on the floor. "How so?"

I shook out the dress, biding myself a moment to think. I didn't want to make him actually mad or offended.

"You're a Guard. That's not meant to be an insult. You're just formal in every way, even how you stand. Observing everything and everyone, you absorb their presence. You're a predator, hunting for the easiest prey. Like how you hold your sword, even while riding. It's one thing that makes other people notice you," I explained, while grabbing my other clothes.

Pax trudged over, picking his bag from its spot next to mine. "You've noticed me quite a bit. I'm flattered."

"You'd like to think so. I'm just making sure you don't kill me when my back is turned."

"You walk around like you'd kill somebody from one wrong look," Pax muttered with snark.

I smirked, peeking at him. "And your point?"

"Wouldn't that scare away potential customers?"

I opened my mouth briefly before shutting it, sighing.

"I don't know how to explain, but no. People trust me because of how I look. Maybe it's because I'm a woman too."

"And why can't I come? I'll dress like a Merchant."

He was determined, but I was stubborn. My stomach gurgled unhappily, forcing me to end the conversation.

"I don't know what else to say. I'm not taking you with me," I said, pushing past him to get to the bathroom.

Shutting the door, I closed my eyes as the nausea filled my abdomen. Resting my forehead against the wooden door, I waited.

My hand found its way to the cage against my chest. The eggs were almost weightless. I knew being pyx-less caused discomfort, but I never expected it to be this bad. No wonder I was guzzling fish tonic like it was dessert.

The feeling slowly disappeared. I straightened, dropping my clothes to the ground and took a moment to splash water on my face and scrub it in. I needed to pull it together, at least for today.

This client was dangerous, and I needed to be on alert. Feeding the leather string through the eyelets of my corset, I looked over my dress in the mirror. It would work. I could still fight, even though my chest was half revealed.

Returning to the room, I folded my sleeping clothes. Already packed, Pax laid out on his bed and occasionally grumbled about not being able to go. He was annoying me in the way a pouty child did.

I glanced out the window and saw the tops of fishing rods as a pair of fishermen walked on the road below. The sight gave me an idea of what I could do with Pax and not be worried about him interrupting my transaction.

Tying the last knot in my bag, I stood over him with my hands on my hips. His head snapped up, wide eyed with hopes I changed my mind.

"Want to go on a trip?" I asked him.

AFTER A FILLING BREAKFAST FROM NORMA, I LED PAX BACK TO the community stables. I needed to get something from my cart, and he wasn't letting me go alone. Giving the horses a quick kiss over their stall door, we continued through the barn to its back doors.

A few carts were parked in a gravelled area. Made of different types of wood, none of the carts were exactly the same size. Mine was somewhere in the middle. It was brand new when I bought it, but there were a few carts that gave me the impression of being handed down generationally. Years of travel worn them all down.

Carefully, I walked around the cart, checking for any hexes or talisman that weren't meant to be there. Pax approached the cart next to mine, his fingers outstretched to touch a trio of long scratches in the wood.

"Don't," I said in a monotone voice, not fully looking at him. Hand frozen, his eyes snapped to me. "You don't know what spells are on that thing. You'll probably lose a hand."

He returned his gaze to the markings, retracting his hand towards his chest with concern. I smirked, bending at my knees. Awkwardly, I reached under one of the cart's shafts and rested my hand against the cedar planks.

A pale blue light illuminated through the grains, my palm warming. Now that it was unlocked, I stood and opened the lid. Warm breath crawled across my neck.

"Whoa," Pax muttered.

"Keep your hands to yourself," I said as the lid locked open.

Leaning into the opening, I ran my hand over top of the merchandise. My cart wasn't full by any means, but what was inside was expensive. Multiple weapons, some brand new and others considered ancient, were secured.

Crates made of different woods, none too big, were packed in tightly. Labels described the contents or listed names and addresses on each item. Peeking over my shoulder, Pax either lost interest or was giving me privacy and wandered back towards the barn.

Spotting the dark coloured tiny crate, I grabbed it. Double checking the name scratched onto it, I dropped the cart's lid shut.

Walking around the perimeter of the barn, I found Pax leaning against the front wall. Unstyled curls hung in his face as he stared at the ground with his arms crossed. He turned his head at the crunch of gravel under my feet. I held the small crate up, showing I was good to go. He held out his hand curiously.

"Follow me," I said, checking his shoulder with mine as I passed.

I knocked on the front door, staring at my feet. A road over, the water rumbled by in the river and waves crashed against the rocks in the lake. I bit my tongue at the look on Pax's face.

With his shoulders pulled back, hand resting on the pommel of his sword, he carefully scanned the crowd of people walking below the busy street. The thought he could hide the fact he's a Guard was humorous, especially when holding a sign over his head would be less obvious.

The door creaked open behind me, and through the crack, a bright green eye was visible. I smiled at the older woman. She gasped, the door thrown open. Her arms wrapped around my middle, and I chuckled, hugging her back.

"Orinthia, my darling. Where have you been?" She stepped back, holding my hands out to assess my figure.

"You look too thin. How tight is that corset? Have you been paid well? I've told you not to save too much money; you need to spend some on food."

Her naturally worrisome instincts filled my heart with warmth. I had experienced no degree of maternal love in a long time.

"Mama, I spend my pesa just fine and, of course, my corset is tight. It'll be uncomfortable no matter what, might as well be too tight and have good posture."

Mama opened her mouth to counter when she noticed Pax watching from a few steps below. Her mouth tightened into a line as she gave him a once over. She tugged me a step closer, grip slipping tightly up to my forearm with her gaze glued on him.

"Why is a Guard with you? What did you do? Are you in some kind of trouble?" Her whisper dropped even lower.

Pax scoffed, shifting his weight, and I grinned at him. He selected his specific outfit, deeming it 'entirely mundane.' He even changed his scabbard to an older, worn one.

"Don't worry, I've kept out of trouble. And yes, he's a Guard, but he's here as a friend, Mama."

Pax stepped onto the porch. "You must be Owyn's mother. Nice to meet you."

We both laughed at the assumption, and she crossed her hands on her chest.

"You sweet boy. As much as I wish this child was my daughter, my son could never snap her up. I've done my best to persuade her otherwise."

Pax's face contorted in confusion, not understanding what she was alluding to, but her suggestion made my eyes roll.

"Come inside, you two. Please." Mama walked inside, leaving the door wide open.

I peered back at Pax, leading him into the house. "Einna is my childhood friend's mother. I stayed here during the school week sometimes."

"I wondered why you were so much paler than her," Pax said as he shut the door. "I was about to suggest you drink blood or something."

Mama chuckled, wagging her finger at him. "I like this boy. I accept it if you consider him."

I hushed her. "Mama, stop trying to marry me off. Especially to a Guard. That's not very nice."

She winked and sat down in her chair. The frumpy blue chair had to be older than me. It was patched up and mended more times than I could remember.

The living space was the same as it always did. A little too dark from the heavy curtains and smaller than some of the other houses in Mye. It was one of the originals. The brick and concrete base was patched so many times, it could be considered entirely rebuilt.

"Where's Cod?" I asked, stepping towards the other chair, but Mama abruptly tsked and pointed at the spot next to Pax on the couch.

I resisted rolling my eyes again and sat down where instructed.

"At work. The fish are overwhelming Lake Kynett ports. He's been there all night," Mama explained, smoothing her dress. "So, what do I owe the pleasure? Are you looking for my son?"

"No, I'm in town for work. Decided to come by for a visit." I paused. "How's Yash? I haven't spoken to him in a while."

She sighed through her nose, pursing her lips. The wrinkles on her face grew more defined at the mention of her son.

"He is fine, I assume. Hasn't sent any letters lately. I don't know the direction he's travelling, so I cannot send him a scolding one either," she told me, thoroughly annoyed.

Yash was an only child, and his parents had been very

good to him growing up. They gave him everything they could.

"If I see him along the road, I'll let him know," I promised, before leaning to Pax. "Her son, Yash, is a Merchant too."

"He became a Merchant to chase Orinthia's tail. Quickly found out it's a hard job where he has to work for his pesa," Mama explained with a smirk.

Even before I was forced into the job, Yash thought it glamorous. His mother always told him otherwise.

I shook my head in amusement at her words. "Anyway, I was hoping to leave this one here so I can finish a transaction. I don't need him scaring my customer away."

"I don't think it'd be that bad if I came with you," Pax muttered, raising his eyebrows sarcastically.

She gave him a sympathetic smile. "You don't understand how people see Guards, do you? Especially the Drao?"

"Apparently I don't," he responded, crossing his arms and sinking into the old couch.

I wondered if he knew just how childish his behaviour could be.

Instead of responding, I stood. "Will you explain it to him, please? He doesn't want to believe me. I need to go. My customer is expecting me soon."

Mama and Pax followed me to the door.

"Who are you delivering to?" Mama asked, holding the door open.

Already knowing she wouldn't approve, I stared at the small piece of lake visible between houses.

"There's a local hunter trying to catch a kelpie," I told her, adjusting my cloak's buckle. "He asked for a specific potion from a practitioner in Dornis."

Mama sharply inhaled, making me wince. She grabbed my face with both hands.

"What were you thinking? I know the man you're

speaking of. That's not a stable man. He's killed three Merchants when transactions haven't gone his way."

"That's a rumour, Mama. The Mye Delegate wouldn't let him survive if he'd killed anyone and so many people know about it," I pointed out. "That makes them look weak."

I couldn't help but steal a brief peek in Pax's direction. His jaw was locked, and I knew Mama's words hit their mark. He understood the reason I didn't want him to come. I glanced back at Mama.

Small freckles were only noticeable this close, the colour so close to her honey skin. Her once black hair was nearly grey. The only woman I still considered a mother figure was worried about me, but I couldn't let her concerns take root in my head.

"I'll be back soon, I promise." I kissed her on the head and walked down the stairs.

Her worries were valid. It wouldn't surprise me if I was about to be paid by a murderer. But it wouldn't be the first time and definitely not the last. No matter what I said, the Delegates would ignore laws when it benefited them.

Walking to the lake docks, I mentally counted the weapons on me. Before we left the inn, Pax was surprised I hid so many in different spots of my outfit.

Pushing through the crowd of Mye, I thought back to the look on his face before I left the house. I didn't explain much to him and almost felt bad about it. I don't know why I felt a whisper of need for him to understand, but I'm sure Mama's words and whatever she was telling him now, he'd get it. She wouldn't take his whining.

Before stepping onto the wooden boardwalk, I glanced back and scanned the crowd. There were a lot of different heads passing by, but not the full head of dark brown curls. Satisfied, I walked into the fenced off district. The sounds differed from in town.

Now, with the water crashing, warning shouts of

incoming nets full of fish and sails hoisting up on boats could be heard. The day was grey from the cloud cover and other than the greenery, the entire lake lacked colour. Different tones of grey with hints of blue and brown were everywhere.

I nodded to the dock workers, each one barely giving me a look, and continued their work. They would continue working as if nothing was happening, unless interrupted.

Rounding the corner that led to the deepest part of the lake's fishing docks, where the old lobster cages and ripped nets piled up, a man stood alone in the small bit of green that survived here. He matched the description I received of who I should be meeting.

The middle-aged hunter leaned against a cedar tree at the edge of the water. He did what was expected by picking a secluded spot. My heart sped up, but I couldn't let it show. Approaching him, I couldn't help but check the water.

Knowing the potion's purpose, I didn't know what the hunter had previously done to kelpies, trying to catch one. Being too close to the water if a kelpie struck was a bad idea. They didn't care if you were the person who wronged them or not. Their memories were long and vengeful.

"Gorrell?" I asked, gripping the strap of my bag.

He nodded, pushing off the tree, and I stopped a few feet away. He had nothing in his hands or around his waist, but that didn't mean he didn't have a weapon hidden.

"Did you bring anyone?"

"I do transactions on my own," I said emotionlessly.

"I heard you arrived with a Guard. Where is he?"

My tongue ran along the back of my teeth, annoyed. Pax really knew how to draw attention.

"I was asked to make a delivery to Jova. The Guard is to make sure it's returned smoothly," I explained. It wasn't entirely a lie.

"Nice to know Janna's mighty successor needs help. She's not entirely unbreakable." Gorrell's eyes sparkled.

He used a joking tone, but he saw prey standing in front of him. My jaw shifted unintentionally. There was a natural temptation to prove him wrong, but that's what he was hoping for.

"Do you want your potion, or should I throw it into the lake? I have no qualms with kelpies and I'm not desperate for your pesa," I asked between teeth.

He smugly grinned, rummaging in his pocket without breaking eye contact. Producing a small bag, he walked forward.

"Stop," I ordered. "Toss it here."

The grin grew on his face, and it made my stomach twist. It was like looking a hungry mountain lion in the eyes. He playfully tossed the bag between his hands. I hated he liked the thought that I was afraid of him. But I wanted to stay alive, and the safest way to do that was from a distance.

"You've heard of my reputation," he said with a shrug. "I can't deny it, so it's best if you stay away while I work. I'll find you if there are any issues."

Some Merchants liked to have people scared of them, to threaten anyone they thought they had to. I wasn't one of them. Expressionless, I stuck my hand out. Gorrell lazily tossed the bag.

Maintaining eye contact, I opened the bag and counted out the copper meso coins I was owed. I took the box holding the potion bottle out and opened the lid. Lifting the bottle out to show him, it slipped back into the crate and then I placed it on the ground.

"Good doing business," I said, walking backwards a few steps, but the smirk on Gorrell's face stayed.

The challenge stabbed me in the spine. Turning my back to the confessed killer, I squeezed my jaw painfully. I couldn't look back. He'd win some twisted game.

I walked past the fishermen with no contact. Once I was out of the Hunter's sight, I dropped back against the wooden fence, my nerves still heightened. My eyelids dropped shut and a shuttered breath slid past my lips.

As I focused on my breathing, my heartbeat calmed. Transactions rarely made me nervous. Janna's name hanging over my head meant people rarely tried to intimidate me or push anything too far. If they did, I can prove them wrong about it. I was trained for it. I can hold my own.

But threats from a shameless killer? It threw me off.

Opening my eyes, I watched people walking by. The town was going through their regular days. It was like the transaction I just finished was its own little bubble in the world. A pair of children dashed by with sparkly batons, ribbons fluttering off the end. I watched them with a smirk when my brain registered that I'd seen something familiar.

Turning my head back, my smile faded. For a moment, I spotted a long facial scar before it vanished into the crowd. My mouth opened slightly in surprise, standing properly.

Looking back to see if Gorrell exited the docks, I moved to where Pax stood. A part of me couldn't believe he'd followed. Lifting on my toes, my gaze weakly searched over heads as best I could.

Mye's market was always busy and today wasn't an exception. I couldn't spot him. But instinctually, I knew it was him. And I better find him exactly where I left him.

The amount of people dwindled the farther I got from the shops. I broke away and turned down the familiar side road. My frustration about being disregarded by Pax built as I got closer to the house.

I quickly spotted him at the bottom of the porch stairs, but not alone. My feet froze underneath me in shock and the frustration disappeared. It was only a head of black hair, but I knew who I was looking at.

Clenching my jaw, my feet forced me to keep walking, knowing that I would be exhausted at the end of the interaction. Pax's gaze slipped past the other man, a half smile appearing on his face. The other man noticed his expression change and peered behind him. A grin appeared on his sharp face.

"Look who finally showed up," Yash Horras greeted, pushing off the bannister.

His arm landed over my shoulders and uncomfortably locked my body against his. Over his shoulder, I looked at Pax, who watched in amusement. My jaw twitched again.

"Good to see you too," I muttered, patting Yash's back lightly.

He pulled back but didn't let go. His grip shifted to putting my neck in the ditch of his elbow.

"Just getting to know your friend here," he said, harshly clapping Pax's shoulder. I visibly saw the impact as Pax fought to keep the pleasant look on his face.

"Your mother said she hadn't heard from you in a while."

I grabbed his wrist and yanked myself out of his grip. There was a moment of resistance, but he released me. I stayed close to his side, though. The hairs on my neck were standing up, and I knew his mother was watching us through the window.

Yash shrugged, bored. "Decided it was time for a quick visit. Just my luck to run into you, sweetheart."

He nudged my side with his elbow. I tightened the corners of my lips into a smile, looking up at him. I didn't truly consider Yash a friend anymore, but his ability to lie to me was still weak. There was something more to his return to Mye than just visiting his mother.

"Heard you finished a transaction. Make lots of pesa?" Yash asked with interest, leaning against the bannister again.

"You'd like to know," I answered with what I hope sounded like a joking dismissal.

The familiar awkwardness yet comfort I felt around Yash was settling. Unsure if it was my Merchant training, or I just grew up, I didn't trust Yash. I saw his selfish behaviour risk lives before. However, I cared about his parents too much to stop visiting them when I could.

"I see you left a mutt here with my mother." Yash nodded his chin towards Pax.

His eyes momentarily squinted, but he smirked at the condescending words. The short time they had interacted didn't create too much tension. They weren't holding each other at sword point. That was some sort of a win.

"He stayed under your mother's supervision the entire time," I said, maintaining direct eye contact with Pax. He looked back with only a polite smile.

"Are you leaving town now?" Yash asked.

"I was planning to. Why?"

"Mama says she won't let you leave without a meal. We should go to Morri's pub after and talk honestly about our lives. Norma won't mind if you rent for another night. It won't throw your travels off that much, will it?"

I ignored his attempt at direct eye contact. No, we couldn't 'talk honestly' here. There was only so much truth his mother could handle. The horrors and truths of Gerennt that Merchants faced were too much for her. I peeked in Pax's direction, who was looking at his hand with interest as it held his sword's handle.

"We'll meet you inside. I need to consult my travelling partner. He doesn't need your dark eyes glaring to persuade him."

Yash glanced at the Guard and nodded, walking up the porch stairs. I waited for the door to close, my fingers twitching at my side.

Once the handle clicked into place, I pushed Pax under the second-floor balcony, hidden from view. He stumbled over his own feet before slamming into the wall.

From the back boning of my corset, I drew a short blade and held it to Pax's throat. He straightened, not expecting the assault. His eyes flicked between the blade and my face as I pressed my hand into the centre of his chest.

"I told you not to follow me," I said between my teeth. "You could've gotten me killed. Being a Guard doesn't make you exempt from causing trouble."

Pax opened his mouth, and in his eyes, he was considering denying it.

"Don't insult me by saying you didn't. If that hunter saw you, he would've slit my throat without a second thought. He's killed for less."

Pax set his mouth, shifting his back to stand straight. I took a micro-step back, not intending to cut him. I'd only pulled it out of anger. Only my fingertips were still touching his chest.

"Repeat yourself and listen, Merchant," Pax said in a low voice. I felt the vibrations under my fingers. "The hunter you willingly met alone was open to murder if you made him the tiniest bit suspicious."

Returning the blade to the corset pocket, I maintained eye contact with him. Out of residual anger, I poked my finger in the centre of his chest while closing the space between us.

"Listen, when I tell you to stay away from my transactions. You don't know how long it's taken for me to gain the smidge of the Drao's trust I have. I won't have some random Guard smash it apart in a second because he thinks his little security job is more important. I will incapacitate you and leave you behind."

Pax grabbed my hand and yanked it down to my side. His chest bumped mine, gripping my wrist tightly.

"I'm here to make sure that necklace ends up back on the Isle. I don't care if I mess with your connections to keep you alive. That's my job. If I think you and those eggs are in danger, I'm doing what I have to. I'll do my best not to interfere, but I have your back," Pax said, dropping to the lowest tone I'd heard from him.

My gaze slipped to his lips, hyper aware of just how close he was. His bangs hit my forehead. His tongue darted out, licking his bottom lip. Glancing back up at his eyes, my bottom lip slipping between my teeth. We stared in silence, his green eyes keeping me frozen in place.

I jumped when people began shouting in the street. I stepped away, clutching my now free wrist to my chest. The sounds of the river thundered in my ears and the world flooded back into focus. With his jaw still clenched, he blinked, but didn't remove his eyes from my face.

"Fine," I muttered. "But if you cause me trouble, I'll kill you."

Pax smirked. "Sounds fair to me."

I stepped out of the tall porch's shadows. Placing my hand on the bannister, I felt eyes from above and I knew it wouldn't be Mama watching.

"Do you want to leave now? I have nothing else to finish here, and we could cover a bit of distance before nightfall."

"I don't mind staying another night. We still have the room. His mother said you two haven't seen each other in at least a year. I'm sure you'll want to catch up with your friend."

I shrugged. "Dinner will be long enough for me."

His eyebrows twitched inwards, but he didn't mention it. "Let's enjoy a home cooked meal at least. I don't think either of us has had one in a long time."

Chapter 11

Stepping through the creaky front door, my eyes rested on Yash lying across the couch, his boots resting on the arm. A beat of annoyance went through me, but I controlled it. He was always careless, and no matter how much scolding or who it came from, he'd never change. Instead, I grabbed the toe of his boot as I walked by and shook it.

"These new?"

He smirked. "I like my boots clean. Helps people figure out who I am a little quicker."

I rolled my eyes at his vanity. It was a personality trait he always sported, but becoming a Merchant and making pesa inflated it. Vanity went along with his superiority complex. Pots clattering together interrupted whatever he was going to say next.

Pushing Pax's shoulder towards the couch, I walked towards the source. In the kitchen, Mama held a large bowl under her arm, mixing vigorously.

"Your muscles must be larger than Pax's," I commented, leaning against the cluttered counter. Mama was always cooking something. "We should compare at dinner."

The old woman glanced at me with the same brown eyes

as her son. Her eyes twinkled, a curl of grey hair in front of her face.

"I raised a son who likes to eat and brought home unannounced friends often. I've gotten used to cooking more than necessary."

I gave her a mostly genuine smile. "You raised an interesting creature."

Slowing the mixing, she leaned to see through the doorway. I followed her gaze to Pax and Yash sitting in the front room. Their mouths were moving, but neither looked at the other. Both sat with their arms across the chair backs they were sitting in. Yash's foot sat across his knee, shaking to a silent beat..

"You like that Guard?" I peered back at her and she was already watching me.

I cleared my throat and shifted my weight between my feet.

"He's nice. Easy to ride with. Hasn't given me a reason to kill him yet."

She acknowledged what I said with a sound in her throat, turning to the stovetop. I rolled my eyes, pushing off the counter. I knew her well, and she didn't believe me. Which I understood.

It was weird for me or anyone to be travelling with an admitted basic stranger. I didn't know how to express the strange feelings I had towards Pax, and I didn't want to try explaining it. Especially to the older, traditional woman. She probably would chalk it up to fate.

"What do you need help with?" I asked, tapping my hands against the countertop.

"Go sit with Yash and the Guard. I'm fine."

I brushed off her instruction, grabbing blindly at the vegetables and knives until she became concerned about my safety enough to give me instructions.

The dinner I helped make was simple: chicken, potatoes,

and homemade bread. My mouth watered as we placed the dishes on the table. Pax had a similar expression. The inns served decent food, but grease covered everything. It did something to your stomach after a while.

While the four of us filled our plates, the front door opened. Pax froze, his grip tightening on the side of the plate. His trained instincts never shut off. The old man brought in a wave of stinky fish smell into the house as the door shut.

Yash's father, Cod, stomped against the hard wooden floor with heavy footsteps. Only after removing and hanging up his heavy coat did he notice the two additions at his dining table. The grey-haired man paused, his squinted eyes landing on Pax first. His mouth opened to question him until he noticed me in another chair. Cod smiled, his hands clapping together.

"Look who's finally crossed our threshold."

I waved to him, knowing better than to try for a hug. It would take so many washes for me to get the smell out of my clothes. It would be easier to burn them.

"Who's the Guard?" Cod asked as he took his overalls off, leaving him in long underwear.

I snorted, and Pax smacked my leg under the table. Biting down on my tongue to stop myself from commenting, but the smile still slipped onto my face.

"Pax, sir. I'm travelling back to the Isle with Owyn."

Cod's gaze flickered to his wife. The couple exchanged a silent conversation with their eyes. I picked my fork up, stabbing at the potatoes.

As a child, I would try to decipher what they were saying to each other, but I never could. Maybe it was because they were married for so long or it was something deeper. There was more in their looks than I could ever understand. When they were done, Cod nodded.

"Alright," he gruffly said. "Glad to have you join us."

Conversing with Yash's family was easy, reminiscing and

sharing stories that left my face red. Pax couldn't stop asking for more stories of ridiculous things I'd done as a child.

Mama and Cod were happy to indulge his amusement. Grinning the whole time, Mama loved to have her table full. She may complain about it now, but she never turned away from any of Yash's school friends.

Pax and Cod swapped work stories with genuine interest. The passion Cod had about being a fisherman impressed Pax. On the other end, Cod had a generation's worth of questions about Guards that Pax was happy to answer where he could. I added a few comments and told a story or two. I didn't give Cod all the details he was digging for about why I was travelling with a Guard.

Merchants kept secrets. He knew that but still tried, interest sparkling in his eyes. Looking at him, it was like seeing the man I knew when I was a child.

The only person who stayed quiet was Yash. He made a few comments, behaving too focused on his mother's cooking. But his eyes rarely left Pax. It wasn't a glare, it was more of a constant observation. I didn't want to compare it to predator and prey, but it fit.

CHAPTER 12

Morri's, the pub I frequented in Mye, wasn't full like I seen in the past. Mye was a town filled with an equal mixture of Drao and Veks.

The range of beings and bodily features that filled the pub were something I found comfortable. It was like Jova, but different. The town was quiet, with less flamboyant behaviour. No assumptions that drunks would flaunt their powers.

"Booth in the back?" Yash suggested close to my ear.

I held back a shiver at the overwhelming scent of his body cologne. He put it on before we left, but I didn't smell it along the walk. I nodded, and he broke away.

Checking for Pax's dark curls behind us, I followed him. Leather covered the seats in the booths lining both walls. Tall tables and stools adorned the rest of the space, only leaving a small dance floor with lonely instruments for the band sitting in the corner.

"Yash, good evening! The usual?" The bar keeper called over the patrons' heads.

A smile appeared on my face at the entirely unchanged man.

"Three, Morri," Yash yelled back, indicating with his fingers.

I slid into the cushioned booth, keeping the bar in my sight. Pax joined me, but Yash pushed by, behaving like he hadn't noticed what he did. Turning my head towards the wall, I rolled my eyes. He hadn't changed. Not giving Yash a reaction, Pax sat across the booth from us.

Morri, the grey-haired owner and barkeeper, placed three heavy steins on our table. He crossed his arms, ready to talk to Yash, when his eyes landed on me in the corner. A natural smirk appeared as his eyebrows raised.

"Look who's come home. How're you, young Owyn?"

I clicked open the clasp of my cloak and let it drop on the bench behind me. The linen white shirt I had on under my corset was thin, almost see through. I felt Yash give me a once over but I ignored him, smiling at the old man.

"I'm fine, Morri. Just passing through."

"Heading back to the bright lights of Jova, I'm sure," Morri said with a smirk, before turning to Pax. "And who's this?"

"A little friend of Owyn's," Yash answered flatly, picking up his stein.

Morri nodded, trying to read the dynamic of our table. Making eye contact, Pax winked, relaxing some of the tension in my shoulders.

Weakly lifting the corners of my mouth, I glanced back at the barkeeper. Eye contact with Morri made me shift in my seat. He saw the wink and was trying to read deeper into it. He nodded to himself, coming to a conclusion alone.

"I'll bring another round in a bit," he said, walking away.

The judgement in his eyes before he left was confusing, but my concerns washed away with the first taste of alcohol. Warmth rushed through my body as I swallowed.

"So, Pax, what's it like being a Guard?" Yash asked, stein touching his lips.

I pause my drink, glaring at Yash through the corner of my eye. A long discussion was had at dinner when his parents asked. Shifting his shoulders, Pax peeked my way before turning to Yash. His index finger ran across the rough wood of the stein.

"It's an everyday job. It's tiring not to have any time off."

"Not tonight, though. And this long trip with my friend here," Yash pointed out. His head tilted, unblinking, as he watched Pax's reactions. "And how long have you worked for the Council?"

Pax's jaw flexed, and our late night conversation at the Warfidd inn replayed in my head. The air in our booth was becoming uncomfortable, feeling more like an interrogation with every passing moment.

I should've known it was a silly decision to put these two in a room where manners weren't required with access to alcohol.

"I was recruited at sixteen years old. Working as a Guard since." Pax examined his ale, speaking with little care. "How long have you been a black-market trader?"

The muscles in my face twitched, but I bit the inside of my cheek, halting the smile. Filling my mouth with alcohol, I peered at the ceiling through my eyelashes until my amusement diminished.

"I assume you don't know how things work if you're calling us black-market traders," Yash said, wagging his finger between us.

I glanced at Pax with raised eyebrows and a smirk, which he returned with a tight smile. The phrasing was intentionally meant to dig at Yash's ego. And it worked. I was a little surprised Yash hadn't caught on to the egging.

Was he just so arrogantly sure of himself to think anyone would try to make fun of him?

Pax's eyes slid back to Yash, who hadn't looked away from the Guard.

"You're right, I'm very sorry. When did you become a Merchant? Veks only, right?"

"I started my apprenticeship at nineteen years old," Yash stated proudly.

"And what drew you to the exciting career choice?"

Pressing my tongue against the back of my teeth, containing my amusement, the weight of Yash's arm disturbed me. Irritation warmed my chest.

"When I saw how much fun this one had, I knew I needed to try it out. Join her on the road."

I scoffed to myself, knowing that was the farthest from the truth. He made his intentions known when I visited the first time, four years into my apprenticeship. His questions proved his genuine reason for becoming a Merchant.

Yash wanted fame and the potential perks that came with the job. Nothing to do with our so-called friendship. Opening his mouth to ask another question, Pax's attention shot to my shoulder where Yash rubbed ends of my hair between his fingers. His mouth shut and jaw shifted.

I cleared my throat, drawing both men's attention. "I'm going to order some potato skins."

Yash stepped out of the booth. Shuffling past, he placed both hands on my lower back. I locked my jaw at the entirely unnecessary gesture. But I knew better than to call Yash out.

When his mistakes were pointed out, Yash would often get loud and defensive. The opposite of my natural reaction is to stay quiet and keep my head down. Maybe I would've said something once upon a time, but Janna taught me to never ruin a contact. "They could always be useful one day."

Manoeuvring through the slightly drunker crowd, I only bumped hips with a few and avoided tripping over some rogue tails. My inelegant steps were ignored, everyone in their own conversations.

Waving for Morri's attention as I sat on a bar stool, I slid three drak coins across the counter.

"Potato skins and a shot of vodka?" I asked, with an obvious hint of desperation.

Morri nodded, and after taking the coins, disappeared into the kitchen. I glanced back over my shoulder. Yash has his arms sprawled across the seat top, appearing casual, but another emotion played around his edges. It hung at the corners of his mouth.

Only seeing a quarter of his face, Pax was leaning back with his hands clasped together on the tabletop. He didn't look tense. The conversation appeared fine until Yash spoke and the second emotion revealed itself. I saw it before. His arrogance. I sighed, knowing tonight was becoming a one sided pissing contest.

Placing a small glass down, Morri filled it with a clear liquid. I raised my eyebrows in thanks and shot it back in one motion. My nose hairs burned from the vapours.

"Who's the Guard you've brought into my pub? I've had a few questions."

I chuckled, placing another drak on the counter. "You know, he's very disappointed he can't live without it being obvious he's a Guard."

Morri filled the glass again, giving me a pointed look. Sliding the small glass towards me, I considered my words. The cage around my neck felt like it was ten pounds heavier. It sat like a ghost, mostly. I'd almost forgotten about it.

"The Council hired me to bring something to Jova. He's my escort. It's fragile, they don't want it jostled too much. Plus, the Council has several doubters." I drank the vodka and waited for the burning to disappear. "Tell the others not to worry. He won't bother them."

The bar keeper nodded, his arms crossed with a rag hanging out the side.

"Thought as much. I know you wouldn't intentionally put us at risk. Yash on the other hand..." his voice trailed off.

Looking down at the wood counter, I raised my eyebrow

in silent agreement. From my pouch, I took a single meso coin and snapped it against the counter.

"I can't disagree, but don't tell anyone that. Will you bring shots to the table for the night? A lot of shots," I clarified.

He chuckled, taking the valuable coin swiftly before anyone noticed. "You have noticed the tension between the two. Good. I was wondering if my imagination was going wild."

I shook my head with a sigh. "I don't understand it. They've just met and will never see each other again. Don't know why one needs to be more superior to the other."

His smile was one of a kind uncle. "You wouldn't, my dear. You don't see things the way they do."

My eyebrows scrunched at him, waiting for an explanation, but none came. Morri only said what he considered enough.

"Here comes one," he muttered, refilling my glass before adding a second one.

"Good man, Morri," Yash commented, dropping onto the stool next to me. His hand rested on my thigh. "Your little friend is interesting."

"I wouldn't call him a friend. We work together. I met him three days ago." Tipping the alcohol down my throat, I casually shifted my leg out from under his grip. It only made him turn towards me instead.

"And how did that happen? You're not one to pick up a stranger, especially some Guard."

We went over this with his parents, too. He was hunting for an inconsistency. I glanced at Morri, pouring a drink for the man on my other side. A hint of a smile was on his lips as he pretended not to listen.

"He's travelling with me back to Jova to finish a transaction."

Yash's face twisted as the alcohol ran down his throat. "And you believed him?"

I watched my hand as my fingers spun the small glass.

"I've read the Council's letter of assignment. And he saved me from being robbed when he could've let me fend for myself." Loosely, I shrugged. "Gives me enough reason to trust him to walk back to Jova with me."

Yash peered back as I smiled at Morri in thanks as he refilled our glasses again. When Yash faced me, we clinked our glasses together before tossing the drinks back.

"Better get back to your pet. Looks like he's drawn some unsavoury attention."

Panic rose in my chest as I spun on the stool and looked across the bar. Now standing, Pax was face to face with the two men. It didn't appear to be a lighthearted conversation based on his tight brow.

A fight couldn't break out. No matter how it started, Pax would get blamed. I pushed past people, the crowd suddenly feeling bigger.

"Gentlemen, can we help you?" I asked, sliding myself between the trio until my back lightly pressed against Pax's chest.

His hand rested on my hip, tightened hesitantly as his fingers curled. The two men, who smelt like they hadn't bathed in a moon cycle, took a surprised step back and gave me a look over. It was a familiar look, my expression staying neutral even if it felt invasive.

"Maybe we'll take your girl as compensation," one said to Pax, grinning. Most of his teeth were missing.

"Yeah, I like her better than you," the other added. His eyes stayed on my chest longer than his companion.

"And what compensation would that be?" Yash asked, stopping beside the group.

The strangers took in Yash's appearance, and for the first time tonight, so did I. He had changed his clothes before we left his parents' house, but I didn't pay attention.

The scabbard on his hip was brand new, as was the cloak

he wore. There wasn't a speck of dirt at the hem. With his shoulders set back, Yash gripped his sword with arrogant authority. He was pompous and the drunk men were going to see it as a challenge soon.

"Your man here's definitely a Guard, but you may be one, too." The larger of the two men faced Yash, resting his large hand on his belt, three blades glinting in the light.

It wasn't a wild assumption he had more hidden under layers. I wished I'd waited on the alcohol, wanting my head to be a little more clear.

"Right, he's not a Guard," I said, pointing at Yash before going to Pax. "And yes, he's a Guard, but isn't here for you nor anyone else in this pub. He's here with me to drink and relax. How about you take your issues to the counter and have a drink on me? Let Morri know I'm paying."

They looked at me with boredom until they understood I was serious. Their eyes went behind me to Pax. I could only hope his expression didn't make them mad. With a shared shrug, they shoved their way back into the crowd.

I let out a built-up sigh and glared at Yash. "Did you have to act like a damn king? I was handling it."

"Obviously not. They looked ready to pounce on you both," Yash snapped, sliding into the booth. Letting my annoyance simmer, I turned to Pax. "Are you alright?"

Pax watched the men through the crowd, his mouth tilted downward. "Fine, but glad you came over. Wasn't sure I'd calm that situation."

I followed Pax's eyes to the men leaning against the counter, speaking with Morri's daughter, Yecca, behind the bar. She peered over their shoulders, hunting for me in the crowd. I raised my arm, and we made eye contact. I nodded. She returned the gesture before dipping her head and speaking to the men again.

"You're probably right," I answered, still watching the counter. "They would've pummelled you."

Pax half-heartedly glared at me, and I winked in response. I stepped past him to sit in the booth, making Yash scoff, showing the empty spot I vacated. I pause, moving back out into the aisle. Yash smirked at Pax and shuffled further into the booth until I stuck my hand out.

"Pass my cloak?"

Yash's smug expression dropped. A dark cloud filled his eyes, but handed my outerwear over. I hung it on the booth divider as I glanced at Pax.

"Would you like me to hang yours too?" I asked politely.

Pax silently chuckled, handing me the fabric. Thoughtlessly, I assessed the cloak as I hung it. The material was worn and obviously used for years. Sections of worn-out stitching were noticeably close to tearing. I held my hand out to Yash, who handed me his cloak without looking.

The assessment I made earlier was right. It was a thick new cloak. Not a gold stitch out of place or popped. I settled in next to Pax as Morri appeared with three full steins and three shot glasses.

"The steins are on your tab," he said. "The shots are on the house for stopping those brutes from causing a fight. The Delegate 'been coming down hard on me lately. He's not impressed with my clientele."

"Do Delegates know how to be impressed or happy ever?" I asked with raised eyebrows. He chuckled, patting Yash on the shoulder and returning to his post.

"Cheers." Yash picked up his glass and shot it back. Pax tilted his own towards me before drinking. The burn was becoming less noticeable as I swallowed.

Our conversation stopped, and we all turned to watch the patrons. Nothing interesting piqued my interest, so with a roll of my neck, my back bumped into the bench. My gaze rested on Yash, who was already staring at Pax. There was a look of disgust in his eyes.

I peeked at Pax through my hair. He peered back with a

neutral expression, spinning the shot glass with his fingers mindlessly. He didn't appear bothered. I drank a mouthful of ale and held it there for a moment before swallowing. This one-sided competition was hurting my head.

"Yash?" The voice caught our attention as a large man approached our booth. Yash exclaimed, getting out of the booth to hug him.

"Shael! My friend, good to see you. You remember Orinthia Kellobyn from school," Yash said, pointing his hand towards me.

I smiled at him, giving a small wave. I remembered him and he was still just as brutish ten years ago.

"Look at you, all grown up!" Shael clapped his hand around my shoulder.

My entire upper body shook on impact. He still threw his weight around. My nails pushing into my palms. The obnoxiousness didn't change either, but neither had Yash's. It's what made them good friends in school.

"And who's this? You towin' around a little friend there, Orinthia?"

Before I could answer, Pax spoke up. "I'm Owyn's partner. Name is Pax. Good to meet you."

Pax rested his arm over my shoulder and purposefully knocked Shael's hand away. He peeked at me with a wink. My mouth tilted up naturally in reaction, and he grinned down at me.

Unexpectedly, my heart jumped at the dimples that formed on his cheeks. He seemed to try a new tactic to avoid detection as a Guard, and I unwittingly helped him. Turning back to Shael, I caught Yash's face. He pushed his jaw to the side, his eyes darker as he glared at Pax's hand, contemplating sticking a fork through it.

"Shael, grab a drink yet? Let's go to the bar," he said through gritted teeth.

"Sounds good. Pax, join us. Orinthia, you too," Shael

grabbed my bicep, dragging me halfway out from the booth. Pax extended his elbow to me once he stood. I chuckled, placing my hand around his arm.

Hours went by and the drinks continued to flow. More old school friends arrived, and the pub continued to get louder. Along with the drinks I bought myself, different men and women offered to buy me drinks too. I tried saying yes, but each time, Yash or Shael appeared and mentioned 'Owyn and Pax are together' with some joke about evaluating my standards.

After he pointed out for the tenth time, I pulled Yash to the side. I let my nails dig into his elbow as we made it to a quieter spot on the pub floor.

"We all know you need to keep inflating your own ego, but what's wrong with you?" I snapped, feeling emboldened by the alcohol in my system.

Yash's jovial attitude disappeared, and he scoffed. "You're travelling with a Guard, behaving like that's normal. Just because you're with him, doesn't mean he's better than the Guards who brutalise Drao and their communities."

I bit my tongue from asking him what he knew about Drao and their lives. He focused on Veks, once saying Drao were too demanding and exhausting.

"I'm the one travelling with him, not you," I said. "Leave him alone or I'll use you as target practice in your sleep."

Yash smirked, pushing my hair off my shoulder and letting his fingers linger. "I like when you're feisty."

I jerked my shoulder away. Not taking the hint, he stepped closer. The smell of alcohol waved off him. It was nauseating and made me realize just how much more he had to drink than me.

"Let me travel with you. Leave that dull mule behind. I'm sure we can have more fun."

Locking my jaw, I took a long deep breath through my nostrils and pushed down the instinct to slap him. No matter how uncomfortable the town made me, Mye was my neutral territory. I wasn't the same person here. Turning on my heels, I walked away from Yash.

Pax stood at the counter, stein in hand with the other on his pommel. He wore a natural smirk, nodding while he listened to the other patrons.

Lightly gripping his elbow, I wasn't entirely sure what I wanted. His head slowly turned towards me as the other man kept talking. I couldn't help but think just how pretty he was. His scar was highlighted under the lights, but his cheekbones were defined. The polite half smile had one of his dimples on display and the only word I could think to describe him was pretty, making something bubble inside of me.

"Hey," Pax said, shifting his attention as he was left alone.

He didn't have time to be confused when I held his face between my hands and tugged him down until our lips connected. It was meant to be a brief kiss, but his palm rested on my back and kept me close. My hand slipped to the back of his neck as all my focus was on his lips, gently pushing against mine.

A booming laugh broke the moment, and I stepped back. The growing sobriety in my brain screamed about what I did. My grip slipped until my palms rested on his collarbone. Pax's face was red and his mouth was open, slightly panting.

"Look at the happy couple!" Shael appeared, slapping his hand against Pax's back.

The jolt brought him back to the present, and deep confusion crossed his face.

Stepping back, my palms felt cold as I lost contact. His hand fell, but he continued to stare. The sparkle in his eye was dark in the low light. Shael moved away, but I didn't know where. I was too confused by my actions.

Returning to the booth with no interruptions, I grabbed my cloak. As I hooked it shut around my neck, I made a path for the pub's front door.

In front of Morri, I left him the pesa that I owed, and he took it without counting, giving me a wink instead. Yash was behind me, his arms crossed and a disapproving expression on his face. I didn't hold back the smug smile.

"By the way," I whispered in his ear as I passed. "He's a good kisser, and from my memory, much better than you."

I didn't wait for an answer, waved to Morri, and exited the loud pub.

Chapter 13

Rolling on my back, a rooster's cry rudely woke me for another day. Reaching for the empty pillow, ideas of murdering the bird bloomed in my mind. Instead of fabric, I slapped bare skin and a male voice called out in surprise. I jolted up in shock, noticing Pax laying beside me, rubbing his eye with confusion.

"Morning?" he said, dropping his hand to rub the slowly growing pink spot on his chest.

"I didn't know you were there."

I slipped my legs out from under the sheets, stretching towards the ceiling as I stood. Under my shirt, the golden cage rubbed against my skin. Scolding myself, I knew I needed to remember it was there more often. Resting back on my feet, my vision got spotty as my head spun. Shutting my eyes, I waited for the dizzy feeling to pass.

"Really?" Pax asked, sitting up. "You told me not to sleep on the couch last night."

I paused, trying to remember. Other than a few fleeting moments, I had nothing. I drank more than I thought. "Oh."

Working to get past the alcohol induced exhaustion, I checked my clothes in the mirror for any mystery stains. Last night, I didn't have the willpower to change into proper sleeping clothes. However, I peeled off some layers, which I only just realized as I spotted the thin shorts meant for under my dresses, and an oversized shirt. Not the shirt wasn't what I had on yesterday, but at least it was mine. I cleared my throat and crossed my arms uncomfortably over my chest.

"What time did you get back?" I asked.

Pax scratched his head, his curls messier than usual. "Not long after you. Your friend did his best to make me uncomfortable."

"Yeah, sorry about that," I said. "I don't know what's wrong with him. He's always a prick, but that was more than normal."

He chuckled.

"Oh, I know why," Pax said, standing up. "Yash is in love with you. He's not happy you brought someone along."

I scoffed, grabbing my bag from the floor. Dropping it on the unmade bed, I rummaged for the pants I wore the previous day. The search was just to keep myself busy; I had no idea where I put them.

"You've misinterpreted the emotions. Did he tell you why he became a Merchant? The truth? He thought I was making so much pesa and popular, his ultimate goal in life. Yash went to Jova and found a desperate Merchant willing to teach him. He doesn't care about what he sells or transports. He just wants to be paid."

I peered at him after not getting a response. He was half bent over his own bag, watching me.

"What?"

"Makes sense," he said, returning to dig his own clothes out.

"I shouldn't sound so angry," I told him, shrugging. "I'm not upset. I was annoyed for a long time, but I think that's from who I was trained by."

I chuckled, standing. "Apparently, there are some residual feelings."

"There's something suspicious about him," Pax commented, collecting his other things strewn around the room.

"Why's that?" I asked, deciding on a shirt. It was dark red and didn't smell too bad. Clean enough for me.

"He was a little too eager to discuss how amazing he is. He has an incessant need to impress, even to a stranger that he claims not to like," Pax explained, dropping a book into the sack.

"Maybe he's in love with you," I said, smiling at him.

Pax chuckled, a gleam in his eye.

"I am irresistible," he said before entering the washroom.

The kiss from last night replayed in my mind as I weakly pushed clothes to make room in the bag. I considered apologizing for the rash behaviour, but I didn't know how other than foolishly blurting it out.

People in my life, Eira included, told me my happiness came out when I was drunk. But last night was an impulsive decision. I knew better than to cross work with whatever this is.

"Should we get some food and then head out?" Pax asked, emerging in new clothes.

I nodded. "Sounds like a plan. I can feel my stomach gurgling."

We treaded along the almost empty street with our bags tossed over our shoulders. I wanted to say goodbye to Yash's parents before we left. I didn't know when I'd see them again.

A crowd of people were gathered around a house's outer stairs as we turned the corner from the main road onto the familiar sidestreet. The people stood with no space to see between them. Their voices were low grumbles and whispers as we came up behind them. As they looked around, their expressions were shocked, hands over mouths and even some tears.

A knot formed in my stomach the closer we got to Mama and Cod's house. Above where we stood, on their porch, the front door was wide open. From the back, I lifted on my toes. Two people stood alone a few feet away, at the base of the neighbouring house.

My heart pulsed roughly with panic as I shoved through the crowd, ignoring the unhappy comments directed towards me. A few swore at me, but I ignored them.

Stumbling out of the crowd with disbelief, I knew what happened to Cod. He stared at the dirt ground, his head lowered. His clipped grey hair was loosely tucked behind his ears, tears streamed noticeably down his cheeks. The ageing man appeared physically in pain, crumpled on the bottom steps using the bannister for some support. His son leaned against the opposite side of the railing.

Yash stared at the trees across the road, his jaw visibly pushed to the side. The tears gathering at his lash line reflected in the rising sunlight, but none had slipped over. The thud of my duffle bag against the ground didn't catch either's attention. My feet moved barely three steps. The movement caught Yash's attention, his eyes moving over to me.

"What happened?" I asked, voice roughly leaving my throat. But I knew the answer. I don't know why I needed to hear it.

Cod released a shuddered breath, head drooping lower into his lap. He couldn't crumple more without falling to the ground. Yash opened his mouth, but the creak of a footstep against the wooden patio above drew our attention.

The sight confirmed my fears, and my stomach dropped. Three Guards began descending the stairs with a heavy bag between them. My throat dried as they got closer. In silence, we stared at the thick black fabric. I couldn't imagine someone I loved was inside.

To fight against the tears, I squeezed my teeth together and focused on the pain. They placed the bag into a large, thickly woven wicker coffin I didn't notice resting across the road. It only had one purpose across Gerennt. A warm hand rested on my lower back. Pax passed by, moving over to his cohorts.

"What happened?" I hissed, stepping closer to Yash.

My eyes darted over to the sobbing man on the stairs before looking back at his son. A chill ran along my spine at the emotionless look in his eyes. Any tears I saw before were gone.

"We woke up this morning. She didn't."

An anguished sob fell from Cod's mouth after his son's empty words. Yash peered at him through his peripheral vision with annoyance. I shouldered past him, resting my knees on the step in front of his father.

"Cod, I'm so sorry," I whispered.

The old man was broken, and he wasn't calming down anytime soon. I couldn't understand how he looked so much smaller than I ever seen. As best I could, I wrapped my arms around his vibrating shoulders. I never thought I would see this calm man in such a state.

I didn't move until Cod could no longer cry. It turned into a short time of hyperventilating, but he breathed through it. He now rested on calm but hesitant breathing. I stood up, blood rushing back through my limbs. The sun was now in the sky and the crowd dispersed. They lost interest, calling out their sympathies before they left. Yash and Pax remained motionless in the road, their arms folded, a silence hanging heavily between all of us.

"Take your father inside to lie down," I instructed Yash.

His brows lifted, but came up to the stairs. He wrapped

his arm over his father's shoulders with care and almost carried the weak man up to their house.

"What did the Guards say?" I asked Pax, wiping the mostly dried tears from my cheeks. He looked down at me with a barely scrunched forehead.

"Best guess? Died in her sleep. They saw nothing intentional."

"You mean someone didn't kill her?"

He sighed, blinking up the stairs. He understood the underlying meaning of my words and where my suspicions lay.

"I can't leave right now," I said. "I can't leave them to deal with this alone."

Pax nodded. "I understand." He cleared his throat awkwardly. "How long do funerals take to organise?"

My heartbeat stuttered over the words. I know the logistics of our trip were behind his question, but it felt so cold. "A few days. No more than a week."

He nodded. "I'll take our stuff back up to the inn and talk to Norma. Stop by the barn and let them know the horses will stay longer."

"Thank you," I said, appreciatively.

He ran his hand along my back, tightening his mouth into a polite smile. "No problem."

I stood at the bottom of the stairs, watching his tall frame retreat down the road with both our bags hanging at his side. When I felt ready, I went up the stairs.

The living room looked the same as last night. The curtains were open, but there were long shadows all around the room. Except for pairs of slippers, everything was neatly put away. Just how Mama liked it. Banging in the kitchen drew my attention. Yash had his sleeves rolled up on his forearms, disjointedly moving around the kitchen.

"What're you doing?" I asked, leaning against the doorframe.

"Delegate's going to be here soon," he grumbled, opening cabinets. "Might as well get something to snack on while I plan a funeral."

"Where's Cod?"

"Sent him to bed. I don't see him being able to handle this," he said, mindlessly checking the label on a wine bottle.

"I'm not leaving town yet," I told him quietly.

"Why? She wasn't your mother."

His words meant to hurt, and I felt it. He glanced at me with no expression, and I stared back. No apology was offered, and I certainly didn't expect one. Returning to his prior task, he turned back to the counter.

"Fine," he grumbled. "Where's your little friend?"

I pivoted back to the living room when a knock reverberated through the house. "Back at the inn, booking a few more nights."

Turning the door handle, I knew who was going to be on the porch. A tall older woman stood in the doorway, hands behind her back. The wrinkles under her eyes were defined like she didn't sleep for the last ten years. But from the rumours, she never took a break, not wanting to give anyone else a chance to take her spot.

"Madame Delegate," I welcomed, holding the door open wider. Two Guards stood a few steps below her, staring me down.

"You're not the child of Einna Horras," she pointed out, entering the house.

"I'm a family friend. Here to help arrange things."

The Delegate made a sound in her throat. "Fine. Where's her child and husband?"

"Her son, Yash, will be out in a moment. Einna's husband is in bed. He's not taking the information well," I told her, closing the door when her security wasn't following her inside.

"As to be expected."

"Take a seat," I said, extending my hand to the furniture.

Sitting in the armchair, she crossed her ankles. The Delegate of Mye was the stereotype for Delegates as a whole. Always composed, she behaved like she wouldn't care if you were choking and hit the ground. She would deal with you once you were dead.

Resting on the couch's arm, I leaned back, trying to see what was happening in the kitchen. I was tempted to yell for Yash, but the Delegate wouldn't appreciate that.

"You're a Merchant," the Delegate said, taking a notepad and pen from a waist pouch I hadn't noticed. In the shadowed light, the pen's gold reflected. I didn't have to look long to know it was genuine gold.

I pressed my chin into my shoulder, looking at her. "Yes, ma'am."

"Einna Horras's son is too."

I nodded, unsure where the line of questions was going. "He is."

She made another sound in her throat, staring at me. I turned my head to the other shoulder, wanting to vomit from the discomfort in the room. In my mind, I went through every flaw I could potentially have.

Was I missing a button? How dirty was my sword? Were the aglets on my shoelaces damaged?

A hesitant sigh slid through my nose as I tried to remain calm. Forget polite formalities.

"Yash," I blurted out. "Let's go."

As if he was waiting for me to call him, Yash entered with a bowl of salted breadsticks and a single bottle of wine. "Madame Delegate."

"Yash Horras, correct?"

Carelessly tossing the bowl onto the coffee table, he dropped onto the couch cushion. "Yes, ma'am."

My head fell forward a little as Yash tipped a long drink of wine into his mouth. One of the Delegate's eyebrows raised. He smacked his lips together once he finished.

"How quickly can we put my mother to rest? I have transactions in other towns to be finished."

My upper lip twitched in disgust at the back of Yash's head. My hands curled into fists on my lap. What was he doing?

"When can we have her cremated?"

The Delegate looked down at her notes. "We are having a funeral bonfire tomorrow night. There's two families in attendance, with room for one more."

"Perfect," Yash said, taking another drink.

I ran my tongue along the back of my teeth, tempted to rip the bottle away and hit him over the head with it.

"Usually families wait a few days since they want to alert family members," the Delegate explained, glancing at me.

I had nothing to add. I only stayed in case Yash wasn't emotionally prepared to decide. Apparently, I was entirely wrong.

"We don't have any family to alert," he said with an exhausted attitude. The Delegate looked at me for confirmation. I gave a small nod. Mama had siblings, but I think they had died years ago.

"Okay. Your mother will be a part of the funeral bonfire tomorrow at sunset," the Delegate said before standing. I followed and at his own leisure, so did Yash. "I'm sorry for your mother's departure."

Yash saluted at her with two fingers and retreated to the kitchen. I ran my hand along my hair, exasperated. Turning to the Delegate, I offered a polite smile. How was I supposed to explain that?

Instead, I said, "thank you for coming by."

She nodded. "It is an important part of my job."

I opened the door again, looking outside. The Guards were at the bottom of the stairs now, turning as the door opened. Like their employer, neither of them had any outward emotion. She paused on the porch, glancing back at me, and her lip twitched to a brief sympathetic smile.

"Everyone reacts in their own way," she told me.

I tried for a more genuine smile than I was giving her and calmly shut the door once she started down the stairs. Tapping my finger on the door handle, anger boiled as I glared at the useless, untouched bowl of salted breadsticks.

Aggressively pushing away from the door, I barged into the kitchen. Leaning back on the counter, Yash had the wine bottle almost upside down as he drank from it. Ripping the bottle from his hands, he cried out as the red liquid soaked his shirt before I flipped it upside down over the sink. It was a short time before it was empty and I let it clatter against the sink. He lunged for the bottle and I shoved his shoulder.

"What's wrong with you?" he barked at me.

His eyes were wild, the actual emotion unreadable.

"Your mother just died!" I shouted back.

I felt a strong desire to slap him, but I took a physical step back as my hands were shaking. He looked at me with nothing to say. I took five deep breaths, instinctual from Janna's training.

"I'll see you tomorrow," I said, keeping my voice even.

I walked out of the house, but let my emotions show by slamming the door shut. I made it halfway down the road before I froze, realising I didn't know where I was going. This wasn't my home, not for a long time.

CHAPTER 14

"YOU SURE YOU DON'T WANT TO TALK ABOUT WHAT HAPPENED last night?" Pax asked, falling in step with me.

Although his official sword hung at his side, he kept his hands in his pockets.

I sighed with frustration. "I already told you no. Stop asking."

"Okay," he said.

He was silent for a minute before clearing his throat and my eyes shut, annoyed at the sound.

"You looked overwhelmed when you came back to the room. It was a little scary. Didn't think you could feel that. Just thought you'd want to talk."

While he spoke, I stopped and glared after him until he realised he was alone. My eyebrows raised a little, teeth bared.

"Right. Sorry. Stop asking," he said, uncomfortably nodding.

I continued walking, staring at him as I passed by. The plot of land used for ceremonial bonfires was at the southern tip of Mye. Only a wall of thirty trees separated the Delegate's house from it.

The bonfire, tended to and added to every day, was huge. Like the stone arches at the entrance, the bonfires were identical in every town. Death didn't need to be fancy.

The pathway leading to the bonfire was inconvenient and long. The construction was almost designed to hide it. I delayed leaving the inn, trying to time my arrival close to the beginning of the ceremony. I wouldn't risk coming face-to-face with the same Yash I dealt with yesterday.

Confusion and emotional exhaustion left me drained. It left me working to control my reactions, knowing that me slapping him wouldn't be appreciated by anyone.

Staying hidden at the back of the small crowd was tempting. Nobody noticed us as the flames crept higher. A row of chairs set up for the mourning families made up the front row. Most of them were full. Two families of adults and children were huddled together. Alone at the end was Cod. His body was leaning forward, elbows resting on his knees. He appeared to be working to keep himself sitting up. A single empty chair beside him.

Keeping still, I scanned the crowd. Yash stood off to the side, looking like a spectator, not a grieving son. He was still wearing expensive clothes, flame light reflecting against the metals. His profile remained emotionless. A sigh slid through my nostrils in agitation.

Cod almost jumped at the slight movement of the chair next to him. He turned back, his eyes red and tears fresh on his cheeks. I lifted the corners of my mouth, reaching across and gripping his hand. Behind us, the dry grass crunched.

Yash moved closer without a word. Unexpectedly, Pax had followed me to the seats, too. The two exchanged uncaring looks. Pax greeted him, and Yash nodded. Clasping his hands together at his waist, he didn't look down at me. That was fine with me.

I witnessed the funeral ceremony many times across Gerennt. More often than not, I didn't know anyone going into the fire. One at a time, the wrapped body was slid into the flames on a wooden board. The officiant only read their names, no other identifying information.

Once the flames were full, and the bodies were engulfed, the crowd watched. A spell kept the aroma of burning flesh at bay. A long enchanted rock sat to collect the ashes of the dead, then given to the family.

As the solemn Guards lifted and placed Mama, the third body to burn, in the flames, sobs filled the crowd. I could hardly blink, not wanting the tears to start again. The smooth sensation of Cod's thumb running over the back of my hand incessantly kept my mind distracted.

With my jaw locked, my lungs were having a hard time getting a full breath. Repeatedly, I reminded myself not to fall apart. My focus was snapped away when a hand rested on my shoulder.

I glanced up at Pax as his eyes appeared hazel with the flames illuminating them. He nodded once and squeezed my shoulder. My teeth grabbed my inner cheek. This was the most intimate funeral ceremony I ever attended.

Yash stood back again. His chin raised, he watched the surrounding trees with barely any interest in the fire. I knew I was looking at a stranger and not the boy I grew up with. I always noticed a change, but this was deeper. And I didn't know where it happened.

Mama's covered feet were the last part of her visible before the flames took over. I sat still, without a thought in my head. When time returned to me, the sky was dark. The mourning crowd dwindled. Next to me, Cod collapsed back into his chair. He continued to watch the flames, eyelids fluttering shut against his swollen face.

Carefully, I slid my hand out of his. He didn't notice. Pax still stood behind me, both thumbs tucked around his belt. Yash was gone.

Chapter 15

Mye disappeared behind us, leaving my grief in its walls. I expected the memories and ghosts to leave me exhausted. Having a person I knew die wasn't new.

But someone I considered family and I could say I loved unconditionally? It left a wound surrounded by black bruises. Would my reaction to finding out my parents have died one day be the same?

Pax didn't speak as we rode. I appreciated it. He looked at me occasionally, his head movement visible in my peripheral vision. Once we returned to the tavern last night, I thought I was fine and overcome my emotions. While I brushed my hair out of its braid, a mundane thing, I crumbled.

As I collapsed onto the bed and wept, Pax watched with a twisted mouth. He was seeing an emotion that I rarely felt. My eyes still felt swollen enough that I was grateful Dill knew to stay on the road.

Pulled from my memory of embarrassment, something large broke branches inside the treeline. Whatever it was, moved far enough back in the foliage that I couldn't tell what it was other than a shadow. My grip tightened on the reins as

I stared between the trees. Worry crept into my mind the longer I couldn't see anything.

Undisturbed forest hugged the roadway, travelling along the mountain base. It was common for predators to wander down when their source of food was scarce. Perhaps the creatures who were tempted by the scent of the dragon corpse didn't return to their dens, instead choosing to stick on flat land and hunt for more food.

"It's fine," Pax said, looking at the trees too. "Whatever it is, sounds like it's alone."

The noises disappeared, leaving much smaller branches snapping under the weight of squirrels. Woodpeckers surrounded us, creating holes in trees. The horses returned to their regular walking pace. It was peaceful.

But then it came back. Jackalopes would dash across the road. Different winged creatures flew above us, calling out their loud squawks. Dill slowed, taking a step away from the woods. I did my best to soothe her, running my hand along her neck. My gaze flickered from the road to the trees. I should figure out if it was something harmless, bothering us for its own amusement or dangerous, deciding when to pounce.

Releasing a sneeze, Dill began walking normally, like nothing bothered her. Marr gave away nothing, bobbing his head as his hooves scuffed against the dirt. From the opposite side of the road, a mother deer stuck her head out, her two headed fawn next to her. The baby grazed, nipping at the grass, but the doe watched us. As we passed, she stepped in front of her fawn. The protective move caused me to smile.

My chest clenched at the sign of a post tipping out of the overgrown tree branches. Multiple little signs decorated the thick post, showing towns and villages and their distances. This sign meant something to me. It represented just how close my childhood was.

The pained cry of a creature screeched from within the

forest and all the horses showed distress. The creature reappeared and was ramping up its teasing.

Marr grunted, shaking out his mane. His body language told me he wasn't too alarmed. For some reason, that didn't make me feel better. Animals smaller than him, no matter how deadly, didn't bother him. I walked up on him eating next to a rattlesnake before.

"Alright, enough," Pax said, tugging Neem's reins.

I did the same with Dill not far ahead. He dismounted, removing his sword from its sheath. Leaves crumpled and slipped as whatever was in the trees must have turned towards the road.

"That's not a good idea," I told him, my gaze flickering between him and the trees.

"I'm going to scare it away. Or take it out if I have to," he explained.

"I know, but…" My words stopped as his boot slipped on the mud, throwing his leg out from under him.

His back hit the ground with a wet thud. The sword landed beside him, covered in dirt. Whatever the creature was, scampered away through the underbrush. Pax loudly groaned, rolling onto his side. I sighed, dropping off Dill's back.

"What I was trying to say." I said, grabbing Pax by his underarm. "There's a lot of marshland here. Everything off the road is muddy."

"You could've said it quicker," he grumbled, allowing me to help him back on the stable road.

Putting his weight down full on his left foot, he couldn't stop the pained groan and his foot lifted into the air.

"Okay, that hurts," he complained, balancing on one foot. His face twisted up, eyes on the sky.

"Can you ride?" I asked, checking for any visible bones.

It looked to be a simple slip in the mud, his clothes taking the worst of it.

"I'm going to have to, but I don't know how long," he answered. "We'll need to go back to Mye. Something doesn't feel right."

I sighed in defeat, dropping my head forwards. It was over two hours back to Mye. Not including the wait to see a physician and have him deem Pax's ankle important enough to look at. We would stay another night, and that's the last thing I wanted.

"I know where we can go," I begrudgingly said, lifting my head.

Pax raised his eyebrows, indicating for me to continue.

"The farm my parents own is about an hour from here and in the direction we're headed. We can probably stop there."

"Probably?" Pax tilted his head. Of course, he caught onto that one.

I led Neem closer to her rider, and with an exaggerated grunt, Pax lifted himself back. Waiting at his feet, I watched as he looked at the sky again. I ignored the wrinkle of his forehead and the distant look in his eyes. He was holding back more emotion. He peeked down at me, nodding. Back in my saddle, I squeezed Dill to walk. Neem and Marr followed.

"So, your parents have a farm?"

"You knew I grew up around here," I said.

"I thought you grew up in Mye. Makes a little more sense that you aren't from town."

I slid my gaze to him. "And that means?"

Pax shrugged. "I've noticed people who grew up in the villages or outside town are people pleasers. They crave attention that thrives in the larger towns."

My eyes squinted, thinking over his words. "I should be offended."

The road widened, and Pax brought Neem to a walk beside Dill. "Don't be. It doesn't refer to you."

A single broken gate showed the road forking off was our spot to turn off. The chipped white wood generated nerves in my stomach. In the almost ten years of being a Merchant, I've passed this cut-off time and time again. There was always a moment of heaviness in my heart, but I never allowed myself to feel more. The night I officially moved spoiled all my wonderful childhood memories.

Dill made an unhappy gruff, her head dipping forward. I ran my hand along her neck, knowing she felt my stress. Her warm, musky scent was comforting. My forehead rested against her neck for a minute and with closed eyes, I embraced the peace of her movement.

"It's okay," I muttered. "I'm sorry, it's okay."

Marr huffed next. Sitting up a little, I looked at the massive horse with a smirk. He may be a grumpy man, but he loved affection. Feeling the weight of another person's eyes had me glancing to the side before turning back to the road. Pax watched the entire interaction, annoyingly more observant than I wanted to give him credit for. Taking another peek, I was met with raised eyebrows.

"The last time I was home, I got into an argument with my father. My parents and I haven't had a relationship for years. I left without resolving it. I don't know how they'll react when we get there."

"How long ago was that?"

"Three years," I said without emotion.

Pax's head turned towards me. "You haven't seen your parents in three years?"

He sounded astonished, and I picked up a bit of judgement.

"And how long has it been since you've seen your parents?" I snapped with a glare.

Pax didn't answer, his jaw shifting.

"Exactly."

Once the word left my mouth, I knew it was rude. My family was a sensitive subject, and I thought I had moved past it enough that I was emotionless.

Obviously not.

I attempted to clear my throat, but it was dry. Reaching to my side, I found my waterskin empty.

"My parents are intense," I said, dropping the waterskin.

"Intense?"

"As in, my father will probably interrogate you when he realizes you're a Guard and my mother will try to marry you off to one of my sisters within ten minutes."

"Why not you?"

I pressed my tongue against my upper teeth, unprepared to say my mother was ashamed that she pawned her daughter off as debt collateral. The first time I visited after being released from the lockdown of my apprenticeship, she couldn't look at me for three days. When she did, it was through tears. I didn't feel bad, and we agreed she would never make a decision for me again.

"She'll say you're too cute for me. A better match for one of my sisters," I lied, forcing a laugh.

"How many sisters do you have?"

"Three, all younger. I'm the oldest." I peered at him. "Don't worry, they're all nicer than I am."

"As long as they don't fall in love with me," Pax said with a genuine smile.

I smirked. "I can't promise anything."

The break in the trees appeared, distinguishing the road from the driveway. Birch trees lined the edge of the driveway. My father planted them when he and my mother first got married. It was a way of welcoming her to her new home. That was the story they told me, anyway. The dirt road became bumpy with gravel and my anxiety soared.

"This is the one," I said.

I suddenly felt hyper aware of myself. Was I speaking too loud? How hard was my breathing? Am I too heavy for Dill?

Pax nodded, giving no indication that I was being weirder than normal. I filled my lungs and released it carefully, trying to be as unobvious as possible. If my parents turned us away, hopefully they would give us water and bread first. They weren't that cruel, but the thought made me laugh. The clucking of chickens was the loudest animal noise, distinguishable before we got to the clearing.

Here we go.

The two-story grey farmhouse stood alone, trees cleared away from it. A couple hundred feet away sat a barn built of wood that once matched the house. The weathered wood became raw and grey, the paint stripped away. Nothing changed in three years. The knot in my stomach squeezed so tight, I was bordering on throwing up.

I did not know how this would play out. My father wasn't naturally an angry person, but I had said some nasty things to him. All of it was true, but still nasty. The cool bars of the small cage bumping against my skin was a friendly reminder I wasn't here to make amends or have a joyful family reunion. It was just a stop on the route back.

Next to the front porch, I slipped off Dill's back. Tying her reins to the hitching post, my back faced the house. Every alarm in my head was going off, warning me how risky that choice was. The front door opened with a loud bang against the inner wall. Closing my eyes, I took a deep, calming breath through my nose. I expected five pairs of eyes as I turned on my toes.

Yet only my sister, Torna, was standing on the porch with crossed arms. We stared at each other in silence. No one came out behind her. I rolled my shoulders and put on the neutral face I used during transactions.

"I expected a bigger hello," I said, letting my suspicions be heard.

Torna's stare flickered behind me. Behind my shoulder, Pax assessed the tension with his hand on the pommel and not hiding his Guard ego. Returning her eyes to me, she pursed her lips.

"This is all you get."

"Parents still mad?" I asked, stopping at the bottom of the porch stairs.

My gaze flickered to the first-floor windows behind her. The blinds hung still. It was easy to sense that Pax was still tense, not knowing what to expect between my sister and me. Truthfully, neither did I. She could've learned how to fight since the last time I saw her.

"Wouldn't know. They're not here."

"Guess I came at the right time." I gingerly stepped up the porch steps until I was in front of her.

She glared at me with a stare as emotionless as mine. Her grey eyes were severe and unforgiving.

"Guess so," she said, dryly.

Stepping past her, I wondered if she was hiding something behind her back. "Where are they? Do I have time to clean up before getting tossed out?"

"I'd say so. Dad died two years ago. Don't know where our mother is. Maybe you showing up will bring them back. Like a bad omen."

The toe of my boot rested against the doorframe as I came to a stop. I looked back at her over my shoulder. She was mimicking the stance. There wasn't a need to wonder if she was lying. My sister was an extremely honest person and I could trust that. Nodding, I finished my step into the front hallway. Not what I expected to hear.

"Who are you?" Torna asked, as my hand gripped the edge of the door.

"I'm a friend of your sister's," Pax hesitantly answered.

My sister was in a hostile mood and I knew it could scare anyone, especially new people. My sisters and I didn't look much alike, but it was an expression we shared.

"Let him in, Torna," I called back over my shoulder.

The house looked the same as the night I left, with blue window drapes that were dirty if you stared too long and a plain green rug in the hallway that my younger sisters, Calla and Laine, vomited on the first time Torna cooked and poisoned all of us. The jug my mother used to make juice was probably still under the kitchen sink. It was demoted from juice duty when she caught Calla and I using it to catch frogs.

A warm feeling of nostalgia wrapped around my heart, and I hated it. Life just continued after I was gone. It was like stepping into one of my nightmares. The stairwell had some noticeable patching as my feet made the wood creak with every step. Trying to keep my eyes on the top of the stairs, the urge to look at the spindles won. A crack ran along most of the dowels. It was only noticeable if you knew it was there.

Laine, the baby of the family, took a headfirst dive into the railing when she was little. It was kidding season and our father was going out in the middle of the night to check on the goats. Laine decided she had to help but made the choice last minute. At the top of the stairs, the rug she tripped on sat, a physical memory just like this entire house.

All the bedroom doors, except Torna's, were closed. The first room at the top of the stairs. My hand wrapped around the door handle without looking. My room until nine years ago. I was prepared for my existence to be gone and replaced with storage.

But nothing changed. My bed on its iron bed frame sat under the front window. The quilt my grandmother made for me was a mess at the end. My vanity, painted white to match the bed frame, was covered in papers and the stems of dead flowers in a vase. I couldn't form a thought past the shock as heavy footsteps thumped up the stairs.

"Your sister said I could stay in your parents' room as long as I'm locked in," Pax said, stopping beside me. "I'm not sure if she's joking."

I didn't answer him. I wouldn't put it past her, whether she was joking or not. Once she set her eyes on somebody, Torna could exist to make them miserable. She rarely did it to me, because I could beat her up. But that was when she was eleven. My guess was, she got better over the years.

Continuing to stare at my unchanged childhood, a dark feeling rose inside me that if I stepped inside, the undisturbed memories would shatter.

"This your room?"

I cleared my throat, and my attention returned from the past.

"Yeah, it is. Surprised it's all here." I cleared my throat again, trying for the emotion to disappear. "But, makes life easier. I don't have to hunt down blankets."

"Let's hope I get the same luck with your parents' room," Pax commented, amused.

Opening my mouth, I turned my head, ready to tell him where the extras were kept. My eyes were the last to move and when they did, I froze. He was much closer than I expected, smirking at his witty comment. My focus jumped between his bright green eyes and cracked lips. My tongue slipped out and wet my bottom lip, instinctively pulling it between my teeth. His expression sobering, Pax stepped closer. His toes bumped into my boot and I jumped back. Words formed in my head and I opened my mouth but it hit a wall and dissolved. Nothing came out.

Cowardly, I spun a little more and looked down the stairs to the first floor. No longer being sucked in by his eyes, I found my voice.

"My parents' room is the last one down the hall. I'll put the horses away. You can check for blankets," I blurted.

The last word wasn't out of my mouth and I rushed down the stairs, my knuckles turning white under how tightly I held the railing. The further I got, the confusion in my brain fizzled out and I became embarrassed again. Being around a man who entranced me in a place that traumatized me was not a good mix. I found that out quick.

Torna stood between Dill and Marr, running her fingers

through their manes. I couldn't see her face well, but she was calmer than a few minutes prior. Neem looked on, jealous over being left out.

"How're the paddock fences? Will they be okay until tonight?" I asked, closing the door behind me.

Hearing my voice, Neem lifted her head. I smirked. After only a few days, Pax's horse wanted my attention, too. In contrast, Torna barely glanced at me as she smiled at Dill, scratching at her neck. The horse rested her nose against my sister's shoulder. Traitor.

"I was there last week, and the fences were okay. You should double check. A few foxes were sleeping in the hay shed yesterday."

"And you didn't…" Biting my tongue, I paused my step to collect my judgement.

Apparently, it was just her taking care of the farm, and I couldn't judge her for how she took care of it. Nodding, I began disconnecting Marr's halter from Dill before moving on, removing his harness. Marr shook his dusty brown mane, relieved to be free of additional weight.

"The Guard. You aren't pregnant, are you?" Torna asked, unknotting Dill's halter.

A snort of laughter shot from my nose and I sent a weak glare at my sister, who was already smirking. Knowing Marr was too lazy to wander off, I turned to Neem. She jutted her head out, asking for the attention she'd missed out on, and I placed a kiss on her nose.

"No, Pax didn't get me pregnant," I answered.

Tossing Neem's saddle on the fence behind the hitching post, I realized I needed a real excuse for coming here. Looking at Pax's ankle wasn't good enough. We could've gone anywhere.

Next to the barn, Torna unlocked the paddock gate before leading Dill through and slipped the bridle from her head. I encouraged Marr and Neem to follow, taking their bridles too.

Pushing up on the lowest bar of the fence, the other end of the paddock came into view by stretching my neck. It was in one piece all the way around. The horses wandered and mingled with the few horses Torna had. They were yet to notice the hay pile, which I'm sure they would empty.

From what I could vaguely remember, the working horses were fairly young, but none of these horses looked familiar. I was tempted to ask, but I didn't. That felt like something she could hold over me. As she leaned next to me against the fence, I peeked down at my sister. Her mouth sat in a tight line and I had a feeling that's how it always sat.

"Where are the kids?" I asked, referring to our younger sisters.

"Calla left a few weeks after mum. Think she's in Rinebur, working. Haven't heard from her in a few months. Laine comes by every few days to help with the animals. She met a boy before dad died. After everything, he convinced her to move to the village when it fell apart here," she explained, staring at the horses.

She was left here with no real help and no options. The frustration that radiated from her was understandable.

"You could sell the farm," I suggested.

Torna sarcastically laughed to the sky and faced me with disbelief.

"You could've come home," she snapped. My head whipped to face her, my mouth agape.

"When would I come back, Torna? I was sent off at fourteen. After that, dad didn't want me here. I was a reminder of their mistakes. If I'd come back when I wanted to, they would've lost this place."

"What're you talking about, Orinthia?" my sister asked, exasperated.

Unable to understand her hostility, I waited for her to say she was kidding, but it wasn't coming. She was genuinely angry with me. Glancing back towards the house to see if Pax came outside. Looking back at my sister, I expected more anger and flung words, but she was as confused as I was. The fire in her eyes was extinguished, leaving a confused child. A lonely child. Sighing, I stepped towards her and rested my hands on my hips.

"Why do you think I left? Do you think I made that choice?"

She opened her mouth, barely any sound came out before crossing her arms and wildly shrugging. I bit on my bottom lip, knowing I had to tell my sister the truth. It wasn't fair to keep it from her. Plus, I needed someone else to know.

"Torna, our parents used me to clear their debts."

"What are you talking about?"

My throat tightened, and I felt shame that how I felt at fourteen could so easily bubble up to the surface. Janna would be disappointed. She worked so hard for me to learn to control my emotions.

"You know our parents used Drao magick to help the farm. Once, they bought a spell during the dry season. The Merchant that brought it asked for a delivery payment which is completely normal. Our parents were familiar with this Merchant's process. They'd worked together before. Our father said he had nothing extra to give and nothing of value to trade. The Merchant promised to come back in one month for payment. And then, our parents refused to hand over any pesa they made. Acting like they didn't know anything about a delivery payment." I scoffed to myself, staring at the dirt piling up as the toe of my boot pushed into the ground. "I don't know what they were thinking. Maybe it was their pride, but the Merchant wasn't leaving. Janna, my mentor, told me years later that our parents even attempted threats. As if they had any strength or knew how to use weapons.

Eventually, they offered their eldest daughter to the Merchant and to keep any earnings I made."

"Why don't I remember this?" Torna asked in a quiet voice.

"The morning it happened, you were at school. The night before, Mother told me they needed my help with collecting vegetables, so I was staying home. It made sense. I knew about the spell and the success we'd gotten from it. Two men locked me in a carriage for two days and tossed me at the feet of a Merchant."

"Where did they take you?" Torna's voice had dropped to nearly a whisper. The wheels were turning inside her head.

"Verceen. I was taken to Janna Cor. At the time, I was given only a few details. Eventually, I was told that she was the Merchant who sold the spell to our parents. I tried to make myself useless as a house employee, hoping to be sent home. Instead, she said I had spunk, and unlike her employees, I was hard to break. Decided I was worth training. From what I understand, our parents never contacted her or tried to get me home. They never paid her back. They never sent any letters. Janna sent me to Mye for my first transaction when I turned nineteen. I came here. Our parents sent me away after a few days. Their guilt ate at them and they couldn't handle me being here. I've had no reason to come back."

Torna turned away to stare out at the paddock. Her eyebrows were pulled down low, lip in her mouth as she went over my words in her head. She peeked at me, analyzing me, hunting for holes in my story. I waited patiently, watching the horses wander and eat.

"The fight you and dad had?" I nodded. The last explosive conversation I had with the man.

"That makes sense," she said. "More sense than what I was told."

Her gaze flickered over my shoulder before returning to the paddock. "The Guard have anything to do with it?"

I glanced back. Pax walked down the porch stairs, the front door slamming behind him. I peered at the ground, lowering my voice.

"Sort of. Somehow, that's the long story."

She snorted, and I smiled politely at him as he got closer.

"Find blankets?" I asked, crossing my arms.

"Didn't have to look very far. The bed was made."

Nodding, I jutted out my chin towards the horses. "Where do you want Neem's saddle?"

"Wherever you put yours is fine," he answered with a shrug.

I nodded and pushed away from the fence. Shooting Torna a brief warning look, I hoped she would keep her mouth shut. As I walked back to where we left the riding equipment, I could hear her boots crackle against the stones as she walked the other way.

CHAPTER 16

"How's the ankle?" I asked, leaning against the living room's door frame.

Pax's amused expression lifted from the book in his hand. His curls were tighter, still wet from the shower he took. The back of the armchair got darker from the water, but the chair had been through worse. My mother bought it for my father after I was born. I was surprised it was still standing.

"Hasn't been too painful."

The room was dimly lit as I stepped in with my arms crossed. "Have you looked at it since we got here?"

"No, just been ignoring it," he answered, teasing.

I rolled my eyes, sitting on the coffee table's edge and waved my hands towards me. He raised his eyebrows, and I waved my hands again.

"Come on, let me see."

He rested his foot on my lap, slipping deeper into the armchair. I pulled the slipper off that looked suspiciously like my father's and his sock. The outside of his ankle appeared fine, but when I tilted it, my eyebrows rose. He had a large bruise running up his calf. My gaze lifted to Pax's face. He jutted out his lower lip as if the bruise almost impressed him.

"You were saying?"

He peeked up at me, barely able to shrug like there wasn't an issue. "Like I said, I ignored it."

"You were going to ride like this?" I couldn't help but scold him.

Maybe it was where we were, but a need to be protective fell over me.

He raised his hands defensively. "Sorry. I'll wrap it up before I go to bed."

Though I wanted to toss it away with frustration, I placed his foot down gently.

"No, I'll do it," I said, standing. "I don't trust you and I don't want our trip delayed even more because you've tripped on the bandage."

"You're the one who keeps delaying it," Pax called as I left the room.

I ignored his comment, even if it was a little true. From the hall closet, I grabbed the small metal medical kit my mother had built. Shutting the closet, I couldn't stop a smile at the wallpaper. Random spots in the house were decorated with it, a choice my mother made when the paint job got scratches or chips. Just one of her quirky choices in the house.

Returning with the kit in hand, I sat on the coffee table again and opened the box next to me. Grabbing the roll of bandages, my gaze flickered to the book Pax stuffed next to his leg. The cover was familiar.

"What's that?" I asked, lifting his foot.

He glanced down and picked up the floral covered book.

"It's a family photo album."

Smirking, I began wrapping his ankle. "What embarrassing age of mine did you pick? You looked like you were enjoying it."

Pax opened the book halfway. "That's the thing. You're not in here. You must be taking the photos."

I paused momentarily, continuing my task. "Check inside the cover. It'll say how old I was," I muttered.

The spine cracked as he followed my directions. After a moment, his head tilted a little.

"You're not on this list but it says Torna was fifteen years old."

I paused, eyes defocusing. I wasn't here, already four years into my apprenticeship. More proof my parents erased me from their lives entirely, just as I was told. Shaking my head to myself, I glanced up at Pax, who caught the change in my expression. I cleared my throat, finishing the wrap tightly.

"Okay, you're good. I'm going to bed."

Pax pulled his foot away as I rushed to stand. Ignoring him as he called my name, I didn't stop at my old bedroom when I reached the second floor. Instead, my knees smacked against the tiles of the bathroom in front of the toilet. My stomach clenched. The little food I had eaten during the day threatened to make an appearance. I waited, but nothing came out.

Dropping to my butt, my fingers brushed my hair into a low bun. Lifting my head, I made eye contact with Torna. Her arms were crossed, no expression as she leaned against the doorframe. We looked at each other for a long moment. There was genuine concern in her eyes for a fleeting moment until she walked away without a word and her bedroom door slammed shut.

***

Last night was the first peaceful sleep I had in weeks. There was a weird feeling of safety being in my childhood home. Nobody was going to steal the cage from around my neck here or focus on how to use the knowledge that I didn't have a pyx. Neither Torna nor Pax knew I didn't have my pyx.

Trying not to get too comfortable in my old room, I kept my duffle bag packed and on the ground. But the familiar scent of the blankets and the early morning sounds of more than just a rooster waking me up broke through my walls.

Opening the top drawer of my old maple dresser, a part of me expected it to be empty or full of my parents' possessions. The clothes owned by a fourteen-year-old me sat, folded neatly. Untouched other than a few moth holes. Holding up a denim shirt I wore while grooming the farm animals, it was obvious it wouldn't fit. I wasn't built the same as I was then. My body was much fuller now. Breasts and hips developed with muscles hidden underneath. The lanky, barely fed version of me would call modern day me 'a venus fly trap'. Attractive and deadly.

After shutting the drawer, I dumped out my sack of belongings on the floor. Clothing, hygiene products, and a few personal items tumbled out with a faint smell of body odour. The bag of dirty laundry was taken out earlier, but I'd have to wash what I considered clean. The smell had clung.

Rummaging around, I found the outfit I had in mind. Shaking the clothes out, I hoped to remove any grass or clumps of dirt that had made their way into the bag. Choosing undergarments, I changed into the most durable pants and a flowy shirt. I wouldn't get rid of the unexpected guilt unless I did some work around the farm. Holding up the small cage, I considered hiding it in the room somewhere. It was a fleeting thought as I dropped it down under my shirt.

Stepping into the hallway, I noticed the door to my parents' room was still closed. Pax must be enjoying the extra time to sleep in. Walking down the stairs, for the first time, I looked at the small picture frames my parents had nailed on the wall. My face was mixed in with my sisters, photos taken all over the property.

My fingertip ran over a small hole where a nail was missing, knowing what photo was meant to be there. It was my fourteenth birthday. Apple pie with a single candle lit sat in front of me. My hair was the longest it had been, hanging around my shoulders. The grin on my face was wide, all my teeth showing. I don't think I've smiled like that since. It was five months before my parents sold me off.

I expected the kitchen to be empty. Pax stood at the sink with his back to me. Staying in the doorway, my eyes ran over his bare back. In the sunlight, the divots in his back from scars were noticeable. The white dimples were uneven, with a few running the length of his freckled olive torso. A nasty and deep one ran from his shoulder and disappeared under his cotton pants. Having scars of my own, I couldn't imagine how painful the original wounds were. He stepped to the side and his broad shoulders blocked the sunlight coming through the window, dropping a shadow over me. I twisted my hair over my shoulder and entered the kitchen.

"Did you forget to get dressed?" I asked, opening a cupboard.

I hadn't thought about where anything was. It seemed my muscles remembered. At the back of the collection of mugs, my old cracked blue mug was hidden. Holding it between my hands, my cheeks warmed. I never imagined my family keeping any of my belongings. Let alone this.

"I was helping your sister take food to the chickens. She roped me into collecting eggs and tossed one when I wasn't expecting it. Cracked on my shirt. I'm trying to wash it out before it smells."

I turned the knob for fresh water, waiting for the mug to fill. Hiding behind a curtain of my hair, I rolled my eyes at my sister's antics. Torna always liked to annoy and poke at anyone. On top of that irritating personality trait, Pax was a stranger. She was going to dig and prod until she deemed him trustworthy. Hopefully, only coming back with one egg cracked on his shirt meant she thought he was okay.

"There's a washing bin and clothesline in the washroom

cupboard," I said. "You can wash it. I was already planning on putting out a line."

"I wasn't sure there was time before we left."

Beside him, I leaned against the counter, taking a slow drink and allowing myself a few seconds to swallow. I stared into my mug as I responded.

"I think I need to stay for a few days. I didn't know Torna was here alone. You can ride ahead if you want. I'll meet you at the next village or Verceen. I'm sure you can find something to amuse yourself."

Pax shut the tap off for unfiltered water. He peered at me while he rang the shirt out.

"You have a hard time accepting I'm here for you. If I didn't want to be, I wouldn't." He shrugged, shaking his hands dry. "I figured you were feeling guilty. You were talking in your sleep when I went to the washroom last night."

"How does that mean I feel guilty?" I asked, swirling the water inside the stained mug.

"I've slept in the same room as you twice now. You didn't make a sound either time. Slept peacefully through the night. Sleep talking is a sign of stress."

Through another drink of water, I considered his words. It was funny he thought I slept peacefully, when my dreams ran wild with nightmares and memories. The front door opened and shut, footsteps thudding towards the kitchen.

Torna walked in wearing a similar outfit to mine. She gave me an apathetic once over. She dismissively waved her hand for me to move. I rolled my eyes and pushed away from the counter, allowing my shoulder to lightly bump into hers. As she turned on the pump's tap, Torna saw what Pax was doing and chuckled.

"I guess they don't teach you to catch in Guard training?"

CHAPTER 17

Missing the chicken coop chores and feeding the other animals meant there was time before other things needed to be done. Putting on a pair of clean underclothes under a lounging dress and grabbing a towel, I enjoyed one perk of the farm.

Walking across the property, I found a path naturally compressed from years of running through to get to the pond first. Several deer stood at the pond's edge on the far side, drinking from its water. Thankfully, what I saw was still as beautiful as I remembered. A pine and floral scent I could never find filled my nose. Slipping my shoes off, I dropped my towel on the ground, followed by my dress.

My nose wrinkled as I stepped into the water. It was freezing, but it wouldn't deter me. Dunking my head under the water, my whole body was much warmer. The deer had disappeared when I disturbed their peace. Outside of the water crashing around, it was silent.

Pushing my toes off the silty lake floor, I swam farther out. Under the water, I opened my eyes. The sunlight penetrated through the water. The pond was my father's pride, and it looked like it was still being kept clean. A few feet ahead of me, a large fish swam by. My limbs paused, confused at just how clear the scales looked underwater.

Needing air, my head broke the surface, a gasp slipping through my lips. I almost expected my sisters to be on shore, lounging in the sun and chasing each other around. They could swim, but my youngest sisters had scared each other with horror stories and it wasn't Torna's type of activity. She preferred being on land.

But no one was there, and I was alone. Sighing, I let myself float backwards. My skin warmed under the rays. Floating here, I could pretend for a little while that everything was normal.

From swimming to gardening. I tossed another carrot into the basket before using a rag to wipe sweat off my forehead. Staring at the hundreds of fronds peeking out from the dirt, I didn't know the last time Torna dug vegetables from the garden; it was so overgrown.

Hooves thundering through the field drew my attention. Pax rode Neem with a grin on his face. He had smiled before, but this was the first time I saw him this free. Navigating Neem to the fence, his hair windblown and falling back into place as he caught his breath. In loose tan pants and a white linen shirt, for once, he didn't look like a Guard.

"How's gardening?" he asked, pushing his thoroughly sweaty curls out of his face.

I stood, ignoring the cracking of my knee. "Not as much fun as you're having."

He grinned down at his horse, scratching her neck with his nails. "I don't get to let Neem just run often. She's having the most fun."

I smiled at the beautiful grey horse. At the sound of her name, Neem huffed and shook out her mane. She was sweating too.

"I'm putting her in the paddock to cool down. I can help after if you've still got work to do."

I rested my hands on my waist. "I'll take the help. Got to dig out a ton of potatoes."

"Happy to be put to work," he said with a grin and a two-fingered salute.

Watching him ride away gracefully across the field, I leaned over to pick up my gloves, but the louder pounding of hooves against the driveway's gravel had me turning straightened in confusion. Torna didn't mention anyone was coming over. I dropped the cage under my shirt, picked up the basket of vegetables and left the fenced garden.

"Can I help you?" I called as I got to the driveway, resting my free hand on my hip.

The giant men didn't stop their horses until one of the creatures snorted in my face. I didn't move, even with the unfamiliar men glaring down at me.

"We're here to see Torna Kellobyn."

"That's nice," I said. "How can I help you?"

"You can't do anything for us, little girl."

I raised my eyebrows at the name. Both men looked grungy and unwashed, with their horses matching. They were noticeably muscular under their dirty clothing. Not highway robbers, but they weren't law-abiding citizens, either.

"If there's nothing I can do for you, have a good day. The driveway will take you right back to the road."

The man who called me the little girl thumped off his horse. The relief in the horse's eyes was obvious, its legs straightening. That man must've weighed a lot. Or it was the smell, I considered as he stopped inches away from my face. I bit down on the inside of my cheek to stop the gag, keeping my expression plain.

"And you would be?" he grunted, crossing his arms.

I smirked. "Thank you for asking. I am Torna's older sister."

"She doesn't have any sisters," the man atop his horse snapped.

My gaze flicked to him, then to the behemoth with almost black eyes in front of me, the corner of my mouth twitching.

"Unless I'm dreaming, you're misinformed."

The front door of the house opened and banged shut as Torna called my name with a slight tremor in her voice. She rushed over, her boots pounding against the dirt. I didn't turn around as she stopped beside me.

"Why're you two back? I told you I'm not selling," she said, crossing her arms.

"We hoped you'd reconsidered," the standing man said as his counterpart got off his horse.

My attention was divided between the two men. Leaning my head back and forth, my eyes darted to the trees. I almost expected more people to come out of the woods.

"I didn't know I had to repeat myself. I'm not selling the farm to you."

The first man with dark, greasy hair opened his mouth, but I spoke first.

"As my sister said, the farm is not for sale today. You'll be leaving now."

Both men stood with their hands resting on their multiple weapons. I would've felt more threatening if I had some sort of weapon instead of carrots and peppers.

"I think I'll go inside and have something to eat," the smelly and greasy one commented, rolling his shoulders.

I was ready to tell him he was incorrect, but I was interrupted.

"Who's that?" the other one asked, nodding his head.

His eyes were as dark as his friend's, but his hair looked better kept. The uneven cuts suggest a knife was used to shorten the sides.

Peering over my shoulder, I already knew. Pax walked out of the barn, his eyes already on the situation. There was an authoritative set to his shoulders that I recognized. The smirk on my face set in as I faced the monstrous men.

"Someone you two won't like."

Pax stopped next to me, hands on his belt. Still in his relaxing clothes, he put his Guard's scabbard and belt around his waist at some point. Matching the height of the two men, Pax met their eyes.

Assessing the men and their horses, Pax's chin got higher in the air. I was seeing his Guard persona for the first time. Stuffed bags hung from the saddles, and just like the riders, nothing was clean or new. It wasn't a stretch to guess that they didn't buy or trade for any of it.

"What's going on here?" he asked.

The less dominant man looked down at Pax's sword. I knew he recognized the symbol sewn into the scabbard when his mouth opened and jaw shifted side to side.

"Finishing a sale with the owner of the farm and her sister, apparently," the dominant one said, looking at me with suspicion.

Leaning forward, Pax looked past me to Torna. "You sellin' the farm?"

"No, I am not. These buffoons keep harassing me," Torna told him, irritated.

Pax made a sound of acceptance in his throat.

"Interesting." He looked at the two men, wagging his finger between them. "And what're your names?"

Neither answered. The one with a bad haircut stood back and watched his partner, waiting for instruction. Their power dynamic was obvious. Pax sighed dramatically, looking at my sister again.

"Are you going to tell me?"

"Carro and Tick," Torna introduced, pointing between them.

The large smelly one was Tick. What a sad name. Was it a nickname, or did his parents hate him?

His lips drooped in disgust when his name was shared. Pax nodded, stepping forward. Tick removed his sword from its scabbard at the movement. The blade wasn't in good condition. It was obviously a long time since it was properly cleaned. Blood and other entrails clung to the hilt. It was gross, and covered in diseases I didn't want to get.

I glanced at Torna. Her eyes widened at the weapon, but the rest of her face stayed flat. It was the face of a woman who'd experienced this before and was tired of it. A fleeting thought went through my mind as I wondered if she'd dealt with more than these two blockheads. Pax crossed his arms, unimpressed.

"Now, Tick. I don't know if you've noticed, but I'm not the right person to pull a sword on."

"And why's that?" Tick asked, pointing the tip at Pax's throat.

Tick's counterpart, Carro, watched his partner with no compassion. I had a feeling if there weren't consequences, he would be vocal about his annoyance. Raising his eyebrows, Pax grabbed the hilt of his sword, turning the scabbard to face the other man. After a long moment, Tick looked down and saw the metal emblem.

His sword dipped a few inches, but he recovered, pushing the sword more aggressively at Pax. Reconsidering the threat, he swiped it in the air to point at Torna instead. I jolted my head back to avoid the metal. Pax and Carro pulled their own weapons, pointing at the opposite person. My hand twitched, wanting my blade.

Unfortunately, Carro caught the movement. The tip of his blade aimed at me. I subtly ran my tongue along the back of my teeth, calming my nerves. Usually, I felt more control in this kind of situation.

"You. Are you a Guard too?"

"No, I'm not, but I will ask you one more time to leave the property and not come back."

Tick cackled, indicating between Torna and me with his sword. "I see the similarities between you now. You don't look nothin' alike, but it's the ruthless personality."

"Again, I think it's time you leave," I said.

Carro smirked, his eyes on mine. He was gaining confidence as his partner continued his behaviour. "Why would we do that?"

"You won't survive if you don't," I said. "And I'd hate to kill you."

From the corner of my eye, Torna slowly reached behind her back and a glint of metal reflected in the sunlight. The weapon stayed behind her. I felt better that we had another weapon, even if it was a third the size of the others.

"Aggressive words for a farm girl," Tick commented, extending his arm to poke me in the chest with the tip of his sword.

Pax's body locked beside me, his sword resting on Tick's throat. Lifting my hand, I wrapped it around Pax's wrist, who accepted my silent request and lowered the sword. His grip stayed tight around the handle. The sharp metal felt like a little pinch through my shirt, but I didn't react.

"Now," Tick said, dragging the blade to rest against my chin. "You three can go inside and collect a few things. We'll be generous. But then you leave. No horses. You walk off our property."

My composure was slipping, and my anger simmered, not being able to handle the men thinking they could push me around.

Behind Tick, Carro read the situation. He appeared to be the more intelligent one as Pax moved his sword to focus on Carro. My poor sister didn't know what to do next to me, her feet shifting back and forth.

"No," I said as the blade pushed into my neck a little more.

I ignored my heart pounding against my sternum. I rarely

had a sword at my throat. With another step forward, Tick pressed the metal a little harder into my skin. His smile was sickening, making sure this didn't end without a fight.

"One more time?" Tick asked, a threatening tone ringing out.

I dropped the basket of vegetables, which caught everyone's attention. My eyes flickered to Carro. With his mouth tightened, I could tell he didn't want to fight. He probably thought they would arrive to find Torna alone and get the farm easily. Releasing Pax's wrist, I turned my other hand over and kept my eyes on the two brutes.

"Torna?"

I didn't need to clarify as my sister placed the dagger in my hand. When my fingers wrapped around the hilt, I used the momentum to knock the sword away from my chin. I felt the tip knick my skin, but I didn't have the time to be worried.

Tick's eyes widened and his mouth dropped open; he didn't notice Torna was armed. I kicked out my foot, connecting it with the edge of his kneecap. And a fight ensued.

With my next targeted swing, Tick blocked his throat with his bare arm. The blade sliced through his forearm. His sword stayed high, and I anticipated the move early enough to step away.

When my foot landed, I registered Torna wasn't behind me but didn't have time to be concerned about where she went. Tick's face contorted with anger, aimlessly slashing his sword at my head. He threw his size like it would help him move closer. Would this be easier if I had my sword? Yes, but the dagger would do.

During my apprenticeship, Janna focused on extensive and intense training sessions. She considered it a basic skill to know different fighter types and how to beat them. The large beast that Tick was, went for the untrained kill, always going for my head and throat. It would produce the most blood without standing too close to his opponent, likely a better trained fighter than him.

Janna's teachings acted like a dial in my head, helping me to focus on an intellectual attack. The years of training formulas flipped through my head like a textbook. Taking a few steps back, I allowed the blade to pass close to my face.

Ducking my head under the flying metal, my arm shot out and slashed across his vulnerable stomach. His vest looked thick, but the sharp edge of my blade sliced through without issue. Tick let out a roar of pain, not expecting the move. From the dagger's weight, I stumbled past him.

Barely swaying, worry dropped to my stomach. Maybe I had only cut the vest. Leaning forwards, his fingers clutched at his stomach, the sword clattered against the ground. His hand looked to dip inward and blood pooled, soaking his ratty beige shirt.

His knees banged against the gravel, dirt puffing up and pebbles shooting out the sides. Knowing it was an impractical choice, I leapt on his back and locked my arm around his swollen neck. The smell had my stomach flopping, my jaw locking so the vomit wouldn't come out. Tick growled under me, thrashing. Both of his hands grabbed at my forearm, attempting to throw me off. One hand released me, and I was only allowed a moment of relief, thinking he'd begun losing more strength until fingers gripped in my hair. The scream barely passed my lips as I was yanked over his shoulder. He still had enough strength to dismount me, but I had enough sense to keep hold of the dagger until I was entirely upside down and shoved the tip towards his body.

Flying through the air, my empty hand caused panic as my spine crashed into the ground, rocks jabbing into my skin and bones. A different type of nausea manifested. Rolling on to my knees, I had to ignore the pain. There wasn't time for it. My gaze shot up to where Tick knelt, violently tapping against the ground in a blind search of the dagger. Grabbing the handle, I realized I didn't need it anymore.

The blood pumped wildly out of the wound, his hand unable to stop it. The colour in his face was gone. Cautiously rising to my feet, his eyes rolled back and his muscles lost all their strength. The brute crumpled to the ground. Gaining control of my breathing, I waited to see if he would stand up. A loud clang took my attention before a sound of heavy impact made me turn.

A bloody Pax hit the gravel as Carro's foot lowered and gained his balance again. My upper body twisted and, with one motion, threw the dagger. The throw was an attempt at distracting Carro, the one left with a weapon in hand. My aim was more spot on than I intended and the blade plunged into his back.

The impact sent him stumbling, "oof" slipping from his mouth. He peered back, attempting to see his back. The distraction gave Pax time to shuffle to his feet, grabbing his sword. The moment Carro faced Pax again, the Guard swung upwards. Only the splatter of blood flying was all I saw.

Carro stumbled back, sword slipping from his fingers. He let out a single cough, a sweat drenched Pax waiting for a response. I paced softly around them, circling the scene. Another cough's vibration ruptured the wound and blood spewed as he collapsed to the ground.

Other than the distant sound of farm animals, the farm was silent. We stared at the bodies, almost expecting the fight to not be done. My attention flickered to Pax as he rested his arm against his stomach. His face was wincing until he caught me staring and he did his best to look neutral.

Stepping around the bodies, I forced his hand away. A grunt slipped from his lips at the jerk. His shirt was unevenly ripped, framing a gaping wound. A gasp slipped out of my mouth, crumpling the bottom of his shirt and shoving it against the wound to stop the bleeding. He instinctively turned away, an uncomfortable groan from the sensation. I mumbled an apology, lightening the pressure so it was just resting on top.

"I guess you didn't need this," Torna called, leaning against the porch with my sword in hand.

She pointedly looked at the bodies with blood soaking into the surrounding gravel. She didn't appear overly disgusted.

"Help me get him inside? He's wounded," I asked.

"Owyn, I'm fine. It's a small wound. It's not that deep."

"Are you sure?" I asked, pulling the fabric away to get a second look.

Pax made a sound of discomfort in his throat, his hand slapping over mine. "I'm sure. Except it's kind of all stuck together and that doesn't feel good. Leave the shirt."

I lifted my hands in the air, letting him control the pressure. He tilted my head with a finger on my chin.

"You've got a cut. We need to wash it out. That sword was filthy," he said with concern.

He pressed his hand against my lower back, guiding me towards the house. I tried to point out his wound was worse, but he wasn't listening.

"I'm fine, by the way," Torna sarcastically added as we passed her on the porch. "If anyone is asking. No wounds here but emotional, permanent damage."

Chapter 18

Leaning against the kitchen counter, I watched Pax move around with one hand pressed to his stomach. His dirty shirt had turned almost entirely blood soaked. Every step made his eyebrows twitch in pain. Not that bad, my ass. I took the half filled bowl of water he was pushing across the counter.

"Gimme that," I whispered.

He resisted until the water splashed out, making him grumble incoherently as I yanked away the dish towel too.

"I'm cleaning your wound first. It's worse than mine, no matter what you say."

"Owyn, stop." Pax tried to push my hand away, but he didn't use a lot of strength. I didn't want to consider whether he had it. "Your wound could get infected."

"And yours won't? It's covered in blood. Which, if you didn't know, isn't a good thing."

Pax sighed with defeat when he saw the scissors I took from a drawer. Muttering a premature apology, I cut up the shirt's front, avoiding the wound. Slowly lifting his hand, I wrapped my fingers around the soaked scrap.

Though my first instinct was to yank it away, I remembered some other bit of training. Doing my best to soak the rag of the shirt with water, I peeled it away as quickly as I could. No matter how hard I tried, a few small spots of blood were dried. My nose twitched as a pained groan slipped from his mouth.

Once it was clean, the wound looked better. The blade didn't go deep enough to cause problems, though riding horses wouldn't be comfortable for a while.

"At least that one kept his sword clean," Pax muttered. "The one you were fighting had a filthy sword. Let me see your chin."

His soft tone had my breath catching in my throat. Pax slid the towel from my hand and found a clean spot before ripping it in half. My eyes dropped when his muscles flexed. I mentally scolded myself. This isn't the time.

Dipping a clean section in the water, he tilted my head back. I watched his mossy green eyes as he wiped at my skin. A dry bit of fabric caught against the wound and I couldn't stop the twitch of my muscles. Pax smirked, eyes twinkling with mischief.

"Now you know how it feels."

I weakly glared at him. "It's annoying. That's how it feels."

He chuckled, dipping the rag into the water again. "It doesn't look infected," he commented. "I think you'll be fine."

I didn't point out it was probably too soon to know if the cut was infected or not because it was nice to have someone take care of me. But as the words came out of his mouth, I yanked the rag away from his hands.

"Great, I'm fine. Let me look at you."

Pax stuck his arms out and slowly spun around. "There, you got a good look at me."

Clicking my tongue in annoyance, I peered down at his stomach again. From the dramatic gesture, the wound was bleeding again. Seeing the red liquid, my hand shot forward and planted the rag against him. He moaned, hands grabbing my wrist to relieve the pressure.

"You need to stop doing that," he said between his teeth.

"Sorry."

The front door opened and closed. A different, vocal groan of disgust echoed through the house.

"I moved the dead giants all by myself, thank you very much. They're in the trees. You have to get rid of them," Torna called. "Not my job."

Her footsteps stop at the kitchen door.

"What's happening here?" She had an amused interest in her voice.

"Torna, go to my sack and bring down the small purple bag with red stitching," I instructed, peeking under the cloth.

"Yes, I'd be happy to do what you've so politely asked," she sarcastically muttered, still walking upstairs.

"You should put something on that," Pax said, tapping my chin.

My head pulled back, but his finger stopped me. My eyes flicked upwards. He was much closer than I was used to. How did he smell good when he just fought and killed somebody?

"The gold in your eyes is brighter today," he muttered, his comment just for me.

"I've been told that happens after a fight," I answered, matching his volume.

"I'll watch out for it," he responded, smirking.

A voice in my head screamed warnings. Did I know what was being said? Not at all. A loud buzzing blocked my ability to hear them. My gaze flickered down to Pax's lips, and our kiss from the pub returned to my mind. Would I enjoy it as much without alcohol and intentions of bothering Yash?

Torna's feet thundered down the stairs, pulling me from the dizzying thoughts. I took a step away and Pax's hand dropped, but he maintained his gaze. Somehow, his eyes were brighter, too.

"When I was hunting for your sword, I poured out your bag," Torna said, holding it out to me. I ignored the 'dumping out my belongings' part.

"Open it and grab the bottle labelled cleaning alcohol. Then get the needle and thread? Thickest needle I have," I instructed, assessing the cut again. "Oh, and roll of bandages."

"Needle and thread?" Pax asked wearily.

"I need to sew this up," I told him. "When we ride, any scab will open up."

"I don't see any thread in here," Torna commented.

"It's not a normal thread, but on the same sort of spool."

"Got it," she said. "On the counter?"

"Table."

I looked at Pax. "I need you to walk with me. I'm going to sit, but you need to stand. Your ankle okay?"

Pax nodded, sweat pooling on his forehead. I wasn't sure if it was from blood loss or nerves. Removing the rag, it was a relief that blood was clotted. Pouring out a small amount of cleaning alcohol on my hands, I pointed to the counter.

"Can you pass the other half of that rag?"

My sister began to leave, but whipped her head back around. "Wait, is that one of my towels?"

I glared at my sister as Pax handed me the fabric. "If you're not going to be helpful or going to be squeamish, do something else. I can't focus on you while I'm literally putting a needle through his skin."

"Did you really have to add that part?" Pax mumbled, wiping his forehead with the back of his hand as Torna backed away with her hands up, but stayed in the kitchen. I peered up at Pax, ignoring the dumb sexual thoughts making their way into my head.

"This is going to suck, okay?"

He stiffly nodded. I already felt guilty for the pain I was about to inflict. Taking a deep breath, I forced myself to smother my nerves. There was no easier way to do this, and it wouldn't help if I was shaking. Starting, I poured cleaning alcohol onto the rag.

"Pass me the rag you had water on?"

"It's covered in blood," he answered in a low voice, intensely focused on what I was doing.

"Torna, I need another towel." She began to complain but I cut her off. "I'll send you a fancy new one when I get back to Jova. Or should I slice you across the stomach to make you frantic? He doesn't want to bleed out on the damn floor."

Torna scoffed, handing me a clean one after soaking it in the water. Careful to not irritate the cut, I patted away dried blood. Locking my jaw, I blocked out his nervous and uneven breathing.

Resting my hand against his abdomen and Pax took a deep breath, preparing himself. I grabbed the needle and dipped it into the jar of alcohol. Thankful no one said anything when my hand shook once as I threaded the needle. Puckering the wound's edges, I look at Pax. His jaw was locked, intensely staring at my forehead.

"I'm sorry," I whispered.

He nodded, grabbing both my shoulders to get his hands out of the way. My chest tightened and my mouth filled with saliva, close to nausea. This wasn't hard to do on myself or to someone else in a dangerous situation. Why did I hate this much?

My heart fractured little by little as I stitched the wound shut. He was doing his best to not whine or flinch. Occasionally, his grip tightened around my shoulder, or a whimper escaped his mouth. Thankfully, the stitches didn't need to be too tight. It wouldn't make sense for riding and cause more damage. Knotting off the end, I used a knife to separate.

Putting the needle and excess thread down, I cleaned up the weeping edges. Pax took his hands off my shoulders when I sat up.

"Done," I said after clearing my throat.

Feeling a slight pressure on my face, I wiped at it. It was a surprise to see my fingers were wet. I glanced up at Pax. His face was flushed, but he was going to stay on his feet. Reaching for the roll of bandages, I saw the doorway was empty. Torna could handle the gory birth of farm animals, but stitching a person's skin together was too much, and I completely understood. I released the bandage's edge, standing up.

"Keep this on and we can change it if you bleed through. It's only until I can cut those stitches," I said, wrapping his torso.

Pax draped his arms over my shoulders to expose his sides again. Holding the end of the bandage to his side, I glanced at the table.

"Shoot, Torna didn't put out the adhesive." I stepped away, but I couldn't turn around without letting go of the bandage.

"Hold on," Pax said.

He shifted, putting our chests flush as he leaned awkwardly around me. His breath heated my neck, my own catching in my throat. Straightening, he ripped off a piece of tape behind my head and held it out.

"This good?" he asked, holding the piece between us with a smirk.

I stared at him, my mind blank. It took me a moment to process he said anything. Nodding, I pulled the tape from his finger. After adding a few more pieces, I attempted to step back, but his hands dropped to my waist.

"You're all wrapped up," I said with weak confidence.

"Thank you very much, doc."

He smirked at me, and it made me want to smack him. I

couldn't understand how I felt like a shy and inexperienced teenager with him. The raw honesty in his eyes continued to send unexplained shivers through me, leaving an urge to kill him, but put him into my bed. It didn't make sense.

"Is it done? Is the blood gone?" Torna's voice flooded in from the hallway.

I twisted in Pax's arms and began collecting the medical stuff. It took a second before his hands let me go.

"Are those two the only men who've shown up here?" He asks her, crossing his arms.

"Yeah. Honestly, I don't know where they came from. Sort of showed up one day," she answered, entering the kitchen. She changed out of her work clothes, still wearing pants, but they didn't look as durable.

I glanced at her as I packed the bag. "You don't know where they came from?"

Filling a glass of water, she shrugged. "No. Like I said, they just showed up."

"Our father probably owed them pesa for something," I muttered. Not giving me a reaction, I knew she had considered the same thing.

"I'm going to ride back to Mye and speak with the Guards," Pax announced.

I paused, looking at him. "Why?"

"Those might be the only two you saw, but you should be concerned that they're alone," he told my sister. "I'm going to arrange for some Guards to come by every week."

"Great," Torna grumbled, walking away.

I rolled my eyes at her bored tone. "You can say thank you!"

"Thank you," she called back in a sickly sweet voice, her footsteps echoing as she walked upstairs.

"It's not a good idea for you to ride into town right now. It's over two hours away, and I've just finished stitching you up."

He shrugged. "It's got to be done. If those two morons found out she's here alone, they're not going to be the only ones."

I tied the ribbons together, closing the bag. "I guess. I'll dig holes for the bodies while you're gone. Are you okay if we leave in the morning?"

"Sure. We got a couple of good sleeps and meals. Might as well get back on the road." Pax walked towards the doorway. "I'm going to put on a fresh shirt and head out."

Ignoring the blood splatters on my clothes, I made my way to the storage shed hidden behind the barn. Finding a shovel in the same spot it was for twenty years, I wandered towards the woods with it in hand. The day wasn't exactly warm, but it didn't take long for bodies to smell.

Once I located the lumps that were Tick and Carro, I didn't look at them. Groaning, I tossed the shovel aside and began dragging fallen branches to the side. Maybe I should've gone back to Mye with Pax and gotten my sister some security. I could afford to make it happen without having him use his connections and have us owe him.

Using the small bout of extra strength in my muscles, I chucked a rock further into the underbrush. It landed, and a coyote darted out of its way. The creature stared at the rock for a moment before looking at me. I could almost read the annoyance in its eyes since I disturbed its potential lunch.

"My bad," I apologised. "I didn't know you were there."

The grey coyote watched me for a second longer before trotting away.

"You wouldn't want to eat these two anyway," I muttered. "You don't know what diseases you'd catch."

After clearing the debris, I picked up the shovel again. The coyote reminded me to dig deep into the ground or these buffoons would become some other creature's meal. Whether it be the entrails and remains or the farm animals being a tempting dessert, I'm sure my sister wouldn't be too pleased.

At least three feet into the ground, my stomach felt funky and nausea was returning. The feeling left me close to feigning ignorance, assuring me the hole would be deep enough. No one was going to come lookin' and wild animals wouldn't dig this deep for half-rotten food.

I put in a few more minutes of work until my stomach made the decision that I was done. Over the edge of the pit, I vomited. The muscles down my bruised left side contracted.

Overwhelmed by the weakness throwing up left me with, I dropped to my knees. The dirt was cool under my hands as I fought to catch my breath. My stomach settling, I leaned back on my feet and pulled the cage out from under my shirt.

Against my dirt caked hands, the gold was beautiful. The eggs were motionless, their colours brightened by the sun breaking through the trees above. Every time I saw them, the guilt reared its head and the feeling would get worse the closer I got to Jova. I couldn't pretend that I didn't pick them up.

If Pax didn't already report it, the Council must be getting reports as we passed through every town from Delegates. It was impossible to believe they trusted me or any of the abducted Merchants to return without a problem.

"You know, that grave isn't for you."

Tilting my head back and staring through the leaves, I scoffed. "Well, if you helped me, I wouldn't feel like just hanging out here."

Torna came closer, her nose scrunching at the vomit on the dirt. "Did you do that, or is that a part of body decomposition I don't know about?"

I snorted, jabbing the shovel into the dirt to help myself stand. Ignoring her question, I continued digging.

"Thia, I think that's deep enough."

The nose of the shovel froze in the dirt, and I glanced at her. Hearing my childhood nickname caused a twisted sadness, almost making me annoyed with her.

Torna stood at the grave's edge, hugging herself. She was older, but there was a hint of the little girl that my sister used to be still in her eyes. No hardness or abandonment there. I couldn't understand how it was still alive inside of her. I had lost any innocence a long time ago.

Tossing the shovel next to her feet, I lifted myself out of the grave.

"Help me with them," I muttered, stepping over to the bodies.

Without a sarcastic complaint, we grabbed Tick's arms first, then Carro's, and let them thud into the hole. I tried not to see the surprised looks permanently left on their faces as I covered them in dirt. A second shovel picked up dirt and tossed it in. I hadn't seen the tool when she came up.

"Dad's ashes are down by the main road," Torna said. "There's a stone marker..."

"Okay," I interrupted her. I didn't want to know. There was no plan to stop when we left.

"Okay," Torna said back quietly.

Chapter 19

With my pack nestled into the back of my saddle, it hooked together easily. This morning, we slept in and took our time. Now the sun was high in the sky, the afternoon just starting.

Standing in the kitchen, I emptied a bottle of fish tonic into my water, the nausea worse than normal when I woke up. I didn't see my sister at the door, but she watched the whole thing in silence. Only looked at me with suspicion. With an excuse at the tip of my tongue, I ignored her.

Braiding my hair over my shoulder, I stared at my childhood house. For once, I wanted to remember it, even though it was burned into my brain just as it was. It probably would never change. I didn't know when I would stop here again. Life was too unpredictable, but knowing my parents weren't here, I felt the encouragement to actually try.

"Got everything?" Pax asked, attaching his own bag to a calm Neem.

The horses were rested, enjoying the freedom of outdoor pens and more food than they've ever had in one sitting. A small voice wanted to leave them here to enjoy life instead of crossing the country repeatedly. But that was my guilt created by the faerie eggs around my neck, talking.

"Yeah, you?"

"Good to go," he said, nodding.

Stepping over to Marr, my hands ran a last check along the harness latches and I peered over my shoulder, hearing my name. Torna jogged over, holding the hem of her dress up.

Behind me, she held out a burlap bag. "Save some pesa on the road."

From the weight and smell, there was bread and more inside. I left her a small bag of pesa on her bed and she hadn't found it yet. The sisterly instinct just never left, I guess.

"I don't know when, but I'll be back," I said, reiterating my thoughts.

She nodded, holding her own elbows. "I'll be here."

Awkwardly looking at each other, neither of us was sure what to do next. When I arrived, I thought my sister disliked me and she thought I left them. Four days later, our mindsets were different. Courage bloomed in my chest as I thought about who she was abandoned to be. The pile of guilt inside of me grew as I pulled her into a hug.

"I'm proud of you," I whispered.

Her hands rested lightly on my back. "I'm sorry."

It took a minute before we released each other. I faced Dill without another look at my sister, almost certain I would cry if I did. Once on the saddle, I looked over at Pax.

"Ready?"

He glanced at Torna and nodded his head in thanks as he picked up the reins.

"Let's go."

My hand ran along the knit of my pants, watching the treeline ahead of us. The sky darkened, and the air was smelling heavier. No animals scampered by in a while and it was eerily silent other than the Histlea River rushing past in the distance. Marr nervously huffed at the thunder rumbling overhead and I looked at the grey clouds for the hundredth time.

"It's okay, buddy. Just a little rain," I muttered soothingly.

"Doesn't sound like a little rain," Pax said. "I think it's going to storm."

I glared at him from the corner of my eyes. No duh. That wasn't a productive comment, though, for anyone's nerves. "We're gonna need to stop. This part of the highway is prone to flooding."

"Can we turn back?"

I rolled my eyes for him to see. "Why do you always want to turn back? I thought your instructions were to push forward, no matter what. Plus, it takes days for this road to clear."

"You know the area, right? You must know somewhere to stop."

I said nothing, examining a map in my mind. It was fuzzy, but a curious childhood helped.

"I know where to go," I said when the answer came to me.

"Of course you do," he said with a chuckle. "Do you know everyone off the highway?"

"We aren't stopping at a house. There's a cave at the top of this hill. It's big enough for the horses inside. We'll stay dry."

"How do you know it's there?"

"My father grew up on the farm with his brothers. They'd disappear for days, exploring the area. When I was little, he showed Torna and I. Said he got lost one night and hid here until morning. He showed it to us, hoping we would be as adventurous as him," I explained.

"And you remembered exactly where it was all these years later?" Pax asked in disbelief.

"I didn't just remember it existed. I've stayed in it before."

He lifted his eyebrows when I didn't give an explanation. I peeked at him twice, hoping he wouldn't push. No luck.

"I tried to run away when I was thirteen. I didn't get far

before logic struck and a storm like this hit all at the same time. Fear burned it into my brain."

"I couldn't imagine you as the kind of child to run away."

I dipped my head under a swaying branch as more thunder rumbled. The rain hadn't started yet, but the growing wind was blocking out the river's noise.

"I was a little different before I became a Merchant. I wanted off the farm." I smirked to myself. "Didn't expect it to actually happen."

Pax chuckled. "I'd have liked to meet you back then."

"I would've eaten you alive."

He grinned at me, amused by my comment, but said nothing back.

I started feeling worried that maybe I forgot where the cave was. There was a rough pathway through the trees, but paths like these were all across the country. Grass and weeds had stood straight, recovered from not being trampled on for years. When I ran away, I didn't have Marr or the cart with me. I ridden Dill and in my memory; it was a shorter ride. Spotting the single red maple tree settled in the middle of pines with its roots gnarly wrapped around the bases of others, the stress disappeared.

The pathway thinned out farther ahead, and I dismounted Dill. Glancing back at Pax, he followed suit. Adjusting their leads to give Dill more length to keep her between Marr and me, I was grateful the rain hadn't started. The cart wouldn't have made it with wet foliage grabbing at the wheels.

Pax took up the rear, more careful where he's stepping than before. Being the grumpy horse he is, Marr was resistant to the muck that gathered around his hooves. He kept stopping, kicking his feet out wildly.

Finally, six pine trees were half fallen over. After my uncle and father found this cave, my uncle had come back and disfigured the trunks. Small branches grew out of the living bases, but the trees were monstrosities compared to the others. They were good identifiers.

"Here it is," I said, more to myself.

Disconnecting the horses from each other, I led Dill into the cave and skimmed my foot across the ground, pushing any sharp debris out of the way. The cave sat the same as I remembered. The flat ground led into darkness until it was pitch black. No plant life grew inside, but years of storms and wind had made piles of dry leaves and debris. The boulders around the entrance didn't encroach but were stacked to block some wind.

"That isn't spooky," Pax muttered, his eyes flickering around nervously.

"You can stay outside, if you want," I told him, tying Dill to a stalagmite. "But I'm keeping myself and these two dry."

He opened his mouth to make a sarcastic comment back, but a crack of thunder interrupted him, followed by the first strike of lightning. Neem whined, backing in fear. Pax grabbed her halter before she tried to run. I focused on Marr, looking into his eyes for any similar desires. His ears were flat against his head, but the weight of the cart kept him on the ground. Running wasn't his safe option.

Nimbly disconnecting Marr from the cart, I used soft, encouraging words to coax him into the cave. He pulled his head a little in resistance towards the dark hole in front of him. The sight of his sister inside seemed to be what finally convinced him.

"What about your cart?" Pax asked, tying Neem's reins next to Dill. The two horses huffed at each other.

"There's a spell on it," I explained. "Weather won't damage it."

"And you couldn't put that spell on us?"

I weakly glared at him before rolling my eyes at his comment. "I'm not Drao. I can't do spell work."

"Not with that attitude," Pax grumbled, removing his bag off Neem's back.

CHAPTER 20

THE RAIN TOOK ITS TIME TO COME DOWN. WE'D BEEN ABLE TO collect enough sticks from the woods before it got too soggy. Pax tended to the fire and I fished out food from our bags. The pouring rain while hiding in the forest grew a sense of peace inside my chest.

After food, we pulled out books and when the clouded sunlight disappeared entirely; the firelight was enough. Once my eyes were having a hard time staying open, I did my best to create a comfortable and warm spot to sleep. Almost like she knew I would need it, Torna insisted I take a blanket from the house. I mentally thanked my stubborn little sister for the forethought as I put it on the ground. My cloak, old and thinning but still warm, would go on top. Getting myself into a comfortable position, I glanced at Pax as he pulled out most of his clothes.

"Do you have a blanket?" I thought Torna had given him one too.

"No, I'll use some clothes," he said.

I sighed, knowing I'd feel guilty in the morning when he was shivering.

"Stop! Put your clothes away. They're clean for once. Sleep

on the blanket with me and bring your cloak. It'll be warmer."

He paused, looking at me hesitantly. "You sure?"

"You don't need to smell like cave dust until you can shower again. People are suspicious enough of you as it is."

As his boots scuffed across the cave floor, fluttering wings echoed against the walls. Instinctually, he dropped his head forwards and used his arms for cover as the noise got louder. In the darkness, small squawks and brief spurts of fire shot through the air. The horses neighed, fussing with the creatures flying over their heads. When the noise was replaced again by the storm, Pax stood and his bewildered expression made a laugh erupt from my chest.

"What was that?" He asked, whipping his head around.

"Dragonnettes," I said through laughter. "This is one of their caves."

"And you didn't tell me?" A small amount of panic slipped into his voice.

"It's fine. They're too little to eat us while we're alive. The worst that can happen is they'll leave burns on us if we get too close."

He looked suspiciously at the darkness and stepped with significantly more care. He sat next to me, his eyes still flickering to the blackness.

I rolled my eyes. "No actual dragons are going to show up. This cave is too small for anything dangerous. I promise."

Pax made a sound of acknowledgement, but it was obvious he didn't completely believe me, so I kept my giggles hidden under my cloak. It seemed Guards weren't exposed to wild creatures often.

I adjusted my sack, punching at it to get comfortable. The rain pattered against the forest muck, bouncing off the cave entrance. Under the edge of my cloak, my sheathed sword rested and, hopefully, didn't need to be taken out.

"You're going to sleep?" Pax asked, laying down too.

"I want to leave early. My back already hurts from the rocks," I mumbled.

He said nothing, just shuffled around and when his elbow bumped me, I stiffened. With the warmth of the fire radiating on my covered feet, my heavy eyes wouldn't stay closed. Every sound from the man next to me caused a twitch of consciousness, my grip on the cage tightening.

It was a weird relief knowing I didn't trust him, this practical stranger, blindly. A part of me kept wondering if I was losing my mind when I agreed to travel with him on that first day.

***

OPENING MY EYES, I INSTANTLY REGRETTED IT. THE SUN WAS already too bright. I rubbed my eyes, hoping to somehow lessen the light. Rolling my neck to the side, my surroundings came into focus. It was a room with only the grey bed I was lying on. Standing, a familiar pain cramped along my ribs.

The bruise on my side was fresh once again. I groaned through a locked jaw, clenching my top in my fist. Tugging at the fabric made me realize I was in an unfamiliar pale dress. Another intense pain shot through my body again, forcing me to bend in a weak attempt to lessen the sensation. Relaxing my grip, I flipped my palms up. The rust smell hit my nose as the fresh blood came into view.

"Owyn?"

My head snapped to the side, the rest of me unmoving.

Eira glided towards me in a white dress. She was backlit, her figure making shadows under the thin linen. Her soft smile put my heart at ease as she reached out with both hands, but I pulled mine away, not wanting to stain her dress.

"Owyn, please," Eira whispered with need. Her voice echoed around the room's bare walls.

"My hands." I showed her, but she grabbed them without concern.

"Hold me," she said, resting my hands on her hips.

The blood came from painless cuts, the white fabric becoming soaked. My instincts changed, and I tugged her closer as her arms around my waist. She smelt like floral and clean laundry. It was my favourite smell. Lips touched my neck, delicately placing open-mouthed kisses, making my eyes fall shut.

"Orinthia."

My eyes shot open, and Eira was gone. Instead, five people lined the other side of the room. Hands clasped behind their backs, they wore dark pants and shirts with long grey robes over top. The Council.

Something behind them caught my attention, and nausea filled my body. On a little gold table, was a floating orb under a glass dome. It wasn't a perfect circle with a tail falling towards the tabletop and smoke rolling off it. It was stormy and grey with flashes of purple and blue lightning from within. I was staring at a warped version of my pyx. My foot moved forward hesitantly, drawn to what was mine.

"Owyn," Eira's voice whispered past my ear.

My gaze jerked over my shoulder, spooked. Eira reappeared on her knees, atop of the bed that was now covered by a fluffy white comforter. I glanced at the Council. The seven men were still watching me, not giving her any attention. Or they hadn't noticed her at all.

Her dress was different, too. Still the same silk white colour, it was a nightie with a much lower neckline and almost see-through. My pounding heart begged me to join her as her large chocolate brown eyes drew me in. My knee smacked into the mattress, but I didn't notice the sensation as her small hand reached for me. Glass clinked when our fingers wrapped together.

We froze and even though my muscles were relaxed, I wasn't sure if it was our choice to or not. My head turned with a sense of pressure against my temple, almost forcing me. My focus was brought to the new person standing in front of the Council. A slender woman held my pyx, watching me. My heart stuttered to a halt and pushed up into my throat.

The room filled with scentless smoke, blacking out most of the light. The stranger grinned at me with sharp teeth. Only her hand moved closer until the pyx filled my vision. Her dirt caked fingernails pressed into the pyx's skin and a scream ripped from my chest. The scream breaking off, I felt like my skin was burning. The sensation grew, overwhelming all of my senses until my legs were too weak to hold me up.

I didn't collide with the floor, my back bounced against the mattress. Eira interrupted the sight of an illuminating white ceiling, tossing her leg over my torso. She leaned forward, running her hands up my chest. The fire inside of me had died and her hands left a familiar tingling. Wanting more, I pressed into her palms.

"Are you missing something?" She asked in a sweet, low voice.

I tried to ask what she was talking about, but I couldn't. Like she knew I couldn't speak, a smile curled on her face as her hand ran down my bruised side. I twitched away, knowing I couldn't tell her to stop, but Eira used her other hand to push me back with an unnatural strength.

The grin on her face twisted menacingly, her nails pinching into my side. My voice returned in a mid-shout of 'stop', but her nails were razor sharp, piercing into my skin. The protesting scream that came from my throat was rough.

Stepping into my field of vision, the mystery woman still held my pyx. Her eerie smile matched Eira's. Her nails were pushed so tightly against the pyx's outer layer, it couldn't last much longer. Eira's fingernails punctured my skin, like her fingers were going into my body. I felt like I was underwater for far too long, my entire body begging for air and I was slipping closer to unconsciousness.

The pain should've killed me, but something was keeping me just conscious enough to feel everything. I couldn't beg or cry. Only a scream.

My eyes shot open, and my lungs were begging for air that I didn't know I was withholding. Sitting up, dry coughs forced their way out as my systems tried to regulate. Fingernails pressed into my palms, I focused on the sharp pressure as my panic dissolved.

A nightmare. Just a nightmare.

Tugging my knees closer to my torso, I scratched my nails against my scalp. My left side felt like it was now covered by just the bruise. My shirt brushed against it, and a sensitive shiver radiated through me. Hesitantly, I touched my shirt, but my hand came away dry. Imagines of Eira's face, the unknown woman and my pyx were stained in my mind.

"Are you alright?"

I jerked away with surprise, forgetting I wasn't alone. Pax sat next to me, leaning back on one hand and rubbed his half-open eyes to wake himself up.

"I'm fine," I muttered. My lids felt like I'd been crying for hours.

"I've seen you restless in your sleep before, but that was eventful," he said in a teasing tone, but soothing.

He was close to me, but not touching, and I appreciated it. Once I could breathe properly again, I laid back down and stared at the cave's roof. He watched me, waiting for something to happen.

"Yeah. Well, cave floors aren't good to sleep on."

It didn't take us long to leave the cave the next morning. Both of us woke with sore backs, but we wanted to get moving. Still half asleep, I scrubbed my fist against my eyelids.

We were getting closer to the Southern Verceen village, another gloomy spot in Gerennt. It was close enough to Mye that my father sold produce here, but kept us girls away. He never explained his dislike for the village, but I followed his lead. I never had a reason to question his choices before. But now it was the closest village to stock up and get some food of substance. I could have taken more food from the farm, but I did my best to keep what I took to a minimum. Even without the cart, I didn't want to be a bigger target for robbery.

When the horses' hooves clattered onto the cobblestone, the villagers' heads turned. Their looks automatically settled on glares of judgement.

Rolling my shoulders back, I mustered some false confidence and tried to look down at them through my eyelashes. Even with my stiff riding corset, the looks made me shrink a little.

There wasn't much grass along the roadside, only tufts of weeds and leaves of unidentified plants sticking up. It left the people standing much closer than I was comfortable with.

"They don't look too happy," Pax muttered.

"They work in the mountains," I said. "I wouldn't be happy either."

I stopped Dill in front of a man leaning in the doorway of a floral shop, who didn't look as disgruntled as his neighbours.

"Excuse me, where is the agriculture shop?"

He lifted his bored green eyes from the ground, having ignored the sounds of hooves and cart wheels getting closer. His eyes assessed across the horses, Pax, myself and stopped on the cart.

The curiosity and greed appearing in his eyes made my jaw lock. Even though Pax's outfit screamed Guard and mine didn't look like cheap riding clothes, the man couldn't figure out what the potential value of the cart's contents were before he looked uninterested again.

"Left down the next road and all the way to the end."

Before I could thank him, he walked into the shop and slammed the door shut. The Council's sigil was engraved deeply into the wood. Encouraging Dill to walk forward, my eyes didn't leave the headless bird until we were entirely past it until the same emblem was on the next door.

I heard how pro-Council the Southern Verceen village was. The whispered rumours were that not a single Drao was left here; they were all driven away. Travelling with a Council's Guard was the safe choice, and that was a wild thing to consider.

The village felt dull and uninviting. The mountains and the goods it produced shaped the village, resulting in greys and dark colours everywhere. From the sun's travelling patterns across the sky, the buildings were always kept in the dark. Shadows never disappeared. No wonder everyone looked miserable.

"You sure we can't give the horses our food? I don't know if I want to get too far from the main road," Pax asked. He looked on edge, eyes twitching around.

"Keep your scabbard in view and there won't be any problems," I told him, adjusting my sweaty grip.

He glanced at me shortly. "What're you talking about?"

"Haven't you noticed the doors? Each one has the Council's sigil. I've never seen it before, not even on the Isle."

His eyebrows twitched as he took in each poorly scratched design. "That's new."

"It's unnerving."

The Council's mark was almost identical to the one they'd given Guards. Still a headless bird with its chest exposed, but for them, the bird was stabbing itself in the chest with its thin and long beak.

Regardless of whether it was a fully detailed and painted mural or a crude scratching with a knife, people recognized it. The villagers continued staring, standing in place as we passed them. The moment his scabbard was noticed, they began to point and whisper.

An unfamiliar mumbling had the hairs on my neck standing up, making me glance back. A small crowd was following us down the main road. They didn't look angry, but I couldn't help watching them. Pax noticed my half backwards sitting.

"What's going on?" He glanced back too and swore under his breath.

"Let's get what we need and go," he said, speeding Neem a little up.

The agriculture store sat independently of the other buildings, marking the end of the road. Sliding off my saddle, I ran my hand along Dill's neck and didn't look away from the crowd of about twenty who followed us the whole way.

Standing far enough back, they didn't give the impression that we'd be rushed. After tying Dill and Marr to the hitching post, my hand ran along their backs as I circled them. Pax already stood at Neem's back legs with his arms crossed, eyes on the crowd.

"Do you want me to wait with the horses and you go inside?" I asked.

"I don't know what'd be safer," Pax commented. "We'll both go in, but you stand by the door and keep watch, just in case."

Pax rested his hand on my lower back, pressing me to walk ahead of him. A small voice called for our attention as soft footsteps attached. Two young boys broke away from the group of watchers and ran towards us. I tugged on Pax's arm as he looked at them suspiciously, hand gripping the handle of his sword.

"Just see what they want," I whispered. I hadn't met many truly dangerous children in my years of travelling.

He raised his eyebrows in agreement. The little boys skidded to a stop in front of us. Well, in front of Pax. Both gazed up at him with wide eyes.

"Are you really a Guard?" one boy with long black hair asked, bouncing on his toes.

Pax glanced at me. Not what he was expecting. I shrugged as he looked down at them.

"I am," Pax answered hesitantly, gripping his sword's pommel with more certainty.

It drew the boys' eyes to the seal. Their mouths fell open and awe grew in their eyes, unable to get any bigger without being painful.

"Wow! How did you become a Guard?"

"Did you have to train really hard?" They asked at the same time.

The corners of my mouth turned up as I watched the interaction. Pax hid his confusion well at the boys' amazement at seeing a Guard. Placing my fingertips against my nose, I hide the natural scrunch at how adorable I found the interaction. Beside me, Pax came around to their genuine curiosity and smirked, bending his knees to be the same height as the two boys.

"I had to work very hard to be a Guard."

The boys hung on his words subconsciously, their torsos leaning forward. The villagers crept closer, more intrigued as Pax spoke. In their long and thick dark clothes, most still watched and whispered amongst themselves.

A few broke away to stand near the horses. Far enough back that I wasn't concerned, they mostly admired Neem. Dill and Marr received very little attention, but that didn't surprise me. She had a Guard's emblem embroidered on her saddle blanket and bags. The whole encounter piqued my curiosity, however. What had the Council done for these people to gain this much respect?

"How old were you when you became a Guard?"

My gaze returned to Pax. His jaw squeezed tighter, but the smile didn't change.

"I was a little younger than most. You're going to have to wait until you're grown up before you become Guards. Okay?" Pax told them.

The boys nodded wildly, too young to understand his meaning. He stood, and without another word, the boys rushed back to the others. Excitedly chattering at the women before the boys even fully had their arms around their legs.

"I guess you have a couple of admirers," I commented, opening the shop's door.

Pax chuckled. "It's nice to be appreciated once in a while."

CHAPTER 21

The store appeared empty and silent. Mundane packs of seeds were lining the first shelf I saw. It was a simpler store than even what I saw in other villages. Stepping around the crates shoved against the baseboards, I walked to the back, where horse feed usually sat. I ran my fingertip along the shelf as I read the labels.

The odd shape of the glass bottles made me suspicious of what the product was, and it was confirmed when a handwritten label with 'Harvest Growth' caught my eye. A chill ran down my spine at the hauntingly familiar words.

"Can I help you?" A burly older man stood at the opening of the aisle with his squinted eyes assessing me.

"Here to buy horse feed. Three bags, if you've got them."

"Keep going down that aisle. You'll have to carry them out yourself. Each one is three hundred pesa, not a coin less."

I nodded, not surprised by the price, and he watched me for a moment longer until he walked away. I took a final glance at the bottles and went for the food. Pax was already standing at the bags, looking at a half grown plant beside the hemp bags.

He glanced at me briefly. "What took you so long?"

I shrugged and grabbed two bags with a grunt.

"Owyn." I paused, looking at him. "Let me take two."

"I can carry two. You just don't want to look bad in front of your friends," I said before walking away.

Behind me, Pax chuckled to himself. "You guessed my intentions."

The shopkeeper stood behind the counter, a deep frown on his face. The suspicion was clear in his dark eyes when I let the bags thump on the counter. Reaching into my waist bag, I put the pesa down for all three bags.

Pax complained, but the man and I ignored him. There wasn't any reason to barter a better price as I ignored the way the shopkeeper picked up the coins and held them up to the lamplight, checking the validity. I grabbed the bags and headed for the exit.

"I could've paid for some," Pax said, holding the door open.

"Don't worry. I was well paid for the transaction in Mye. I can afford an extra bag of horse feed."

The crowd outside had moved even closer. Their whispers stopped when we emerged. Pax walked ahead of me and he was exactly what they wanted. The villagers reached for him, showering him with words of gratitude.

Older women cut me off, swarming him entirely, and he was halted by his admirers. They were all touching wherever they could reach. Rolling my eyes, I stepped around them.

Dropping the bags between my horses, I ran my hand down Neem's muzzle. She tilted her head, indicating a want for deeper scratches.

"Your rider draws a lot of attention. How fun for you," I said to her, planting a kiss on her nose.

The look in her eyes said that she agreed. I began undoing the buckles around Marr's face. Might as well feed them while Pax was being adored. He might be occupied for a little. I glanced at Dill when she huffed, turning her head away from me and letting her pale mane shake out, making me smirk at her wordless attitude.

"I'll be with you in a moment. Impatient."

"You!" an angry male voice shouted. I turned, expecting it to be directed at Pax, but a small group of men barrelled towards me. Dill huffed again, a little more determined.

"Okay, I get it. You were trying to warn me. Sorry," I muttered to her.

Some villagers shrunk away from the men, grabbing their children. Instinctively grasping the pommel at my side, but I didn't move. "Can I help you, gentlemen?"

"What're you doing in our village?" A large man barked, sticking his thick finger at me.

He stopped far enough back that I couldn't smack his hand away. His eyelids twitched, looking over me accusingly. Four other men stopped with similar expressions.

Hostility. A behaviour that I knew how to handle. "We needed to buy food for our horses. We're on our way out now."

"What's your intention of stopping here?"

My eyebrow raised high, restraining myself from rolling my eyes. "I just told you."

"Who invited you here?" Another asked, hateful aggression in his voice. Some men turned on the other citizens, hunting for the culprit.

"I don't know what you're talking about."

"You were overheard discussing a transaction. Tell us who invited you to our village," he barked.

It took a moment to remember that I'd mentioned the Mye transaction in the shop. Glancing back over my shoulder, I made eye contact with the shopkeeper. He retreated inside silently and I turned back to the men, squeezing my sword.

"As I said, we're on our way now."

"You people should know better than to stop here," the group leader growled.

His accomplices nodded. They all seemed tough, but gave me a feeling that alone, I would win. However, they weren't alone right now.

"And what people are you referring to?" Pax asked, finally free of his admirers.

The men straightened, getting a look in their eyes similar to the boys' minutes ago.

"We don't refer to you, sir. Only talking about the diseased creature you're transporting."

"I'm diseased? Didn't know that," I said with a sarcastic tone, putting my hand against my chest with mock offence.

Pax snorted at my reaction. "Would you like to explain how my companion is diseased?"

"She's a Drao. They aren't welcome here," one explained, glaring at me with disgust. His bony hands curled into fists and I could tell this would not end peacefully if we continued the conversation.

Pax stepped in front of me, holding his sword with intent. He rolled his shoulders for them all to see, his eyes not leaving the men. Falling into his Guard mentality, he grew taller. Genuine fear was written on the faces of the adults, their children watching with naïve wonderment.

"Like I said." I turned back to the grimy men. "We're leaving. Thank you for the information."

Monitoring them, I returned to the horses and put the bags of feed on to their saddles. Marr snorted, unhappy he was teased with food. I tightened his bridle.

"Sorry," I whispered.

A single pair of footsteps got closer. Wanting to behave like I had no fear of an attack, I didn't turn around. In my peripheral, familiar scarred hands moved at the back of Neem's saddle. Tightening a strap around the feed, I moved to the bag at Dill's feet. She huffed, watching me closely. I met her large eye before giving in and peeking back.

A few steps closer, their attention was on me. A shiver ran

down my spine as two instincts fought against each other. One was to get in their faces, demand why they thought I was Drao and what was so wrong with it. The other, a voice that always sounded suspiciously like Janna, told me to leave. Leave fast and not provoke them further. The way a proper Merchant would do it.

I fumbled hooking the bag to the saddle as half my attention was on the threat. I wasn't sure if the hemp bag would stay, but I got on Dill's back, anyway. Pax walked around to the side of Neem, staring at the men.

"Thank you for your hospitality. Enjoy your day."

The men wholeheartedly thanked him for his work as a Guard, taking steps backwards. He mounted Neem and, without getting comfortable, he squeezed her sides. This was the first time I felt genuinely thankful for his assignment.

I couldn't help glance at each headless bird on the houses and shops. The entire village was standing on the main road. They waved and smiled at Pax, but as soon as he passed, their faces changed to fear and disgust. The unruly teenager inside of me wanted to react, to give them something to fear. Again, Janna's voice in my head reminded me I knew better.

"You won't earn pesa if you behave like that," the static memory of her voice repeated in my head.

Once the village was far enough behind us that the worry slid off my shoulders, I dropped the reins and spun my hair into a bun at my neck. My shoulders sat tense for too long, but letting my body move naturally with Dill's step, rocking back and forth helped.

Taking the reins loosely in hand again, I peered at Pax behind me. Our eyes met as he was already watching me.

"Are you alright?"

A humourless laugh slipped out as I faced forward. "No, I don't think so. Though if you ever need a confidence boost, you have the perfect spot."

Pax chuckled. "Jealous?"

I wasn't; I was angry. Drao did good things for everyone, even if they didn't know it. Yes, some Drao committed crimes and killed people. But those weren't the majority and Veks did the same. The Council frowned upon thriving Drao culture. They allowed vicious rumours to flourish and grow through the population. The dark truths, like the Cursed, were only known by Merchants and Drao, who experienced it.

I responded with a snort. "Sorry, I'm not into praise for something hundreds already do."

Just shaking his head, he quietly smiled to himself.

"By the way, our stop in Verceen needs to be short."

"Since when are we stopping in Verceen?" Pax asked.

I glanced at him, rolling my eyes at his childish tone.

"I have to finish a transaction. I'm not coming all the way back here to deliver it after. You don't have to stop with me, but I've had these crystals for a full moon cycle."

A sigh came from behind me. "You know I can't do that."

"Glad you agree. We'll only be there for a few hours. The crystals are going to a man near the ocean port, so it's a straight shot."

"Verceen is the halfway marker of our trip." Pax pointed out. "If we're stopping, it could be a night or two."

"In and out will be fine," I said with a tight voice. He made an inaudible sound in his throat, and my gaze slid over to him. "What?"

"Nothing," he responded, jutting out his lower lip and bringing Neem next to Dill. "Just sounds like there's a story behind those words."

"You're hearing things," I mumbled, staring ahead with a blank face.

It was already a risk to enter Verceen uninvited. With a Guard too?

Staying one night was beyond pushing my luck.

Chapter 22

Sunlight woke me up with a grumble. Stretching my arms above my head, my brain was forced into consciousness by the bright light. Next to me, Pax groaned and dropped his arm onto my mid-drift. Adjusting my bag that was a makeshift pillow again, my eyes opened, and I looked over.

Facing each other, he laid on his side, eyes shut and mouth open. A string of drool stuck to his cheek. I smirked at his goofy expression.

"Are you awake?" I whispered, my voice thick.

Nuzzling his face against his own bag, he made a lazy sound. Sitting up, his arm slumped into my lap. The horses stood where we left them, munching on the overgrown grass.

Through the sparse birch trees, a herd of deer grazed. They didn't give us any attention, and my stomach let out an audible rumble as I watched them.

"What're you thinking about?" Pax grumbled, his eyes still shut.

"Meat," I answered immediately.

He stayed silent and unmoving. Until, "we can catch some rabbits if you want."

"I have a better idea," I said, watching the venison.

"Hm?" Pax shifted, lifting on his elbow. His barely open gaze followed mine and his shoulders slumped. "And how do you expect to catch those?"

Digging through my cart, I revealed an old bow and arrows I was paid to deliver to a Drao halfling. After attempting to flee without paying, I've been stuck with them since. Slinging the quiver over my torso, I tucked my pants into my aged riding boots. I didn't need to stumble over ratty hemlines.

"Have you ever used a bow before?"

I peered at Pax leaning against a growing oak tree. He was still half asleep. "No, I set traps."

He sauntered over, lazily holding out his hand. "You don't get to wear the quiver. Pass it before you shoot one of us in the foot."

I rested my hand on my pushed out hip. "You'll need to teach me then, so I don't shoot anyone in the foot."

"A good plan, since you can't survive without me. I don't know how you have until this point."

Giving him a mocking smile, I made no move to hand over the quiver, but his eyebrows raised, towering over me as he waited. His hand inched closer to the buckle, and I rolled my eyes, pulling the strap over my head.

"Good girl," he praised. My heart dropped at the double meaning of his words, which he didn't appear to notice.

Not far from the impromptu camp, we found a lone jackalope. Pax convinced me to stay away from the deer. With its curled antlers, it shuffled forwards a little, nibbling at the grass. I refused to think of how cute the creature was.

Between the bushes, Pax knelt and set up for the cleanest shot. My gaze ran along his jawline as he tightened and released it multiple times. The tip of his tongue poked out, running along his bottom lip. He lowered the weapon, glancing at me.

"Do you want to try?"

My gaze lingered on his lips, the lower one poutier than the top. I nodded slightly when the question processed in my head. He indicated for me to crouch in front of him and I hesitated, highly aware of the intimate proximity. Either better at ignoring it or he didn't notice and tugged lightly on my elbow.

I lowered onto my knee, keeping my other foot planted. I allowed him to adjust me into the best position, pushing at my limbs. Other than the cold dirt I could feel through my pants, all around me was his warmth.

"You see it?" He whispered against my head. My skin raised in bumps where his breath hit.

I looked through the bush, moving my stance to get a clear view of the small creature through the bushes. My tailbone brushed against his thigh. The contact made his hand snap out and grab my hip. I peered at him over my shoulder. His face was close to mine but didn't look down at me, keeping his attention on the jackalope.

After I nodded, he wrapped his arms around me without hesitation, placing the bow and arrow into my hands. I felt like a doll, being positioned just how he wanted.

"Raise the bow to shoot it after you've clipped in the arrow," he instructed. "Don't pull your hand back yet."

In the confined space, I did my best to remember how Janna instructed me to hold the bow. I hoped the eight-year-old muscle memory would come back.

"Bring the nock to the corner of your mouth. Look down the arrow. I tend to shoot higher than I aim. Keep that in mind."

Janna's voice in my head spoke over Pax's. Her instructions, worded almost the same, were burned into me. Overshooting sounded familiar, too. I set up and had the arrow tip rested against my finger.

"Okay."

Pax shifted closer, his chest heavier against my back.

Leaving one hand on my hip, his other slid up my stomach and rested under my breasts. My attention snapped from the jackalope to the weight of his palm. My ears were ringing.

Focusing on the animal, I pushed through the fog that the physical contact created. A loaded weapon in my hand was a good reason to not be distracted. Pax's hand shifted, fingers squeezing gently.

"When you're ready, take a deep breath and release. Be confident. You can't do it twice."

My heart hammered, but Janna's voice was there, snapping at me for being distracted and not being faster. The arrow slipped between my fingers before I realized I released it. Before I could blink, the tip was lodged into the jackalope's neck. The oversized cousin of the rabbit attempted to take off, but made it ten feet before collapsing.

"Good job," Pax said, a little louder than a whisper.

Something in his gravelly tone made me look back. His tongue stuck out and his green eyes had shadows as he stared down at me. I expected him to pull back, but he didn't. Neither did I. It felt like we were frozen, hot water bubbling and lulling up into a sense of security. Without thinking, I pressed my lips into his.

Still expecting him to move away, I was surprised when Pax pushed against my sternum, keeping me close. My focus was entirely on him and the kiss. A wolf could have run by and stolen the jackalope for all I cared. Lowering the bow, and I placed my hand over top of his. His heartbeat thumped against my back erratically. A rush of adrenaline shot up my spine, wanting to feel his hands on more parts of my body.

That unfamiliar, needy feeling woke me up, and I sharply pulled back. I landed on my butt from not judging how fast I moved away, and the spell broke. He released me as I fell. I was teetering on throwing up and I couldn't explain it. It wasn't the same nausea as not having my pyx.

Shutting my eyes, I begged my heart to calm. It needed to

be enough of a deterrent to not vomit. The back of my head felt heavy, indicating a headache was coming. A hand rested on my knee, stroking it comfortingly.

"Are you okay?" he asked, sounding entirely normal.

Nodding, my eyes were sluggish to open. He watched me with concern, like I tripped on a tree root and my knee was bleeding. The shadows were gone. His eyes were back to their regular colour. The moment had passed. It seemed to leave no effect on him, even though I felt like I was burned.

WHEN THE NUMBER OF OAK TREES THINNED AND THE FOREST ended, Verceen's archway was revealed and my back muscles tightened. It was an unwritten rule that no Merchants entered Verceen and did transactions. It was Janna's territory. She got all the transactions without question or complaint. She never left the town for work. She didn't need to. All her customers came here. I was about to break a cardinal rule that was all but burned into my brain.

Verceen's archway was pristine. The rocks sparkled, and I was sure there was some kind of quartz inside. The Delegate must hire someone to clean it weekly. Other than Jova, Verceen was the only town to have functional gates. They never closed in my lifetime, but I met a Drao who remembered it happening once.

"We need to ride along the coastline to the mountains," I said, tension growing into my stomach.

I scanned the first buildings as they came into view. It was all shops in this section of town. The people who would recognize me. Under me, Dill let out a brisk snort, feeling my stress. Knowing it did her no good, I tasked myself to calm down, even if I could only think of everything I should've done to hide who I was.

"Are you worried?"

I glanced at Pax. "About?"

"That what happened in the village will happen here."

I smirked without meaning to. That's definitely the furthest thing from my mind. "It won't."

"How are you so sure?"

I pursed my lips. This was a question with two answers, and I could only give him one. "Verceen is a Drao-centric town. Trust me, no one will harass me here."

Looking at him, I see my answer wasn't satisfying as he studied me, trying to figure out something else.

Passing under the archway, my jaw locked as the town came into view. Unsurprisingly, Verceen hadn't changed since I lived here. The magick moved freely through town, a glitter-like sparkle almost existing in the air. It kept all the buildings appearing brand new and the environment flourishing. Flowers grew all year, even during the few cold months we had. Trees never died unless it was intentionally. Colours stayed bright. Not painful on the eyes, but alive even during storms. I almost wished it looked completely different.

As the horses crossed onto the colourful cobblestones indicating the shopping district, fuzzy memories from the day of my abrupt arrival in Verceen danced in my head. I was a terrified fourteen-year-old.

As a farmer's kid, I barely saw more than five Drao at a time. Mye didn't center them out. The ones who lived there were quiet, they didn't flaunt their differences. In Verceen, however, Drao never hid behind disguising potions or hooded cloaks. I remember shaking for days. Going into town only made it worse.

Swarms of horns, tails, a multitude of different eye colours and a few with coloured skin beings intertwined with plain looking Veks. The unchanging shops looked like my memories had come to life. During my training, Janna made me create relationships with every shopkeeper. It was a good thing then.

But now, it worked against me. Approaching the first apothecary, the judgemental old Drao named Roke, who ran the shop for over two hundred years, took a second glance as we passed by. He placed his hands on his hips, staring.

There was barely any time to hope he was losing his memory when he tapped his wife on the shoulder and conspicuously pointed. Her mouth dropped open, whispering to each other. Averting my face didn't do me good. People on the other side were staring, too.

I regretted my choice not to leave Dill and Marr at the community stables that sat right inside the gates and made the trek to the customer's house on foot. My nerves clouded my judgement, ending with a reckless choice. My hand twitched to pull my hood up, but I knew in my heart, it was too late.

"Am I being paranoid, or are Verceen townies not fans of Guards?" Pax asked in a low voice, moving Neem to walk closer beside Dill.

He peered back and forth across the street. I shrugged, staring ahead. Knowing the inevitable was coming, I kept Dill at a steady pace. I think we were both happy when we were past the shops and on the isolated road up the coastline.

Chapter 23

I leaned against the cracking kitchen counter, arms crossed. Forgetting where I was, I felt in my element. This is what I knew how to do. The small velvet bag filled with magickally grown crystals sat next to me on the counter. The bag was visible enough for the client to see, but I could grab it quickly if he tried anything.

My dagger was exposed along the front of my thigh and not a single emotion would cross my face while I was here. Rolling my neck, the light footsteps of the homeowner coming back towards the kitchen echoed through the tiny house.

The short man, a goblin with a large crooked nose and glasses, appeared. He gazed at me, pushing his mouth to the side.

"I know soliciting you with these crystals is frowned upon, but I figured since you are Janna's prized protegee, it would be okay."

I flashed a look at Pax, where he stood at the kitchen door. He was a little surprised when I suggested he come inside for the transaction. Better than explaining why he shouldn't be outside.

Heeding my advice, he stayed silent during the transaction. His forehead twitched at the goblin's words, his eyes returning to me. Ignoring the questions, I held out my hand.

"It's not an issue. Just a stop along my way. We're heading out today."

The Drao held out six coins totaling 1400 pesa, and I pushed away from the counter, keeping my tone careless. There was a sense of satisfaction as he shrunk back when I passed him.

"Good doing business with you," I said, passing the stuttering man as he thanked me again.

He should be nervous, Janna won't be happy with him. I don't know if he'd be able to get any product for a while because she would likely cut him off, ostracised. But that wasn't my problem.

A flicker of realization at my callus emotions knew it was from the town. I grew to understand that there was a sick sense of power I felt here. It radiated from Janna and I absorbed it.

Pax led us out of the house without a word. The questions could wait until we were back on the main highway before questions were asked.

I dropped the pesa into my waist pouch, and gazed out at the Ocean of Tepstow, walking down the porch steps. It was a relief the transaction went smoothly.

Verceen triggered anxiety deep inside of me. The rhythmic crashing of waves on the shoreline hundreds of feet below was encouraging my headache to worsen.

Pax awkwardly cleared his throat. "Owyn?"

Following his gaze, two teenage boys stood on the rocky pathway ahead of us. Their hands crossed under their cloaks, sword handles exposed. Expressionless and patiently waiting. I shut my eyes. A naïve part of me hoped Janna would let me leave town without an issue.

I rested my hand on Pax's upper arm as I stepped past him. "Give us a moment."

Maintaining eye contact with the older boy, I left a space between us.

"We're leaving now. I was dropping something off," I told them.

"She wants to speak with you. It's rude to come into town without stopping by," the older of the two said.

His dark hair was slicked back, tied at his neck but a few strands too short and tucked behind his ears. He didn't have a single laugh line on his face, just a hard jaw and a practiced dead face. I looked at the younger boy for a brief second, not much older than I was when I was first brought here. He was new. I could almost smell it on him.

Ignoring the light brown hair that stuck away from his head like he could never master how to keep it down, she had the stone's expression drilled into every apprentice. However, a twinkle still shone in his eyes, revealing that he hadn't been exposed too much.

"Thanks for the lesson on manners, but like the lady said, we'll be leaving." Pax's voice got closer as he stopped beside me.

I'm sure he was standing with all the confidence of a Guard talking to teenage boys. But neither gave him a second of attention, regarding only me. I didn't move my eyes either. I wanted to leave, not go in front of Janna.

"Owyn?"

"Show me," I stated.

"What?" Pax muttered with a crinkled brow, but the order wasn't for him.

The older boy released his grip on his own wrist and the movement triggered Pax to grab his pommel. Barely checking the reaction, the slender teenager removed his cape and dropped the heavy fabric in his younger partner's arms. Giving us his back, he pulled the collar of his purple shirt down enough to reveal the healed scar on his shoulder blade.

I nodded when he looked for approval, but Pax stared at the teenager's shoulder, not understanding what he was seeing. A part of me hoped he wasn't marked. If he was fresh like his companion, I would've ignored them and left fast. But Janna had faith in him and wanted everyone to know it.

My chin dropped an inch, and I watched the unmoving pebbles. "We need to go with them. We can leave after. It won't take long."

My words had no confidence in it whatsoever. Pax tried to understand what happened between the two teenagers and I. But he didn't know what questions to ask, so he agreed.

I mounted Dill and faced the teenagers. "Do you have horses or did you walk?"

Using his fingers, the older boy let out a sharp whistle. Two horses galloped out of the treeline. I should've known. Dill was trained to do that, but I never used it.

"Cool trick," Pax commented from atop Neem.

I almost wished they didn't have horses. There would be more time to prepare for what was coming.

Riding down Verceen's main road, the gawking intensified. My arrival flew through town and everyone was out of their houses. The town came to a stop. No one was trying to hide the fact they were talking about us. It felt like I was being led to slaughter.

I couldn't look at Pax, my cheeks burning with embarrassment. He had to be more than confused. At least he understood the stares had nothing to do with him for once.

The boys' horses trotted ahead of us, chins high in the air. I didn't have to wonder if I appeared that arrogant once. It felt like my mentor's name was branded across my chest, and I could do nothing wrong. I suddenly became hyperconscious that my own chin was tilted up and my shoulders rolled back even without my riding corset and the casual position I sat on

Dill's back. I couldn't change it, Janna ingrained this posture in my behavior, and I had once painful scars to prove it.

Verceen seared itself into my dreams. I thought about it as little as possible, but every nightmare I had was here. The houses were as beautiful and just as well kept as the shops. Stained glass windows adorned every house in at least one window. Full gardens were dug at the sides of houses with tomatoes, peas, and peppers, all grew without stopping. Ivy grew on the street lamps with fire salamanders crawling up and down, looking to sleep in comfort. The colossal pine trees were like a wall leading into the forest. Thousands of them indicated the end of town and the start of the Crewnyr Mountains. It was a beautiful sight. Cherry trees blooming near the Delegate's house were special only to Verceen. Wild creatures didn't hide, they didn't have any predators here. It was safe for them.

The house was nestled in the middle of the wilderness, approaching faster than I was prepared for. A sense of panic built up in my chest. I wanted to yank Dill to a stop and run the other way, but I couldn't. I wouldn't be able to live with myself.

A few growing cedar trees stood in a mock fence, showing where the drive ended. The property was like its own little oasis, and the house I lived in for my teen years stood in silence. It looked like a cabin but didn't match the size. It was two stories and huge. I counted twenty-five rooms once during a sleepless night.

Both outside and inside screamed wealth and unquestionable power. It was one of a kind. Unknown if it was done by manual labour or magick, the cobblestones with flowers and moss specifically planted to appear more luscious than they were. A well-packed dirt path led to the private stables hidden in the trees, along with several other buildings. It was all too familiar and didn't change at all.

On the porch was the most detailed and terrifying

memory I had. Unsurprisingly, she wore beautifully tailored pants and a flowing top with her hair in a low bun with strands carefully placed. As always, she looked perfect. It was a mask, though. A dangerous and scheming mind lurked behind her dark blue eyes. I would never fall asleep unguarded if I had something she wanted.

Feeling the pressure of her eyes as I dismounted Dill, I reminded myself to keep a straight face. Practice what she taught me.

Tying Dill to the hitching posts on the side of the house without being told, I realized more habits were ingrained than I thought. I didn't wait for the apprentices or Pax to approach the porch. I stopped at the bottom of the white porch steps, peering up at the woman who moulded me.

Chapter 24

Janna Cor never seemed to age. There must be a magick practitioner in town well compensated to keep her that way. There was something in her eyes, a blend of familiarity and unimpressed disinterest, that I instantly recognized. It wasn't often she didn't look at someone with it at least once a day.

Her hands were at her waist, fingers braided together. The only movement other than her eyes evaluating me was a single finger tapping against the back of her opposite hand. Her apprentices stopped beside me. She didn't look at Pax. He was a Guard, and she had no time for him.

"Cyrell, Regis, help Doe finish dinner." She never looked away from me as she gave orders. It was hard to guess her thoughts. At one point, I was good at it. Not anymore.

I felt a nauseating pinch in my spine at her voice. For years, her voice echoed in my head, but in person was a completely different experience and I reminded myself I wasn't fifteen anymore. I knew better to be overly confident.

Fear and respect still filled me, and I had to pay attention. I wasn't free of her wrath and pettiness. The teenagers nodded, rushing into the house. As they opened the front door, I noticed another person on the porch. With a flickered glance, it was another teenage boy. He was older than the others. It surprised me that Janna didn't send him to wrangle me back here. But as she felt towards Pax, he didn't deserve my attention.

As the door shut behind my mentor, we didn't look away from one another. We were still sizing each other up. We weren't familiar anymore and the lack of trust was thick in the air. I hoped I became a mystery and a threat to her.

Pax broke the tension by stepping onto the first stair. Before his foot landed, the teenager stepped next to Janna, his eyes locked on Pax.

"You must be Janna Cor, Owyn's mentor."

My eyelids fell shut as a groan of embarrassment tried to make an appearance. Janna wouldn't respond politely if she said anything at all. The boy's thin mouth twitched, thinking the same thing. He took a long look at Pax, a secondary scan, before returning his heavy stare to me. In his eyes, I was standing next to a bunny rabbit.

"The Guard won't be coming inside," Janna said. "He will stay here while we talk."

"I'm not staying long," I told her. "My presence is needed in Jova."

I was proud of myself that my voice didn't waver or crack.

The corner of Janna's mouth twitched, amused that I put my foot down. "I'm aware of your situation. You will stay for as long as this conversation takes. There's a room ready for you with Marllon. And when dinner is prepared, we will eat with my guests." Janna sent Pax a side glance of disinterest. "I would hate to leave the Guard out here when the bears come for scraps. He can come inside at that time. Come."

My lips parted, ready to insist we weren't staying, but it died in my throat. Walking up the stairs, I glanced at Pax. His entire face was scrunched, his mouth open with confusion, but in his eyes, there was another emotion. Was it disgust?

"I'll be back," I said. "You can walk around. It's gorgeous.

But don't wander out of sight of the house. She's not lying about the bears."

He nodded in slow understanding, watching Janna. The teenage apprentice, with his dark hair tightly curled against his head, opened the front door and stepped aside for us to pass. Janna strolled through without a word. I felt the door silently shut behind me.

A shudder vibrated through my spine. It was like going back in time and I was a naïve, weak fourteen-year-old trying to be tough and like nothing could break me. My fingernails curled into the skin of my palms. That wasn't who I am and Janna made sure of it.

I trailed behind Janna, but I didn't need it. The house hadn't changed one bit. Coming through the front door, guests encountered tall ceilings and a single large room extending to the back wall of windows. There were multiple different paths through the house, including the stairwell and a hallway underneath leading to staff rooms, the kitchen and offices. It was warm and gave the illusion of comfort.

Janna was called lucky by guests all the time and she agreed, knowing her guests weren't privy to the weapons and secrets stashed in the walls.

Crossing through the threshold of her office, stomach cramps made an appearance. My nightmares were familiar with this room. Matching this side of the house, towering windows looking into the forest at the base of the Crewnyr Mountains. Snow crusted the trees, and eagles constantly flew across the view, their nests deep in the pine trees. On the other side of the mountains, the country of Ynoms sat like a mystery. Hundreds of paintings depicted this very scenery.

"Shut the door," she instructed.

When I faced her again, a different person waited for me. With a genuine smile, Janna spread her arms.

"Orinthia, my darling. Come, give me a hug. It's been too long since our last visit."

I felt a shaky smile on my face and, not knowing what else to do, I accepted the gesture. It was formal and, if not for the tiny squeeze of my sides, I'd say cold. It was as caring of a gesture as I knew she was capable of.

Gently releasing me with a push back, Janna sauntered to her high-backed chair, angled to look out the windows. Crossing her ankles and resting her hands on each armrest, she gave a sense of false royalty. I placed myself on the couch, my ankles resting to match hers. It was one of two positions I used while sitting during a transaction, depending on the situation and how I needed to be seen.

Her office was clinical. A grand oak desk with a wall of bookshelves, boxes filling most of them. I didn't know what was inside, only they were her little treasures from years of work. All of her time was spent here. It wasn't a welcoming environment.

"You have three apprentices?" I asked, trying to start with a simple conversation.

"Five. Four boys and a girl. One is off collecting something for me," Janna said, leaning back into the cushions.

"I never expected you to take on so many at once."

She shrugged carelessly, like it wasn't hard or a big deal. "Merchant numbers are low. We need more people on the road. I've been asked to do my part."

Mentally, I pointed out that those 'people on the road' would be under her command as I ignored her comment about being asked to do her part. She wanted me to fish, to give her the opportunity to brag.

"Are you training them to work with Drao?"

"Two of them. The girl, Doe and my eldest boy, Tyress. They hold similar skills to those you showed when you first arrived."

"I wasn't aware I had any skills at fourteen."

She kept her smile tight, her eyes glimmering. "You arrived to me with undiscovered and obvious potential,

Orinthia. The desperation to impress me and return to your parents was a bonus."

My upper lip twitched in disgust and I caught it before the reaction could show, but her eyes shot down my face. She saw enough to feel satisfied her comment landed, her natural behaviour to squish any potential confidence was still present.

"Their parents have debts, too?"

A single eyebrow lifted along with the side of her mouth in mocking amusement. "Not as far into graves as yours, but just as prepared to sacrifice their children."

I nodded twice, but tried not to move too much. Janna always said I was too obvious with my physical reactions. It was like I was back under her thumb, needing to remember every little thing to avoid a scolding.

"The one at the door, your oldest?" I asked, with a head nod.

"Tyress," Janna confirmed. "Eager to please. He's decided he won't work on the road. He plans to stay and work directly with me."

"How did you convince him to do that?" I asked in disbelief. She ignored the obvious tone.

"He has a very commanding personality. I enjoy it. I will admit I've encouraged him to stay in Verceen, but I didn't make that choice. Tyress did."

Janna never encouraged me to stay. She wanted me on the road and claimed I was a brutal force she wanted representing her name. I didn't see it as a teenager, but I understand now. I wondered what she saw missing in Tyress to allow him to stay.

"So, what prompted you to come into Verceen?" she asked to the silent room.

She knew the exact reason I was here, to the smallest detail. I wasn't naïve enough to think she didn't or to hand over all the information at once.

"I received a letter asking me to pick up a bundle of magickally grown crystals."

"And why didn't you drop them off on your way to Rinebur?"

It felt like an interrogation, but Janna was just rudely blunt. "I had other things on my mind."

Janna made a sound. "We will discuss that shortly. I don't appreciate the lack of information regarding your transaction beforehand."

I pressed my tongue against the back of my teeth. "It wasn't a large transaction. I'll remember not to do it again."

She noticed I wasn't apologizing.

"I will be speaking with the recipient of your transaction." Unsurprising. "I'd like to know why he felt the need to search outside of town."

She was angry, like I knew she would be. Not insulted, only angry. The man I sold to was in trouble and probably not safe. For his sake, I hope he was already running far away from here. I began to ask a question, but Janna raised her hand. The gesture killed my vocal chords, the hand signal still holding its power.

"It was shared with me you've gotten yourself into trouble."

The urge to roll my eyes was tempting. "That's not correct, but you could say that. I guess."

Janna threaded her fingers together, unimpressed.

"Tell me, how do you plan on fixing this? I don't like my legacy dragged through mud. Especially by you."

There was no point in explaining that I didn't set this into motion. The trouble was forced on me, just for being a Merchant. Which was technically thanks to her. But if I said that, I could expect a look like she was watching a toddler throwing a tantrum.

"I've already collected what the Council asked for. If I deal with no other snags, I'll be on the Isle in another week and my pyx will be returned," I explained, giving Janna the answer she wanted.

She scoffed, beginning to pace around her office. I didn't move, waiting for her reaction. It was like watching a wolf make up its mind if it was going to attack or not.

"How could you be so reckless as to let your pyx be taken? I'm disappointed. I thought you were the best I taught. Yet the Council has taken it upon themselves to teach you a lesson about arrogance."

Counting to ten in my head, the irritation disappeared. Feeling the bruises already forming from her critiques, I needed to stay away from the student mindset and remember I was her equal. I could handle this and myself without her approval or help. Whether she liked it now, she made sure of it.

She interrupted my thoughts. "You'll be grateful to know I have a solution to buy your pyx back. No need to embarrass me more by breaking my clients' trust."

My eyes flickered away from the pile of books on the floor to Janna, arms crossed. Her eyes reflected the sunlight, making them an even deeper blue as she watched me intensely with an unreadable emotion.

"How?" I asked, clenching my fingers together.

"A Councilman owes me a favour, and another has asked me to produce a few unsavoury transactions for him. Some will require me to leave Verceen and I don't have time for that. With five apprentices, I'm needed here."

She went silent, looming over me from across the room with her arms crossed.

"You want me to handle these transactions for you?"

"And deliver them to the Isle. You will get your pyx back at that point. After payment, you'll return and hand the pesa to me. I'll give you a cut, of course."

Oh, of course. Handing faerie eggs to the Council was bad enough. But working for Janna?

Her influence would hang even heavier over my head than it does. I knew Janna better than what she was saying, too. It didn't matter if she had five apprentices. The client was a Councilman. She would want to see him in person, to insist on a larger pay out and remind him he owed her now. She was offering the job to hold over my head. To see how loyal I still was. I would owe her for the rest of my life.

"What would I be picking up?" I asked, scratching my eyebrow.

"Ingredients. I have specific addresses and you'll have special permission to harvest yourself. It's easy enough."

My stomach dropped. There was a single location in Gerennt you needed written permission for.

"You mean the Forest of Som."

"I do, but you'll be going to the Forest of Islenng too," Janna added, like she didn't say I would enter a physical nightmare.

I wanted to say no. Actually, I wanted to yell that she was out of her mind and if she thought it was so casual, to go into the Forest of Som herself. Creatures and humanoids with no control over their lust and hunger for flesh and darkest magick were contained behind physical walls there. The dark magick was so potent in the air, a person could vomit from choking on it. Yet, if you got out alive with whatever you went in for, you would be the richest person in Gerennt. Or the most dangerous.

"Can I think about it?" I weakly asked before clearing my throat.

Janna sighed, pressing her lips together, unhappy with my hesitant response. "Only because you have never let me down before. This situation with the Council will be a onetime occurrence, I hope. Before you leave in the morning, I expect a yes."

I pressed my tongue against my lower teeth, focusing on the sensation. It was better than having my response beaten out of me. A tentative knock echoed off the door and without breaking her stare, Janna called them in.

A lean girl with shallow cheeks and blond hair braided down her back noiselessly walked into the room. She allowed herself a quick peek at me, but her attention went directly to Janna.

"Your first guest is arriving," she told our looming mentor in a soft voice.

"Excellent. Doe, take Owyn upstairs to change into something more appropriate. Have Regis give the Guard clothes that don't disgust me."

Janna didn't address me again before striding out of the room. The girl cringed closer to the door to avoid being run into. Standing from the couch, the apprentice opened the door wider for me. I smiled kindly at Doe, indicating with my hand for her to lead the way.

Watching her braid swing back and forth over her stiff shoulders, I remembered what it was like to be her. She wasn't allowed to be her own person while living here, meant to follow every rule and request given. Her quiet voice was natural, a timid reaction to the countless ways Janna could behave. Eventually, she would grow to sound confident again, but in a way that didn't question our mentor. It's the way to reap benefits and stay alive.

Doe led me down the giant cabin's second floor long hallway of bedrooms. The walls were plain, with a few large scenic paintings. She opened a door midway, making me shake my head in disbelief. I could imagine Janna laughing maniacally to herself.

Identical to when I left it, the sheets were dark with a flannel blanket sticking out. The standing mirror was pushed into the corner with a matching desk and dresser. The worn green reading chair was pushed into a new spot and a new pillow sat on top. It was obvious somebody was using this room, and it gave me a weird feeling to see a different pair of shoes pushed under the bed and weapons on top of the dark wood dresser when everything else was exactly the same.

"Janna offered my room for you to change in," Doe muttered, holding the door handle. I nodded, noticing the red dress hanging from the curtain rod.

"For me?" I asked, pointing to the garment.

"Yes, ma'am."

I scrunch my nose, peeking at the teenager. "Please don't call me that. Owyn is fine. I was in your position five years ago. I'm too young to be, ma'am."

A hint of a smile appeared as she nodded. I ran my hand along the smooth fabric. The dress was almost burgundy with gold metal accents synching the material. My arms would be bare with a layer of silky tulle around my shoulders. I hadn't worn anything so elegant in years. The last time may be here when Janna considered me 'ready'.

"Do you need help to get changed?"

My finger ran along the boning built in the bodice.

"I wish I confidently could say no." I glanced over my shoulder. "Do you mind hanging around?"

A smile broke on her face, even as she tried to dim the twinkle in her eyes.

Unsurprisingly, I needed Doe's help to tighten the lace detailed bodice. I felt like a fish out of water. The dress was gorgeous, complimenting my skin tone, and the tulle skirt flowed out from the corset at my hips.

Looking in a mirror, I recognized it was one of Janna's old dresses. I don't know why I would think she would give me a new dress. It felt like a weird way of being claimed. The bodice ribbing dug into my ribs, the dress not moulded for my shape. My body was fuller than Janna's.

Doe cinched the corset once more at my waist, forcing my spine straight. The air bubbles popped at the movement. I adjusted the gold cage between my breasts and the dress. It wasn't a comfortable fit, but hopefully, the confined space would keep it from falling out, but it looked like I was wearing a long and chunky chain. Janna's eyes would sparkle with lust over the valuable items if she saw it. Doe didn't mention the necklace.

I took my time coming down the stairs. I didn't want to owe Janna a new dress if I ripped this one. Thankfully, Doe stayed next to me. She was ready to help if I slipped, but wasn't making it obvious. Even though I didn't want to, I couldn't help noticing that she was good and will become a good Merchant.

Reaching the first floor, my hand twitched to mess with my hair. Doe pinned a few bits back after adding some little braids. I wanted to put my hair in a ponytail, but Janna wouldn't appreciate a style she deemed casual.

Rolling my shoulders, I glanced around the familiar house to settle my anxiety. I hoped Pax was allowed to change his clothes inside the house. I have witnessed her send people she didn't like to the barn before.

A pair of house staff scurried past me, completely silent. My eyes followed after them. The staff did everything unless apprentices were assigned work as punishment. Originally, I was brought here to work as staff but after that short period and then my punishments for rebellious behaviour, I knew every employee's name. Pulling my bottom lip into my mouth as they disappeared down another hallway, wondering if I knew anyone still here.

Across the room, Pax stood with another man in a conversation. He had already spotted me, his mouth in a tight line and attention no longer on the older man, who hadn't noticed his audience wasn't listening. His eyes slid along my outfit and when he reached my face again, the scar across his face crinkled with a smile.

The man said something else, his deep voice reverberating across the room, and Pax's smile dropped, his gaze returning to the older man. The shorter man adjusted his stance, making his profile visible. It was the Delegate of Verceen. I should've known from the perfectly placed hair. No wonder Pax didn't wander over.

Preferring to stay away from that conversation, I checked the clothes that Janna lent Pax. He had washed up, his face clean, and his damp curls were slicked back. It gave a mature appearance, but I preferred his curls falling onto his forehead. The clean black riding pants and dark grey tunic were a stark contrast to the scuffed riding boots on his feet. The tanned leather jacket across his broad shoulders fit well. It wasn't tight, but there was no way to hide how muscular he was. I never seen him so un-Guardly. He should be proud.

"Owyn?" My attention was pulled to Doe, stopping beside me.

I didn't notice she disappeared. Though not as regal, her outfit changed too. It looked familiar and extremely worn, the different coloured threads used to hem and mend the pale blue dress were visible. A part of me wondered if I wore it.

"Janna would like you to meet someone outside."

I smiled at her gratefully. "Okay, thanks."

Doe returned the smile, more genuine this time and her youth showing. She was beautiful but living with Janna, smiles and 'thank yous' weren't common.

"How long have you been with Janna?" I asked, following behind her.

"Two years. My mother left me in Janna's care when she died."

Moving past my surprise on how she landed here, an apology for her misfortune bubbled up, but she likely heard enough of that.

"Janna mentioned you're training to work with Drao. How's that going?"

"Good. I've seen things I never thought I would," Doe said with a knowing smirk.

I chuckled. "I thought the same thing. There are a few Drao that make me feel like I'm in a dream when I see them."

Doe nodded, her expression still soft. Two years into my training, Janna had me face what she called the 'the worst thing I'd ever see'. It was a lie, purposefully making me feel secure before sticking a worse nightmare in front of me and enjoying my failure. I didn't want to consider this frail girl going through the same ordeal.

On the back porch, Doe pointed to Janna standing with a tall, unfamiliar man. I stepped away before pausing.

"If you ever have a question you feel too silly or scared to ask Janna, I'm happy to answer. Whenever, but it might be easier for you while I'm here."

Her expression turned meek. "Thank you."

Chapter 25

Appreciating the flats Janna provided, I crossed the raised porch without pain shooting through my feet. Stopping next to her with my hands crossed, my mentor looked down at me. Of course, she would put on heels for dinner. Sticking to her traditional colour palette of dark blues and purples, Janna's dress had a similar silhouette to mine, but her long sleeves were off the shoulder and every inch was structured. She would have no bad angles.

"Cormitt, this is Orinthia, my most successful apprentice. Orinthia, this is Cormitt Thaxton. He's a highly recommended art dealer from Jova."

My heart paused when our eyes connected. The man's eyes were a light green with a cat-like reflection as the late afternoon sun hit them. His long hair was pulled back in a band, leaving a few strands loosely hung around his forehead. I couldn't quite tell if the colour was called cocoa blonde or champagne brown. His hair was unique and for most people, that would be the most distinguishing feature about him, but he was wildly handsome, and it distracted from the hair somehow.

Peeking at Janna, I knew she thought so too. She looked at

him with sparkling lust. She didn't feel weird wanting him, even if his age sat somewhere between her and I. Looking at him, I was having a hard time reading what his true age was and it made me think he was a Drao. A very old Drao. Glancing back at the stranger, our eyes met again, but I couldn't maintain contact without butterflies growing inside of me.

"Nice to meet you, Cormitt. Call me Owyn. Orinthia is a bit of a mouthful," I said, politely smiling.

He smirked, a dimple appearing deep in his cheek. Could this man be more visually appealing?

"I've never understood why you go by Owyn. Thia is a kinder name," Janna said, putting her hands together.

My eyebrows twitched, glancing at her. I racked my brain, trying to remember when I shared the nickname my youngest sisters used before they could pronounce my whole name, but I would never remember. Over the years I spent here, Janna gained my trust and only she would remember something so specific for personal gain.

"I've heard good things, Owyn. Your name is whispered in Jova," Cormitt said, moving past Janna's comment.

I felt my own lips pulling upward, my cheeks warming. My natural attraction to him made me sceptical, but in this environment, I had more predators to focus on.

The older of the two apprentices I met earlier, Cyrell, if I remembered correctly, stepped up beside me with his hands behind him. I noticed a pink scar along his jawline and knew he was going through physical testing. It was a straight scar with no puckering from stitches. A blade and Janna had him let it heal on its own, no salves to keep the scarring minimal. A punishment. A similar one ran along my collarbone.

"Dinner is ready, ma'am."

"Thank you, Cyrell. Please tell our guests to sit."

As Cyrell followed the instructions, Cormitt stuck out his

elbow with a smirk. His eyes glimmered down at me. "Owyn, please."

Before I could move, Janna wrapped her hand around his upper arm. "Cormitt, you'll sit with me. I'll introduce you to the Delegate of Verceen. He's quite the art collector himself."

Cormitt's eyebrows creased, surprised by the interruption but recovered, politely smiling at Janna. She'd let her true side slip for a brief second, selfish and cutthroat.

"Of course. Please, lead the way."

I watched my mentor lead the handsome art dealer to the long decorated table. It was just one of her many personas, a flirtatious saleswoman. She wanted something from him, and she was likely going to get it.

The five apprentices filled the seats around Janna after covering the table with cutlery. I took my time finding a seat. The Delegate, a man friendly enough, smiled when he passed me. He was a perfect ruling match for Janna. He cared most about his wealth and the appearance of Verceen to the rest of the country.

Five other people were already at the table. I didn't recognize them and Janna didn't introduce them. They wore clothes as expensive and well made as mine. All huddled together, the men and women were at the far end of the table. I caught a set of horns peeking out from a tall woman's hair and as she sat, hooves stuck out from the hem of her dress. A faun. I should have known Janna would invite Drao to dinner.

"Shall we eat, or do you want to continue glaring?" Pax asked, leaning over my shoulder with a smirk.

Rolling my eyes, I walked away from him. Janna was calculating, and it was easy to assume the empty spots were on purpose. One was next to Janna, and the other was at the opposite end of the table. It was well known she had no respect for Guards. I leaned down to the youngest apprentice sitting next to Cormitt.

"Regis, right?" The boy nodded. "Do you mind taking the seat at the end? I'd hate to make a guest of Janna's uncomfortable by putting him at the end of the table away from the only person he knows."

I let my voice travel for Janna and the others at the table to hear. The young boy's eyes flicked to Janna, where I was already focused. I didn't ask her for permission and he didn't know what to do. She nodded her head once, and he stood up without a comment.

I moved to the other side, sitting in the chair to the right of Janna at the head of the table. Irritation rolled off my mentor. Smoothing out my skirt, I peeked up at an amused Cormitt and I held my mouth together to keep from matching the half smile he had. Pax sat, nodding his head politely at Janna. She didn't give him a response.

Lifting my glass of ice water, I allowed myself to glance at my mentor. The only emotion was in her eyes, the rest of her face a smooth rock. Politely smiling at her as I lowered the glass, I didn't look away. My confidence was coming from the number of witnesses, though she was paying most.

The back door of the house creaked open and a gruff voice called out. "I apologize for being late. I hope you didn't hold off eating on my behalf."

Janna broke eye contact first. A buzz of adrenaline filled my head. It was like a weird win. Led by an unfamiliar staffer, the High Drao of Verceen walked towards the table. A grin naturally appeared on my lips at the old man's arrival.

After he scanned the guests at the table, a similar smile appeared when his eyes landed on me. I was the only one to stand as he walked over, and we grasped each other's forearms in a welcoming embrace.

"It's good to see you, my dear. It's been too long," he said, placing a kiss on my forehead.

"You too, sir."

Janna stood, and they exchanged a similar embrace. The

two were good friends, knowing each other longer than I could imagine. He was an old Shifter, often choosing the form of a twisted deer, who accepted bribes without hesitation. But he was sweet and always treated me like an equal. She introduced Cormitt and Pax with a warm voice, almost like she didn't hate Pax.

Sitting back in my seat, my attention landed on Pax and the High Drao. When they gripped each other's forearms, it was formal. The 'good to meet you' sounded genuine. I wouldn't have known they met before. The High Drao sat next to the Delegate, sharing a friendly exchange. They worked together daily, making sure Verceen didn't implode of its magick and ridiculous citizens. Their personal relationship was a mystery, but the two men showed no dislike.

Two pale staffers carried a cooked pig out with a section of pre-cut meat hugging it. Others carried plates filled with vegetables and additional foods that I didn't recognize but smelled amazing. Guests dove into the food, using large spoons and forks to pick at what they wanted to eat. The staff walked around the table, hands full of drinks and shifting plates of food for others to reach. My gaze roamed around the table, noting that I didn't recognize any of the staff. I suspected once that everyone who worked here was Vek and from how homely they looked, Janna picking them for those two reasons alone.

"Owyn." My attention turned to the High Drao. "How has the work been across Gerennt?"

I nodded, chewing through a chunk of melon. "Good. I haven't been asked to pick up anything too ridiculous lately."

"What sort of ridiculous things have you been asked to get?" The Delegate asked.

I placed my cutlery down, running my hands along my thighs. "Oh, I was once asked to bring someone's newborn baby from Jova to Delf."

Everyone around me chuckled in shock. "You cannot be serious?"

"It's true. I said no for many reasons."

The Delegate looked at Janna. "Do you still get requests like that?"

She chuckled to herself, placing a piece of meat into her mouth.

"No. I only get serious requests nowadays. I'm lucky for that." Her eyes flickered to me before smiling at the Delegate.

There was a moment of silence that hung in the air. Maybe everyone sensed Janna meant something else with her words or it was just me. The High Drao cleared his throat, scratching his beard.

"Cormitt, Janna said you travel between Ynoms and Gerennt."

He nodded, taking a drink of a dark liquor. "Yes sir, I do."

"What's that like? Do you always have to come through the ports?"

As Cormitt explained his process of travelling down the mountain range to one of the three ports in Gerennt, my eyes flickered to the Delegate. He was staring at the High Drao with squinted eyes, unhappy with the question.

Ynoms was supposed to be a mystery, and I had a feeling he would report it to the Council.

The sun was kissing the horizon, hundred-year-old pine trees hiding it. Staffers cleared the table and filled it with large candles and lanterns. Janna's apprentices disappeared, dismissed with jobs to do. Around the porch, we stood with glasses in hand and chatted. If Janna had something to announce, it would've already happened. Janna didn't host people for no reason. Pax and I stumbling on a casual dinner party felt suspicious.

I leaned on the railing, an oak tree truck that was stripped of its bark and varnished. The same use of tree trunks wrapped around the entire porch. It was built off the second floor, overlooking a huge grassy space with a mixed garden of flowers and vegetables. I stared at the tree in the centre of the yard. It was as if I could see the crack in the trunk from the axe I whacked against it, trying to ruin her perfect yard. It was three months after I arrived and I wanted to go home, thinking if I acted out would get me sent back. Two months later, my apprenticeship started.

Past the natural scar, how familiar was it all six years later? Were all the crushed paths still the same?

Janna had a training space inside the trees for apprentices. It was far enough back that shouts and grunts wouldn't be heard from the house. I bled a scary amount on those structures.

A deer coming out of the tree brought me out of my thoughts. It nipped at leaves on the grass. I kept a mouthful of alcohol in my cheeks as the deer froze, noticing the crowd above and debated its safety.

"I'll give you a hundred pesa if you can get a dagger through the deer's eye from here."

Cormitt leaned on the railing beside me, watching the creature. His dark blue jacket was taut against his shoulders, hugging the linen shirt to his chest. A wave of energy radiated off him like sparks, causing the hairs on my arms to lift. His pale green eyes shone strangely as he watched the deer before flickering down to me through his lashes.

Was he a Drao, and no one mentioned it? Did anyone else know?

"I don't have a dagger to take that bet."

"Really?" He smirked. "I assumed you had one strapped to your thigh under that lovely gown."

I pulled my lower lip between my teeth, carelessly shrugging. My thigh muscle subconsciously twitched under the leather strap that indeed held a short blade. A playful glint shone as he glanced down suggestively. A rush of heat shot to my cheeks as a smirk made my cheek twitch.

"I don't think Janna would appreciate hunting during her dinner party," I muttered, turning my back to the trees. His hand pressed against the railing next to me.

"You sure? It might liven things up," he teased.

"There's enough going on you don't see. Trust me," I said.

Biting down on the tip of my tongue, I chastised myself. That was a slip. I felt at ease in his presence and the words fell out of my mouth. Peering at Cormitt, he looked at me with his eyebrows furrowed and I shook my head, a smile politely slipping onto my face. My words were enough to risk whatever Janna planned with or for this handsome stranger. And that was worse than doing a transaction on her territory.

Cormitt shifted closer, his eyes staying on mine. I stood and faced him, my back no longer touching the railing. If we both took a deep breath, our chests would touch. My thoughts stuttered with his eyes staring directly into mine. It was almost predatory, in the way his eyes reflected the light.

What was it with men bewitching me into wanting them lately?

The surrounding conversations became a hum. My legs were losing stability, making me sway closer to him.

"Why are you in Verceen?" I blurted, without thinking.

His forehead wrinkled, pulled from the moment too. Processing my question, he cleared his throat. "Just passing through."

Without a second glance, he walked away and stiffly approached Janna. She looked at him with a smile that fell after a moment. The pair spoke quietly, Janna nodding in understanding with what he said.

After sharply nodding to the Delegate and the High Drao, he entered the house. With his hand around the door handle, he glanced back at me and the only change in expression was a nostril flair. No one else appeared to notice Cormitt's strange departure.

A moment later, Pax wandered over with a half empty

glass cradled in his hand. "Having a pleasant evening? I'm enjoying it."

I snorted, taking another drink. "Janna would've made you eat on the front porch if the High Drao wasn't here. She's being generous."

He shrugged, finishing his drink. I watched his throat contract around the drink, wondering what he thought of this weird gathering. Before I could ask, Janna left her conversation with the Delegate and the High Drao, walking to us.

"Guard, I'll speak with Orinthia now." Her eyes never left my face as she spoke.

Pax nodded once, accepting the dismissal, and left. My gaze followed him, but she moved into my sightline.

"Have you thought about what I said?"

"No, Janna. I've been enjoying the dinner your staff and apprentices made," I answered.

It could've been the alcohol in my blood, but it came out with snark. Maybe sitting at the table with all the guests made me feel like a true equal. Or it was wisdom that came with life experience because she wasn't as all knowing and powerful as I once thought. My shoulders naturally sat back. Her eyes skimmed along my face, taking in the change in posture and her tongue sat between her teeth.

"Why are you travelling with the lackey?" she asked with a touch of disgust.

"You know why. The Council assigned him to make sure I arrived at the Isle, alive. It wasn't my choice," I answered, unintentionally matching her tone.

Janna sighed, changing from the strong Merchant to the confidant I was used to by the end of my apprenticeship in a blink of my eye. She placed her hands on the railing, stress falling from her shoulders.

"I hate having Guards around. They're judgemental and unintelligent."

I chuckled, placing the glass next to her hand. "You think that about a lot of people."

A laugh huffed through her nose, half her mouth lifting to a smile. Her profile faced me as she gazed out at the forest. The candle light made her naturally severe features almost soft for once.

"We'll be leaving for the night," I said. "Thank your apprentices for supper. It was delicious."

Janna grabbed my arm as I turned to walk away. I was prepared for her to scold me, but her eyes were even. The professional persona was present with everyone watching.

"I'd like you to meet me at the wandmaker's tonight. I have a transaction that needs to be finished, and I want to hand off the second half to you in Dornis's Northern village. It's barely a detour from your route."

I stared at her, waiting for something else. But she stopped after those instructions. I nodded slowly, a strange feeling festering in my stomach.

"Good. Don't bring the Guard. He'll spook the shopkeeper."

Janna released my arm and returned to looking at the trees. I found Pax speaking to Tyress and one of the strangers, whispering that I was ready to leave. He nodded, his eyes roaming around my face, looking for something wrong.

Leading me through the back door, I remembered I was still in the borrowed dress as my foot caught the hem and I almost tripped.

"Oh crap," I muttered, looking down at the dark red fabric.

"Janna would like you to keep the dress. Consider it a present."

In the sitting room, Doe and Cyrell stood with their hands behind their backs. They were doing their best to mock Janna's natural expression. It was like looking in a twisted mirror, seeing myself how other people saw me five years ago and I was only realising it now.

"Do you have our clothes?"

Doe held up a thick bag stuffed to the brim. Pax took it from her and dropped it over his shoulder. This dress would suck on the ride to the tavern, but I couldn't insult Janna's generosity, and I wanted to leave.

The horses were ready at the bottom of the porch steps, their reins being held by two barn hands. I didn't recognize either of them. I ran my hand down Dill's neck, doing the same thing to Marr, giving them a quick inspection. They both looked fine and unharmed.

"Your horses were fed," Regis told us, standing back.

He appeared older than what I initially thought when we met hours earlier. But Janna had that effect on people.

"Good to know," Pax commented, mounting Neem.

I tossed my leg over Dill's back, knowing I'd likely flashed more than my legs to the apprentices. The fabric bunched up around me, making it hard to not feel like I was going to fall off.

"Shall we?" Pax asked, a smirk on his face after watching my struggle.

He led the way down the dirt drive as anxiety built in my chest. I didn't know where it was coming from. Glancing back at the house and all its illuminated windows, I caught movement on the second floor. A chill ran down my spine as Janna stared down at us.

"Your mentor doesn't seem too bad," Pax said as we came back into the town.

The shops were still open, but the streets were almost empty. A few shopkeepers either recognized me or saw us leave the road coming from Janna's and waved. I didn't stop myself from waving back.

"She was in a good mood tonight," I muttered back.

Pax glanced at me. "What do you mean?"

I shook my head, politely smiling at him. "Nothing."

Chapter 26

I sat at a pub table, my finger running through the precipitation from my beer. Pax was supposed to meet me soon, but I felt on edge, questioning everything happening around me. Being away from the house, my sense of security vanished. Any time I made eye contact with someone, I wondered if they were in Janna's pocket. Verceen wasn't safe.

It was a constant party of Drao and Vek, mingling with endless smiles. How much of it was true? I didn't know anymore. It felt like facing a stix, a giant carnivorous bird, when it was in a cage and then having the cage vanish. I was vulnerable.

Taking a drink of the weak alcohol, I stared at the wax running down the side of a thick pillar candle against the wall. The entire building was dark, keeping a sense of mystery and maybe to make its patrons feel less alone.

"Excuse me, miss?" My eyes flickered to the young boy at the booth's edge. "The High Drao would like to speak with you."

Nodding, I took another drink of beer. "Lead the way."

The child waited until I stood before leading me to a private back room. Each room was magickally protected, allowing for private and secret conversations. I don't know how strong the magick was after hundreds of years, but the High Drao trusted it.

"Didn't get enough of me earlier?" I asked the old man as the door shut.

He stood with a knowing smile on his face. He was wearing the same silky embroidered jacket from dinner.

"We didn't have much time for a conversation, and I believe we have some things to discuss."

The High Drao of Verceen and I exchanged a welcoming grasp. I pulled out the opposite chair and sat across from the man who'd shown me genuine kindness while I was stuck in Verceen. He was a little older now, the creases in his face were a touch more set. His age was a mystery, but I'm sure he'd been around longer than he looked.

I peered into my half full mug. "I was surprised to find out there was a dinner party without an agenda. Unless I missed it entirely."

His eyebrows lifted in agreement. "Yes. But what question is burning you the most?"

My eyes met his. Straight to the point.

"Why did you meet with Pax, and how did you know?"

He smirked. "High Drao are privy to plenty of things. Being around for hundreds of years gives us that all knowing privilege."

"You knew what happened on the Isle?"

He nodded. "Yes, but not until after. The Council worked hard to hide their plans. It sounds like none of the High Drao knew."

"How much do you trust that information?" I asked, taking another drink.

"I don't get to choose if I trust the other High Drao, Owyn."

"That's terrifying," I commented.

The High Drao weakly shrugged.

"You get used to it. Secrets don't stay secret ever. The truth always comes out whether you want to or not." He intertwined his fingers on the table, his mouth falling to a more serious expression. "Now, for your Guard. When the information reached us, the High Drao met. None of the others were prepared to act without an explanation from the Council."

"And that leads to you meeting with the Guard, how?"

"I was made aware the Council was sending a Guard out to meet you. I knew you were likely to kill him out of self preservation. I gave you a helping hand."

"I'm glad you have faith in my self control and defensive skills," I muttered.

He smiled, canines on show. "That I have faith in, as well as your abilities to murder."

I pursed my lips before taking a small drink. I didn't know how to take the compliment about my ability to create bloodshed. Weirdly, I enjoyed it.

"I gave the Guard a talisman to increase his chances of survival. Your return would be much harder without him."

My eyebrow raised dramatically. "Meaning?"

He swirled his bright green drink around in the glass.

"I can't tell you that. There's only so much I'm allowed to say, no matter how fond I am of you. The others weren't impressed when they found out I helped you."

"That doesn't surprise me. You're a very secretive group."

"Shall I point out again that some have lived for hundreds of years? Revealing secrets isn't the best chance for survival."

I rolled my eyes, making the old man chuckle. "Fine. How were you so sure the talisman would stop me from killing him?"

"I trusted your training would have stayed with you. You'd remember what it meant."

I tapped my finger along the mug, silent. Staring at the powerful man, I considered what he said. He was right, the

High Drao kept their secrets when they needed to and I wasn't naïve enough to think he would tell me the whole truth. He stared right back, not letting anything show on his face.

"Pax told me it was the Council who sent him after me. Or was it really you?"

"It was the Council," the High Drao said, nodding. "Pax was chosen for a specific purpose, I'm sure, but only a few Guards could've been chosen to travel with you."

"If I were to ask what you meant by one of a few Guards?"

"They would need a certain temperament for you not to kill them, even if you trusted my endorsement. Or for them not to kill you."

"And the specific reason?"

"I will have to keep that answer to myself," he said, eyes sparkling with amusement.

"Do you actually know why he was chosen?" I asked, squinting my eyes with cheeky suspicion.

"I will keep that to myself," he repeated.

I nodded, suppressing a smile. "I understand."

"Was my talisman all it took for you to trust that Guard?" High Drao asked after we both paused the conversation to take a drink.

I wrapped both my hands around the cup and stared at the wood. My instinctual answer was yes. I trusted Pax because of the talisman. Or was it the deeply set draw I felt to him? I felt something positive towards him, even before I saw the talisman. So what was my answer?

The High Drao made an amused sound in his throat with a gleam in his eye, taking another drink. He knew more than he was letting on. And I couldn't answer him.

"Since you won't say more, can you tell me about the most suspicious dinner party ever?" I asked, changing the subject.

"From what I understand, Janna was alerted that you were heading to Verceen. I don't know if she knew you were coming for a transaction. That's when I was informed about the dinner. When you came through the gates, the news spread like wildfire. Everyone knew within an hour. Janna's successful protégé returned. It was more of a scandal when you were seen with the Guard."

"He doesn't blend in well, does he?" I said, chuckling.

"That may be an understatement," he answered, raising his eyebrows.

"And the art dealer? I was surprised to see Janna invite a stranger. Her dinner parties usually hold a different tone."

The High Drao's eyes flicker around, long enough to let me know he was about to lie. "I've heard his name before. He's a strong seller of both legal and illegal art. I believe Janna is procuring something from him."

I didn't give him an answer, only nodding my head and emptied my drink into my mouth. What was the point of more questions when I wasn't getting an honest answer?

The private room's door opened, and the young boy cautiously entered. His stance became more confident when High Drao approved the interruption. He stopped next to the table, hands behind his back politely.

"The Guard from Jova has arrived looking for Miss. Kellobyn."

"Thank you, Jonah," the High Drao said, rising from his seat and handing the boy a coin. I followed, and we exchanged goodbyes.

"Be careful out there, Owyn Kellobyn. Your future relies on gut and properly placed trust," he commented as I reached the doorframe. I looked back at him, dramatically rolling my eyes.

"That's mystical of you." I ignored the look in his eyes that made my gut twist, knowing he wasn't joking. A more sober mind would go over his words later.

I exited the back room, empty mug in hand. I changed from the dress to be more low-key. Not only for the transaction I was going to later, but I hoped to deter the stares from people who recognized me. It didn't help.

Slipping between patrons, I sat down on a bar stool at the counter. A new bartender was behind the counter, and recognition flashed across his eyes before we exchanged a nod.

"Where have you been hiding?" Pax asked, resting his elbow next to me on the counter.

I glanced up at the Guard. His dark hair was loose, curling under his earlobes. He was back in his regular clothes, too. The outfit Janna gave him was back at the tavern, probably shoved to the bottom of his bag.

"Had some old friends to catch up with," I answered, wagging my empty mug in the air.

The bartender stepped up, exchanging it with a full one. Taking a sip, I didn't wonder how he knew what I was drinking.

"From the gentlemen over there." The bartender indicated with his head.

Pax and I glanced across the dully lit bar. Both men were older, and I recognized the grey dust covering their skin as a sign of Drao miners.

Verceen was littered with entrances to the crystal mines. Their shifts went on for days. It took deadly labour and magick to grow certain crystals. I went into the mines a handful of times, wanting to see where the materials were coming from. I didn't stop coughing up dust and sparkled shards of minerals for three days.

I raised the glass in thanks. Both nodded, returning to their conversation.

"How do I get free beer?" Pax asked in amusement, sitting on the stool beside me.

"Be a woman or get trained by the woman who supplies the whole town with their secrets and vices," I muttered against the glass. "Up to you."

We drank in relative silence. Strangers approached me, knowing my name and commenting on how nice it was to see me in town. It was uncomfortable, to say the least. Across Gerennt, I was recognized as a Merchant. It came with years of training. But in Verceen, it was a different identity. Forever, I would be Janna's protégé and that's it.

As it got later into the night, I allowed myself to enjoy a few more drinks. Pax matched me drink for drink until he surpassed me. The patrons ignored the fact he was a Guard and started including him in their conversations. Maybe it had to do with my recognition, since half of them attempted to flirt with me after talking to him. I watched him wander around the pub, slowly sipping on my drink.

Two females with pale lilac skin approached him. I wasn't concerned with Pax potentially being seduced and hanging all over his possessions. They were sylphs, air spirits who collected hairs to build nests. I didn't interact with them much as sylphs had little need for Merchants.

Leaving Pax in the pub with Drao women holding his attention, I walked out the front door. My first stop was the community stables. I approached through the treeline, hoping anyone outside would be less likely to notice me.

Opening a secret compartment in my cart, I slipped the necklace and cage inside. Slowly, I stood up and looked around. No one could be seen, but that didn't mean I was unnoticed. At least I knew nobody could get into the cart.

I remembered the way through town without a second thought or doubt. A part of me hoped I forgot, but that was a silly hope. The shopping core of Verceen fell silent, the only noise spilling from open windows. A few shops, mostly food related, were still open. By sundown, the whole town was usually closed.

Above my head, wings flapped loudly in the sky. Looking up into the darkness, I couldn't tell what was making the noise. It could be an eagle, one of the giant bats that lived most of their lives in the caves of Crewnyr Mountains or a dragon that called the mountaintops home.

I nodded to a couple walking together. The woman with glowing eyes smiled and the man, spinning a handful of flames, nodded back. I stuffed my hands into my pockets, lowering my head as I kept walking. Verceen was safe for me. I wasn't worried about getting mugged.

Nestled between two other shops, the wandmaker's windows were dark. Odd. I tugged on the front door. Locked. A few voices could be heard nearby when I remembered the shop was in front of a small courtyard with back entrances to the buildings. Maybe I was meant to meet them there.

I found the cobblestone alleyway and fiddled with the ends of my hair as I walked along it. If I couldn't find anyone, I would go back to the tavern and see if Pax made any more friends.

The shadows were looming, only a few lamps illuminated the pathway from either end. Turning into the courtyard, the volume of the voices didn't change. My feet halted when the single orb of light came into view. My heart dropped. It was an imitation spell, and I walked right into its trap.

The orb faded away; the voices went with it. A shoe quietly scuffed against the ground, making me spin and reach for a weapon. My hand found nothing against my hip as I came face to face with Janna's apprentice.

Cyrell couldn't be more than sixteen. Even with his neutral mask, I could tell. The childish sparkle still lived in his eyes, even if Janna tried her best to break it during training. A dagger was wrapped in his hand, hanging at his side as he stepped farther out of the shadows. The short knife strapped to my ankle pressed into my skin, but there wasn't time to grab it. His gaze flickered over my shoulder as a pebble bounced against the pathway, echoing off the brick walls that surrounded us.

Peering back, two large men stopped behind me. They

both lacked emotion in their eyes. Both held daggers too; though not nearly as nice as Cyrell's. His was made by a Drao blacksmith and enchantment with numerous spells. Mine was the exact same. A gift from Janna. I got mine for successfully negotiating a price through intimidation.

I should've known this was Janna's plan. I betrayed her and her image. And now, I was dealing with the consequences.

Cyrell's eyes revealed how nervous he was. I understood. Doing Janna's dirty work, whether for the first time or the tenth, never felt good. Even if you executed everything she asked, she was still critical. And if he didn't do it, Cyrell would have his own price to pay.

"It's okay," I whispered, nodding once in understanding. "Do what you've been told."

"She says this is for losing your pyx," Cyrell whispered back.

His grip flexed around the dagger. It didn't surprise me that was the reason she gave him, but it made me sick to say I knew Janna better. She was furious. I embarrassed her. Her image was power, and I made a crack in it.

"It's okay," I answered, giving him a reassuring smile.

He nodded, determination cementing on his face. I hoped for his health that he satisfied Janna.

With one sharp movement, Cyrell jabbed his hand forward and stabbed my bicep. As the dagger ripped out, I groaned and crumpled away.

Looking up at him, he stared back with wide eyes, and I knew he had never done something like this before. I straightened with a deep sigh and waited for the next blow. His gaze shot to the men behind me as he shifted his weight.

"She expected you to fight back," Cyrell commented, his eyebrows almost touching.

As a hand clamped around my shoulder, I winked at Cyrell. I allowed myself to be spun, but when I faced the man,

I kicked and connected the sole of my boot with his stomach. He stumbled back, clutching at his torso. The reaction made the second man realise I was fighting and lumbered over. His dagger was held high in the air. It was a dumb angle, but the stinging of my wound buzzed in my ear, leaving me disoriented.

I gave too much attention to the dagger that I didn't see the fist before it connected with my eye. My head snapped sideways, a wave of nausea filling my mouth mixed with blood. Keeping my eyes shut, I tried to stop the dizziness. A hand grabbed me again and a cold pinch jabbed into my stomach. My knees collapsed under the sudden pain and my gaze fell to the hole a blade left in my body.

I was losing much quicker than I expected.

"Enough," Cyrell commanded with a single tremor in his voice.

Almost blinded by tears, I lifted my head. The two men on either side of me, heaving with adrenaline and daggers, ready to attack. I should've noticed the burning rage in their eyes before. They would only respond to commands.

Janna had the men under a controlling spell. Unable to hold back the whimper of pain, I weakly got to my feet. Another wave of sickness hit as the edges of my soaked wound pulled with the shift of my torso. I grabbed my stomach with my wounded arm, feeling like I was keeping my organs in their proper spot. Cyrell watched me stumble to him, his mouth open.

"She'll have expected me to fight back," I said, metal on my tongue.

As his eyebrows crinkled together, I swung my good arm. My fist connected with his cheekbone, sending him flying.

Without looking at the unknown men, I dragged my feet towards the main road. No one was going to follow me.

Chapter 27

I opened the inn's front door with my elbow, not wanting to leave a bloody handprint on the wood. Marllo wouldn't appreciate it.

The woman at the front desk stared, not knowing what to say or do. She looked close to passing out. With her loose hair framing her face, it was easy to notice that she was close to my age. How different our lives were.

"Have whiskey and vodka bottles sent up to Orinthia Kellobyn's room," I commented, holding my stomach tighter as I shuffled by. "And an empty glass."

She stiffly nodded, her mouth never closing.

I slammed the door to my room shut. I was on the verge of passing out if I didn't sit down soon. With my uninjured arm, I peeled my sweater and tunic off. The ruined shirt was new, but I didn't feel guilty wrapping it around my bicep. Violently, I shook a pillowcase from a pillow on the bed. My clothes weren't clean enough to use on my torso.

Pushing the fabric against the wound, bile rose in my throat. Swallowing it, I could barely lift my feet off the ground as I did my best to lie down without covering the sheets in blood.

I'm not sure how long I laid unmoving, forcing myself to stay awake. At one point, an inn employee dropped off the alcohol I requested. I didn't see them, nor did they say anything, but I heard the clinking of glass on wood. A second person scarred this evening. I'm surprised Marllo hasn't come by yet, whether to yell at the mess I left in her hallways or to see if I was dead.

Eventually, I was no longer on the edge of unconsciousness and I could awkwardly shuffle myself off the bed. I was thankful Cyrell didn't wound my dominant hand. This would've been so much worse. I grabbed the two full bottles by their necks, ignoring the glass. As carefully as I was currently capable of, I let them thunk against the desk next to the standing mirror. I uncapped the whiskey bottle and took a long drink, almost able to feel the alcohol mix with my blood. The pain in my body was just a sense of burning nerves now.

I shuffled into the washroom to grab the medical kit. Carelessly, I knocked things onto the ground. I'd grab it later. Back in front of the mirror, my teeth ground together, dumping the items out. Thankfully, the roll of bandages was large. Dried blood covered my stomach, clinging to the fabric. Humming a low grumble, I peel off the crusty shirt.

Glaring at the bottles, I knew this was about to feel worse than being attacked. Unscrewing the vodka lid with a shaking hand and, without a second to reconsider, I poured some on my forearm. A cry slipped out before biting my tongue. The bottle slammed into the desk. The nausea returned with force and I stared at the roof, blinking back the tears spilling over. I considered my two options as I checked both gashes in the mirror. Get someone with two hands to stitch me up or do it myself and end up with an ugly scar.

Was it worth waiting for Pax and letting him know I snuck away?

Realistically, if I did it myself and changed only in the

bathroom, I could hide it. He was already critical of my relationship with Janna, not that I didn't know it was messed up.

I hated her and was afraid of her, but yearned for her approval? He truly might get angry at me for this one.

Tapping my fingers against my thigh, I remembered something I bought in Warfidd. Rummaging through my rucksack, a black velvet bag stuck out. Dumping its contents, the ornate purple bottle was what I was looking for. Taking it back to the desk, I carefully twisted the topper out. A rotting smell filled my nose. Healing potions smelt horrible. Oddly, like death.

Squeezing my teeth together, a few drops landed on the wound. Focusing on putting the lid on correctly as a burning intensified over my arm wasn't easy. I did my best not to watch my flesh slither back together. It was another minute before a filmy layer of scar tissue settled and it would have to be enough for the night. I would visit the practitioner tomorrow before we leave.

Ignoring the prickling sensation as I moved, both hands were now free to unravel the bandages. I covered my bicep with gauze before grabbing the medical tape. It was messy, but enough to keep from scratching in my sleep.

I looked in the mirror. It was a long time since I saw myself in such a dishevelled state. Maybe since my days as an apprentice. Fitting. My face was pale but almost green. For once, I looked as weak as I felt. I could fall to the ground and sleep, but I ignored the more serious injury long enough.

I was glad the pillowcase still stuck to me, meaning there weren't any poisons stopping the blood from clotting. My stomach rolled as the pillowcase crunched away from my skin. A few beads of blood escaped when the crust was taken away.

Thinking the worst was over, I let out a relieved huff. Bad idea. The sudden movement sent pain through me and I couldn't keep my composure. I emptied my stomach into a large planter beside the desk and mentally; I apologized to the plant it housed.

The unlocked door squeaked open as I cautiously stood up, waiting to see if anything else would come out. In the mirror, I made eye contact with a furious Pax. I considered joking about his timing, but my legs chose a different route. The muscles relaxed and my body slumped to the floor. I heard a deafening thud as I fell asleep.

MY EYELIDS SCRUNCHED AS MY BRAIN AWOKE. I WASN'T SURE where I was. Leaning on my left arm to sit up, the forgotten injury sent an uncomfortable pressure through my body. Switching to my right arm saved me from slumping back onto the bed. My finger ran along the bandages lightly. No blood seeped through, but the sheets were stained. Marllo would be pissed. I would buy her a new set still.

Resting my head against the headboard, I smacked my mouth in disgust, still faintly tasting stomach bile. Time to get up. We needed to leave and if I walked outside like this, somebody would call Guards.

Compared to last night, my feet felt solid underneath me as I wandered into the bathroom. Cupping my hands in the clear water and ignoring the blood under my nails, I filled my mouth. Swishing it around before spitting out, I leaned against the counter. Curses ran through my head directed at Janna as I had a moment of dizziness. I knew she was selfish, but I could've died and she didn't care.

I examined my body in the mirror. Still in the dirty undergarments from yesterday, my torso was wrapped in fresh bandages and assumed I must've woken up and changed them at some point.

While picking at the tape, I spotted a few cuts on my skin I didn't see before. I expected dried blood to have spattered the gauze, but it came away clean. My stomach was cleanly stitched shut. I ran my finger along the wiring, knowing I couldn't have done that without remembering.

Loosely re-wrapping my stomach, the room door opened. My gaze briefly flickered to the reflection of the man behind me. Pax let the door slam shut in a passive aggressive way.

"Thanks for sewing me up. I couldn't have done it so cleanly," I said, placing a new piece of tape against my skin before leaning back and forth, checking how much it would pull.

He didn't respond. Cleaning up the desk, I reached for the gauze pads. On my back, the bandage folded. Instinctively, I reached to fix it, but froze when the stitches tugged. My face tightened from the sensation and I took clumsy breaths to suppress the screaming. I glanced at Pax in the mirror.

"Do you mind?" I asked. "I don't want to ruin your handy work."

He stayed leaning on the doorframe, staring me in the eye with his arms crossed. Facing him, I responded by placing my hands on my hips. He gave up, sighing with an eye roll before coming over.

Turning back around, I watched through the mirror as he straightened the bandage. His lips were tightened in a line, staring down at the fabric.

"Is it more twisted than I thought?" I asked, trying to lighten the mood and get his scar to lose the unnecessary crinkle.

He let the bandage snap against my back and I felt his breath against my shoulders when he sighed again, continuing to stare downwards.

"What's the matter with you?" I asked, softly running my fingertips over my stomach.

"Where were you last night?"

I cleared my throat, stepping around him towards the bed. "Nowhere."

His hand gripped my arm, jerking me back. His face was inches from mine.

"You're saying you got that from sitting here all night? Because you weren't here when I came back from the pub."

"Must've missed me. Probably in the bathroom," I answered, ignoring the dark tone in his voice.

I weakly shrugged my shoulder back, trying to roll out of his grip. His grip lightened, but he didn't let go. The anger boiling in his eyes wasn't going away and, to anyone else, it would be intimidating. But having someone behave protectively made me shudder.

"Fine," I whispered, knowing he wouldn't drop it. "Janna asked me to meet her for a transaction last night. It was a setup. One of her apprentices attacked me on her command."

The darkness in Pax's eyes deepened, but it was no longer directed at me.

"I'm going to kill them," he muttered, dropping my arm from his grasp, but I grabbed the front of his shirt. His chest was heaving under my hand as he tried to control his anger.

"You can't."

"And why not?" Pax snapped. "You could've died."

"Janna thinks I embarrassed her. To her, I lost my pyx through my volition, and that looks bad on her. This was my punishment for it. It's fine," I explained in a rush.

His scrunched eyebrows flattened out, and he became emotionless, his eyes flickering around my face. My fist squeezed tighter around his shirt, trying to keep the shaking in my hand to a minimum. He would make things so much worse if he did or said anything.

"How is it fine?" He pointed at my stomach. "Is this fine?"

"It was my punishment. I should've realized sooner," I repeated, unemotional.

We stared at each other, neither saying a word, until his heartbeat slowed.

"What did she do to you?" he asked.

Maybe it was supposed to be a question with a stronger voice, but it was hushed. It hit my heart like he punched me in the chest.

My hand slipped away from him and dropped to my side. It was a more personal question than he probably realized. Weapons. Bruises and blood. Being broken down to skin and bones. No food for days. Every chance Janna got, my life was on the edge of death. I almost forgot it all. I tried anyway. But he didn't get to know that.

"If it's okay with you, I'm going to rest for the day. I'll be ready to leave in the morning."

Reaching down to pull back the bedsheets, the edges of the wire stitches scraped into my wound and I whimpered, trying to it in my throat. Pax stepped forwards and lifted me in his arms. I let out a quiet protest that he ignored. He laid me down, dropping the blankets into place.

"You can't ride like this, anyway. I've checked on the horses and they're okay. I'll go down and get you something to eat after you sleep."

He knelt next to my head. Gently, he brushed my hair away from my face.

"You're taking your job of getting your ward to the Isle safely very seriously," I mumbled.

The corners of his mouth lifted, his fingertips brushing against my forehead as he continued the motion.

"Something like that," he answered.

Chapter 28

I stared at my riding corset with disgust. I consumed healing elixirs and herbs all night. Pax visited the few apothecaries in town and bought what they recommended.

To his annoyance, the shopkeepers recognized him as my travelling partner and gave him the product for free. I was grateful that my arm was almost healed completely. It felt like a very fresh bruise now.

When I woke up, my abdomen had turned into a large scab that was getting punched over and over by ghosts. It wasn't good to ingest that much magick in a short time and my stomach would be unhappy with me later, but we needed to leave.

Pax's invasive question from the night before continued to bounce in my mind, and it was making me feel claustrophobic.

Glaring at my inanimate enemy, a knock sounded on my room's door. "Come in, Pax."

His dark hair appeared around the door as it opened. I flashed a brief smile at him before picking up the small bottle of fish tonic. He chuckled as my face contoured around the nasty taste. Leaving the door wide open, he threw his washing bag onto his bed.

"Someone was asking for you downstairs. She looked a little suspicious, but I brought her up anyway," he commented.

Clicking footsteps approached the room, and I snapped my head to look at Pax. He tried to hide a smile, which made me feel a little better that I wasn't in too much danger. My alarm changed to a grin as Lyris Pennev stepped through the doorway.

"I heard there was a hypnotically beautiful Merchant in town and I could only assume it was you. Had to come see for myself," Lyris said, dropping her bag with a thud.

My friend and I wrapped our arms around each other with giggles. The last I saw Lyris was minutes after our pyxes were taken and our orders were given. Pulling back, the difference about Lyris's dark skin was blatant, and she appeared sick. The usual brightness of her gold eyes dulled and the whites behind the pupils were turning grey.

"Are you feeling okay?" I rested my hand against her forehead. Her skin was concerningly warm under my hand.

"I haven't felt well since leaving the Isle. I've barely been able to keep food down. My pyx is gone, if you don't remember," she teased poorly.

I glanced at Pax, watching us with crossed arms. If he knew she was one of the Merchants, he wasn't letting on. I opened the drawstring of my bag, hunting for the fish tonic again.

"Do you have what the Council requested?"

Lyris shook her head. "I've asked everyone I can think of. No one knows how to convince a werewolf to hand over bone marrow. It's not something I can go to any accessible practitioner for."

I indicated for her to open her mouth before letting a few drops fall in. Lyris's face twisted at the bitter flavour as I ran my hands up and down her biceps soothingly. I felt the side effects of not having my pyx, but at least I had the faerie eggs. The end was in sight for me.

"Can the Council give her another assignment?" I asked Pax. "She will not get bone marrow if she's this ill."

Pax looked at his feet, clearing his throat. His eyes flickered between Lyris and I, rubbing on his lower lip.

"The Council was very exact with their instructions. They don't change their minds. Merchants must bring back what they've been instructed to. It's the only way to get your pyx back."

"Pax, she's sick because she doesn't have her pyx. No amount of fish tonic is going to recover the month she's gone without it. She's obviously been affected by it more than me and isn't going to get the damn bone marrow if she's writhing in pain on the ground," I hissed.

"There's nothing I can do. The Council has their instructions."

My lips tightened, glaring at him. He looked almost sorry but resolute in what he said. I huffed, turning back to my friend.

"Did you talk to any of the High Drao?"

Lyris nodded, her eyes almost dropping closed. "Gave me a bottle of fish tonic and said the same thing. There's nothing to do for me without my pyx."

"What're you going to do?" I asked, trying to reserve my panic.

"I plan on riding back to the Isle. Hopefully, if the Council sees how ineffective I am for this job without my pyx, they'll give me a different one or something."

I nodded, rubbing her arms again.

"You're not riding alone. I'm not letting you collapse in the middle of the road and die because someone isn't paying attention." I turned to Pax. "She's coming with us."

"Fine," He said. "But we need to leave. I'd like to get past Delf before nightfall."

I noticed the twist of his lip when mentioning the town, but I ignored it.

"That's fine. I know an inn's owner on the other side of Delf. We'll get there by nightfall and have a room."

He nodded, snatching his bag and leaving the room. Lyris looked back at me with her eyebrows raised.

"Is he always moody?" she asked with an amused smirk.

"I still haven't figured him out," I muttered, gaze flicking back to the empty doorway.

Leaving Verceen lifted a weight off my shoulders. I know it was my imagination, but my wounds felt better. I took up the back of our little group, not wanting Lyris behind me and falling without being noticed.

Pax tried to ride next to me, but the road was uneven in width and he ended up between us. Lyris's horse, Scholl, had no desire to socialize with Neem or either of mine. He wasn't old, just stuck up. I wasn't even sure he liked Lyris that much.

"Why were you in evil's lair?" Lyris asked, glancing over her shoulder at me.

I snorted, knowing who she was talking about. "I had a transaction."

She dramatically widened her eyes, her eyebrows shooting up. "Really? Wow, that person is brave."

"Or stupid," I said, loud enough for her to hear.

"Or that," she agreed, laughing.

"Lyris?" she hummed, glancing at Pax. "Was your mentor as psychopathic as Owyn's?"

I rolled my eyes at the back of his head as Lyris laughed.

"Well, my mentor married my brother. She was strict but I love her very much, so no, she isn't a psychopath like Janna."

My gaze flickered to Pax, smirking at the shocked reaction on his face.

"It gets even better," I said. "Our mentors were trained together."

"Very different results," Lyris added over her shoulder.

"No kidding," he mumbled.

HISTLEA RIVER ROARED A FEW DOZEN FEET TO OUR LEFT. Getting over the bridge that covered the offshoot to the ocean was easy and without concern that we were going to crash through.

The Council spent pesa getting it back to standards after five people had died from rotted boards breaking under their feet and they plunged into the fast moving water. Wouldn't that have been an ironic death?

In the near distance, the uneven and crude wall built around the town of Delf was visible. Unlike the rest of the country, no wildlife or foliage grew outside the walls. The grass was dead and yellow. Trees were crumpling over and were so empty from rot, they would knock over if an eagle landed on one. Dark green treetops were visible at the other end of Delf. A shadow lived over the Forest of Som, proving just how unsettling the restricted zone was.

In front of me, Pax's hand tapped without rhythm on his thigh, keeping his head turned away from Delf. Neem's head bobbed from side to side, a recognizable stress motion for a horse but an unfamiliar movement for her. Questions pressed against my lips, wanting to know what his issue was.

Our three heads shot up in the air, a piercing squawking making our ears hurt. My stomach dropped, recognizing the incoming glow pressing against the clouds as I tried to keep control of a disturbed Dill.

"Firebugs," I said, my hands squeezing around the reins.

"That swarm looks gigantic," Lyris said nervously. "Owyn, you don't have a fireproof shelter inside that cart, do you?"

"Would've pulled it out by now," I answered, not looking away from the swarm. "We're going to have to stop in town."

Pax made an unhappy sound in his throat, but his eyes didn't leave the slow-moving swarm.

"Unless you want to get thousands of little burns until they kill you?"

He glared at me, but I could see a desperation in his eyes. "Fine. Let's go."

The sky brightened as the firebugs got closer, still making the worst sound. Neem and Scholl passed through the archway first, their riders looking back with concern as I did my best to have Dill and Marr speed up.

The usually unaffected Marr was agitated with his ears turned back and weaving on the road. Dill was being jerked around by her slightly larger brother and her fear was becoming frustration. When I could finally get them through the archway, the sounds of rain began. But it wasn't raining. It was little spurts of fire from the bugs.

Every once in a while, dead firebugs hit the ground too. Some caught fire and those flames were bigger. These were the ones that usually caused problems before actual rain followed and put out the fires.

Lyris and Pax rode their horses right into the community stables as I jumped off Dill and quickly disconnected her from Marr. Smacking her butt, she wandered into the barn and I released Marr from the cart.

Pax was talking to a stable worker, arranging how long the horses would be here. Others were rushing around the enormous barn, trying to make sure everything was locked down and no firebugs could get in. Fire was an obvious issue, but so were terrified horses.

"Help me put the cart away?" I asked Pax, as Lyris pulled out her coin purse to pay the keepers.

Outside, the firebugs were swarming. My heart pounded in fear, but I ignored them. A couple landed on my arms, but I didn't flinch. Agitating them was like bothering mosquitoes, but a lot more painful.

We each grabbed a bar and yanked the cart close to the barn wall. Pax took all the straps in his arm and followed me back into the barn. I'd have to cross my fingers that the protection potions worked. Everything inside was protected by magick, but the cart was expensive and custom-made.

"We're going to be here for a couple hours," I commented, walking back into the barn.

Behind me, the workers closed the large doors. It got darker, the minimal sunlight coming in through the windows. There had to be ventilation somewhere, even as I was overwhelmed by the smell of hay and poop. Pax made a sound of agreement that caught my attention.

Lyris stared up at Scholl, petting him along his snout.

"The keepers said there's a small inn three buildings down. They should have a room for us to wait in. At least we won't be stuck in here," she told us.

Going through the open stall door where Neem was, Pax unclipped his bag from her saddle. He left the wooden door wide open and walked past me without a look.

He was tense, not even reacting, when his elbow smacked into a post. Lyris and I exchanged a look as he left the barn.

Chapter 29

Delf pubs weren't as fancy as some of the other towns. Fewer windows, more lanterns and overhead lights.

Similar to Verceen, the Drao didn't hide their differences, but here, the characters were much seedier. Some of them lived here for the illegal merchandise that came out of the Forest of Som. Others wanted to feel the dark magick radiating off the forest.

Sitting at the bar top, I stared down at the half-empty mug of alcohol. Lyris sat next to me with a large sweater on and a toque tugged over her ears. She'd found herself freezing, even after the three hour long firebug swarming over the town. I was sweating, but I didn't point that out. Pax stayed at the inn, claiming he didn't need to go out. Since we arrived in town, he entirely forgot his manners and I was irritated beyond reason.

After making some unnecessary comments about my corsets and weapons, I counted to ten in my head to keep from hitting him. Lyris awkwardly suggested we go to the pub for a quick drink, and I accepted her offer without looking at him again.

I finished the rest of my drink, letting the mug clunk

against the countertop. Rolling my neck back and forth to loosen the muscles, I sighed through my nose. Lyris chuckled, holding her own stein to her mouth.

"What?" I asked, squinting my eyes at her.

"Pax really gets on your nerves, doesn't he?"

"He's a Guard. They have no social courtesy," I muttered, staring at the stein.

"I don't know. He's pretty socially adept. I think the two of you have a lot of ignored sexual tension."

I let out a single bark of laughter. "I'm sure he'd love that. He's been bossing me around for weeks now. Maybe it's all just a sexual need."

"Bossing you around or keeping you alive? Because I'm certain you won't be able to see the difference."

I glared at her. "And what do you mean by that?"

She sent me side-eye, but stayed quiet by taking another drink. I rolled my eyes and searched for the bartender. A man with tightly curled horns leaned against the counter beside us. He gave us both a once over and suggestively smiled over his shoulder but got the hint when neither of us smiled at him, just stared until he became uncomfortable and looked for the bartender too.

Returning my attention to Lyris, I said, "I've taken care of myself for years. I don't see how it's any different now."

"Because something is missing in your life and Gerennt isn't a friendly country. You are just extremely suspicious," Lyris pointed out.

I raised my eyebrows in agreement before sliding the stein to the bartender and repeated my order. I saw a change in Gerennt since I started as a Merchant. Customers were quicker to rip you off, suspecting you were doing the same. Veks didn't want Drao Merchants doing business in their shops. The Council's negative influence over an already rocky country was becoming dangerous. The divide was found everywhere.

"Doesn't mean I don't have fun. It also doesn't mean I'm not careful."

"We both know you're only careful enough not to kill those horses. Your safety doesn't cross your mind often. Don't think Pax didn't mention what happened with Janna last night."

"Of course he did," I said with an eye roll. "Guard training is different from a Merchant. Janna was decent as a guardian. She's strict when it comes to her training. To her, I've failed the first rule of being a Merchant, never give up a weakness. I let the Council take my pyx and now they're using it against me. Pax doesn't get that."

"We both know that isn't how it happened. And to point out the obvious, there are better ways to punish you. Especially since you're Janna's prized pony." Lyris rolled her own eyes. "You're an adult that has travelled alone for years. She shouldn't be punishing you for anything."

I shrugged. "I was her apprentice. Even if she disowned me, that can never change. I assume she still feels some sort of responsibility. Doesn't Tian give you trouble for things occasionally?"

"Tian and my brother are travelling the country. I haven't seen her since the birds first sang at the beginning of the year. But my mentor was a lot nicer to me as a child than yours."

"I hadn't seen Janna for almost two years. Trust me, I was happy with it."

"Why did you go? It's her territory. You were just asking to run into her."

I shrugged. "The pay was good. Plus, I was trying not to be noticed. I also got it before everything happened. Obviously, I was wrong."

Lyris snorted, finishing her drink. "Do you want to go back to the inn? Or should we get drunk and let you rant a little longer?"

My head dropped back, and I stared at the roof. Staying

here seemed like a better choice. I was sore from riding and my healing wounds. Every time Pax glanced at me, it was like he thought I lost my mind. But he insisted we needed to leave before the sun rises tomorrow morning.

"I guess we should leave. I don't like carrying this thing around after dark." I tapped the cage over my shirt.

Seeing us stand, the bartender came over. We handed what we owed and thanked him.

"You're lucky you were tasked with something so easy to get," Lyris commented.

"Maybe, except what I have is murderously valuable," I said in a mumble.

Weaving through the pub's crowd, I could feel eyes staring. In every town but Jova, two Merchants weren't seen together. It caused attention and greedy minds started wondering what was so valuable nearby. Delf wasn't a normal town and being on the edge of the Forest of Som caused more curiosity. Maybe we should have reconsidered wearing leathers that helped identify us as Merchants.

"People are staring," Lyris commented as we stepped outside. "I'm sure those men would happily help you destress from Pax and his attitude. A few of the ladies, too."

I rolled my eyes at her dramatics. "I'm sure that'd go over well. He'd probably hunt me down and drag me back to the inn."

"I'd like to watch him fight for your honour," she said. "That would be very attractive."

Stepping around a crowd outside of another pub, I scowled at her. She shrugged dramatically, sticking out her lower lip but broken into laughter. The sound broke my serious expression, and I started laughing too. A night of drinking made her skin glow a little, looking a little more awake, and my concern diminished.

Most buildings were still open, shops still getting customers and restaurants still feeding people. The drunks were spilling into the street, slumped on the ground and talking to themselves. One person was lying on some grass with a ball of fire spinning over their head. I wasn't even sure if they were awake.

Starting down the lamp-lit road, I slid my hands into my pant's pockets. Nights were getting colder. Autumn lasted a long time in Gerennt, much to my pleasure. We walked in comfortable silence, staying alone in our own slightly drunk thoughts. The night smelt like rain and the residual smoke in the air. The dark magick of Som slithered into town, giving an almost peppery smell to the air.

Each step around me caught my attention, and I picked up on bits of conversations. Lyris was too. Either born with it or it trained into you, Merchants were aware of everything.

Ahead of us, some pebbles clattered across the sidewalk. Unfortunately, I made eye contact with a man being serviced in an alleyway. He was enjoying it enough to have knocked away some rocks. Lyris snorted, covering her mouth, having seen it too. I knocked her with my elbow and we both started giggling.

Being raised to think all Merchants did was trade and sell items, Janna gave me a very different opinion of being a Merchant. Merchants were no longer a simple aspect of life in Gerennt. They supplied the public, but kept the underworld of Gerennt thriving, too. It would be so easy to let an ego to grow.

"Excuse me, ladies."

We slowed our pace, glancing back. Nobody was behind us or anywhere around. The spot of road we stood on was quiet, in the shadow between two lampposts. We exchanged an unsure glance, but continued to walk. Maybe the call wasn't for us.

Turning forward again, I stumbled to a stop. Two hulking men appeared mere feet from us. They almost looked like twins, tall with dark hair, except one was hulking and the other was severely underweight.

Next to me, Lyris gasped and her hands shot up in surprise. My foot stepped back, but I was halted when a hand clamped around my throat. Knocked off balance, he yanked me towards him. My hands scratched at his, yanking at his fingers, opening my mouth to scream, but it was filled with a rag. Next to me, Lyris was trying to scream around the fabric shoved in her own mouth. The horrible scent triggered my poison's knowledge.

As the name manifested in my mind, my eyes couldn't stay open any longer.

CHAPTER 30

The discomfort of an aching neck woke me up. I didn't know how long my chin was pressed against my chest, but a headache pounded through me like someone took a hammer to my skull.

Trying to open my eyes, my eyelashes were pressed down. Whatever was over my head was scratchy, tight, and making me claustrophobic. Lifting my head and adjusting my shoulders to loosen the tension, it didn't surprise me that my wrists were tied together with the same fabric. Though it was surprising, my hands were in front of me. Using my thumbs to push the blindfold up, I expected to be inside some empty building.

Instead, I was surrounded by treetops so thick that the sunlight barely seeped through. The weeds, both dead and alive, were tall and any small creatures were invisible to the eye. Where I sat at the base of the tree was clear, like most of the other tree bases. Fog was slithering through the plants and along the ground. A sense of dread ran through me as my brain accepted where I was.

The Forest of Som. Regular citizens weren't allowed beyond the enchanted fence. Expensive products meant only for Drao could be procured here and I stayed far away from them. I wouldn't reject them if they fell into my hands, but I would do a transaction quickly. People murdered each other over what comes from this forest.

Trying not to move my head too much, I scanned the area. Male voices could be heard, but I wasn't sure how far away. Not letting my eyes focus on anything in particular, I tried to gauge the distance. In my peripheral vision, I caught movement.

Glancing down, my heart jumped in my chest as a giant snake passed by. Having disturbed it with my slight movement, the snake lifted its head and looked at me. It didn't seem interested in such easy prey, giving me a blank look of boredom, and I pressed my tongue against the roof of my mouth as it continued by. I wasn't afraid of snakes, but its body was thicker than my leg and the scales were the size of cherries. I didn't want to know how big its teeth were.

A few trees away, dry weeds crackled. My heart jumped, but I looked carefully. Grunting, Lyris sat up with her hands tied and a blindfold over her eyes. She began coughing as the potion wore off, drying her throat. Not knowing where she was, she wasn't being quiet, and I leaned to the side, trying to get a peek at the men who brought us here.

From the small amount of light, it was still daytime, but a live fire came into my sight, keeping away any unwelcome creatures with flames and smoke. Lyris groaned again, mumbling to herself. I couldn't tell if it was all the shadows, but her skin was looking worse.

The men finally noticed her noises. One of them grunted as he stood and his feet thundered against the forest floor. I dropped my head, leaving the blindfold pushed up.

Once my gaze was lowered, I noticed my feet were tied too. Fighting and running weren't options. Feet got closer to me, and before they could do anything, I raised my head. Two men stood between Lyris and I, only one facing me.

Both were grungy and gross, their layers of clothes were drenched in dirt and sweat. It wasn't the ones who grabbed us and I couldn't see Guards letting these men wander freely around Delf.

The lankier of the two reached down and pulled Lyris's blindfold from her eyes. Her face scrunched, adjusting to the light before realising where she was. Keeping my eyes on her, I let no emotions slip through as she looked from me to the men with wide eyes.

"So," the other man said, staring down at me.

His face was covered in fresh scratches. Dried blood bubbled along the wounds.

"You two ladies are going to tell us where your stash is. Then you're free to go."

Lyris and I made eye contact with blank expressions. Stash?

"Come now. We know you're Merchants. It's a little obvious. And from your eyes." He pointed at Lyris.

"And how your eyes look right now." He pointed at me. "I know you're both Drao. And Drao Merchants have the best goodies."

Falling into the same mindset as me, Lyris maintained eye contact and no expression. To anyone else, her eyes were bright yellow. But after knowing her for so long, the colour was duller than usual. I knew what they saw, referring to my eyes.

Stressful situations triggered something, and my blue eyes darkened to almost black. My under eyes felt warmer than normal, the sign that my skin was appearing grey. My parents told me when I was a little kid, a Drao put a curse on me because my father fell in love with my mother. Other than getting weird looks sometimes, it never really affected my life and I didn't question the story.

"Are you going to tell us the easy way to find where your goodies are?" The fatter man bent in my face.

My stomach rolled, and my mouth filled with saliva. He hadn't bathed in months. Food and other things between his teeth. I contained my disgust, locking my teeth together to stop the vomit from coming out. Gaining control over myself, I looked past his shoulder.

Receiving no answer from me, the man sighed. "Alright. We'll find a harder way."

He stood up with a grunt and a loud crack of his knees. The lankier man smirked maniacally at his partner. They looked at each other and seemed to have a silent conversation. Both nodded and the lankier man stuck his lower lip out and rocked his head to the side. Lyris and I looked at each other while the conversation happened. Stepping around his companion, the fatter man dealt with Lyris. Her eyes widened as the man grabbed her upper arm.

Being dragged past me, her whole body shifted awkwardly and she didn't get a chance to get her feet underneath her. The fabric of her pants caught on weeds and sticks, tearing from how roughly she was being treated. The whimpers coming from her mouth made me bite down on my tongue. Coming to her defence would make this worse. Merchants travelled alone for a reason. If the companionship between us was revealed, they would likely use it against us later. Even if I wanted to kill the man for what he was doing, I had to keep myself quiet. The lanky man watched them disappear behind trees and tall grass with a glimmer in his eye before walking up to me and crouched in my face.

"We'll have a little fun before you tell me where your stash is," he said, a grin on his face.

Like his cohort, his teeth were in disgusting condition. I could count at least four missing. Rocking back and forth, he got closer to my face to intimidate me.

But I kept a blank expression, looking past him into the dark forest. He inhaled bitterly, not like he wasn't getting a reaction. With more intelligence than I expected him to have, he recovered quickly once he realized I wasn't giving him what he wanted. Lanky's disgusting breath warmed my cheek as he reached behind him.

A small pin was attached to his collar as he moved. A silhouette of a raven. Vek Merchants. And not the good kind. They weren't good kidnappers, either. If one of them wasn't inches from my face, I could work my hands and feet out of the bindings. I'd be more likely to run away than fight because it wasn't a one-on-one situation. There were at least five others sitting around the fire, and I probably wouldn't survive.

Lanky revealed a small dagger and placed the tip under my chin. I didn't break eye contact with him. I didn't want to think about the last time it was cleaned.

"This is my last time asking. Where's your stash?"

I considered spitting in his face. But a piece of Janna's advice stuck out to me. She burned into my brain to hold my tongue until the day I die. Never give people what they want. I had scars on my inner thighs from that lesson.

Lanky huffed. "Fine."

He drew the dagger down my neck, then across the collar of my shirt. Keeping direct eye contact, the tip dug into my skin. Allowing myself a long blink, I used the extra time to internalize the pinch. With a sharp jerk, Lanky sliced across my collarbone. My jaw clenched to hold back a vocal reaction.

Opening my eyes again, my heart pounded as the fabric of my shirt stuck against the cut. He smiled, noticing the twitch of my jaw. Keeping the blood-covered blade against my skin, he twisted his wrist to run it up my neck. He purposefully caught my skin again before holding the blade in my field of view. My blood rolled to the hilt.

"Do you have anything to say?"

I shifted my jaw forward, not moving my eyes. He huffed with childlike frustration and it was rewarding to see. In a new tactic, he roughly grabbed my hands and lined his blade against the back of my hand.

"I bet you know how to use a sword. You people need to defend themselves. What'd you do if I damaged your hands beyond repair? I'm sure your life would be ruined."

The sting of the blade pressing across the bones and tendons forced my jaw to lock. Blood began pooling instantly. I focused on the curves in the bark as he moved the blade to my next finger.

Shouting from around the firepit drew our attention, our heads snapping at the commotion. I couldn't see clearly, but even crouching, Lanky could. His jaw dropped, eyes wide with fear. Rising slowly, he stepped back with a tight grip on the dagger. With Lanky's attention gone, I leaned on my hip, trying to see what was happening on the other side of the tree.

A flash of tan fur could be seen through the weeds, and I knew. Walking through the camp and fog was a fully grown sabertooth tiger. The tiger's fangs gleamed in the bit of sunlight and my back smacked against the tree. Now I was afraid. The creature was probably hungry, and the boisterous voices of the men drew her in. I peered up at Lanky, seeing if he had a plan, but he was frozen, unblinking. Useless.

The men screamed for somebody to take out the creature. I turned again, trying to see if anyone was doing anything. She paced around, waiting for something to happen. A man lunged for the tiger, snapping the rest of the Merchants out of their daze to scramble for weapons. He lost the fight with his ill-thought out move. The tiger ripped his arm away.

I twisted my wrists to loosen the bindings, watching the feline move around. I hoped the blood covering the tiger's face masked the little bit trickling from me. The weapons in the hands of trembling men were no match for the tiger. It was pathetic.

Lanky forgot about me entirely. In a sense of duty that

most of his group probably didn't feel, he started walking towards his dwindling crew with a hand raised. Watching the two threats, I began pulling at the knot with my teeth.

One man stumbled over the burning fire pit as a more unlucky man tripped with the sabertooth tiger's eyes locked on him. He attempted to scurry backwards, but it was a weak attempt and he was the next target. With a single pounce, the tiger landed against his chest. The knot fell away from my wrists as his throat was ripped out. Blood sprayed across the weeds, barely moving them with the weight. The Merchants continued screaming at each other and with the death of another cohort, they finally ran.

Lanky followed the mob, yelling and disappearing into the forest. Apparently, I wasn't valuable enough to grab before they made a dash. Reaching for my ankles, I was grateful the knot was much looser than my wrists, and I got my finger through in little time.

My body stiffened when a low growl vibrated through my bones. It was closer than before. In a jerk reaction, I scrambled back until I hit the tree and held my breath. Over the fading yells, the dry ground crunched under heavy paws. Pressing my head against the bark harder, the sabretooth tiger came into view. Her shoulders rolled as she stalked towards Lanky, who seemed to find every single stick and rock hidden in the undergrowth to trip over.

The tiger launched, and I blinked once as the lanky man hit the dirt. In the single movement her head made, he died. The men used their companion's death as a last opportunity to run. Lanky's skull was crushed between the tiger's jaws, bits of human spraying out. The tiger lifted her head, blood and flesh hanging from her jowls. She lowered her head again, but the man's sickening odour hit her and she pulled away, letting out a sneeze-like sound.

Unable to take my eyes off the predator, I reached for my ankles, tugging at the remaining knot. The wounds on my hand and shoulder pulsed. The first knot was easy and the second one wasn't complicated, only tight. Nibbling on my lower lip, I weaselled my fingers under the rope and forced the knot loose.

The blood made my fingers wet, and it soaked the rope. The hemp dug into the wound on my fingers as I lost grip and the raw skin on my ankles. A pained hiss slipped between my teeth, my eyes snapping down to the fabric. A grumble vibrated in the air.

Barely moving, I straightened my back, already feeling the tiger's gaze. I shortly met her topaz eyes framed with blood-soaked fur. The sabertooth huffed, abandoning her easy meal. I was relatively calm seeing other people die. But watching death approach me as an elegant cat? I could've thrown up my heart.

The tiger stopped inches away. Her reeking breath washed against my face. I couldn't stop myself from meeting her gaze. Her nose pressed against my shoulder, her fur brushing against my skin.

Shutting my eyes, I pushed my tongue against the roof of my mouth to stop the sob that was building. Did she want to play with her food, hoping I'd run like the others?

The tiger bumped my unwounded shoulder with her nose. She pulled back and the look in her eyes was different. Almost docile, no longer hungry. With my heart still pounding hard enough in my chest to make me dizzy, I hoped my imagination wasn't making it up. She let out another softer chuff, her tail flicking behind her. The tiger took a small step back and, as if I could suddenly understand her, I knew I would not be attacked.

CHAPTER 31

A THUNDERING OF HORSE HOOVES ECHOED THROUGH THE underbrush. The sabretooth tiger leapt back in surprise, growling as her head whipped around. It was a terrifying noise that I felt in my core.

glancing around, I spotted the moving shadow as it got closer. Appearing from between the trees, Neem with her ears pinned low with Pax on her back, his sword drawn. Upon seeing the predator crouched on the ground, Neem reared on her back legs and whinnied, kicking in self-defense. The tiger hissed aggressively, showing off her deadly teeth before running away. I watched her tail disappear into the weeds, my fingernails digging into my ankles. I didn't move during the entire exchange.

Staring into the darkness where the sabretooth had gone, my heart still pounded against my eardrums and chest. The sound of boots colliding with the ground broke through the daze, startling me, and my head whipped around. Pax dropped next to me, frantic as he looked me over with his hands hovering in the air. His hair was a mess from riding at full speed.

"Are you hurt?"

Through the nauseous feeling of my life being at risk twice in the space of ten minutes, I smirked at him. "I'd like to say this isn't my blood, but I've been tied up on the ground the whole time. Couldn't inflict much pain from here."

"Where's Lyris?" He asked, straightening his spine to look around.

The last of the shock wore off and the realization hit that I heard nothing from Lyris. My fingers went back to fighting with the knots, my eyes continuing to look away and searching for her.

He pushed my hands away and my legs fell apart as he cut the rope away. Shoving myself up to my feet, I launched off in the direction Lyris was dragged, but I couldn't even get from sitting to kneeling. My legs felt like jelly. Pax grabbing my shoulders and holding me down.

"Whoa, Owyn, stop. Stay down. You're bleeding and your wounds are dirty." I pushed his hands away, my legs flailing to move. "Stop moving!"

My body went rigid, and a hiss slipped through my teeth as he swiped across the cut on my collarbone. Pax mumbled an apology as I ignored, continuing to push past him. Unfortunately, he had all his strength and blood and I wasn't winning.

"They took her away. They went that way. I don't know where she is," I mumbled.

"Owyn." Pax put my face between his hands, forcing me to look at him. "We have to go. Let me clean your shoulder up and then we need to leave. We don't have time to look for her."

My eyes twitched across the trees, looking for some movement. All the Vek Merchants ran, and I didn't know if they took Lyris with them. Yanking my head back, my hands cupped around my mouth.

"Lyris!"

Pax slapped his hand over my mouth, looking around

frantically. "What're you doing? Are you trying to get us mauled? I just chased a sabretooth away from you! There's a lot worse here other than a giant cat."

I shoved against his chest with my hand and only when both my shoulders shot forward did I remember my wrists were still tied together. Having a moment of clarity, I held my wrists out to him and raised my eyebrows expectantly. With a shake of his head, Pax cut my hands free. Like my ankles, the skin was raw. It wouldn't feel good for a while.

He grabbed my wounded hand and reached for something in his jacket pocket. Seeing he was distracted, I knocked him backwards. As he hit the weeds and dirt, I scrambled to my feet and something close by skittered away from the disturbance. The world around me began spinning as my feet flattened under me. Trying to run to where the fat Merchant and Lyris went out of sight, everything slanted in front of me.

My upper body slammed into a tree and another wave of nausea hit and this time, I couldn't hold it down. My fingernails dug into the bark as whatever alcohol and food left in my stomach spewed onto the forest floor. Weakly wiping my mouth with my sleeve, my heart dropped when I realized Lyris wasn't here. Whipping my head around, I placed both hands on the tree as I got dizzier. There were no signs of her. Hands grabbed my waist, keeping me steady. I was already halfway back to the ground without knowing.

"Owyn, I'm sorry. We need to go right now! I had to barter to get in here. The guards will only allow us a short time to come back through the gates."

Unable to respond through the panic inside my head, he could pull me back towards Neem. Whatever potion was inside my system kept me in a dizzy fog, as I wanted to keep looking for Lyris. For a moment, there was clarity and I was on the saddle. Slipping back under, I felt a slight pressure on my back as Pax rested behind me. A weight inside my head had me slumping forwards, and I closed my eyes, expecting the jerking shock of falling off the horse.

"Owyn, listen to me," he said in a calm voice, and my eyelids opened a little. We were thumping up and down as Neem ran through the forest. "Do not make eye contact with any of the Guards, okay? Keep your head down."

I nodded, hearing the words, but didn't really understand them. A pressure around my waist adjusted and a rush of warm air shot across my neck. The weight of my head was too much, and it dropped back against the solid chest behind me. But I didn't care.

The world came back into focus when the sharp squeal of metal caught my attention. It was a monstrously large gate, entirely rusted, sliding open enough for Neem to slip through. Her tail barely passed through when it slammed shut. The quiet headache that was festering grew and suddenly, it felt like something inside my head was trying to escape from both sides.

A high pitch ringing began and my eyes instinctually shut to keep myself from throwing up again. The sound was familiar. A powerful source of magick was taking effect. The gates were reactivating to keep the nightmare-ish creatures out.

Neem slowed to a trot, and I opened my eyes carefully, now enveloped by significantly more sun than in the Forest. Five well armoured Guards were in front of us. They all looked mean, with deep scowls and broadswords resting on each of their shoulders. I'm sure they were working at the Som gates since they were old enough to walk.

Pax's instructions rang, and I dropped my head, letting a few strands loosely hang in my face. Did they not know who he rescued?

My eyes were aching from the dark magick inside the Forest. I'm sure being exposed to it without protection wasn't healthy.

"There's another woman in the forest. Her name is Lyris Pennev. She wasn't where my companion was and I didn't have time to find her. She doesn't know how to protect herself in the forest," Pax told the Som Guards. There were unspoken instructions in his words.

"Yes, sir."

My eyes flickered up instinctively at the feminine voice. I wasn't expecting any female Guards, especially around the Forest of Som. Through strands of hair, I made eye contact with the small woman in her layered metal uniform before looking away.

Pax kept his arm tightly around my waist as he instructed Neem to walk again. The swaying made my stomach turn, and I shut my eyes, focusing on breathing through the movement. None of us would appreciate it if I threw up on Neem.

"OWYN, WE'RE HERE."

The world stopped shifting, and I opened my eyes. We were at the other end of town, Delf's community stables in front of us. Black singe marks were across the wood, results of the firebugs swarming.

"I need to go back. I have to get Lyris," I said, feeling strong enough to speak.

"We can't go back. The gates are closed, and the magick is sealed. The Guards will find Lyris, okay?" Pax told me, rubbing his hand across my stomach. "I'm going to let go of you. I'll help you get down after me. Can you stay up?"

Getting down smoothly, he rested a hand on my thigh to help guide me across Neem's saddle. Underneath me, it felt like the horse was staying extra still, knowing I was a fall risk.

Once he was certain I would not fall, his hands shifted to my waist. I let him half lift me and place me down. My leg muscles vibrated uncomfortably from the impact, making me grip the leather saddle in fear of collapsing. His hands lifted from my waist and turned my head. My eyes opened when Pax quietly mumbled my name. His lips parted as if to say something, and the warmth of his palms woke me from the remaining daze. Leaning away from his hands, I felt uncomfortable from the intimacy.

"We should go," I muttered.

Mostly having my stability back, I walked into the barn. A single barn-hand was at the other end, tending to another of the horses. It was fairly quiet, with a few stalls occupied. Dill's head peeked over the stall door, already waiting. Sliding the wooden door, I expected her to step back and let me in. Instead, she continued to stare with patient concern.

"I'm fine. I'll do my best not to throw up on you," I assured her, running my hand down her neck as I moved around her.

Marr stood with his head in the straw bin, eating breakfast. Lyris's horse, Scholl, stood against the barn's wall. He barely glanced at me before gazing through the window at the back of the stall, knowing something was up.

"You," I called, re-entering the hallway.

The young man jogged over, standing at attention when he got close.

"That chestnut horse? If his owner, Lyris Pennev, doesn't return within three days, have this horse transported to Jova. Ask for Eira Khrom and tell her the owner's name. She'll claim him. Understand?"

The barn-hand removed a piece of parchment out of his pocket and, using a dense piece of lead, he scribbled out my instructions. He nodded after finishing. "Is that all?"

"Yes." He turned to go back to his work, but as I bent to grab my saddle, the barn spun around me.

"Wait," I called him back. "Put my saddle on my tan horse and the halter on the darker one."

He nodded, abandoning his prior task. Slumping against the timeworn wood, I shut my eyes and took deep breaths through my nose. Having my head feel clear again, I knew whatever potion the Vek Merchants used was still in my veins, even though throwing up helped a little. It was a hefty dose, and I still felt miserable. It was worse than being hungover. I groaned, bending to rest my hands on my knees, knowing I would need to throw up again.

"Miss? Your horses are ready."

I shoved my hand into my pesa pouch and...it wasn't there. Annoyance shot through me, knowing the Merchants took it while I was unconscious.

"Hold on," I grumbled, stomping outside. Pax stared down at his sword until he heard my footsteps and looked at me with an eyebrow raised. "Can I borrow some coins? I've got to tip the kid."

He nodded and pulled out a couple of smaller coins. Good enough.

I slapped them into the worker's hand as I took the reins. Leading the horses outside, Pax watched me carefully. He was waiting for me to fall apart again. Honestly, so was I.

Crappily typing Dill's reins to the hitching post, I attached Marr to the cart. Bending over to adjust a buckle, a lack of pull from around my neck made me realise I was missing something.

There was a shot of panic through my heart before I remembered where the cage was. Kneeling beside the cart, I rested my hand against the wood. In a risky spot just behind Marr's rear, a small compartment popped open.

As I reached for the chain, I paused and winced at how dirty my hand was. Peering down at my outfit, everywhere looked the same. I'm surprised the barn-hand spoke to me in the first place. Once out of Delf, I would clean myself up at the river, Knowing I'd need to look somewhat presentable going back into Jova.

"Are you ready to go?"

Clicking the compartment back into place and rising, I nodded. With the single rein of leather, I clipped Marr to Dill. I glanced at Pax across our horses. The scar along his face looked darker, almost bruised.

Seeing I was settled on my saddle and I would not topple over, Pax encouraged Neem to walk up the dirt road back into town and I stayed close behind.

CHAPTER 32

Town buildings were coming back into view as two Guards on horseback drew closer, restricting us from going around them. We slowed, expecting them to step off the path, but they stopped.

The clouds moved in the wind, revealing the sun again. Dill shifted, rays shooting directly into her eyes. The sunlight hit the metallic cage, and the shine caught the Guards' attention. Knowing it would look suspicious, I didn't move to hide it, instead keeping a neutral face and a tight grip as Dill got comfortable with the growing light. The men's gazes left my necklace and flickered to the cart behind the three horses.

"Can we help you?" Pax asked. Neem stepped forward to draw attention.

"We have a few questions for yourself and your travelling companion," a younger Guard said, his honey coloured hair pushed back as if it sat under a helmet for a long time.

"Okay."

Unexpectedly, the Guards dismounted their horses, and anxiety jumped inside me. I glanced at Pax, unsure what to do. Only able to see a quarter of his face, I could barely see him stare at the Guards. Thankfully, he peered over long enough to shake his head once. Okay?

The duo passed Neem entirely, more interested in me and my animals. The other Guard, older than his partner, with more wrinkles and darker hair, reached for Dill's reins. She attempted to step away, but Marr, too close, let out a neigh of discomfort.

I told him to back off when a blade plunged into the old Guard's neck. A pause of shocked silence filled the trail before he dropped. In the next second, the light-haired Guard's sword was out and Pax was next to him.

I moved off the saddle when Pax barked, "don't".

He and the living Guard circled each other with their swords drawn. As if the potion was gone from my system, I shifted to sit properly into the saddle, tugging Dill to move her and Marr back a few paces.

On the opposite side of the fight, Neem did the same by herself. My eyes flickered between her and the exchange. If she ran, I couldn't catch her. As Pax's sword swung, my heart jumped to my throat as it clanged against the Guard's. The two Guards' horses uncomfortably stepped back, disturbed by the clang of metal.

The bright sunlight made watching the Guard's sword clash against Pax's sword clear to see. A gasp slipped out at the deadly move as I waited for Pax to topple over. But when he continued to circle, my pounding heart fell from my throat as I noticed his leather chest plate. It had an obvious slash in it but had taken the brunt of the metal. The motion left the Guard's neck vulnerable.

From his years of Council's Guard training, Pax knew his options, and the answer was clear as his jaw shifted. Stepping into optimal range, he swung across the Guard's neck. The blade connected, but the young man barely registered it with only a jolt of his head before swinging again at Pax. It was a weak swing, though. Pax only needed to take a single step back. The Guard's arm lazily dropped, unable to hold up his sword. Along with the blood now pouring from his neck, it bubbled from his mouth as he coughed. With a few ugly sounds, he crumpled like a bag.

We stared at the men, their blood soaking the dirt. It was over. Carefully I dismounted Dill, watching for a reaction. Toeing around the mess and staying far away from the sweat soaked Pax, I grabbed the younger Guard's armpits. Tugging, I ignored the discomfort shooting through my body. It was the only way I could get him off the road without falling over, too.

"What're you doing?" Pax asked in a grumble, putting his sword back in its sheath.

"You said we have to leave," I said, keeping my voice even. "We need to move them out of the road or we won't be leaving Delf anytime soon."

Being so close to the dead Guard's face, it was clear just how young he was. He looked around Torna's age. His skin was dirty but no wrinkles or sunspots, probably having started patrolling the Som Gates within the last few months. I thought of his family, either in Delf or in another town of Gerennt.

They wouldn't know their son was dead. If they found out, it wouldn't be for months. I rested the body far enough into the brush that he couldn't be spotted right away. It would be when he smelled he would be found.

Pax pulled the other Guard to the opposite side of the road. He stared down at the dead man. Guilt bit at me as I stepped back into the road, being the reason Pax killed his comrades. I kicked the dirt off the road around, trying to disguise the blood a bit.

It dawned on me how unresponsive I was to death. I turned into the final form of a Merchant, not sure how I felt about it at the moment. I peeked at Pax again as he joined me. My hand raised, intending to rub his arm in comfort, but he moved away, avoiding the contact. He didn't look at me as he went back to Neem.

We rode in silence, following the main road to Delf's gates. I couldn't stop looking at Pax. For once, the quiet wasn't soothing. It let my anxiety and guilt grow. Maybe it was the fact he didn't want to talk or acknowledge me, but I was itching to know what was inside his head.

The Guards at the gate, less concerned with protection than their companions at the Forest gates, barely looked at us. Being covered in grime and blood wasn't a cause for a conversation. I was almost tempted to stop and ask them what happened in Delf for how I looked not to be concerning.

But outside the gates and crossing the wide bridge that reached the other side of Histlea River, the magick hovering over Delf cleared. My need for confrontation was gone, all that was left was the body aches and tense muscles. The skin hidden under the bandage around my stomach was itching, making me uneasy that the Forest of Som's dark magick reversed the healing potion.

Eventually, the weight of my continuous stare caused him to look over, and Pax sighed in defeat when we made eye contact. Adjusting himself on the saddle, he cleared his throat and gazed at the road ahead. He waited for the river's roaring to quiet a little before talking.

"That was the first time I've been back since I was eighteen." My eyebrows twitched in surprise. I didn't consider where he was from.

"My parents were royal supporters. Believed Gerennt should still be under their rule and the Council was created for rich people to have power without consequences. As you know, the Council frowns on that belief and punishes anyone who thinks it. I was ten when my parents were exposed. Don't know how. No one ever said. Guards were sent to kill my parents, but maybe history or their own amusement, they left them alive and used them instead.

Illegal stuff mostly. Took their only child, though. I was kept in Delf, probably because they had no way of sending me anywhere else. My parents were ordered not to contact me. Could walk past me, talk to people I was with, be in the same shop but were to never look or speak to me. When I think back, I'm surprised I wasn't taken to be a Som Guard. But there's some honour in being a Council's Guard, even a low one at the Som gates," he said, with a self-deprecating smirk, his head dropping forward. "They left me at a blacksmith. I don't know how they convinced him to take me. I'm sure there was some sort of exchange or payoff. Or he just wanted someone to beat. But that's where I was for six years." Pax paused, dropping his head to avoid a low-hanging branch.

"How did you leave?" I asked, the question coming out as a whisper.

"The blacksmith figured if he was stuck with me, might as well put me to work. When I was sixteen, the Chief Guard rode through Delf. He ordered a sword from the blacksmith I was at. No idea why he came to pick it up himself. The blacksmith smacked me for not getting the sheath fast enough. The Chief Guard was impressed with my obedience as a teenage boy. He didn't realize I was hit so many times, I was numb to it. Especially on that side of my face." I knew he was referring to his scar. "Ultimately, the blacksmith offered me up, asking for almost nothing. A few messo, maybe. The Chief Guard said he could always use assistants."

He glanced over, checking that I was still listening and I was hanging onto every word, unable to look away.

"I came back two years later, weeks into my official Guard training. Wanted to see my parents. I thought maybe they would apologize." Pax shrugged. "I got through the gates, and it hit me how bad the idea was. I realized I didn't want an apology. I wanted my eight years back. Got to the road where my parents' house was, I saw them sitting with two children. Their children. They replaced me, like the blacksmith always said."

He fell silent, and I waited for him to continue, noticing he never said the blacksmith's name. But when his lower lip jutted out a little, it told me he was done. I tried imagining Pax fifteen years ago. I assumed his hair was just as shaggy, even curlier. The image of a sad, deserted ten-year-old I created broke my heart.

"You never have to go back there again," I told him.

I wasn't sure if I was telling the imaginary child or the actual man riding with me. He released a shuddered breath, and I glanced across the space to see him looking at the saddle but with a smirk.

A tear run down his cheek as he nodded mindlessly. Whether he agreed or was letting me know he really heard them, I didn't know. Pax glanced at me, and the smirk softened.

ATTACHING DILL AND MARR TO THE HITCHING POST, I HAD A sense of relief. No more personal nightmares. From here until Jova, I was safe. Opening the creaking cart door, I took out my coin purse. I grabbed a handful of pesa coins and a small hip bag to keep them in.

If the Vek Merchants broke into my cart, I wasn't sure how much pesa I would have to my name. I knew there was some stashed at Eira's townhouse, but it couldn't be much.

"We can finish the ride today, but I hate getting to Jova on an empty stomach. Some of those sweets shops by the gates are too tempting," I said, slinging my bag of clothes and toiletries over my shoulder.

Pax chuckled, holding out his hand. "Lead the way."

I opened the door to the warm inn, a wave of spices

flowing over me. Voices could be heard from the dining room, as could the smell of a fire in the library.

At the front desk, a dainty girl with pale blonde hair sat on the top, watching a large feather hang in the air. I smirked as the feather did figure eights and spun around her head like a bird. She seemed bored, head held up by her hands, elbows against her knees. Pax's eyebrows met on his forehead as he watched her, too.

"Pardon me…" he started, but I raised my hand.

I adjusted the strap across my back. "Table for two, if you've got it."

She lifted her hand and flicked it to the side. Her illuminating blue eyes never moved from the feather. Over the chatter in the pub, two chairs scraped against the ground. A small candle's flame on the table shot over a foot in the air. I glanced at Pax, indicating for him to follow.

"How'd you know to do that?" Pax quietly asked as we stepped into the next room.

"I've been here before. She doesn't really talk to anyone. Pretty sure Gerna has only spoken to her about ten times in seventeen years."

Once we sat, the flame extinguished with a sizzle. I draped my bag over the back of the chair. Pax doing the same but did not look away from me. "Gerna?"

"The owner. I think she's owned the inn for fifty years."

As the words left my mouth, the back of my neck went cold and I knew I was heard. A chuckle slipped from my lips, and I peered back as footsteps approached.

"Young lady, how dare you age me like that in public?" a sharp voice scolded.

The grey-haired woman glared down at me with hands on her hips, and lips pursed. Gerna didn't age a day since I last saw her six months ago. I'm sure she didn't age in the eight years I knew her.

"Might as well tell him the truth before you swindle him into staying here forever," I said, standing.

I bent slightly at the waist to wrap my arms around her shoulders. The spices I smelt radiated from her.

"I'll have to get to know this young man a bit before I convince him of that," Gerna said, releasing me.

The corners of my lips tightened as I held in a smile.

"Gerna, this is Pax. He's travelling with me back to the Isle. Pax, meet Gerna, the lively and very youthful owner of the Som Inn." Pax nodded in greeting and Gerna did the same.

"I'll get you some soup. It will be damp out tonight and I'm sure you'll be halfway to Jova when you realise you should've stayed the night."

I thanked her and sat back down. With a quick glance around the room at the other occupants, I faced Pax, expecting questions. Except his skin looked grey and his hair was sticking to his forehead, profusely sweating.

Shifting to cover himself with his cloak, his leather chest plate was revealed, and it caught my attention. There was a jagged tear across the bottom. I saw the damage, but it didn't look that bad. He protested when I rounded the table and bent down next to him. Slapping his hands away, I yanked his cloak aside and nimbly unbuckled his chest plate. He didn't get out of the way like I thought.

The Guard's blade went straight through the leather, slicing Pax's abdomen. His grey shirt stuck to his torso, soaked in blood and sweat.

I glared up at him. His mouth was open, but he wasn't trying to apologize, he was trying to breathe. Tossing my bag over my shoulder, I grabbed Pax's too and his armpit, awkwardly dragging him to the front desk.

"I need a room," I snapped at the ditzy Drao. "Now!"

Unfazed by the attitude change, she swiped her hand

again and up a single set of stairs, a door slam open. Pax stumbled next to me, trying to keep his grunts of pain quiet. I slid my shoulder into Pax's armpit, wrapping my arm around his waist. How did I miss this before? I was too distracted by his story.

I directed Pax to remove his cloak at the bed's edge as I threw our bags on the second bed. With a dry throat, he finally tried to protest, but giving him a single glare, he shut up.

I rushed into the bathroom and grabbed the first aid box, knowing I should try to do something first before I called for a physician. Tossing it onto the bed, I finished taking his chest plate off. He hissed as some blood dried to the leather. I muttered weak apologies, but it was his fault he was like this. He should've said something earlier.

The blade didn't go deep enough that removing the plate made his organs fall out. That was good, at least. I grabbed a pair of scissors and with a flickered look at Pax's paling face; I cut open his shirt. I held the already soaked fabric to his abdomen, absorbing the blood from the irritated wound. His skin was darkening near the edges of the cut as his body tried to stop the bleeding.

"I'm going to help you lie down and then I'm cleaning this," I explained.

For the first time since I knew him, there was fear in his eyes and with the tears, it was hard to ignore. I was proud of myself for not breaking down, too. Kneeling on the bed behind him, I slid my hands under his armpits, cautiously lowering his torso onto the mattress.

I rushed back into the bathroom when he was settled. Feeling pressure against my throat that was causing panic, I frustratedly unbuckled the cloak and let it fall to the floor.

Picking up the small washing bowl, I waited impatiently for it to fill with water. It took longer than necessary due to continuously peeking out into the bedroom, making sure a dead body wasn't waiting for me. Grabbing a face cloth, I submerged it into the water.

After placing the pan carefully onto the bed, I worked on peeling back the ruined shirt. I had to block out the whimpers and closed mouth groans if I was going to do this. Resting my free hand against his hipbone to hold him down, I wiped carefully at the dried blood. I continuously whispered apologies as he shut his eyes and his face scrunched. My eyes jumped around his body, watching so many points to keep track if he was still breathing.

Dropping the stained cloth into the washing pan, my shaking hand grabbed the large healing elixir from my rucksack. He would still have to see a physician when we got back, but this would keep him alive for now.

"This is going to hurt," I warned, but didn't stop to let him think about it, removing the topper.

Biting on my lower lip, I let drops of elixir fall on his wound. Pax sharply inhaled and his eyes shot open, squirming to get away.

"No, no, no." I pushed on his shoulders, but he wasn't thinking clearly, overwhelmed by pain.

Doing what I could to hold him down and not dropping the bottle, I swung my leg over his lap. I fought to recap the bottle and when I got it, my hands were free to hold his shoulders still. Unexpected tears slipped down my face as I desperately waited for the elixir to make its way through his veins.

Pax's back slammed against the mattress unexpectedly, tears welling in his eyes. I rubbed my hand along his ribs to create another sensation for him to focus on. I was relieved to see the bleeding stopped. All his veins were closed and healing. I needed to drop a bit more elixir to be sure and then I could put on the potion I used on myself days ago.

Pax squirmed towards the top of the bed as he saw the

topper get removed again. I dug my hips into him, stopping him from going farther.

"I'm sorry, it's not as bad as the first time," I whispered, releasing a few drops.

As the elixir soaked into his skin, his eyes shut. His shaking hands grabbed my thighs and pressed his fingers into my legs. A wave went through him, making his body curl and instinctively yank me forward. I stared at the healing wound, forcibly ignoring the warmth generated from the friction. I was trying to save his life; I scolded my body.

With only his panting as the noise in the room, I grabbed the sealing potion. Resting one knee on the bed next to him, I leaned forward to get a better angle. I started asking what he was doing when Pax sat up a little, but he wrapped his hand around my other thigh and encouraged me to straddle him again. My cheeks burned. Doing what he wanted.

The muscles in his abdomen contracted as the potion brought the sides of his wound together. Knowing the process grossed me out, I looked at his face. His nose was crinkled as he felt the healing potion work. My thighs twitched when he started running his nails along my pants, causing the skin to rise. His chest glowed from the drying sweat as he caught his breath. Dirt and blood speckled across where his skin was exposed earlier.

Once the open wound turned into an angry red scar, I cleared my throat.

"How are you feeling?" I quietly asked.

He loosened his grip, but didn't remove his hands. Lifting his head, he looked at the scar before dropping his head back down.

"Like magick, just forced a hole in my body to close," he muttered in exhaustion.

Half my mouth turned into a smile, glad to hear sarcasm from him. "Good. Sit up, I'll bandage you."

Shuffling back to remove myself from Pax's lap, his grip

tightened on my thighs again. Having anchored my body to his lower half, he sat up with a loud groan. My heart thudded at the movement that ended with our chests touching. His warmth radiated through my shirt.

I took a deep breath. My gaze flickered to his bare chest. I never seen his scars so close and my fingers twitched with desire to run along them. Forcefully, I cleared my throat and grabbed the large roll of bandages from the first aid box. After unrolling the end, I wrapped my arms around Pax's torso.

"I can do it," Pax said.

Our chests bumped, and I was thankful he ignored the small whine that slipped from me.

"It's okay, I'm almost done."

Feeling his gaze, I forced my hands not to shake and finished wrapping. Leaning back, I could see the bandage better to adjust it. His fingers slipped upwards, fidgeting with the hem of my shirt before lightly brushing my stomach, and I peeked up to see his eyes squeezed shut. In silence, I snipped the bandage and taped it together.

"Done," I whispered, tossing the equipment behind him.

Pax didn't entirely release me, just loosened his grip to lean back on his elbow and assess my handy work. No longer concerned about his preeminent death, I allowed myself to shamelessly appreciate his shirtless chest for a second before trying to reel my feelings in and my gaze continued downwards. Wrong decision.

I was now staring at the dip of muscle into his pant line. The skin was smooth and appealing. I pinched my lower lip between my thumb and first finger, rolling the skin back and forth. My other hand gripped the first elbow to my body, holding in the temptation.

Pax sat up, my eyes drawing a line up his chest. Intentionally or not, his finger flexed on my hips and my heart skipped a beat. My lip popped out, and I jumped at the quiet sound of him clearing his throat. Gaze snapping up to his face, I realized I was staring for too long. I opened my mouth, and a sound came out, but not words.

Flooded with embarrassment, I tried to get up, but he gripped my jaw. My hands dropped to rest on his scarred chest, and the tip of my pointer finger fell on a scar along his collarbone. Absently, I traced it. He weakly coughed for my attention and my eyes snapped up to his face, expecting him to tell me to stop, but the heat in his eyes didn't say that, though.

Instead, I got an urge to kiss him, but he moved his head away and his hand flexed against my jaw. A shot of rejection ran through me. He didn't want to kiss me. He was holding me back. My hands slumped into my lap, my lower lip pouting. I felt silly. Could he just let me go?

His eyes snapped down to it and cleared his throat again, more strongly this time.

"Thank you for finishing my stitches," he said, his hand resting on my neck.

"You're welcome," I whispered.

When he didn't let me go, a shot of uncalled for confidence hit me and I placed his face between my hands. My thumb ran along his lower lip in the same moment his tongue shot out. A small gasp and a grumble were released from both of us at the contact. Pax sat up again, his hands still in the same positions, still pressing against the inside of my thigh.

"Are you sure you're done thanking me?" I whispered.

His hand swept my hair back, leaving my neck exposed. I watched his jaw flex a few times as his eyes ran up my neck and met my own.

"Are you sure? Even after all you've seen of me?" His grip on my neck twitched and my heart ached for his vulnerability. I angled his head up, my breath washed over his lips, and I raised myself higher on my knees.

"I haven't seen all of you."

Without another word, Pax wrapped his arms around me, yanking my torso flush against him. His lips pressed against mine. The world became blurry before I shut my eyes as electric charges surged through me. I latched my fingers into his curls, holding Pax where he was. He grunted in his throat, my eyes flying open.

Did I do something to his wound? His eyes were already open, surprised by the sound too. I smiled, tugging his hair playfully.

Pax bit his lip, a slight shake of his head in amusement. "You're right. I'm not done yet."

His lower lip was slick with saliva. It was alluring. Allowing the unnatural vulnerability to control me, I sucked his lip into my mouth and bit down. He released another throaty sound, almost like a growl. This one I didn't find amusing, my hips pressing into his, encouraging the fuzziness inside me.

His arms wrapped under me, standing. I gasped, stopping the kiss. I didn't expect the barely healed man to have strength and my hands clutched at his back. But the need in his eyes was like fuel. My mouth fell open as I was no longer wrapped around Pax. I bounced against the mattress, my arms splayed out to catch myself. He watched me with a satisfied smirk and one knee resting on the bed.

The pounding of my heart stopped for a beat as he shamelessly stared at my body. He froze on my waist, his hands resting on my ankles. I glanced down to see my dress flew up, revealing my legs and underwear. The mud caked on my dress and boots had me scrambling to sit up, but his light hold on my ankle tightened.

"What're you doing?" He asked, his voice gruffer than usual.

"I'm covered in dirt," I started. "I need to…"

"No, you don't," Pax said, tugging my legs, jolting me

back down. "I can't wait, knowing this feeling isn't just me. I almost died, you almost died. We're both close to expiring here."

Playfully, I rolled my eyes at him. He crawled up my body until our faces were even and my nerves melted at his words. He picked up my hand and my gaze unintentionally flickered to his bicep, the muscle shifting under his skin. His muscles weren't sharp and obvious, but toned and defined when he used them. The back of my hand touched his mouth, placing several light kisses against the skin. A smile slipped out from the gesture.

Releasing my hand to drop back to the bed, he gently kissed my cheeks and moved down my body, placing the occasional kiss. I couldn't hold back the ticklish wiggle when he stopped at my pubic bone. We made eye contact and he looked back with an intensity causing my whole body to shiver.

He stood, and the dominant look conflicted with questions. I sensed from his flexing grip against my calves that he wanted to take control, but he wouldn't until he knew it was okay.

Maintaining eye contact, I shuffled out of my dress to reveal a well loved corset. His eyes soaked up my newly revealed skin. His head dipped, and I felt disappointed when he only removed my boots and socks. A long scar ran up the inside of my calf and as he stood, his nose brushed against it. Then a soft kiss.

Eager for more contact with him, I all but ripped off my under corset. I'm sure I would've whined if it was more than clipped together. His hand gripped my bare ankle tighter, but was quick to disappear when I rolled onto my shins and held my hand out. He walked around the side of the bed, my upper torso following him.

The look in his eyes was softer as his hand slipped into

mine. With a small curl of my lips, I tugged lightly, silently asking him to join me. He didn't take the invite, instead yanking me towards him. Flying onto my knees, his other hand grabbed my waist to stop me from falling.

Our noses brushed, and I pushed on my tongue to the roof of my mouth, fighting to control the breath that wanted to rush out of my mouth. My free hand ran up his chest, fingertips catching in its hair as he started our kiss again.

Pax hummed, his lips pressing harder against mine. My hand splayed at the crook of his neck, pushing my thumb into his collarbone with his natural heat radiating against my palm.

As we chased to taste every inch of each other, my hand slid to the waistband of his pants. I was almost naked, and he still had pants and boots on. He put his now free hand behind my ear, but didn't intensify the kiss. He left this as my decision and that made my core temperature rise more. I was used to once an article of clothing was removed, it was a go. Pax's way made my thighs rub together.

I couldn't make rational decisions, my brain swimming in lust. With a finger, I followed the waistband to the string, holding them up. My other hand helped remove the knot.

As I did, Pax's hand on my waist slid lower, massaging the skin as he went. The material fell around his ankles and the final wall crashed down. Pax paused our kiss for a second to nuzzle our foreheads together.

Softly, he placed a kiss on each of my cheeks as he pulled at my underwear. His head pulled back for a moment and we both looked at each other, a meek smile on each of our faces.

Carefully, I was guided to my back. We were both still healing, after all.

A dull throbbing under his grip caught my attention, making me remember the ugly bruise still covering my side. I wiggled away from him, trying to hide it. His gaze moved down to where his hand rested. With just a twitch of his eyebrows, he bent down.

Flickering his eyes up for a moment, he placed kisses atop the bruise. The feeling of his lips and breath on my skin on the tender bruise created warm shivers. My head tipped back and my eyes fell shut as Pax kissed lower.

Chapter 33

My eyes fluttered open, being woken up by a satisfying tightness across my muscles. Releasing a content sigh, I turned my head to the side.

Pax lay on his back, mouth hung open as he quietly snored. I delicately ran my finger along his lower lip, remembering how during the night, I touched every part of Pax's body and he did the same to me.

It was like a fire every moment that reignited the more I thought about it. Now in the morning light, we didn't need to ravish each other. Soft and gentle fit the atmosphere. The tip of my finger ran along his scar. I felt how deep it was and understood how serious the wound was.

"If you keep that up, we're going to mess up the sheets again. It took us long enough to fix them last night," Pax mumbled, his eyes still closed.

I quietly laughed, letting my finger finish its trail to his chin before I laid my hand on his neck. The feeling of his pulse gave me a sense of comfort. My small smile disappeared, taking in his features over and over again.

"My parents were facing a bad growing season on the farm," I said, staring at his pouty lips. "They always used growth potions, but there hadn't been a lot of rain. The potions they used could only do so much. They needed something stronger if they were going to survive the season."

Pax opened his eyes. With a sliver of sunlight beaming across his face, he listened. I licked my suddenly dry lips.

"Janna was still a travelling Merchant at that point. She didn't do it often, but she had loyal customers." I was vocalizing my nightmares for the first time that I could remember. "My parents bought from her yearly, so she was who they requested the potion from. Two weeks later, Janna had it. They paid but didn't give a transaction fee. And for someone like Janna, you pay for her time too. She let it go because she was busy, but when she stopped by two months later and they gave her nothing, she was beyond insulted and told my parents they had five days to get enough pesa to pay the potion's fee again with a generous transaction fee. They didn't get any of it. I don't know if they tried. Instead, they offered their first-born daughter to cover the debts. I didn't know any of this when it happened. Janna told me years later and my parents confirmed it."

Pax's hand came into view and wrapped it around mine. He nodded his head once, encouraging me to finish the story.

"I was thirteen. My mother said I had to stay home to help on the farm that day."

The memories flashed through my mind. Eating breakfast. Two huge Drao entered the kitchen ahead of my father, who didn't say a word. My mother, leaving the room. My screams begging for help, and tears echoed in my head. I peered at Pax, still watching me with wide eyes and weakly shrugging. Tears were swimming at my lash line, and I peered down to hide it.

"Did your sisters know?"

"No. I assumed they did and never cared, but Torna told me when we were there that my parents said I chose to leave. They thought I abandoned them."

His thumb rubbed against my hand, and I watched it. "I have a question. You don't have to answer if it's too much."

I nodded, knowing there were a lot of things he could ask about.

"Your apprenticeship." Pax paused, licking his lips. "Was it as miserable as I imagined?"

I opened my mouth, weighing the experience in my head. A chuckle thoughtlessly slipped out.

"I have a symbol burned into my shoulder that's recognizable across Gerennt. And most of my scars came from the few years in Verceen. How's that for an answer?"

A smirk grew across Pax's lips. "You know, your humour towards that situation is a little messed up?"

I grinned, laughing. "I know."

Pax released my hand, gripping my face instead. He pulled me forward, smiling into the kiss.

***

THE SUN WAS JUST HITTING THE TREETOPS WHEN WE FINALLY GOT the horses ready to finish the last leg of the highway. Running my hand across her mane, I could tell Dill was ready to not travel for a while and I couldn't blame her.

I wanted to lie in a bath for a week and then in bed for the week after that. A few blacksmiths I knew would be happy to give Dill and Marr a new set of shoes.

"What're you thinking about?"

I peered over my shoulder at Pax as he tightened the last buckles on the saddlebags. His hair was wet from a morning shower and slicked back on his head, except for a few curls that popped forward to frame his face. A wave of adoration swelled through my heart.

"How I'll be pampering the horses when I get back to Jova," I said, looking back at my well loved horse. She shook out her mane, agreeing with me.

"I should think about that, too."

"Don't Guards have official horse handlers?" I asked, lifting myself onto her back.

"They do, but most Guards have their own horse. There's more responsibility for you."

I chuckled. "Sounds like my father."

"What do you mean?"

I tossed my damp braid over my shoulder.

"When they bought Dill, she was entirely my responsibility. No exception. Unless I couldn't get out of bed from a deadly illness or something happened while I was at school, everything about her was my job."

"Weren't you eight years old when they bought Dill?"

I nodded. "Something like that."

He gave a single nod before settling on Neem's back with a grunt. With full stomachs thanks to Gerna refusing to let us leave with anything less, we returned to the highway.

Trees surrounded the inn like most of the way across Gerennt. Wild flowers carpeted the grass with small creatures sticking their heads up from underneath every once in a while. I never knew they were there. The air smelled like the time of year, either fresh or floral, or it was cold enough for nose hairs to freeze. It was always colourful scenery, and I never hated a second of it. Maybe that was what I got from my apprenticeship. An appreciation for nature and its beauty. Or I was seeing everything brighter this morning. I peeked at Pax and wondered if that was normal.

The quiet between us didn't need to be filled. It was a constant I was only truly appreciating now. I never ridden this far with anyone and truthfully, I always figured it would be painful. Maybe I could contribute my appreciation to the lack of traffic. Or it was the attention he gave me last night and this morning. Shaking my head to myself, I knew I would have to contain my cheerful mood soon. It wouldn't do any good on the Isle.

APPEARING FROM BEHIND THE TREES, THE GATES OF JOVA LOOMED over us. Music and voices poured out of the worn red gates.

The town was designed to have a market directly on the opposite side of the gates. It was a smart tactic. People arrived hungry every day. I fell victim to the tactic often. Ten feet ahead of the open gates, a handful of Guards were clustered at the edge of the roadway. Talking amongst themselves, their heads all turned and watched us get closer, hands on their belts. I nervously looked at Pax.

"They're here for me," he said with a sigh, rolling his shoulders. I saw him physically change back into a Guard.

Neem trotted ahead by a few paces as the Guards welcomed him back. A few of the men patted the horse's rear as Pax dismounted her. Dill continued past them slowly as I watched from the corner of my eye. He glanced over his shoulder, barely sending me a polite smile before joining in on the Guards' conversation.

I snapped Dill's rein, speeding her and Marr up, and ignored the loud whispers about the Drao Merchant. Pressure started behind my eyes as I passed under the shadow of the gates' arch. Okay. I guess that's done. His assignment ended at the gates. We didn't know each other anymore.

Children ran close to Dill's and Marr's hooves as they played in the streets. The school bell was still chiming across the bridge. They were free for the rest of the day. Some shops were closing as parents headed home to take care of their children. I nodded to familiar faces, feeling myself relax a little and fall back into the mentality I had most of the time, contained and professional. I didn't live in Jova, but I stayed with Eira enough that it was a familiar environment.

The wooden bridge across the Rinals River, connecting the Histlea River to the Ocean of Tepstow, generated a clicking sound under the wheels of Marr's cart. I would know it with my eyes closed.

A few more shops later was the turnoff for the communal stables. It was well kept and appeared to be gleamingly new, though it wasn't. Jova liked to focus on its presentation to its citizens. A smaller stable was nestled closer to the port at the other end of town, but this one was two stories and showed just how many people travelled through Jova.

Dill let out a thankful huff, knowing she was going to be treated like royalty. Even beside me, Marr trotted with a little more pep.

Outside the tall front doors, I dismounted Dill and removed my rucksack from her saddle. Berna, the head stable keeper, walked out of the barn and called to my horses. Her best and admittedly favourite clients.

"You work them hard?" she asked, running her hand down Marr's hair.

He huffed against her in appreciation. I sometimes thought he liked her more. He probably did, since she gave him most of the meals.

"It was a long trip for all of us," I answered, patting Dill's neck. "Give them the full package, yeah? They deserve it."

Berna nodded with amused eyebrows, waving over some of her subordinates to remove the cart from Marr. I placed a kiss on both horses' snouts and watched them be escorted into the barn. I wasn't worried. The stable had taken good care of them for years.

With my bag slung across my chest, I slid my hands into my pant pockets. The walk to Eira's townhouse wasn't long, so I took my time. Nodding to the shopkeepers I made eye contact with, I was determined not to stop. I wanted to get into my borrowed bed.

An elderly baker noticed me and a grin appeared on her face before grabbing a fresh bun off her cart and held it out. I smiled at her, taking the baked goods with thanks. The crystal I'd collected for her knee pain was still around her neck.

Finally, spotting the house I was looking for, my pace sped up. The ivy vines were as bushy on the stonework siding as when I left a month ago. I would have to trim those back soon or else it would start attracting salamander faeries.

Unlike the creatures I had the eggs of around my neck, salamander faeries made nests in their ideal spaces and when one got comfy, hundreds more arrived. They were hard to get rid of, and I did not know what their point of existence was.

I bit into the fresh bun as I bounced up the tall stairs. Thinking of the comfortable mattress I claimed made my knock on the door more energetic than I intended, knowing I shouldn't just walk in after months of being away. I looked backwards at the town, seeing people enjoy their lives.

For the first time in two months, the cage didn't feel like a hundred-pound weight around my neck. The door opened behind me and when I turned, my cheerful mood dropped like a rock in my stomach. Only Eira's amber eyes were revealed around the door. She tried to hide, but I saw the bruises and cuts cluttering her skin.

"You're back," her voice cracked out.

I pushed the door open further so I could step in and she awkwardly stumbled back. The curtains in the house were shut, but with the front door open, I could see the bottom half of her face was bruised too.

Dropping my bag heedlessly, I grabbed her face and tilted it towards the light. She hissed and pushed weakly against my stomach.

"Who did this?" I snapped, my hold loosening, and ran my thumb over the gash in her forehead.

The scab was rough with dry blood poking through. Her black and purple bruises were on show under her honey-coloured hair. Fresh wounds. Eira turned her head out of my hands and walked into the house.

"It's fine, Owyn."

Roughly letting the door close, I followed her into the sitting room. Whipping around, she glared at my riding boots, leaving mud on the hardwood floor.

I crossed my arms, not removing them until I got answers. She mimicked my pose, raising her eyebrows. We stared at each other stubbornly. It would be funny in any other situation, so I sighed in defeat. This wasn't worth the fight, and I knew she would win in the end.

Barely undoing the laces, I yanked my boots off in the front entrance and let them thud against the floor. Eira was sitting in her armchair, head in her hands. Gesturing to my now shoeless feet, I dropped into the other chair facing her. Crossing my arms, I leaned back into the cushion.

"Are you going to tell me now?"

"No, I'm not. I've got it handled," she said from her hands. "Will you please get up and go bathe? I'll need to throw out that chair."

I rolled my eyes and stood up. I cleaned up in Som Inn, but I'm sure it wasn't to Eira's standards. I wanted a bath anyway, but I wouldn't tell her that.

Leaning over her, I pushed the free strands back and placed a soft kiss on Eira's forehead. She glanced up at me with wide chestnut eyes. The darker room changed their colour entirely.

"I'm glad you're home," she muttered as I walked away.

THE BATHTUB FILLED SLOWLY AS I EYED THE BOILING POT OF water. In front of the floor-length mirror, I let my hair out of the braid I put it into this morning. Running a brush through the strands, a few leaves fell out. I couldn't even say where they came from in the few hours I rode.

Dunking my hair into a basin of cold water, I scrubbed my

nails against my scalp. Even though I'd washed it last night, I knew the water would still be dirty. There was never any time to make sure every speck of dirt was gone.

Being back at Eira's, the stress inside my head dulled. I could clean myself without worry of being ambushed or something bad happening. Standing up and reaching for the brush again, my gaze rested on the cage through the mirror's reflection.

The three fragile eggs sat unmoved and the familiar guilt filled my heart. I hadn't let myself think of the actual consequences of what I had to do. On a regular day, I knew better than to hand the eggs to the Council without knowing their intentions. Fairies didn't lay eggs often, maybe every hundred years. Though the High Drao of Rinebur promised these eggs were stillborn, I shouldn't have taken them. But I had to, and that didn't feel like enough of a reason.

I soaked a rag in the boiling water, impatient to wait until I got in the tub. Ringing it out, my thoughts went to Pax. He was swept away by the other Guards before we made it through the gates. They were expecting us. I didn't know what would've happened if we were seen in Jova together. Probably have gone straight to the Isle. It would be the least suspicious. But last night...

The memories played through my mind as I scrubbed at my face. My body shivered over the ways he touched me.

I turned off the tub's spout and dropped the last of my clothes. Dipping my body under the water, I was enveloped by the familiarity of the bathroom. I used this room for years. I stayed with Eira often, most of the time I wasn't working transactions.

Shutting my eyes, I tried to relax in the hot water, but her bruises came into my mind. Her job as a Companion was safe. Sleeping with their clients wasn't normal.

They got security from the secrets they kept for the people who hired them. They were just people to talk to.

I slipped lower in the water, thinking of all the ways I could hurt the person responsible.

CHAPTER 34

I TIGHTENED THE BELT ON MY ROBE AS I ENTERED THE BEDROOM. Barely glancing at her, Eira sat on the edge of my bed with a pile of clothes beside her. I sat down at the vanity to detangle my wet hair. I peered at Eira through the mirror, my attention going at the purple bruise around her eye.

I couldn't stop the heavy sigh. "You going to tell me what happened?"

Her eyes flickered from the window to meet mine. Quickly, tears built up. She cleared her throat, looking at the grey carpet under the bed.

"A client I've had for a few months thinks I shared confidential information. He showed up the other night, screaming. I denied it, which angered him more. He started hitting me, thinking he could beat the truth out and it only stopped when my neighbours knocked on the front door. They heard him yelling."

"Did you report this to the Delegate?"

I already knew the answer before she looked at me with her eyebrows pinched high. Companions couldn't freely go to the Delegate or the Guards to report an issue. The assumption would be they're sharing secrets and if their client didn't put a bounty out on their lives, the Companion would never make another dollar again. Word spread fast.

Tears sliding down her cheeks, Eira watched me walk over and rest on my knees in front of her. I placed my hands on her thighs. The tears made my heart ache as the anger built. I knew she didn't leave the house since the attack. The potential embarrassment and rumours weren't worth it. So she was cooped up here, not even calling a physician to look at her.

"Who did it?"

Her gaze dropped, wrapping her hands around mine, and her shoulders shook. It didn't happen often, but she only cried when she was truly hurting. I knew she would tell me when the corners of her mouth twitched downwards, and she peered up at me through her lashes. I recognized the name that came out of Eira's mouth. She watched me as I went through the faces of Jova's rich men in my head.

"Why do I know him?"

"He used to be a Guard Captain," she said.

As she said it, I remembered exactly who he was. He was a very large and fit man who had an abusive anger towards his subordinates. Rumour was that he killed at least three Guards by beating them to death. He must've paid well if Eira agreed to work for him. I removed my hands from her grasp and used her knees to stand up. She reached for me frantically.

"Owyn, don't do anything, please. Let it go. I've heard he knows it wasn't me who told. It'll pass."

"Has he apologized? Or give some compensation for what he did to your face?" I asked in a clipped voice.

Her mouth opened, but nothing came out. I raised my eyebrows, leaning my head forward, and her mouth snapped shut. I didn't want to make her feel worse, but I wasn't backing down. Capris Accora was going to pay for his actions.

"Exactly," I stated, before undoing my robe.

Tossing it on the bed, I grabbed the undergarments. She stayed silent while I adjusted the chain around my neck. I glanced at her, pulling my underwear up between my legs. She freely looked at my body, stopping at my chest for the longest. The appreciative look on her face warmed my body, but I ignored it.

"Eira, I'm finding that creep. You don't get to say no to that. All Companions have someone who watches out for them and you have me. I wasn't here when it happened, but I'm here now."

She took a deep breath, eyes staring into mine before nodding her head. She bit down on her lower lips as she glanced back at my body. If I wasn't determined to make a man bleed, I would pull her under the sheets.

I grabbed my bra next and turned away from her, sliding it on. If I kept watching her look at me, I was going to let lust black out my anger. Reaching around to pull at the strings, Eira walked behind me. Her hand resting on my unbruised side before taking hold of the strings, her light touch made shivers run along my spine.

Once she tapped my back, indicating she was done, I stepped forwards to grab my shirt, but she yanked me back by my waist. I looked back at her mischievous smile. I playfully rolled my eyes as she tilted her head up and grabbed my wrist, turning me around.

Cupping my hands around her jaw, being hyperaware of her injuries, I pressed our lips together in a light kiss. Eira's grip tightened as she tried to deepen the kiss. I pulled away, but she followed onto her tiptoes.

"I haven't kissed you in two months. Let me have my fill," she whispered, her gaze on my mouth.

Chuckling, I pressed a harder kiss to her lips before running my tongue along her lower lip. Before she could respond, I removed her hands from my waist and stepped away.

Turning to grab my clothes, I let myself grin at the dramatic pout on her face. Sliding the tunic over my head, my laughter grew at Eira's now crossed arms and even more childish expression. I rested my hands on her shoulders, my smile turning gentle.

"I promise, once I know you're safe, we can stay in bed and do whatever you want. Okay?"

With her lower lip still pouting, she smiled. "Okay."

I pecked her on the lips before grabbing my trousers.

Sitting in a stiff armchair, I swirled topaz coloured alcohol in a short glass I found. The chair was conveniently next to the front window, where I shifted the curtains open enough to see the road and front door.

The man unknowingly kept me waiting, thus breaking into the man's alcohol cabinet. Shooting the alcohol back, my eyes zoned in on a large, old dresser sitting on the other side of the room. There was an odd smell when I got into the house and had a nagging feeling that it came from within the wood.

Moving quietly enough to still hear the activity outside the house, I opened the first drawer. It overflowed with parchment. Running my finger down the top page, it was a list of names. Some last names rang familiar, but I couldn't place them.

In the next drawer, a few more pieces of parchment were scattered, but the hairpins drew my attention. The metal pins and the gems decorating them were old. Sections of the corroded metal were dark and my brain flipped between rust and blood until I picked up one, tilting it to catch the minimal light. It was dried blood, and I turned it over in my hand, recognizing them. A few older Drao in Verceen wore these during ceremonies. These were period pieces and Veks didn't own them. It was a weird find, but I moved past it. Many people in Jova had secrets and were collectors of antiques.

The smell got worse as I slid open the third drawer, radiating from multiple hemp bags. Breathing through my mouth, I untied the strings to reveal full sized dragon scales. I never seen them stored this poorly before.

Usually kept in jars of preservation fluids, these were dried out and useless for any magick work, but this wasn't what I smelt coming inside. I bent at the knees, opening the cabinet door below and slapped my hand over my mouth and nose. The dark space was packed full of jars and boxes.

What caught my eye was a large jar shoved towards the back, with a small humanoid body floating in a thick fluid. Reaching into the damp space, my fingers barely wrapped around the side as I dragged it forwards. My eyes adjusted to the dim light and a small gasp fell from my mouth.

A faerie. Dead.

Her body was curled inwards around an engorged stomach, the dried slash across her neck visible. She was murdered. To have this was illegal. It was illegal to interfere with a faerie funeral, because of specific rituals. Not to mention murder was a punishable offence by death. Behind the jar, something else caught my attention. Guiltily pushing the jar to the side, I grabbed what appeared to be a shadowbox.

My heart dropped further with disgust. It was a Dragonnette, dissected with pins. The scales were sliced poorly, flaking off. Behind it, more jars and frames sat with dead creatures. All of them crudely displayed. A hacking cough snapped my attention to the front door. Shutting the cabinet and toeing my way back across the room, I peered around the curtain's edge.

Through the gap, I watched a man climb the tall porch

steps to the front door. As the lock turned and the door opened, I let the curtain fall into place to make the room pitch black. He kicked off his boots and walked with lazy footsteps into the room.

Silently, I watched him click on the one large lamp hanging from the roof. When the light flooded the room, he jumped at my revealed presence by the window.

Capris Accora stared at me, his hand slipping from the wall switch. I saw Accora around Jova. He stepped down as Guard Captain a few years ago. The official story was that riding his horse became excruciating from a permanent injury to his knees.

The people across the country, Jova especially, accepted it and welcomed him as a regular citizen. The rumour amongst Merchants was Accora wanted to make a play for a Council spot and was just waiting for someone to step down or die.

"Hello," Accora carefully spoke, his puffy eyes roaming over my body.

Intentionally, I wore tight riding pants and an old riding corset of mine that Eira found somewhere in her house. Other than that, I had a long-sleeved white shirt hiding the cage pressed between my breasts. His eyes rested on the blade prominently attached to my hip. It was alluring, hopefully enough to distract him, but with no extra fabric to work against me.

"I'd like to speak with you for a moment," I said casually, pouring myself another small amount of alcohol.

It was good, and didn't burn too much. Expensive. Shooting the liquid back, I let the glass clunk down on the small table beside me. Stepping further out from behind the chair, Accora taking an instinctual step back. Usually the frightened move would pet my ego but, in this case, it made me suspicious. Even though he was no longer a Guard, the man still towered over me.

"What can I do for you?"

I turned most of my back to him. Pouring more of the alcohol, I kept him in my peripheral vision. I was being bold, not dumb.

"I've been presented with damning evidence that you acted towards a lady with non-gentlemanly behaviour." I put the stopper back in the decanter's opening and faced him with the glass in my hand. "We need to discuss it."

Realization dawned on his face. I took a long sip from the drink as he scratched the prickly beard on his ageing face. His eyes roamed over my body again with more suspicion in his eyes than before.

"Did Janna send you?"

I kept the reflexive confusion inside. Janna? Saying my mentor's name, fear showed in his eyes. He knew who I was, at least. That worked in my favour most of the time.

"And why would that concern you?" I tried to ask with mystery and amusement in my voice.

I was curious to know what he did to put the fear of Janna in him. But if he wouldn't tell me, that was for another time. He sighed, his head drooped a little. His eyes flick back and forth across the carpet as he frantically tried to think of what to do next. I raised my eyebrows with fake interest, waiting and drinking his alcohol like it was mine.

I looked into the empty glass. "You know, I came with a very specific and to-the-point plan. But now that I'm seeing your face, I've been a little more dramatic."

Fear was still bright in his eyes. I smiled and chucked the cup at his head.

He wasn't drunk enough to be hit with it, jerking his head to miss it. Good. I wanted him to feel everything. After it shattered on the wall, the glass rained down on him. With his body bent in on itself, I pulled out my dagger and went for his known weakness. It wasn't much of a jump across the room to stab him. He made a little sound as I plunged the blade into his knee.

As I ripped it out, his arm rammed into my stomach. The force knocked me down, my hands shooting out to catch myself and the impact didn't feel good. My gaze fell to my dagger as Accora picked it up.

The old Guard Captain smiled, spinning the dagger to hold it in an efficient stabbing position. He took his time walking over me, thinking he had the upper hand. I reached into my boot and out of the tiny sheath sewn inside; I gripped the hidden small knife handle.

With one flick of my wrist, the goblin steel planted into his stomach. Not knowing what hit him, Accora crumpled in pain. Shoving to my feet and launching him, I grabbed for the blade. It was an impulsive move as my hand wrapped around it, the dagger in his hand sliced through my thin sleeve. I recoiled from the shock of cold metal, but kept my grip.

Blood sprayed from the gap in his gut, hitting my face. Not disgusted by blood often, the heightened emotions of the situation caused me to gag. Straightening, I shifted my grip, taking the goblin blade with me, and stabbed it into his collar. If I thought I had the time, I'd appreciate the goblin steel breaking through bone.

Going to pull it back, my heartbeat paused when the blade wouldn't move. My jaw cracked to the side, with my head and body following. I stumbled before feeling an impact on my chest, making my throat close up and the back of my head slammed into the wooden floor. I groaned, rolling to the side. With all my still healing wounds and pyx-less body, I was quick to feel nausea and dizziness.

Accora walked towards me with my dagger in hand. Trying to regain my equilibrium, I shuffled backwards along the slick wood floor. I didn't get far before bumping into furniture.

My eyes jumped around, searching for a weapon. As he stepped over me and leaned down, a ridiculous idea came to mind. I swung my foot up, connecting between his legs. He sobbed, leaned into the tender spot. The rest of his body reached, his eyes crossing as he stumbled back. I halted his ability to catch his balance by hooking my foot around his ankle and yanking.

Accora toppled backwards, dropping my dagger as he crashed into the floor. I leapt and grabbed the dagger's handle, stomping my foot onto his chest. He groaned, body curling away from the pain but staying on the ground.

Knowing he wasn't getting up, I took a moment to catch my breath before leaning down and jabbed the dagger into the space between his ribcage. He gasped for air, but from the hissing, I knew I nicked his lung.

"By the way," I whispered. "Janna didn't send me. I'm here for Eira Khrom."

His eyes widened. Guilt crossed his face before starting a coughing fit. His face turned red as he fought for more air. I twisted the blade in a full circle before yanking it out. Against my hand, I sensed the metal grind against bone. Ignoring the blood, I put the blade away. I had to leave.

Picking my cloak up, I glanced down at Accora with my lip curled. He glared back, his hand pressing into his abdomen as I calmly popped the clasp shut around my neck. Blood pooled around his fingers. He would not last much longer and we both knew it.

I lifted the bottom of my cape so it wouldn't drag through the bloody mess as I walked by. Shutting the front door behind me, I draped the hood on my head. I had blood all over me, but thankfully, the cape was covering enough that no one would call the authorities.

Chapter 35

It was a beautiful night in Jova. Ironic. In the sky, the moon was almost full, stars brightly joining it. The bustle of the day had quieted, but it wasn't entirely silent. Jova was never silent.

The restaurants and bars were still open; patrons enjoying their night without responsibility. Halfway across the bridge, a group of Guards began crossing in conversation. Leaning my elbows on the brick railing, I slid the hood off my head but kept it bunched around my neck. With shoulders bunched up to my ears, I tried to keep myself as small as possible. A hood up at night was more suspicious than someone walking alone at night. I turned my head away from them. Hopefully, they wouldn't notice the blood covered woman.

They were boisterous as they passed, and all sounded fairly young. One Guard strolled behind the rest, sighing at their behaviour.

"We've got duty in the morning. You drank way too much to take any decent assignments, and I'm going to have to babysit you."

Another one looked at the exasperated Guard, throwing his hands in the air.

"Oh, come on, what's the worst we could get? Rounding up the Merchants and all our goodies?"

My gaze shot up from the rippling water against rocks, staring at a point in the distance and listening. Another Guard obnoxiously snorted.

"No, the worst assignment would be to deal with the problem Guard."

"Who, the one that came in with that famous Merchant? What's his name, Pat?"

"Pax." The sober Guard cleared up.

My nails pressed against the railing tighter. I was tempted to follow and hear more, but knew better. It felt too convenient that I was overhearing this conversation.

"Duh!" one man yelled out. "Rumour has it, he's fallen a little too deeply in with his assignment. Guard Cap' isn't impressed, but that's what happens when you send a weakling to the Council to experiment on."

"How'd you hear?"

"Ryak was assigned to follow them and keep a close eye."

"From what I've heard, I'm surprised he made it back alive with that Merchant. I guess she's too daft to realise what was in front of her," another said, laughing.

I peeked at the men over my shoulder. They made it off the bridge and were too far away to hear anymore. I put the hood back up, resuming my walk. A foul taste formed in my mouth as the words rolled over in my head.

Another Guard was following us? What hung in my face?

Pax was a Guard for ten years. Did he trick me into believing his dedication was less than it really was? Why did he share the things I told him with the Council? Did I get played?

My head turned to the side, hearing horses loudly neighing from the barn across the river. My fingers twitched to get Dill ready. Hop on her back and leave. But where would I go?

I thought of the cage hanging against my chest. I was just as stuck as I was this whole time.

Rocks clattered together on the cobblestone, and I froze, my gaze snapping up. Blocking the entrance to Eira's street was a ghastly thin woman. Holding up a lantern next to her head, her image swayed with the wind. She wasn't a physical being. The edges of her body were translucent.

"Orinthia Kellobyn?" A sweet voice shouted my name.

From her staring eyes, she didn't need to open her mouth to speak to make her voice rattle through my brain.

"Yes?" I answered.

My fingers twitched at my side. Maybe the Guards wouldn't have time to find me if the ghosts got me first.

"The Drao requests your presence."

I sighed, my face dropping. I would not try to walk the other way. You couldn't outrun spirits. I glanced up, and the being was walking away from me along the centre of the road. I tugged my hood tighter around my head. I passed Eira's street without a glance and continued further into town.

The Oxbo Castle was the only home to the generations of Gerennt royalty. History says it stood strong until the last moments of the mutiny that led to the Council's reign.

Two hundred years later, the castle sat in crumbles and was picked over. I hadn't visited the ruins in years and never at night. I wouldn't be shocked if the land was haunted. I heard once, the Drao celebrations and parties here were memorable. Tonight, complete silence. The few buildings that mostly survived were boarded up, with nothing inside for looters to get. Rabbits and gnomes filled the bushes surrounding and growing inside the ruins.

The spirit stopped at the mouth of a crumbling arch and uneven stairs.

"You will need this," she said, holding out the lantern.

I nodded, hesitantly taking it from her. I wasn't expecting it to be tangible. Holding up the edge of my cape to stop myself from tripping, I placed my boot on a large, stable rock to step through. The remains archived what happened on that fateful day.

Enormous boulders dug into the ground with ivy and weeds encapsulating them; trenches followed deep in the dirt. Standing walls were missing chunks of rock, being caught in the projectile's collision course. Magick wasn't used. Everything was done with people's hands and mechanics. I don't know why.

In the daylight, I could look up and see into the remaining towers, bare rooms once holding royalty that overlooked Jova. But in the dark, I kept my focus on my feet and the unstable hallways ahead. I had no clue where I needed to go. From history books, I knew trekking through the main hallway that I would enter the great hall soon.

Crickets spoke to each other, almost like music in the night. Water surrounded the castle ruins on three sides. Two were ocean, but I could barely hear it. It felt like being in the middle of a field.

Coming to the end of the hallway, a loud chirp caught my attention as a hundred small balls of light shot into the air. I paused, unsure, until one flew close to my face. Fairies masquerading as lightning bugs. My hand grabbed the cage around my throat, as if they didn't notice the eggs already.

Along the remaining walls and where the walls once stood, the faeries formed a pathway for me to follow. I stared ahead, too ashamed to look at them.

My boot squeaked against a chunk of remaining tile, and I entered a new room. Hundreds of small wings whooshed past, my muscles locking. More fairies appeared and with previously unseen candles sparking to life, what remained of the great hall was revealed.

The faeries created a roof, illuminating the entire space. If I wasn't familiar with a map of the blueprints, I wouldn't know where I was. The rubble of both interior and exterior walls was piled up. Some still had art and paint attached. Above where two piles of rubble that were once thrones sat was a large rectangular hole, half of it intact enough to know it was once a window.

With the lights, three people were revealed in the centre of the room. An enormous man flanked a young woman. Not far to the side, another man sat casually on a boulder. I stared at him with furrowed eyebrows, unsure if the light was playing tricks. He looked back with no indication we met before, throwing a rock in the air to himself. It was different from the persona I met in Verceen. Cormitt Thaxton.

I walked over carefully, unsure of what to expect. The other two were not Veks. I would believe anyone if they told me the man was half-giant. The sword hanging at his side was close to my height. Dark, tight curls sat on the top of his head and I'm sure his eyes would be pretty with how brightly they reflected the dull light if his face wasn't in a permanent scowl. He was intimidating. I would hate to even see him get a paper cut.

The woman was closer to my age and height, but obviously lived a very different life. Her complexion appeared to glow from within. Her eyes glowed, a trait she shared like her mountainous companion's. Hers were the colour of honey, though.

She stepped towards me, and I wasn't certain that she wasn't a spirit. Almost a foot shorter than me, I never seen anyone move with such elegance. I felt the weight on my face of the gigantic man as she approached. I peeked at Cormitt. He looked bored, an apple now spinning in his hand. I placed the lantern on a boulder next to me, wanting my hands free. She stopped far enough back that I knew she was being careful, her youth even more evident.

"Orinthia Kellobyn, correct?" she asked, extending her hand.

Her voice sounded like bells. An immediate sense of truth for her flooded through my veins, making me suspicious.

"I am," I answered, tentatively holding out my hand.

We clasped each other's forearms. I almost expected her skin to be cold from how regal she was. Warmth radiated from her instead.

"My name is Heathlyn Davvins. I appreciate you came to speak with me."

Her last name poked at some deep memory. My gaze flickered to the hulking man still watching me like prey.

"That would be Driftenn, my guardian. He's harmless, I promise. We'd like to talk with you." The way she said it made him sound like he was a puppy.

I hesitantly nodded, giving him a once over. If I needed to fight him, I'd lose. Immediately. No competition. The crunch of an apple shot my attention back to the third person. He examined his apple, but gaze briefly peeked at me. He gave me a cocky smirk, taking another bite.

"That'd be Cormitt. He isn't as harmless as Driftenn, though it's his bark, not his bite, that causes issues. He collects intelligence for me."

So much for art dealer. Cormitt nodded his head, amused by the introduction. Did she know we met before? I weakly rolled my eyes, looking at Heathlyn.

"You've brought me here. What would you like to speak about?"

"The cage around your neck. We know you're to give it to the Council. I was hoping to discuss other options with you."

My hands twitched at my side. Whether I was going to reach for my dagger or the necklace, I wasn't too sure. Another peek at Cormitt. I knew in my gut that his trip to Verceen was to confirm I had the cage. I felt ill that more people knew about the eggs but said nothing.

"What do you know about the history between Drao and the Council?"

I cleared my throat, resting my thumbs on my weapon's belt. My mouth opened, but I shut it again, awkwardly looking around the ruins and the hundreds of faeries above me to compose myself, before coming back to Heathlyn.

"During my training, my mentor taught me what I believe is all I need to know. She strictly works with Drao, as do I."

"I'm aware of Janna Cor and her extensive transaction history with the Drao," Heathlyn said with a soft authority. "But do you understand what restrictions the Council has placed in recent decades?"

"I've heard rumours."

"The truth is much worse than any rumour could be."

Heathlyn raised her hand out to the side. Cormitt slipping off the rock, he sauntered over, tossing the apple core to the opposite end of the room. Smiling at me with a smug attitude, his heady scent made my mouth water. He drew me in and it made me want to hate him.

Stopping beside Heathlyn, he didn't take his eyes away from mine as he tugged his shirt sleeve up. Where we stood grew brighter as a dozen fairies fell out of formation, falling closer. He was as handsome as I remembered, more so in the glowing faeries' light.

My eyes slid along his arm to his revealed forearm. What should be a smooth palette was tattered, burnt, and scarred. There wasn't a spot of his warm skin unmarked. Some scars reflected blue and green from magick. Unfocused, my hand lifted, and I ran my middle finger carefully down the longest scar. He released a quivering sigh. My hand snapped back at his sound, realizing the oddness of what I did.

Heathlyn spoke, acting like I hadn't just done that. "His entire arm and ribcage look like this. The Council performed nonconsensual experiments on him. They've done this to countless Drao, some ending in significantly worse condition.

I've known a few who've had their blood replaced with a Veks to see if they would lose their magick."

That was something I didn't hear. I glanced at Driftenn. No longer staring at me, his chin dropped as he stared at the ground. It was pensive and mournful to look at. Seeing a burly man so vulnerable made a knot grow in my stomach.

"I know of the Cursed. I've seen them before. What are the numbers of the dead?" I asked, feeling rather overly formal, but I didn't know how to talk to these strangers.

Cormitt pushed his sleeve down. A shadow crossed his face, and the fairies returned to their hovering positions.

Heathlyn sighed. "We don't know the exact numbers. It's been going for two hundred years. But personally, I've lost three friends in the last year."

I was surprised I didn't throw up. My hand lifted, fingertips running across the smooth bottom of the cage. I so badly wanted to take the cage from around my neck and put it in her hands.

I was unwillingly a part of the annihilation of the Drao, but the bruise on my side wasn't going to just disappear. It began pulsing as a reminder of why I bought the eggs in the first place and why I couldn't hand them over. My heart sank, knowing I wouldn't survive if I did. My eyes dropped in shame.

"If I told you I had to give them the eggs without giving you an answer other than I have a good reason, would you believe me?" I asked, staring at the cracked tiles and glass ingrained in the floor.

With a masculine scoff, Cormitt walked away. I knew I sounded ridiculous. A second sigh filled the air, but it wasn't in annoyance. It was disappointed. I glanced at Heathlyn. Her eyes sparkled more as she analysed me, head tilting to the side.

"Once you give it to them, will it be safe for you to share?"

The feeling of trust bubbled up again.

"If I'm returned what I'm owed, it'll be safe to share." I realized I didn't come here by myself. I was brought here. "Will you explain why you've requested me? Besides wanting me to hand over the eggs."

"Many Drao respect you and thank you for continuing to keep our society functioning. There are many Merchants who think less of us and believe we should be left to fend for ourselves. You have a solid reputation," Heathlyn explained. "If you feel this strongly about giving the eggs to the Council, I ask you to continue supporting Drao, but only the Drao afterwards. Not the Council, and as little of Veks as possible. We're fighting for our lives, and we'll only survive if we keep allies close. I would appreciate your help as a part of my inner circle. We've had many Drao contact us that Guards and Vek Merchants have stolen important heritage pieces from them. I'm aware you have talents in that department."

I already knew my answer. I was prepared to accept, but stones crunching together had me whipping around, grabbing my dagger. In the dull light, the new addition made me wonder what kind of magick they were using and for what purpose.

"Korta, thank you for coming. You mentioned wanting to see your daughter when I was finally able to speak with her," Heathlyn said.

My hand dropped, speechless. The woman I haven't seen in nine years stood with her hands together and a loving smile on her face. I could feel a need to throw my arms around her neck and cry. But those were the thoughts of fourteen-year-old Owyn.

The Owyn standing here was in control and I didn't move other than clenching my jaw. The day I was taken from my family's farm played in my head.

"Hello, my darling."

Chapter 36

Her voice wrapped around my heart and squeezed. It produced a warm and comforting feeling inside me. A cough pulled my mind from the spiral it was about to slide down. I turned, tightly smiling at Heathlyn and her accomplices. If they wanted the known Merchant Owyn to help them, they wouldn't want to see the emotions trying to burst free.

"I'll speak with you as soon as I can. If you need to find me, I'm staying at Eira Khrom's house by the community stables. Thank you for providing me with this information. I look forward to working with you." I stiffly gave them a nod and grabbed the lantern, but let my other hand squeeze into a fist.

My nails pierced into my palm, the pain keeping my focus on leaving. My mother stood near the door and I stared past her. She was far enough in the room and I didn't need to be too close.

"Orinthia, please." My mother placed her hand on my arm gently, but the touch froze my feet to the ground.

A pounding grew in my head as I looked at her hand, then back at the strangers. Heathlyn watched with sympathy in her eyes. If my mother and she were friendly, I wondered how much of the story she knew. Or what side of the story she knew. Was it what my sisters were told?

Cormitt's gaze went between my mother and me. His eyes squinted briefly at my mother until he looked at me. He kept my focus and wet his bottom lip. I couldn't tell what he was thinking of the situation, so I faced my mother again.

"I will speak with you, but not in front of other people," I mumbled. "I don't have a lot to say to you, anyway."

I exited the grand hall, coolly taking my arm away from her. As my feet left the grand hall, the fairies dispersed; the sound of their wings rustled in my ears. The ruins fell into blackness.

Once outside the destroyed castle and in the courtyard, I faced my mother. She aged, but her wrinkles showed that she often smiled. With a few hairs loose around her forehead, she twisted her dark hair–the same dark hair my three sisters shared–into a low bun. It bothered me she looked to have a simple life while wherever they were, my sisters suffered.

"Torna could use your help," I said, resting my free hand against my dagger.

The lantern hung low at my side. The moonlight was bright, and I didn't want to see much of her face, anyway.

"Torna doesn't need my help. She has your sisters," she said with a tone like I didn't know what I was talking about.

I snorted. "Glad to see I'm not the only child you abandoned. Quick update. Torna is the only one left at the farm. From what she told me, she rarely sees Calla and does not know where Laine is or what she's doing. You've left your daughter with a lot of heavy responsibility and to suffer for the rest of her life."

My words didn't seem to phase her. "I didn't intend that when I left. The Drao saved me."

"You had three daughters, not to mention a fully running farm. I would like to know how the Drao saved you other than giving you the chance to abandon your responsibilities."

"Not when your father died. I felt alone. I heard rumors of the Drao massacre and I came to them. I owed them a debt, and the least I could do was help them."

My nose wrinkled in disgust.

"You seem to owe a lot of debts. However, I'd like to sleep in a familiar bed for the first time in two months. It was..." I cut myself off because saying it was good to see her was a lie. "Have a good night."

I didn't wait for a response. The need to yell was growing inside of me, but I knew she wasn't worth it. There was almost ten years of resentment inside of me. I placed the lantern on the grass and allowed the crunch of gravel under my feet to guide me back to the main street of Jova. My head was spinning with too much new information.

My feet slammed against the wooden stairs up to the townhouse's front door. I closed the door hard enough to make its frame shudder. Standing in the foyer, I took several deep breaths and stared into the kitchen at the other end of the hallway. Once I knew I would not scream, I calmly hung my cloak on the rack as footsteps tapped down the staircase.

"Are you..." Eira froze with wide eyes, taking in my appearance.

My hand dropped away from the cloak, staring at the roof. Ignoring her, I bent down and removed my boots silently.

"Soooo..." Eira began, extending the vowel.

I glanced over as I stood up. Leaning against the bannister, her arms were across her chest. Her hair was resting on her shoulder, complimenting the blue night coat she was in. Her lips were pressed firmly together, amusement twinkling in her eyes.

"How did it go?" She asked with a singsong voice.

Locking the front door, I walked past the stairs with a flickered glance at her.

"You seemed more worried before I left," I grumbled.

"Yes, because...Don't sit down!" I flinched at her shout, glaring back at her. "You're covered in blood."

Dramatically, I rolled my eyes. "Not the first time."

"Can you just sit on the arm? Don't ruin the cushions," she begged.

Pulling the corners of my mouth down, I sat on the uncomfortable armrest, and she smirked.

"I've come back covered in blood and you're in a better mood."

She stood across the room with her arms crossed, entertained. "You came home with a dramatic attitude. No matter how much blood you're soaked in, I know you're fine."

Her hip cocked to the side, and the night coat opened, showing off her bare leg to the hem of her sleeping dress. I recognized it as something I bought her. Distracting me, I nodded and stood up.

"You won't have to worry about Accora anymore. Though if you want some illegal Drao contraband, his house is overflowing with it. If not, I have a couple of people to send over before someone finds the body."

She gave me a questioning look, but I shook my head. It already felt like a weird dream that I wouldn't forget.

"I'm going to clean up. I have to write Torna before bed," I muttered, running my hand across her hip and stomach on my way to the stairs.

"This may be a silly question," she said, following behind me. "But why are you writing to your sister? You haven't spoken to her in years."

Trudging through my borrowed room, I began peeling off layers. She already had the sheets pulled back and the side table lights on. Guess I wasn't sleeping alone. I shrugged, emotions finally contained.

"I saw her on the way through. Need to write and say that unless I spoke to a ghost, our mother isn't dead."

"Excuse me?" Eira exclaimed, stopping at my washing room door. "You saw your mother? When?"

Taking my time giving her an answer, I washed my hands thoroughly. Once the blood was gone from under my nails, I soaked a facecloth. Ringing the extra water out, I glanced at her.

"Can I tell you tomorrow? I'm exhausted and need to deal with this," I said, pulling my shirt collar aside to reveal the wound that stopped bleeding ages ago.

Her jaw dropped and began stuttering out a few words, but shook her head and walked away.

"Thank you for not getting killed!" She called back.

I smirked to myself as I scrubbed away the scumbag's blood. I knew Eira. She was a little annoyed that I hadn't shown her the cut right away, but she would get over it.

It didn't take long to clean off the blood and bandage my shoulder. My wounds from Delf were pink and healing. Grabbing a slip of parchment and pen, I sat at my desk. Staring out the window, I tapped the pen against the wood, considering how I wanted to start. This was surprising news, and I wasn't sure how she would take it.

> Torna,
>
> I'm writing because I needed someone else to be as shocked as I am.
>
> To skip a long story that will only generate more questions and ironic comments from you, I saw an old acquaintance of ours today. Our mother.
>
> Living and breathing. Well. Grey hairs and wrinkles too, if that makes you feel better. She says the Drao saved her life. Do you know what she's talking about?
>
> Send your response to this house - Eira Khoms.

Your older, amazing sister
Owyn Kellobyn. Jova.

My eyes snapped open, ripped from a peaceful sleep by the irritating sound of pounding against the wall. Sunlight slipping through the curtains, I groaned and rolled over, yanking the covers up over my chin. The pillow next to me was empty, still pressed inward from a head laying on it. What was she doing?

"Eira!" I called with my eyes shut.

The noise stopped. I smiled, rubbing my forehead against the pillowcase. My brain slowly began quieting again, with a hope she was going to come back to bed after whatever noisy thing she was doing.

My ears perked at Eira, shouting from the floor below. I didn't hear what she was saying, but in one movement, I threw the blankets off. My foot got caught in the sheets, making my half conscious body stumble. I searched wildly for my robe as the bedroom door opened.

Three Guards entered, all looking hostile and armed. They came in and covered most of the room by standing side by side. No longer concerned with the thin dress I wore; I started looking for my weapons. I cursed; all were behind the Guards against the wall.

My brain was now fully awake, and I saw my robe slung on the back of my vanity's chair. Forcing my mind to slow down and work out how to get downstairs, I calmed my breathing.

"Good morning. What can I help you with?" I asked, making it obvious that I was walking over to the vanity and not going for the weapons.

"You arrived in town yesterday, correct?" the first Guard

asked, resting his thumbs in his belt. His tone was casual but accusing.

I slid my arms through the robe's sleeves and stared at the Guards, watching them shamelessly look over my body, each stopping at my chest for an extended time. Whether it was the cage with faerie eggs they were looking at or not, I didn't appreciate it. Pursing my lips, I folded the robe closed and tied the sash. "I did. I assumed that was already known since my arrival was with one of your comrades."

"Just confirming that our information was correct," he said. "Are you aware your instructions were to deliver your task to the Council as soon as possible?"

"I wasn't aware. I've got plans for today but I will bring it by tomorrow. Thank you for stopping by," I said, my next aim being the washing room.

I took barely any steps as two hands grabbed my upper arms. I was spun to face the man who spoke to me. My gaze flickered to a long gold bar pinned on his jacket. Guard Lieutenant.

"We've been instructed to bring you to the Council and deliver the package," he told me, rolling his shoulders with authority. He was tall enough that I was basically looking under his square jaw.

The two Guards tried to pull me towards the bedroom door, but I yanked my body backwards. "As much as you'd enjoy it, I plan on changing into regular clothes."

The Guard Lieutenant smirked. "The Council would prefer you to be in a suitable dress."

He nodded to the others, their hands releasing me. I wiped imaginary dust away from my robe and collected an outfit containing pants and a corset I set out last night.

"Like I said, a suitable dress."

I glared at him. The look on his face said I wasn't leaving until I picked a different outfit, whether I wanted to. I dropped the clothes on the bed dramatically while keeping direct eye contact with the Lieutenant and went to find a dress. Might as well put it on willingly. Grabbing an old dress, I made for the washing room.

"If you choose to go out that window, just know we are taking someone to the Council. Whether it be you or your little friend downstairs."

I studied the Guards with my hand on the doorknob. With the growing smirks at how quickly they got my attention, I knew they weren't lying. Shutting the door without a word, I changed.

Before my pyx was removed, I'd never experienced such consistent ugliness from Guards. Yes, Guards weren't always the biggest supporters of Merchants but it was a symbiotic existence.

Was it because I travelled with Pax? Did he share just how compassionate I was with Drao? I paused, yanking on my cross-breast corset strings. Did he brag about the details of our last night?

Shaking my head, I continued putting on my clothing, knowing I had more to deal with than details of a sexual interaction. I only checked my reflection when I finished, a blue dress with long bell sleeves that ended above my feet. It was presentable and I could move in it. I wore it many times before, mostly when I wanted to be taken more seriously and I knew I had the underhand. The grey corset on top held a small blade against my ribs, but only I needed to know that.

The Guards barely stepped away from the washing room door to let me through. Their eyes roamed my figure and stopped on my chest. There wasn't a single dress I owned which didn't show off my full chest; I couldn't help it. I was used to the disgusting looks, but it didn't mean I didn't want to hit every single one of them. I grabbed my boots and tried to ignore the cage swinging in my face. If I was going to the Council, I didn't need to hide it. They were just going to hide it, anyway.

The three men surrounded me as I walked down the stairs. Eira came into view, sitting on the front room couch in her night coat. Two Guards crowded her attention already on me. She was terrified, teary-eyed, as we looked at each other. The tears and her healing bruises were like an attack on my heart. It didn't make me upset, though, only angry.

"I'll be back later," I dryly commented to her, taking my day cloak from the wall hook. "Don't worry. I'll see you soon."

She said nothing as I was escorted out the front door.

Chapter 37

Five horses waited in front of Eira's house, covered in garb that screamed Guards and the Council. Children surrounded their legs but, seeing the Guards, they scattered. The Guard Lieutenant mounted his horse and held out his hand to me. I stared at it.

"You could walk. I'm sure everyone would enjoy it."

I squared my shoulders and took his hand. I didn't like wearing dresses while riding. I was forced to ride sideways and keep a tighter hold on the Guard's waist not to fall. It was almost a straight road to the Isle's bridge. We would pass schools and fresh food markets. I was being put on display. Without cuffs, people were left to speculate why I was on a horse with a high member of the Council's Guard.

At first, the normal curiosity was seeing the Guards passing, but when they noticed me on the back of the lead horse, the staring grew and facial expressions changed. I wouldn't know what to think if I was in their position.

The morning was almost over, the sun high in the cloudless sky, and most of the boats were usually emptied by now. I wondered if it was just my luck that the Port of Jova was still busy.

Baked goods, fish, fresh meat, fruits and perfumes soaked their air with their smells. More boats than normal must have come in. The shopkeepers, far enough from the docks themselves but lucky to be near the edge of the port entrance, noticed the Guards, hoping to make a quick sale. When they didn't make instant contact with the men on horseback, they moved on to the next potential customer.

A Drao butcher I dealt with, his name slipping my mind, made eye contact with me, a look of horror crossed his face, the slab of meat in his hands was forgotten. I didn't know what the correct response was. So, I just stared until he was out of view.

Following the slight left away from the Port, the bridge was going to come up soon. Clutching my hands together around the Guard Lieutenant, I considered leaping off the saddle and making a run for it. It was busy enough they couldn't chase me on horseback without creating a trail of panic and chaos. But what would I do after I jumped?

The closer the horses got to Long Bridge, more and more Guards appeared. It felt like I was being led into a bear's den. Eyes watched us. Conversations paused as we passed by. Instead of keeping my head buried in the man's back, I searched around for a familiar face, but I knew he wouldn't be there. Did I want him to be? Or was I just looking for comfort?

Another man with a long gold bar on his chest strolled over when the horses stopped at the bridge, glaring at me. He turned to his cohort in front of me.

"What's this about?"

"Evasive Merchant here to meet with the Council," he stated.

The man sent me another look, one of total disgust, nodding. The Guard snapped the reins, his horse walking again. At the edge of Long Bridge was a set of gates. Much less glorious than the ones at the edge of town, but these wooden doors worked. One end or the other was closed every night when most Isle Guards went to sleep, only a small crew was left to patrol.

Crossing Long Bridge left us exposed to the freezing winds that rushed across the strait. Magick surrounded the bridge like a bubble, making death by drowning impossible. My arm muscles instinctually tightened around the Lieutenant's waist. He didn't react, as I'm sure he was just as cold as I was. Or at least, he was used to it and didn't care about my reaction. At the other end of the bridge, Guards appeared again.

The Isle was constructed entirely differently than the rest of Gerennt. The Council's Chambers stuck out above the treetops. It was the tallest building in the country by far, at seven stories. Within the first hundred years of the Council's control, it was built and was something grander than the royal family's castle. The Council's Chambers held their lives, both personal and professional. It was beautifully built, almost a C shape, but not quite curved enough and hugged the second building. Snuggled next to it, in the courtyard of the outer building, was with only a wide path between the two and a hallway connecting the two at the third floor, was the building that contained all the Gerennt workers' offices. It was only three floors tall, but still imposing.

Riding along the road, I noticed that the only shoreline seen from the mainland was packed with pine and cedar trees, not giving any regular citizens a chance to get a hint of what could be happening. The Isle was much the same but with trees that let in more light. Staying on the main road, there were two cut-offs.

To the left, housing for the Council's people who worked on the Isle, giving them almost no need to cross the Long Bridge other than to restock their pantries. And to the right, a grey and unremarkable building sat at the other end of the Isle. The country's jail.

Janna said the official claim was that the worst people the Delegates didn't know what to do with other than killing them lived there. But more rumours continued that Drao were held here, between experiments which left most of them Cursed. Other than housing for Guards and substantial stables, the Isle was bare.

A handful of men stood at the slabs of stairs, waiting for our arrival. Three were Guards, obviously by their polished armour, but the other three were in thin and worn clothing. One man didn't even have shoes on. Prisoners, I could only guess. I never seen anyone labelled as one before. Tugged off the horse at the front door of the concave building by one of the lesser Guards, I was left unshackled.

Maybe the Council didn't want their brainwashed subjects to know what they were up to. With the Lieutenant leading, I was taken up the ornate front stairs and through the front doors of an ugly grey facility. The lobby continued the sterile look from outside. It was almost silent, with the only sound being mumbling from the receptionists and Guards. I stared at the expensive clothes of the Isle's Guards, different from their regular associates. I wondered if the rest ever felt jealous.

A Guard who stayed silent during my transit opened a glass door, revealing the first of multiple flights of stairs. I held back a groan and mentally thanked myself for choosing a dress that brushed the tops of my feet. Holding up a skirt got tiring after a while.

I allowed myself to crumple forwards and take a deep breath when we reached the large platform between staircases. We were on the fourth floor, and I might not know most of what happened on the Isle but I knew the first of three floors held Councilmen housing.

Sweat poured down the back of my neck. Maybe this was how all the Guards stayed fit. Each flight of stairs felt longer than necessary, but I never walked up so many at once before.

I could be wrong. Straightening, knowing I needed to keep going whether I liked it, when the Lieutenant approached a door and yanked it to the side.

It wasn't another set of stairs, but a closet. It was then I remembered the Isle had elevators, and I was filled with relief. Stepping carefully into the enclosed car, I peeked at the prisoners in shabby attire standing next to the crank. Their muscles were huge, bulging out from their thin dirty shirts. I'm certain they were relieved that only three of us were going up and the other two stayed in the stairwell. Behind them stood two Guards, armed with multiple swords and what looked to be whips hanging from their backs. Like most Guards I saw, they appeared bored.

I could feel my heart pounding in my chest and it was more than just being out of breath. I barely remembered the last time I saw the Council. What would occur now that I had what they wanted?

From the corner of my eye, I watched the two men crank the elevator upwards, going round and round. I knew there was magick that could levitate items and people, but had it not been expanded to fuel something so large as an elevator cart?

Without knowing their crimes, I felt bad for the men. Even with their engorged muscles, they were exhausted when we got to the last floor.

A lesser Guard slid the door open when we stopped moving. The room that was revealed made my breath catch. The room matched the nightmare I was repeatedly forced through over the past two months. I didn't make the connection.

The morning sun shone through the wall of windows, illuminating the occupants as they watched us. Not moving fast enough, I was nudged forwards. I stumbled over my feet, not expecting the contact. Catching myself, my gaze landed on bodies piled at the base of the windows. I recognized their faces, even if I didn't know all their names. The other Merchants from that day. Were they killing us?

I stared until the movement of their chests registered in my brain. Breathing. Not dead. Turning towards the people who inflicted my pain, another body lay in the centre of the room. The greying skin was facing me as the body lay in what seemed to be an uncomfortable lump. Lyris.

I convinced myself she died in the Forest of Som. Seeing her now made this feel more like a dream. Her breathing differed from the others. Unconscious, too, but she looked like she was fighting to breathe. Each breath stuttered. She looked much worse than the last time I saw her.

"Orinthia Kellobyn, it's good to see you."

A hand clamped down on my shoulder and shoved me harder than before. My hands barely caught me as I slammed into the pale grey floor. Three men sat in large chairs that could only be described as thrones. The Councilmen wore twisted looks of satisfaction now that I was on my knees. My gaze flickered to the people lined behind the thrones. All Guards, wearing the familiar sweater with the Council's emblem on the chest. Not a single one in actual armour.

A few watched me or the other Merchants' bodies, hands casually resting on their swords. The rest looked straight ahead as if the room was empty. My gaze returned to the Councilmen. It was ironic how they behaved so much like the royalty they overthrew. Suddenly, I wasn't as scared as I felt in the elevator.

"To what do I owe the displeasure?" I asked, rising to my feet.

A Guard from my kidnapping party gripped my upper arm. I glanced at him, raising my eyebrows, then down at my arm. Really? What was I going to do with easily a dozen Guards in the room? Use the small blade hidden in my corset?

I couldn't get it out without someone noticing. His face

stayed emotionless, but his lips slightly pursed. I pressed down on the smirk, trying to grow from his indecision.

"If you followed our instructions, we wouldn't have dispatched Guards to collect you," the centre Councilman, oldest looking of the bunch, commented.

"My deepest apologies," I said, slowly returning my gaze to the men. "I didn't realize there was a time limit on your little mission."

The dark-haired Councilman on the left barely turned his head, eyes still on me. "Bring them in."

The Guard to his left nodded, striding across the room. At one of the white doors lining a wall, he opened it enough for his torso to stick through. The bass of his voice reverberated into the room before propping the door open with his hand. A girl of at least twelve stepped into the throne room first, pushing a sparkling gold cart. Two glass domes rested on top. My jaw locked and I couldn't look away.

Contained underneath were pulsating globes the size of my fist, icy blue with veins of more blues and purples inside, smoke wrapping around it. It was my pyx. A surge of adrenaline filled me, encouraging me to rip myself from the Guard. I calculated how long it would take to cross the room and how quickly the Guards would stop me. In my peripheral vision, two more people entered and the familiar wide strides of one drew my attention.

A tall, lanky woman approached; her shoulders rolled back with her chin high in the air. White-blonde, stick straight hair slicked back against her head, ends brushed against her thighs. She was confident, even in a dress that was semi-sheer draped over her body. A shadow of her figure was visible through the fabric. The look gave her away as a practitioner.

And the person to enter with her before the Guard let the door swing closed?

Yash Horras.

My childhood friend was dressed like he had in Mye,

expensive clothing with his hair styled. Now I understood how he afforded the wardrobe. In the two weeks since our interaction in Mye, his face was thinner. He wasn't sickly, almost haunted.

Yash stopped beside the practitioner and folded his hands together. He looked down his nose at me and I was overwhelmed with anger. The feeling shot to my stomach, and I threw myself away from the Guard, emptying the little food in my stomach onto the floor.

My arm was released, the Guard making a sound of disgust. Spitting out the last bile, a throat cleared in the room. I stared at the vomit, knowing it was the least disgusting part of my day so far.

"The spell has affected her. Shall we see if it has affected the other one?"

Another door opened, and formal footsteps entered, with another uneven pair out of sync. With my hands resting against my knees, I peered at the new occupants. Three more Guards entered, and I weakly rolled my eyes at the middle person.

Pax's skin was bruised and cut up; eyes sunken from just a day. His cheekbones protruded in the sunlight. He hasn't slept. It wasn't possible we arrived in Jova yesterday for him to look this bad. Guards stood close at his side, almost touching him. They appeared tense, anticipating a reaction. His eyes stared ahead, and I wasn't sure if he saw anything.

"Did he throw up outside?" the old Councilman asked.

"Yes sir," one of Pax's Guards answered.

He faced their practitioner, but the room paused when Lyris released a painful groan. Next to me, the Guard stepped closer.

Her dark hair splayed across the floor, lying on her side. In the sunlight, it looked more purple than black. She groaned again, curling in tighter. She was waking up. Avoiding the vomit, I dropped to my knees and reached for her shoulder.

As I inched closer, her body spasmed wildly. I flinched back, falling on my tailbone. She rolled to her back, arms splayed across the ground, and she gasped. Her eyes were still closed. I glanced at the Councilmen. They sat with small smiles on their faces. They were enjoying whatever was happening.

Looking back at Lyris, her muscles were twitching, but not in a regular way. It was like bugs crawling under her skin. Hundreds of them. I rolled to my knees, reaching out again, wondering if it was an illusion.

"Lyris?" I whispered.

Her eyelids shot open, but she wasn't seeing anything. Her eyes were shining gold, her pupil entirely disappeared. Her facial muscles curled in rage but continued twisting to be inhumane. My hands hovered over her, unsure of what I could do to help.

What happened looked like it was in slow motion, but her body was morphing. Coarse fur sprouted, and the Council mumbled approval. I couldn't imagine this coming from a spell or potion.

My friend went from umber skinned to tawny fur. She disappeared; and at the end, a cougar took her place.

Chapter 38

Once the cougar stopped twitching and the cat's eyes shut again, the Council applauded amongst themselves. I couldn't stop staring, unsure if what I saw was real, even from this close. I waited for the laughter to start. It had to be a spell from the practitioner, or I was hallucinating.

"Now." The youngest Councilman on the right pointed lazily at Lyris. "If you put the pyx back in her, will she still be able to do that?"

The practitioner grinned with satisfaction. "Yes sir. This is her first full shift to cougar form, I believe. From my agent's information, she got sicker and sicker the further she got from her pyx. Now that she's so close, her body can relax itself."

The young girl bent behind the cougar, moving fur to the side, inspecting the skin underneath. She paused, looking at the practitioner with concern.

"Ma'am?"

Under the fur, there were freely bleeding wounds. The practitioner sighed.

"There are still a few kinks to work out. A body isn't supposed to change forms unless it's born for it." She snapped her fingers. "Take the creature to the hospital wing. I'll inspect it there before we return the pyx."

Still in shock, I rose to my feet as a Guard picked the cougar off the ground. Her head flopped to the side.

"You poisoned her?" The words slipped from my mouth as I watched the Guard leave before turning on the practitioner.

As horrified as I felt, I was also in awe. I couldn't help it. The transition a regular Shifting Drao went through was smooth and nothing like what I just saw. I couldn't imagine this being possible or something a sane person would try.

"A spell to turn her into a Shifter. I wrote it myself," she said proudly.

The mysterious illness she faced. The body aches and her eyes being dry and hurting. It all made sense now. The werewolf bone marrow she got sent for. They knew she would never be able to get it. They were just testing the spell.

"And now your turn, Orinthia," the young Councilman said, nodding at the practitioner.

She stepped forward as the Guard forcibly straightened me with a new grip on my arms. The bruise covering my left side noticeably throbbed. Heavy breathing replaced the silence of the room, but I couldn't pin where it came from. My focus was split between the woman getting closer and the discomfort in my body.

Her hand reached for the cage, my heart pounding in my chest as I could only watch. Her hand wrapped around the cage, but jerked to a stop with a hiss, snapping her arm protectively to her chest. Staring down at her palm, she glared at me.

"What did you do?" she snapped.

I couldn't answer her, barely able to shake my head. I didn't know what she was talking about. She whipped around to Yash, pointing a bony finger at him.

"You told me it could be removed!" Her arm swung back

around, ending dangerously close to my face. "You come get it off her."

Yash's mouth fell open, but he thought better of speaking. His eyes dropped to his feet as he crossed the room. Stopping before me, his mouth twitched in discomfort; then, with determination, he reached forward. His hand bounced away, the same way the practitioner did.

With wide, scared eyes, he scanned the room, his fingers curling. I held in my smirk and sent thanks to the High Drao of Rinebur for whatever magick was on the cage, whether it was put there for me. The furious practitioner looked to the Councilmen for her next instructions but we all knew. They wanted the eggs. She did whatever was necessary.

She stormed back to the cart. The young girl cowered away, not wanting to be in the woman's enraged path. The practitioner snatched a brown translucent bottle off one of the few shelves on the cart. Facing me, she uncorked the bottle and sprinkled droplets of the mystery liquid in her hands. Shoving the bottle to the girl without looking, the practitioner stared into my eyes. Rubbing her palms together, she mumbled.

I couldn't hear the words, but she didn't blink. My already pounding heart got faster and faster the longer she stared. I couldn't remove my eyes from hers. When my eyes opened after my next blink, the practitioner was four feet away, making me gasp and sink back into the Guard. The practitioner flicked her fingers. A few droplets hit my forehead.

When the liquid hit my skin, every muscle in my body locked up. Inside my head, I was trying my hardest to move away, but nothing happened. She motioned her hands downward and with it, my muscles gave out and I dropped.

Unable to slow my fall, my head smacked the floor with a thud. All the muscles throughout my body steadily tightened until it became painful. A quiet sob was squeezed from between my lips. On my back, I saw the practitioner. Her hands shut, nails pressing into her palms with a look of almost pleasure in her eyes.

I experienced muscle spasms before, but this was excruciating. It was like my muscles were trying to keep from shrinking, but my bones were in the way. It was a tight pinch at a thousand different points under my skin. If my abdomen relaxed at all, stomach bile would make its way up.

Her hands opened, letting my muscles free. My chest heaved as I desperately tried to catch my breath, but couldn't stop coughing. A full body sob broke from my mouth as my body considered throwing up again. The pain vanished, leaving an emptiness that hurt just as much in its wake. I tried to roll onto my side, but my limbs were liquid.

"Will you hand over the eggs now?" a booming male voice asked.

I regained feeling in my arms again and had enough strength to push my torso up. The Councilmen watched me from their thrones with intense eyes. A sense of defiance bloomed in my chest, angry at what I just went through. Like a child learning to walk, I rolled to my knees, and I stared back at them. The centre Councilman sighed with his hand covering his chin and peered at the practitioner, lowering his chin. She smiled maniacally, returning her eyes to me.

The practitioner began talking, her words slightly different. My forearm snapped backwards and my shoulder and head collided with the tile. I was useless at protecting myself against magick. Slumping around, I landed on top of the newly broken bone. As if someone else was doing it, the broken forearm twisted under me. I didn't care enough to stop the scream.

And when my voice eventually failed…"Will you hand over the cage now?"

I wanted to. Every cell in my body begged me to hand it over. Make the torture stop. But what Heathlyn told me last night accompanied images of a dead Drao in my mind. The things stored in Accora's cabinet like they were forgotten knickknacks.

I couldn't give up the faerie eggs so easily. I was too stubborn for my own good. If I died here, they still couldn't take it off my body. The practitioner began a different spell. Inside my boots, I felt all ten of my toes dislocate and continue to pull away from my body. I whimpered, bringing my legs into myself.

Over the thundering of my heartbeat, I was forced to hear the practitioner. My freshly broken arm tingled and grew into a burning sensation. My insides were on fire. From around the room, it must look like I was lying there, crying and whimpering. Not a single scratch.

"The eggs, child?"

My gaze rose and contacted the old Councilman at the centre of the trio. His tone was more contained than before. I hoped my fury was clear through the tears streaming down my face. The practitioner waved her hand and my head was rammed to the opposite side. My nose burned in pain, like someone had broken it with their foot.

I wasn't sure how much more I could take. The room was silent other than my cries and the Councilmen quietly conversing between themselves. Squeezing my eyes shut, inhaling sharply through my nose, I focused on breathing through the swelling. I could taste my sweat running into my mouth, mixed with tears and snot. Was there blood, too?

There had to be more coming. The low voices of the three men were the only sound in the room.

Instead, the Councilman spoke again.

"Take her away. Maybe she'll change her mind overnight while her wounds heal themselves."

The ground rumbled under my head before hands grabbed under my arms. I wailed out at the rush of new pain. Violently twisting my torso, I worked to yank myself away from whoever was holding me. The hands let go of me, but fighting to stand, I forgot about my toes until the pain shot up my legs. I did a better job of catching myself.

"Pick her up. She'll be fine in the morning."

Another person chuckled. "You heard the woman, Pax. Pick up your little friend."

Behind me, a thump hit the floor with pained coughing to follow. My body vibrated. In shock or from pain, I didn't know. Hands rested on my back and I tried to shuffle away. Even with the overwhelming fire in my body, the touch was too familiar. I didn't want Pax to touch me. Ever again.

He grunted as he lifted, working to keep me in his grip. I didn't want to fall and make my wounds worse, so I begrudgingly settled but kept my eyes shut. I couldn't look at him. His neck would still be littered with proof of the other night. How could I've been so naïve?

Something rough bumped against my hair and I instinctively turned my head away from it. My forehead rested against his chest, his comforting scent was overwhelming. Pax inhaled sharply, his arms tightening around me.

More tears welled in my eyes. I experienced lots of broken bones, but I never felt this bad. Not just my body, but my heart ached in waves of pain.

Chapter 39

I opened my eyes when a heavy door squeaked open. I unintentionally fell asleep as Pax carried me and now I had no clue where I was on the Isle.

My head injuries turned into a debilitating migraine, and I meekly looked around. The torches propped against the stone walls gave it away. I was in a cell. Great.

Pax stepped through a doorway. It was set up with a dingy bed and a toilet. He placed me as gently as he could on the bed. I held my breath as my back pressed into the lumpy mattress and my skin started tingling; the pain returning to the surface. It wasn't the worst bed I ever slept on, but it wasn't comfortable. Pax's eyes glistened in the low light as he peered down at me. Being forced to look at him, I pushed as much betrayal through my eyes as possible. We broke eye contact when the door shut behind him. Spinning on his toes, he grabbed the handle and shook the door aggressively.

"What the hell?" he shouted through the barred window.

A Guard looked back at him with a smirk. He pointed at a bucket on the ground next to the door.

"Council wants her clean. Wash your girlfriend and you can go back to your orders."

Panic filled my heart at the thought of him touching me.

"I can wash myself. He can leave." I insisted, trying to swing my legs off the mattress.

The pressure against my elbow sent a cold pain up to my shoulder. The joint gave out, and I fell back on the bed. I stared at the dark ceiling, holding in the sobs gathering in my chest. I couldn't imagine healing properly. I was permanently broken. I would never be able to travel and work again.

"Clean her wounds, boy."

The footsteps walked away, and Pax sighed from across the room. I continued to stare at the ceiling as he picked up the full bucket. The mattress dipped at my feet. Even the light movement caused discomfort to ripple in my body. He must have seen it, muttering an apology. My foot twitched and a deep throbbing enveloped around my toes. Lifting my head, I watched Pax loosen my laces.

"Stop, I can clean myself. I don't want your help," I said, weakly trying to pull my foot away.

"Owyn, you can barely move," Pax said, continuing to unravel the laces.

"Don't call me that," I said, but gave up on the tough act. He was right. I couldn't do anything right now.

"This is the last time you touch me," I added.

Pax peered at me, eyebrows scrunched together. His forehead wrinkled more than I'd seen, reminding me of how sickly he seemed.

"Why are you angry at me? I had no part in the Council bringing you in."

I rolled my head against the lumpy pillow, looking through the small barred window. I envied the only thing I could see, the blue sky. My nose twitched as he peeled my socks off. My entire foot was swollen, not just my toes. I couldn't understand how my skin wasn't shredded. It felt like it.

"Why were you sent to travel with me?" I asked, my voice barely above a whisper.

Pax carefully wiped the wet rag against my skin.

"You know why. The Council told me that you had a package that needed to be brought back. You needed a travel partner for the safety of you and what you had."

I focused on breathing through the pressure of his touch, tiptoe-ing closer to nausea or blacking out. Resting my feet on the bed, he got up and dragged the bucket of now murky water across the ground. He held out his hand. Ignoring it, I attempted to roll over, but it wasn't easy. I hissed as Pax gripped my bicep of my broken arm. Tomorrow I was going to feel so much worse.

"Did you know what I was carrying?"

"Yes. I was with you for weeks. I saw the cage plenty of times."

"Do you know why?" My voice wasn't loud enough for anyone else to hear. I couldn't make it any louder.

He glanced at my face, but focused on my broken arm instead. "No, Owyn. I didn't."

I scoffed with my mouth closed, keeping my head turned away from him. His grip twitched tighter, and I cried out. My head whipped back around, ready to curse him out.

"Dammit, Owyn. I didn't know what they did to you," he snapped.

I glared at him, and he looked back at me with sadness.

"What would you've done if you had?" I asked.

His mouth opened and shut; a crackle of sound came from his throat. His gaze wandered to the wall behind my head, searching for an answer with his mouth still open. I rolled my eyes and looked at the window again.

"Exactly."

After the blood and little bits of dirt were washed away, Pax dropped the rag into the bloody water. He stood, looking down at me. I was frustrated, and staring at the cracked roof, unable to stop tears from rolling down my cheeks. I wasn't in a lot of pain, but I was embarrassed and felt raw. He placed his hand on my forehead. I didn't move away.

The part of me that craved touch won the momentary fight. I shut my eyes, embracing the warmth of his palm. He shifted, and I thought he was pulling away, but instead, lips pressed against my forehead.

"I'll do my best to get you out, but please give them the eggs. I can't watch that again."

With that, he pounded his fist against the door. A Guard appeared, assessing Pax's work through the window before opening the door. He left without a look back and I heard the door shut. The tears continued to roll down my face. I lifted the cage and stared at the fragile little eggs.

Was it worth it?

I could live without my pyx. I'd be sick, on the brink of death, for the rest of my life, but I could live. However, did I want to be in the Council's talons for another sixty years?

Resting the cage back against my chest with my hand around it, I didn't expect Yash. In Mye, he wasn't acting suspiciously. I thought he was behaving more pompous than usual, sure, but that didn't shock me. My stomach knotted, knowing he left his parents in that old, falling apart house on Histlea River for years and he wore the finest furs and clothes, all paid for by the Council.

Staring at the ceiling of the cell and even with all the pain I faced today, I knew.

Seeing Mama and Cod's faces in my head, my decision was made. I wasn't giving the cage over easily. I tried considering what could force me to hand it over, but I stopped. If I got to that point, I'd know. I didn't need to torment myself.

Chapter 40

I barely had the goop from my eyes when a hand wrapped around my arm and yanked me up. My stomach rolled, anticipating a pain that never came.

Standing, I couldn't feel the swelling in my toes. I glanced at my forearm. It didn't look broken or even bruised. I healed overnight. I was almost relieved they used magick on me, but then I realized the Council wasn't leaving any evidence. If they wanted to kill me, they could make it look like something else entirely.

"The Council would like to see you," the Guard said, dryly.

"Shocker," I muttered, letting the Guards roughly escort me out of the cell.

I thought they would keep me in the jail building, but coming up the stairs and after someone shoved me through a door, sunlight blinded me. I was back in the foyer of the Council building.

From how white and pale the colour scheme was, the sun reflected off everything. Like the day before, it was only secretaries to be seen. Tripping over my feet, half blind by the light, I was dragged through the next stairwell door and I was forced to make the climb again.

Pushed through the door to the Council Chambers, my body slammed it open. I expected my blood to be stained across the slatted tile floor. But it was so clean it looked like nothing happened. No people piled in a corner. The door clicked shut behind me. I was alone in the room. No Guards or Councilmen. Well, almost alone. A woman stood with her back to me, looking out the windows at the ocean with her arms crossed.

"I don't think I've ever travelled so quickly before," Janna said, turning.

"But when my top protégé is being difficult with the Council, continuing to give my name an unacceptable reputation." She paused. "Well, I had to fix that myself."

"I'm not being difficult," I said. "I'm doing what I think is right."

She approached me, running her tongue across her top teeth. A dry swallow rolled down my throat. Janna may be graceful, but she hit me enough times to know better. She pinched my chin, tilting my head to look me in the face. Her dark blue eyes shone.

"They told you to collect fairies' eggs. Albeit, it wasn't a kind way of asking." Her thumb nail pushed into my chin. "Give them the eggs. Get your pyx back and fix the stains on your reputation."

She paused, tilting her head a little.

"Actually, you don't have a choice, Orinthia. No one will work with you if you defy the Council. And that affects me. I won't have that."

I felt the glare settle on my face. Her back handed threat poked at the fire smoldering inside of me. I was tempted to spit in her face, but I clenched my jaw hard enough that she felt it. Her voice dropped, a hiss to each of her words.

"If you don't give it to them, I will find a way to. And I

won't be leaving this building to pick up more eggs." She leaned closer. "It will be the ones around your neck."

After letting her words sink in, she pushed my head away.

"Now get washed. You won't be seeing the Council looking like a low level housemaid," Janna directed, pointing to the other end of the room carelessly. A single door sat open.

I bit down on my bottom lip, still glaring at my mentor. The irritation was replaced by indifference, but would return if I didn't follow her directions.

Looking at myself in the mirror hanging over the sink, my messy hair and a smudge of dirt on my cheekbone was evidence I didn't peacefully sleep. The blood was gone. Pax did a good job.

My eyes held the only permanent evidence of my torture. The gold flecks in my eyes that were always noticeable in the sunlight were dull. It wasn't a bad dream. Running my hands under the water and then through my hair a few times would have to do.

I barely exited the washing room when Janna had a hold of my wrist and dragged me by the arm to stand in front of the thrones. She adjusted my hair to hang smoothly behind my back.

"The Council is coming. You think you would move quicker," she grumbled. She placed her hands gently on my face. "Make me proud."

The maternal words didn't match her expression. She was still violently disappointed in me.

The large intricately carved double doors hidden behind the thrones opened, voices flooding into the room. Janna stepped behind my shoulder, showing her responsibility for me. It was almost the guardianship behaviour I'd wanted from her. It added to my guilt, which annoyed me. First to step into the sunlight were three Guards. Each took their position behind the thrones as their bosses came into view.

The same Councilmen as yesterday. Janna rolled her shoulders, standing taller.

As the Councilmen settled in their chairs, the practitioner slinked around the end. She looked as elegant as yesterday. Apparently, I was the only one tired from the torture. My tongue pressed against my upper teeth when Yash appeared, stopping next to the practitioner. He glanced at me from the corner of his eye; chin tilted high. I got the urge to smack him. The door connecting to the private quarters shut and the door I entered through opened in the same beat.

Three more Guards came in with Pax between them, sickly as yesterday. He was at least standing by himself this time. My heart clenched as we made eye contact. His eyes were dull like mine. What happened last night to make him look like this?

The oldest Councilman in the centre stood, and the room went silent. "Janna Cor. Good to see you on the Isle again. It has been too long."

"Thank you, Councilman Sunnif. It's lovely to see Councilman Wilmot and Councilman Erom too." Janna's voice was sweet, searching for approval.

"What has brought you to the Isle?" Councilman Sunnif asked, running his hands along his robe.

"I was contacted by a friend of my pupil that she did not deliver the faerie eggs upon her arrival in Jova. I was concerned for her wellbeing and thought I could help."

He didn't respond and sat down, making himself comfortable. My eyes slid to Yash. He was watching Janna intensely. Apparently, I had two friends in Jova when I arrived and Eira would never call Janna. I didn't trust him, but knew he was slimy enough to get himself in the good graces of my mentor. Everything was piecing together.

"And have you been able to help?" The dark-haired Councilman asked, resting his ankle across his knee. It was casual, but he became more smug.

"I hope so, Councilman Wilmot."

His gaze flickered from Janna to me.

"Our attention turns to you then, Orinthia Kellobyn. Has your experience yesterday changed your mind? Will you hand over what we asked of you?"

A small voice in my head screamed for me to do it. A slight movement caught my eye. Pax, shifting his weight, watched me with wide eyes, begging me. I pressed my lips together and felt a light nudge to the back of my arm, taking my attention away from him.

Two Councilmen, Sunnif and the youngest who hadn't spoken, Erom both met my gaze. Their eyes were steady, anticipating my response. The third Councilmen, Wilmot, watched at the cage. Different from his cohorts' looks of anticipation, Wilmot's eyes burned with hunger. He knew the potential of these eggs and what it could give him. His gaze flickered to mine, and I watched him change entirely, becoming an easy-going old man. It encouraged my decision.

"No," I said, turning to Sunnif. "I'm sorry, but I won't be handing over the eggs."

Janna sighed in disappointment and Sunnif's face matched, his wrinkles deepened.

"That's your decision," he said. "However, I must attempt to convince you once more."

My eyes peeked at Pax before joining Sunnif's look at their practitioner. We both knew yesterday was about to be repeated. He was angry at me for choosing it to happen again. Impassively, the practitioner nodded and moved to the cart brought in by the neglected girl.

My pyx spun, flexing under the glass dome. The practitioner rested her hand around the lid's metal knob and stared me in the eye. She paused, waiting for my reconsideration. Breathing became harder as my heart rate sped faster, but I stayed silent.

Lifting the lid, my heart slammed against my ribs. The

need to lunge for my pyx became almost unbearable. All eyes were on me, prickling my skin. I couldn't say I was hiding the feeling well, my fingers moving aimlessly at my sides. Guards shifted their weight, seeing how restless I was becoming. I considered all the different ways I would get across the room and how much blood I would have to spill before slamming my eyes shut, trying to remove the sight of temptation.

When my heart was no longer throwing itself against my breastbone, I reopened them and looked at the practitioner directly. Her mouth twitched, enjoying how hard I was fighting. She watched herself put down the lid, and after making eye contact again, she wrapped her hand around my pyx. The organs inside my chest vibrated and my blood stopped flowing. She swung her arm straight ahead, giving everyone a clear view.

Whimpering, I fell to my knees and my joints popped at the contact; the sound echoing around the room. As if every movement was through a microscope, she pressed into the ball. All the saliva disappeared from my mouth and my lungs tightened. My body tensed, but not in the same manner as yesterday from her spell. I sensed my veins trying to pump blood. My upper torso crashed to the ground, my vision going black. I rolled onto my back as I fought to breathe. Every part of me was on fire as my body worked to stay alive. Trying to scream, I needed someone to remove my corset.

I barely heard Councilman Sunnif's voice. "More".

Everything around me was slowing down. The blood moved towards my heart at the speed of molasses, not a drop going anywhere else. I felt my organs dry out and beg for blood or moisture. My stomach ached from repetitive contractions, but all that was left against the tissue was acid.

The practitioner appeared in the single spot I still had vision, with my pyx in her hand. With the smoke gone, her fingernails looked close to piercing its outer skin. She placed her other hand on top until it did the same thing. My heart wasn't beating, only forcibly expanding, blood overwhelming it.

"Will you give up the eggs?" Her voice booming through my ears, satisfied with her work.

I was going to die any second. I had to. I wanted to. Hopefully, the cage wouldn't come off when I did, and they would be screwed. With the small bit of rationale I had, I felt terrified. My ego wanted me to hold out, die, and make them all feel dumb.

The practitioner bent at the knee, putting my pyx inches away from my face. I was only seeing shadows, and she was now the darkest part.

"You will not die, child. I've made sure of it. Your heart may explode or your organs fail, but you won't die. You'll continue to feel every second if you don't give up that cage."

I wasn't in a position to test if she was bluffing. Cowardly, I nodded as best I could, surrendering. A grin grew across the woman's eerily smooth face. Her fingernails released their grip. It was like a damn broke in my chest, my heart releasing all the blood it collected and continued its regular rhythm.

The acid in my stomach reappeared, shooting to my throat, and on to the floor as I rolled over. I vibrated from terror, ripping the cage over my head as quickly as I could and threw it away from me. I didn't know how long I had to hand it over before she stopped believing me and started the torture again. My heart thumped as if I had run for hours, trying to return my body to its normal cycle. My mouth filled with saliva as if I needed to throw up again, but my stomach had nothing left, not even acid.

I don't know how long it took to stop feeling each of my organs beginning to work again. I could've laid in that spot for a year and not care. I almost felt seasick, something I'd only experienced once in my life. The room was swaying, and happily, I was getting ready to sink. Already closed, my eyelids felt even more weighted down.

"Orinthia Kellobyn, I ask you to stand."

I tried to ignore the command. They could wait. I gave them what they wanted. But hands grabbed both my wrists and lifted me to my feet. I was grateful whoever it was didn't let go until my body stopped swaying. With my head dropped, gently my eyelids opened.

Puddles of blood were across the floor, indicating where I was lying. Under my dress, I was feeling itchy, like the fabric was tightening. My pulsing nose drew my attention. I lifted my fingers to my upper lip, where my skin felt warmer than normal. Blood covered my fingertips.

"Good, child. Good," Janna whispered praises in my ear. There was no care in her voice. She was cold again.

Focusing on the Councilmen, my guilt had replaced the discomfort at how satisfied they were. Someone retrieved the cage from where I threw it and it sat in Councilman Sunnif's hand, holding it up to the sun. The metal of the cage shot rays of light around the room. The eggs didn't crack when I threw the cage. I might have enjoyed that.

"Bring the boy forwards," Sunnif ordered to no one in particular, still watching me with pride.

I expected Yash to step forward, but the Guards pushed Pax. He looked at the Councilmen with confusion. They placed him next to me.

"Now that we've received all payments, we can sever the final spell," Sunnif announced, looking at his practitioner.

For once, she looked hesitant.

"Yes sir. However, the spell cannot be broken without both parties having their pyx, as that's where the bond is," she explained.

He let the cage twist in his hands. "Fine."

With my pyx still in her hand, the practitioner stepped closer.

"Wait, if you please, Councilmen," Janna interrupted.

She stepped forward to be seen by everyone. She must

have moved away when the Guards were hauling me off the ground.

"May I suggest you keep Orinthia's pyx? You'd have a worthwhile Merchant at your disposal. A Guard too, if the spell is correct."

I was too exhausted to admit I wasn't surprised Janna was selling me out. I wore her symbol. I would always be her toy.

"The spell is correct," the practitioner said between gritted teeth, glaring at Janna.

The corner of Janna's mouth twitched, but she gave the practitioner an emotionless look.

"It was just a suggestion," she assured, innocently.

"Thank you for the suggestion," Councilman Wilmot said. "But return her pyx. We made a promise and I do not intend to leave this unresolved. We gave payment to all the other Merchants."

The practitioner smirked at Janna, nodding her head. I planted my feet as the woman stopped in front of me. I hadn't noticed she was taller by a few inches. My eyes slid down to her extended hand. My pyx levitated off her palm. All the blues move like smoke. It was mesmerizing. She began speaking an incantation. The more she said, the higher the pyx rose until it was level with my eyes.

She spoke the last words, then snapped her fingers. My pyx shot forward and instinctively, I shut my eyes, but didn't feel more than a breeze against my forehead.

After a moment of nothing, I opened my eyes. I was looking at the ceiling, the floor underneath my back. I hadn't felt the fall or hitting the ground. Pax was bent down beside me with his hand on my shoulder. I got a sudden throbbing headache. My brain had to be bruised over the multiple impacts I experienced over the past few days.

"Come on," he encouraged, hoisting me up with both hands under my armpits.

"There, Merchant. You have your pyx. We are even and clear now," Councilman Wilmot said.

I nodded once. I had nothing to say, and he wasn't looking for an answer. I watched the men in thrones, but could feel Janna's eyes on me. I had a feeling if I turned, I would punch her and that wouldn't look good or end well.

"Now, let's end this. Cut the spell." Sunnif waved his free hand, covered in gaudy bracelets and rings, as he stared at the cage in the other. It was like he was enchanted.

"What spell?" Pax frustratedly blurted.

I felt the same, but didn't have the strength to talk, and there was a sense of fear inside me. I didn't know what could get me into trouble. The Councilmen began jovially laughing at his question, shivers running down my spine. My entire body ached, but the defiant part of me that was still conscious wanted to run. Whatever spell they planned on removing, the connotations around it didn't sound good.

"I'm surprised you have to ask, Guard. We didn't mask the smell of magick on you two," Councilman Erom said, the first words he spoke.

They were full of amusement and hunger. The man who stayed silent gave me the strongest sense of danger.

But something in what he said hit a memory. I noticed the smell a couple of times, but never thought too much about it. I assumed it was the faeries' eggs.

"We may as well tell you what you don't know, but are wondering," Erom said, smirking. "Before pyxes were removed, the Council tested how best to get Merchants to return efficiently. You, Orinthia, drew the card of a bonding spell between yourself and the Guard we assigned to escort you back. It was activated when you made eye contact for the first time."

I remembered the moment, in the underground Rinebur Drao bar. Pax sat at a table with the other Guards. In the dim lights, his eyes shone, and he stuck out. I noticed him.

"Pax felt a desire to return. He was drawn to your pyx, but as a loyal Guard, he had to bring you along. If he were any other Guard, the restraint he showed not to leave you behind would surprise me. But the boy was always a fighter, even when it didn't serve his best interest," Erom continued. "We fixed it so you were drawn to each other. We were warned Miss Kellobyn was a flight risk. This was the best option."

Pax's hand ran along my lower back softly. I so easily trusted him, barely questioning the behaviour. I had assumed my trust had to do with the talisman, but it was magick all along. My gaze snapped up as the practitioner began speaking again, palms up with her eyes shut.

I peered at Pax, who was already staring at me with wide eyes. He reached across to hold my hand, but I pulled away. My trust dissolved. Disgusted with him again. What part did he have in this? He had to know.

Hurt filled his eyes before he squeezed them shut, thumping his fist against his chest, shouting in pain. My heart jolted in my chest, feeling like it bounced against everything around it. My knees dropped out from the surprised feeling.

I curled towards the floor, grabbing at my chest. My heart beat against my esophagus until it slowed and the acidic burn subsided. I shut my eyes, panting as, once again, my body felt a lot of new pains.

Gratefully, I slipped into unconsciousness.

CHAPTER 41

I JOLTED AWAKE AS MY BODY DROPPED THROUGH THE AIR. I WAS on the mattress from the night before. The cell's heavy door shut. I tried to push off the bed, but I moved too fast. Dull pain shot through my spine; making me pause.

"Wait," I groaned. "Why am I here? I did what they said."

The Guard stared at me through the barred window. "The Council will decide what to do with you. Can't send a familiar face back out on the streets looking so messed up."

I planted my feet on the ground, hands gripping the scratchy blanket. I handed the faerie eggs over and the guilt of that decision sat in my throat, even knowing it was self preservation. It stuck out over all the throbbing discomfort the rest of my body felt.

Glaring at the dirty concrete floor, I thought of what happened in the chambers. I couldn't remember the extent of the pain. My brain blocked it out, but I knew how it felt. It was a small degree of the pain that the Cursed went through, before they were cast out onto the streets. Their lives, ruined. Families ruined.

The Council would have to let me out. I would find Heathlyn, explain what my last two months were and promise to help her cause. I didn't know the specifics of what she wanted, but anything could be better than what the Drao were being subjected to.

I would move past the betrayal that I felt from everyone I once trusted. I was a Merchant. My job was to keep going and ignore ties and heartbreak. One of the most famous Merchants, the person I was supposed to trust to help me trained me.

My fingers slipped together, and I tapped them against my knees. I wasn't going to just roll over and go on with my life.

About the Author

© Emily Grey

Emily Grey, a Canadian author from a town near Toronto, finds inspiration in both the vibrant energy of summer concerts and the introspective calm of Ontario winters spent immersed in thought-provoking literature. Raised on a diet of diverse book and movie sagas, Emily is a passionate advocate of fanfiction, weaving eerie tales of magic and romance that resonate with readers. Guided by her two opinionated cats, Remus and Kenobi, Emily crafts characters who provoke strong emotions —either adoration or disdain—reflecting her belief in storytelling's power to illuminate real-world issues and challenge societal norms.

instagram.com/emilygreybooks
tiktok.com/@emilygreybooks

www.ingramcontent.com/pod-product-compliance
Lightning Source LLC
Chambersburg PA
CBHW031200310726
48969CB00001B/151